THE SECRET KEEPER FULFILLED

(THE SECRET KEEPER SERIES #6)

BREA BROWN

WAYZGOOSE PRESS

CONTENTS

For the readers who have been through it all with Peyton and Brice and who have waited so patiently for this final installment. I hope everything I imagined lives up to everything you've imagined.

Special Dedication
In memory of Amy, a loyal friend and inspiration.

SOMEWHAT CONTROLLED CHAOS

*a*granola cluster sails past my head. My arms full of baby, I can do nothing more than glare over my shoulder toward the kitchen table and growl, "Cut it out, you guys."

Four-year-old Max informs me at high volume and maximum whine that his nearly-three-year-old brother, Harris, is eating his cereal with his hands. In his righteous indignation, Max dips his elbow in his own cereal bowl, sending milk and granola bits flying. Aidan, almost two, giggles at the sight of more airborne food. Harris's twin, Brooks, observes disdainfully, like he can't believe he's a member of this herd.

It's a typical late summer Monday morning in the Northam house. Five kids under the age of five. You do the math. I'm living it. It's messy. And loud.

Holding a hungry, increasingly impatient eight-week-old Addison in one arm, I give the anti-Norman-Rockwell tableau barely more than a glance as I retrieve a baby bottle from the fridge.

Brice steps over the puddle of milk on his way into the

kitchen and says dully, "Good morning. I'll get that." He plucks the roll of paper toweling from its holder and steps into the fray.

"Much obliged," I drawl, then firmly instruct Max to put his bottom in his booster seat and be quiet while his father deals with the mess.

Max complies with the first request but wails about being "wet and sticky," before screeching at Aidan, "It's not funny!"

"Lord, deliver me," Brice mutters, peeling Max's milk-soaked pajamas from the boy's body.

"He will," I point out to my husband. "In about fifteen minutes, when you get to leave for work."

Crouching to mop the floor with Max's castoff pajama bottoms, Brice says, "I'll be taking the mouthiest one with me, though. Lucky you. How thankful are you for Monday morning preschool?"

"Very." I pour his coffee and set it on the narrow slab of counter next to the stove, out of reach of any spill-prone hands. Focused once again on warming Addi's bottle, I turn my back to the room and stare into the cup of warm water, as if that will heat the formula faster.

Before the bottle's ready, Brice returns to the kitchen, having made short work of de-stickifying and dressing our oldest child. He snags the mug of coffee, draining half of it in three swallows. Reaching over me to pull down a box of cereal from the cabinet next to my head, he lightly kisses the back of my neck.

Testing the temperature of the formula against my wrist, I smile quietly and face him as I begin feeding the baby her long-awaited breakfast. "Good morning."

"Something like that," he replies wryly. His hand rests on Addi's fuzzy blonde head. "And good morning to you,

Ladybug! Someone could forget about such a well-behaved, quiet baby with these bozos around." He jabs a thumb in the direction of the squirmy boys at the table.

She blinks up at him but continues gulping.

"No, don't stop on my account. Pretend I'm not here. I do. Often."

"It's not that bad, is it?"

He shakes bran flakes and raisins into a bowl, then reaches into the fridge for the milk. Nudging the appliance closed with his elbow, he answers, "I'm only kidding."

He's not very convincing, though. And that's not exactly what I was fishing for. I need him to tell me, like he does most days, that this is temporary. And I need him to give me an encouraging estimate for life returning to some semblance of order, preferably a figure smaller than "eighteen years."

I chalk up this morning's uncharacteristic ennui to fatigue. Neither of us has had a full night's sleep in months, unless you count that six-day sleep I took back in June, which wasn't as restful as it may sound.

Now he levels a playful scowl at me. "I do have a bone to pick with you, though."

I pull back my chin and widen my eyes. "Moi?"

"Yes! Mitzi is so desperate to get in touch with you to set up a play date with Sasha and the boys that she's resorted to using Jared and me as go-betweens. What the higgety-heck is the deal with that?"

"What the hack?" Harris echoes, then tips his bowl toward his face.

"Exactly," Brice says, pointing to our son with his spoon, before flattening his flakes into his own bowl.

I focus on Addi's button nose and mumble, "I don't know. I just—" Raising my head to meet my husband's eyes,

I whine, "Do I have to?" Immediately, I regret the unfiltered question that wrinkles his forehead.

"Not if you're too tired, but you should probably answer your friend's calls and tell her that. Are you feeling okay?"

I sigh. That settles it. I have to do it. Otherwise, he'll think all this is too much for me. And we'll have to have that conversation again. I hate that conversation, the one that makes me feel like I'm an eyelash away from being classified as "unstable" and observed for risky postpartum behavior. It doesn't matter that he'll couch it in the "Remember-you're-still-recovering-from-a-major-medical-ordeal?" talk.

As if I would or could forget. People are constantly reminding me of it.

The response to my health crisis and recovery has been nearly as overwhelming and daunting as the recovery itself. Peace held a 24-hour prayer vigil while I was comatose, with people taking shifts to pray for me. Me! When I found out, after the fact, I had to go to bed for a couple of hours.

Of course, I'm grateful. That goes without saying. But the mere thought of such an event in my honor, while I slept, oblivious, a few miles away in a hospital room, threatens to smother me more effectively than a pillow to the face. If I had been aware of it while it was happening, I would have been hesitant to wake up. Ever. Don't try to make that make any sense. It doesn't. But it's true. Even while deeply unconscious, I want nothing to do with that level of attention.

When yet another long-suffering exhalation is the only answer his latest inquiry into my health receives, he suggests, "Why don't you have Mom come over and sit with Addi and Aidan, so you only have to keep track of the older boys? And go somewhere they can wear themselves out. Like the pool or one of those bounce places. You and Mitzi can watch from the sidelines and catch up with each other; the kids can go nuts without either of you worrying about having a disaster area on your hands when everyone goes home."

My mouth stretches into a brave smile I don't quite feel. "Good ideas. I'll give her a call."

He nods while chewing and swallowing a mouthful of cereal. "Excellent. I want a full report when you come to pick up Max." Before I can tell him where he can shove his half-serious "full report," he winces. "Oooh, except I won't see you today, actually. I'm supposed to call Dr. Glenden-ning at that time."

"Who is this Dr. Glendenning, and why does he take priority over me?" I wink and pull the bottle from Addi's mouth, holding it at eye level to check her progress. When I see she's made it to the halfway point, I transfer her to my shoulder, not bothering with a burp rag or towel.

He chases a raisin around the bottom of the bowl with his spoon, finally capturing it and shaking it into the center of the utensil. Holding it to his lips, he answers, "You know, Dr. G. Vince and I talk about him all the time. He was our favorite professor at Sem."

Although Vince and Brice didn't attend Concordia Seminary in St. Louis at the same time (Vince was ordained a year before Brice enrolled), many of the same professors were still around by the time Brice came through. Dr. Glendenning was one of those professors. I know that much from the stories he and Vince love to trade late into the night while I doze nearby. But if Brice is going to quiz me about the particulars of those tales, I'm in trouble.

"Oh, yes. Dr. G. I remember now. And you have to call him precisely at 11:30? Isn't he retired by now? Doesn't he have all the time in the world to shoot the shi— breeze with you?"

My near-curse in the presence of the children fetches a glower over the rim of Brice's bowl as he drinks his milk like an overgrown kid. Finishing, he reaches behind himself and puts his dirty dishes in the sink, earning him an equally severe frown. Which he ignores, in favor of continuing his explanation.

"He may have all the time in the world, but I don't. I'm squeezing him in, because he said it was important. I hope it has something to do with brainstorming how to get Peace behind the idea of hosting a vicar."

I groan.

"What's wrong with that?"

"Do you remember Jared's vicarage? Or have you blocked that out? Because I remember it. I was on vicar duty 24/7."

"It's not going to be like that this time, hon," Brice promises, digging at his teeth with his tongue.

"And you think that, because…?"

He chases rogue bran flake remnants with the last of his chilly coffee. "Well, I'm not the only pastor this guy would be shadowing, for one thing. Yeah, ultimately, I'll be the supervisor, but Jared and Wes would be better mentors, anyway."

"I guess."

Addi burps her opinion on the matter.

He makes an amused face at the baby's noises and taps his wedding ring against the side of the ceramic mug. "Really. You won't have to be involved at all this time. Other than making the guy feel welcome. Plus, nobody could be as high-maintenance as Jared was."

I settle Addi in my arms for the second half of her bottle. "You're a glutton for punishment, you know that?"

Before he can respond to the charges, another skirmish breaks out at the table. Sighing, he sets his mug in the sink with the rest of his dishes. "And with that, I'm off. Good luck." He plants a peck on my lips, then kisses the top of Addi's head. "Although you don't need luck with this one, because she's an angel. Right, Ladybug?"

His daughter's answer is an uncoordinated punch to his chin.

"Okay! I'll leave you alone to eat." He straightens and rubs his face, as if she truly hurt him. Crossing to the table, he barks, "Max! Enough of the reign of terror in here. Let's go to preschool, where you can boss around some people unrelated to you, for a change." He pulls out Max's chair and angles it to give his son room to hop down.

"I yanna go to school!" Brooks wails.

Harris blindly follows his twin brother's lead in the chant.

"You guys get to stay home with Mommy and Aidan and Addi! How fun is that?" their dad gushes, struggling to speak loudly enough to be heard.

Aidan joins the chorus. Much square-mouth crying and gnashing of baby teeth ensues.

With Addi on my shoulder for another round of burping, I approach the table and shoo Brice and Max toward the garage. "Just go. Please. They'll be fine as soon as you're gone."

Not helping matters, Max tosses his left-behind brothers a smug smile while his dad slides the straps of his backpack up his wiry arms. "See ya, suckas!" he flings gleefully over his shoulder on the way out the door.

I try not to react to my oldest child's new favorite catch phrase.

Brice, on the other hand, stands with his back against the open door and watches after his son, then turns his head and says to me, "I really hate that."

"I know." Placing Addi in her swing, I free up the two hands necessary to clean the hands and faces of the sniffling younger boys before releasing them from their boosters. "But what're you gonna do? It's technically not a bad word, so…"

He snorts and shakes his head. "You and your technicalities. I guess I'll have a talk with him about it on our way to the church."

"Yeah. I'm sure he loves those as much as I do," I mutter. "Have a nice morning."

With a final, limp wave, he descends the stairs into the garage and pulls the door shut behind him.

Almost immediately, the remaining three boys stop wailing. Brooks and Harris run to the dining room. There, they jockey for position at the window, where they receive their dad's daily wave and short horn-honk (which I'm sure the neighbors love) as he backs from the driveway. Aidan follows more unsteadily but gets there just in time to wave his dad and brother off.

And another week commences.

"I don't know why you don't get some help around there."

And I don't know why I subject myself to these calls with my mother every other day. Oh, that's right. Because my dad died. And I feel bad that I'm hundreds of miles away, an absentee daughter.

So I answer for what feels like the hundredth time, trying not to let the exasperation bleed into my tone, "I don't need help, Mom."

"Yes, you do. You're still recovering, but you push yourself with those kids and the house and the stuff at the church. Something's gotta give!"

"I'm fine."

It's nap time, which means I'm picking up the toys the boys have strewn about the main floor. I methodically make my way from living room to dining room (crawling under the table is the worst) to kitchen in my search, while I talk to Mom on the phone. Because it's best I don't pay 100 percent attention to our talks.

"There are three colleges in that town. I'm sure you could find a childhood development major to come in a couple of times a week and take the kids off your hands. Or clean your bathrooms."

"We can't afford 'help.'"

"Can you afford to collapse and end up in the hospital again? Or worse?"

"That's not going to happen."

"Nobody thinks it's going to happen. I didn't think I'd wake up one morning next to—" She chokes and trails off.

I wait, trying to swallow past the lump in my own throat.

Recovered, she continues, "Just promise me you'll leave more for Brice to do."

"Okay, Mom. I promise." I dab at the corner of my eye with my pinkie.

If I were being honest with her, I'd tell her these phone calls are more taxing than all of my kids put together on their worst day. But I don't have the heart. Anyway, something tells me nagging is a necessary diversion for her.

Quietly, she adds what she always says. "I worry about

you. That's all. In the course of a week, I lost my husband and almost lost one of my daughters. That scares a person."

"I know. But I'm okay. I get tired, and I rest. If I don't manage to accomplish a critical task during the day, Brice takes care of it when he gets home."

"He makes it sound like it's business as usual there, like you're such a trouper, and you never ask for his help on anything. He comes home to a hot dinner and five kids scrubbed for bedtime and a wife who's in denial that she fell into a coma after an emergency C-section two months ago. It was only two months ago, Peyton!"

"Yeah, yeah. I have a calend— Wait a minute! You've been talking to Brice about me? Since when?" I drop an armload of trucks and loose Legos into the wicker chest in the living room and slam its hinged lid, already planning my confrontation with Reverend Benedict Arnold about his collusion with the enemy… er, Mom.

"I've called him a couple of times to voice my concerns. And Mary, too. They both say the same thing, so at least I know they're telling me the truth. But I can read between the lines. By the time Brice gets home, you're probably nearly as comatose as you were after having Addi. You're just faking consciousness better."

The afternoon round of tidying complete, I plop onto the couch and flap my lips. "Mom, please don't worry. And please stop calling my husband and mother-in-law to talk about me behind my back."

"If you don't watch it, I'm going to drive there and stay on your couch indefinitely."

Now there's a prospect to scare me straight. It's time to start talking, fast, even if it means I have to make some mighty promises I may or may not have any intention of keeping.

"If it makes you feel better, I'll call on Mitzi and Mary and Marianne to take the kids for an hour or two during the week."

"And you'll use that time to rest, not to get more stuff done without the children underfoot?"

I cross my fingers, toes, eyes, and legs. "Yes, Mother."

She doesn't sound at all convinced; however, she relents with an, "Okay," that she immediately chases with, "But I will ask Brice if you're following through."

"I don't doubt it."

And that little traitor will probably tell her everything, too.

2

CHILLIN' AT THE POOL

*I*t feels weird to be out of the house for something other than church or Addi's doctor's appointments or driving Max to preschool. I haven't done the grocery shopping since… well, it feels like forever. Brice took over that chore while I was in the hospital, and he still does it on Friday mornings. I'm not in any hurry to take it back.

Frankly, it's a challenge to get myself to church on Sundays. Being in a hospital bed for months on bed rest—while maddening at times—broke something in me. I grew accustomed to my little fiefdom of blinking, beeping machines and round-the-clock nursing staff. While stuck there, all I wanted to do was go outside. Now that I can do that whenever I want, I have to force myself.

No matter what I said to my mom, I still tire easily, although I try not to give into it or let it show. And my tolerance for noise and activity is practically non-existent. Imagine what a complication that is in my house. I'm often on edge. I live for nap times (the ones that don't include calls to my mom).

At the same time, I'm so thankful to be alive that sometimes the mere act of living is borderline painful. My emotions hover close to the surface, poignant and over-whelming. I'm sure it'll pass. I'll get used to being alive and awake and able to move around and communicate with people and hold my children and function. Eventually. Right now, it's still a novelty. At least an appreciation for life is a positive outcome to this whole thing. It beats some of the other repercussions.

And as tiring as it is to tend to all of my children alone during the day, I prefer the solitude. Children under five rarely notice when you're on the verge of tears, especially if it's a regular occurrence. After a while, that's just the way Mommy looks (wrinkly chin, red-rimmed eyes, runny nose) and sounds (wobbly voice). Adults aren't as oblivious. And when they're your best friends, they rarely let emotional episodes go unnoticed.

Despite that, I took Brice's suggestion from two days ago and set up a play date with Mitzi and Sasha and the three oldest boys at the neighborhood pool. It's taken us nearly thirty minutes to set up close to the edge of the baby pool, but now that the kids are slathered in sunscreen, strapped into swimming vests, and splashing in the glorified toilet, I flop into my chair in the shade of the umbrella and hope I can last long enough out in this heat to make all that work worthwhile.

Mitzi stands in front of me, in the pool, keeping a firm grip on Sasha, protecting the baby from the older kids' rowdiness—and fun. Mitzi and Jared seem determined to perfectly act the part of typical first-time parents, complete with their twenty tons of baby gear, multi-page lists of instructions when they have to leave Sasha with a babysitter, possible—but not officially diagnosed—health issues, and their parent-related mobile phone apps. Sometimes it's endearing; most of the time, it's exhausting to be in their presence.

"Man, it's hot out here!" Mitzi says, adjusting Sasha's sun hat.

A simple walk from the car to the house leaves me winded and sweaty lately, so I'm no help judging whether it's truly scorching or I'm merely experiencing my usual autonomic nervous system's response to being mobile. Considering the time of year and where we live, I'd have to guess it's hot for everyone, not just me. I merely agree with her observation and try not to think too much about it.

She squints at me, studying my face, obviously not satisfied with what she can see of it around a pair of sunglasses that would make Jackie O. proud. "I know you hate when people ask you this…"

"Then don't."

She giggles. "Nice try. How are you feeling?"

I survey the crowded pool area for a diversion, but nobody has the decency to come down with so much as a leg cramp, although I'm considering my own attempt at fake-drowning, rather than answering her question. That would require a lot of energy I don't have, though.

Instead, I supply shortly, "I'm fine."

"But?"

"But I'm sick of answering that question."

"Well, we all know you're not going to volunteer the information if you're not feeling fine, so we ask. In case you're not in the mood to lie."

I roll my eyes but laugh at her astute observation. "And what if I said, 'Terrible. I'm so tired and run-down that sometimes by the time I get the kids in bed, I don't even have the energy to crawl under the covers, much less brush my teeth, put on pajamas, or 'visit' with my husband'? How would you react to that?"

"I'd ask what I can do to help."

"You'd offer to help with my husband's needs?"

She turns a red that has nothing to do with the heat or the sun, clicks her tongue, and sighs.

I yawn. "I appreciate the concern."

"No, you don't."

"I'm glad you care about me. But what I need most is time. I have to build up my stamina. And I can't do that if people are constantly doing things for me." Or tormenting me with their worries.

Dipping Sasha nearly as far as her bellybutton (Careful now! She's on the verge of having a good time!), Mitzi allows, "Fair enough. As long as you're not overdoing it."

"I admitted to going to bed fully clothed without brushing my teeth. I'm cutting plenty of corners."

She purses her lips in a way I know means she wants me to stop joking and listen to her. "No, that's what I'm worried about. I'm worried you're 'cutting corners' with yourself, at the expense of your health, so you can do all the things you need to do for your family. For the church. If you don't have the energy to put on pajamas for bed—or take off your clothes and sleep in your underwear, for goodness' sakes—then there's something wrong."

She has a point, and I'm about to concede as much—if for no other reason than to get her to stop harping on it, since there's only so much harassment a person can handle —when something behind her grabs my attention.

Without warning, I bellow, "Harris James Northam! Do not drink that water!"

He stares me down like he's considering to choose this day to do a one-eighty on his personality and be a rebel.

After a few tense seconds, however, he drops his jaw and lets the chlorinated water cascade into the pool.

Max turns to face me, shields his eyes from the sun with his hand, and brags, "I'm not drinking the water! Because I'm a big boy."

I give him a thumbs up and shout, "Awesome!"

Brooks waddles up the ramp that leads from the pool and plunks himself on his towel next to me.

"You already done, Screamy?" I ask.

He nods solemnly, then shivers. After helping him remove his swim vest, I wrap one of the extra towels around his shoulders and tuck it tightly to him, pinning it under his legs. "There. Now you're a Brooks burrito."

He giggles, then undoes my hard work by clambering to his feet and climbing into my lap. The unpleasant peed-on feeling resulting from his wet bottom against my legs goes ignored while I hug him to me, resting my chin on top of his clammy hair. "Maybe you should have stayed home with Gammy and the babies, huh?"

His vehement head shaking contradicts his disinterest in the water play in front of him. "I can watch."

"Sasha's going to get out, too," Mitzi declares, setting her daughter outside of the pool, then rushing to wrap her in a towel, clucking and tutting the whole time about "more sunscreen" and "chills."

I think we've already established it's two billion degrees out here. Nobody's going to be cold long enough to get a chill.

I do take advantage of the change in subject, though, and as soon as Mitzi takes her seat with Sasha in her lap, I say while watching my friend smear more sunblock on her daughter's fair face, "What's this I hear about Wes being engaged?"

Mitzi laughs. "Well, we know he's not one to waste time. Have you met her yet?"

I try not to take it personally, because truthfully, I'm not all that anxious to meet Jen's successor. I've been too distracted lately to properly feed my grudge against Peace's assistant pastor for breaking up with my other best friend (and breaking her heart). In any case, he was just as heart-broken and conflicted about the whole thing as she was. But that doesn't mean I'm ready to see whom he deems more worthy of his affections.

"No. I take it you have?"

Finished with the sunscreen application, Mitzi moves on to combing Sasha's curly red locks. "Yep. Tamra. She goes to one of the other Lutheran churches in town," she says in a mock-haughty tone while looking down her nose. "She's a graduate student at Missouri State."

"A grad student? How old is she?"

"Old enough to be in graduate school."

"Does she know how old Wes is?"

"I'm assuming it's come up in conversation. Anyway, he's not that old."

"Pushing thirty. Too old for someone still in college."

"Graduate school."

"Whatever. So, dish. Tell me about her."

Mitzi glances at me, then returns her concentration to a knot in Sasha's hair. "This feels suspiciously like gossip."

I roll my eyes. "Oh, and you're morally against that now that we're pastors' wives? Puh-lease. I'm going to meet her eventually, so you're just describing her to me so I know her when I see her."

Mitzi's chin thrusts forward as she tries to stifle her amusement and justify her urge to appease me. "I'm surprised you haven't met her yet. The two of them are always together."

"I'm not surprised at all. Wes is afraid of me, or something. You'd think he'd have gotten over that after seeing me lying helpless in a hospital bed for months, but it's almost worse since I've recovered."

"Maybe he thinks you're a vampire—or a witch."

We laugh at the prospect of Reverend Lurch believing in such nonsense. Then I say, "Come on!"

She rolls her eyes. "Fine. She's... very sweet and innocent."

I stare at my friend's profile. After several seconds, it's obvious she's blushing. That tells me everything. "Seriously? He nabbed a virgin?"

She widens her eyes and shrugs. "There's no way to know. But it appears they're a matching set."

"That figures," I grumble. "And of course, he put a ring on her as fast as he could. Virgins are an endangered species, you know."

"Now, now. It's probably for the best that he found someone close to his age—"

"Ha!"

"Who has as little experience as he does. Don't you think that will make things less awkward for him on their wedding night?"

"That sounds like a miserable time, if you ask me. 'Wait a second... is this where it goes? Let me consult the manual...'"

"Peyton!"

I peek around the front of Brooks to confirm he's fallen asleep against me, then say, "Sorry. I'm just— I'm mad for Jen."

"Don't be. She's happy where she is, in Florida, tooling

around on Vince's boat on the weekends, working on her cancerous tan on the weekdays, doing her freelance web designing whenever it suits her. Maybe she and Wes would have been happy, too, but it wasn't meant to be. I still don't know what caused their breakup."

She casts a pointed look at me that I pretend not to notice as I watch Harris and Max paddle around the pool with some kids I don't recognize. "But it must have been something serious. Lord knows Jen had a lot of stuff in her history that might have caused tension in their marriage. Not everyone is as understanding as Brice."

"And Jared! It's not like you were Miss Vestal Virgin of the Year when you two met."

She smiles sheepishly. "True."

"You've always been able to get away with anything with your sweet, innocent act."

"It's not an act. This is my personality. I don't claim to be innocent. People simply infer."

"Must be nice."

"It's not always good to be underestimated, even if it is usually to my advantage. There are times I think people see me as two-dimensional and uninteresting, and I'm tempted to tell them a few stories about… days gone by."

"Our Trippin' Trio days?"

"I'd never call them that, but yes. Those would be included. But you know, it's immature to brag about that stuff. It's not that we did anything most people our age weren't doing, but we did stuff I'd certainly never do now." She sniffs.

"We're married moms; of course, we're not going to go clubbing on a quest to scratch various itches. I get my itches scratched at home now. Preferably in a bed. Before ten o'clock."

"Exactly. And it's nice. I'm glad I don't feel nostalgic for those other days. I don't regret them, either. I think of them as part of what's shaped me as a person who can appreciate where I am now."

I bob my head in agreement. "Yeah. Well said."

"See? I can be deep." She stretches her legs in front of her and wiggles her toes. "And you know, it helps that we have husbands who are okay with that, who feel the same way and don't make us think we have to regret everything—or everyone—that came before them. No pun intended."

My head falls back against the canvas of my chair as I laugh up into the spokes of the sun umbrella.

She titters at herself. "Seriously, though. I don't think Wes would have been able to pull that off."

I clutch my side and squeal, "Stop it!" waking up Brooks, who grouches at the noise and grinds his head harder against my chest.

Mitzi slaps my shoulder. "I didn't mean that last thing like that!"

"I know! That's what makes it even funnier."

"I just meant, he probably would have made Jen feel bad about everything. Maybe not intentionally. But by saying little things or making his point by not saying things."

"You're right. I know, it was for the best. And I hope he and Tamra are very happy, once they get the hang of things." I bite my lower lip to keep from cackling.

"You're terrible."

"I know! I'm sorry."

"Stop thinking about it!"

"I can't!"

Sasha mutters something unintelligible at Mitzi, who speaks that language, apparently, and roots in the cooler next to her chair, coming out with a sippy cup of milk that she hands to the toddler. Ultra-casually, she says, "Jared didn't… know… all that much when we got married."

"But I'll bet you were a fine teacher. And what he lacked in experience, I'm sure he made up for with enthusiasm. Wes…" I shudder. "He's so… robotic. 'This position does not compute! Abort, abort!'" As soon as the last two words leave my mouth, my immature glee fizzles. "Anyway…"

"This is so wrong."

"Yeah, it is." I rub Brooks's back. "And when I finally do meet this Tamra, I'm going to be unable to look her in the eye. And she's going to think it's because my best friend and her fiancé used to be a thing. And it's going to be a deal. Ugh."

"Maybe it's best she thinks it's about that, though, rather than the truth: you like to poke fun at her imagined future sex life."

"Poke!"

"I give up," Mitzi murmurs, gathering her hair at the base of her neck and holding it against the top of her head. "I guess near-death experiences don't change some things about people."

"Nope. I'm pretty much the same person. Which is what I've been trying to tell people for two months. But nobody's listening."

She tilts her head, drops her hair, and reaches for my hand.

I give it to her.

"I'm glad you're back. And I'm glad you're the same old Peyton. Sort of."

"You're sort of glad, or I'm sort of the same?"

"Sort of the same!" she chides. "Because you're not, are you?"

Ah, damn. The zero-warning waterworks activate.

I squeeze her fingers and shake my head.

"That's okay, you know? And, frankly, it would be weird if you weren't a little different."

"Yeah. I know. I just…" I take a deep breath. "I hate the 'spot-the-differences' game everyone seems to play when they're around me now. Half the time, I feel like they're disappointed the changes aren't more pronounced. Like I should suddenly be this angelic person, with all of my priorities straight. Which implies I didn't have them straight to begin with."

"I don't think—"

"Mrs. Whitney asked me if I 'saw the light.'"

"She was talking about the white light in near-death experiences, though, right?"

"Still… They want me to have had this transcendent experience that I can take with me on a lecture circuit, or something."

Mitzi snickers.

"When really, I remember very little. I remember the green curtain obscuring my view from the C-section. And I remember Brice holding my hand and kissing my forehead. Then I was waking up. Only I couldn't move or open my eyes or make it all the way to wakefulness. But I could hear… things."

I stop. It's not right for Mitzi to know exactly what I heard when I haven't even told Brice.

"And I had memories of weird dreams. Talking to my dad and stuff."

"Do you think they were dreams or… something else?"

"Dreams," I immediately answer. "My brain desperately trying to fill in the gaps. My subconscious putting together everything that was going through my mind at the time."

"You never know."

"I'm pretty sure I know."

"Did you tell Brice about these dreams?"

"Yeah," I half-lie.

I've hinted at it and joked about it, but I've never seriously shared with him what I saw. Until recently, I didn't remember much of it. It was just a hazy feeling. Like I seemed to know things without knowing how I knew them. Then more details emerged, often at inconvenient times. And lately, it's morphed into a full-blown dream-memory.

Reverend Vision Quest, who "saw" our future daughter in the urologist's office right before he was about to get the ol' snip-snip, would think it was more than a dream, for sure. Part of me wants to believe it, too. But another part of me thinks I'm losing my mind, and sharing the details of the dream I'm starting to remember will only confirm my slipping sanity. I understand now why Brice doesn't share with the world what he claims to have experienced.

"And...?" Mitzi says.

Instead of digging myself deeper into my lie, I merely say, "I think I can tell the difference between a dream and reality. Or a spiritual experience outside of reality."

"I guess."

"It's not exciting, but it's the truth. I fell asleep; I woke up. I'm not rockin' it at parties with that story. And it's like people are disappointed."

"Everyone's glad you're okay. Period. Maybe you're disappointed it wasn't more dramatic or that you don't feel more changed because of it?" she suggests gently.

I sniffle. "Maybe. I'm too tired to feel changed."

She releases my hand as Max and Harris run up to us, demanding fruit snacks. Since she's closer to the cooler, she takes care of distribution, making both boys "say the magic word" before opening the packets and dumping them into their pruney, outstretched hands. While everyone else is otherwise occupied, I take a moment to compose myself, swiping Brook's towel between my sunglasses and my cheeks.

The truth is, the biggest differences in the way I feel and act aren't positive. And who wants to break that to someone who took a middle-of-the-night shift at a prayer vigil for you? Or to someone who has you in their prayers every single day? I can't be the bearer of that bad news.

3

JOB OFFER

*R*ainbows dance in the water droplets arcing through the sun slanting over the top of the privacy fence. Each drop takes its place in predictable patterns on the freshly mown grass, stirring the scent and wafting it our way, almost as effectively as a rare August shower and not the city water we're buying. The kids don't care. Their delighted squeals and screams prove this old-fashioned activity is still one of the season's greatest joys, no matter where the water originates.

Since our trip to the pool the other day, the boys have been begging for an encore. While I can't quite muster the energy for a repeat performance so soon, I did ask Brice if he'd set up the sprinkler and fill the kiddie pool in the back-yard after he mowed this afternoon. That way, everything would be ready after dinner.

The water toys allow me to participate in one of my favorite summertime activities, too: sipping a post-dinner margarita next to the love of my life on a relaxing Friday evening. It's almost as good as the vacation we can't afford this year. So what if I'm not the only girl occupying Brice's attention (the other one's slumped between his legs and looks a lot cuter than I do in a onesie), and my feet aren't buried in sand, and I'll eventually have to move from this spot to clean eight grass-covered velvety legs and tender feet before overseeing what will surely be a tearful and tiring bedtime routine? That's okay. I know now I need to savor these moments.

We're the picture of domestic bliss. As a matter of fact, when I think about how we must appear right now, in this instant, I realize this isn't far off from how I imagined my life to be in my wildest fantasies when I was still single. There are more kids in this reality than I ever would have dreamed (I would have woken up in a cold sweat if this many kids had been in any of my dreams), but otherwise, we cut a fairly idyllic vision.

From the matching Adirondack chair pushed against mine, Brice inquires, "What if it were like this all the time?"

Assuming he's speaking philosophically, and not actually reading my mind, I think before answering, "Then it wouldn't be as special. This feels amazing, because it's not every day we do this."

Brice nods at the scene before us. "Maybe not always like this..." He pauses to snort at Brooks tumbling head-first into the baby pool. Before either of us can rush to his rescue, he comes up spluttering and frantically wiping water from his face, unsure if he should laugh or cry. He takes his cue from his dad and laughs.

As Brooks runs off to tell his brothers about his new diving skills, Brice continues, "But what if— What if things could be different?"

"Different how?"

"So different."

"You're scaring me." Change hasn't been historically awesome in our marriage, to date.

He grins but says, "I'm a little scared too, actually."

"What's going on?"

"Nothing. Yet. Nothing ever, if you don't want it to." He releases a huge breath. "This is hard for me to talk about, because if I say it out loud— If I say it, it means I'm thinking of doing it, and if I'm thinking of doing it, what does that mean about life as we know it?"

"I'd tell you, if you'd clue me in. You want to write it down and send it to me in an email? Text me?"

He shakes his head as if my suggestions are serious. "No. Remember how I talked to Dr. G. Monday?"

"Yes." Oh, no. *Different* has to do with some fresh-faced vicar who's about to ruin my life, doesn't it? Please, no. Please, please, please. Don't spoil this wonderful evening.

Oblivious to my internal panic, Brice says, "The call didn't go as I expected."

"Oh?"

This could be good. If they were supposed to discuss a vicarage, and that's not what they discussed, maybe that idea's been tabled. Maybe I'll be granted a reprieve.

"He's been trying to get in touch with me since May, but with things so unsettled here, I haven't had a chance to do much more than answer his emails with, 'Yes, we definitely should catch up.'"

I think back to May, when I was still confined to strict, supervised bed rest, pumped full of drugs to try to stave off Addi's birth. I smile over at the dozing infant in her father's lap.

Brice picks up the two-month-old's dimpled hand and waves it at me. "My bad," he squeaks, making both of us laugh so hard, we wake the baby and bring the older kids running.

After I've convinced the boys they're not missing out on anything in the "grownup" area and should return to their water toys, I recover from Brice's joke and say over Addi's grousing, "Tell me what Dr. G. had to say that has you so scared or excited. Or whatever you are."

Shifting Addi to his shoulder and rubbing her back to soothe her, he answers, "He said Concordia's president has been in touch with him and asked him if he has any candidates for new professors. Dr. G. gave him my name. And, long story short, they want me."

"Like a job offer?" My heart rate quickens.

"Technically, it's a call like any other, just not from a congregation." His intense eye contact clearly conveys one question, though: *What should I do?*

I swallow my excitement, imploring my racing thoughts not to get too ahead of things. "And are you hearing that call?" I finally manage to ask.

He gazes across the backyard, but I doubt he's watching our sons chase each other through the sprinkler. Rather, he's staring into the middle distance, searching for an answer in the sunbeams.

Quietly, so I have to strain to hear him over the jollity before us, he answers, "Maybe. It feels like I'm not very good at leading a congregation."

"That's not—"

He turns his head sharply to make eye contact. "I punched a retired minister."

"Shhh!" I look around, as if suddenly worried the yard has filled with adults who can understand what we're discussing. "Only a handful of us know about that, and none of us is ever going to talk about it."

"Doesn't mean it didn't happen."

"Okay, but it also doesn't mean you're a failure."

He shrugs then gently taps the silky sole of Addi's left foot with the back of his hand. She twitches and whimpers in her sleep.

I set my margarita on the ground to the left of my chair and reach across the small space between our chairs to rub his upper arm with my knuckles but don't say anything. Instead, I wait for him to collect his thoughts. My patience pays off.

"Some days it feels like my ordination was yesterday, like I'm floundering around, trying to find my footing, trying to figure out how all the moving parts are supposed to work together."

"You do just fine."

"Maybe, but 'just fine' doesn't cut it some days. Or if it does, it doesn't feel all that great. I—" He chuckles ruefully into his lap. "I had this vision…"

Oh, shit. Not another vision.

"…of myself, when I was attending Seminary, like I was going to be some kind of pastoral rock star." His expression tells me he's laughing plenty at himself about it, and it's safe to share in his amusement. (I'm also relieved he wasn't referring to one of those visions.) "You know, like, I was going to take Lutheranism by storm, or something. I was going to be a champion of all that was right in the doctrine and a force for change on the non-doctrinal things that could stand improvement. I was going to be innovative and breathe new life into the Church." His fist punches the air.

"A real renegade, huh?"

Thinking about it, he drops his hand to the armrest. "No, not really. But someone who would be part of the next phase in the church, not one of the ones clinging to all the old ways that aren't working anymore, traditions mere mortals have set down throughout the years that we Lutherans tend not to be able to separate from our faith. But it hasn't worked out that way, has it?"

"What? You haven't set the Lutheran Church on fire? Your church was destroyed by a tornado. Is that close enough?"

He bobs his head from side to side and closes one eye, pretending to consider it. "Maybe. Maybe that's the closest I'll ever get. Granted, it's a more literal 'rebuilding' than I'd hoped." More seriously, he continues, "Or maybe being a senior pastor isn't conducive to effecting change. There's too much business to be done. I'm too busy looking after people—which I love—and keeping all the balls in the air to keep the church running—which I like less—to think about how things can or should be done differently."

When I open my mouth to contradict him, he anticipates my objections and says, "I'm not talking about moving VBS from July to early June, hon."

"What about the Communion thing? That was a relatively big deal."

"Yeah, but it wasn't even a change."

"Perception is everything. And people perceived it as a big change."

"Yeah. It almost had disastrous results, too. I had to call some big bluffs and play spiritual chicken with a group who would have been happy to see me defrocked. I... I can't ever go through something like that again. I was an idiot to try it the first time."

"A successful idiot."

"A successful idiot with a lot more gray hairs because of it." He runs his hand through the still-dark hair that seems to back up my argument more than his. "You know what it is? I don't have the charisma required to get people on board with my ideas at the congregational level."

"If you don't, then nobody does."

"No, really. You should see some of these pastors at conferences and symposiums. They're forces to be reckoned with. But they make me uneasy. Like, they're steamrolling their congregants, trying to mold them into what they want them to be or what they think the Lutheran Church wants them to be. That's not how it works, either. You have to meet people where they are. Like Jesus did."

Since it's obvious he's already thought a lot about this and is rehashing his musings for my benefit, I move on. "What would this job at Concordia entail? Teaching the next generation of pastors to do all the things you claim to suck at so much?"

Pausing to send me a long-suffering look, he answers, "No, that's just it. Dr. G. said they most desperately need professors in Homiletics."

"English, please."

"Sermon-writing and delivery."

"Ah. You are awesome at that."

He beams. "Thanks, hon."

"It's true, so you're welcome. What else?"

"He told me they're looking for someone to teach a section on family and marriage counseling."

"Also in your wheelhouse."

"And serve as the seminary's adjunct professor at Wash U, teaching a course in the Religious Studies department. Not during my first year, but eventually."

My initial excitement at this prospect fades. "Wow. That sounds like a lot of work."

"Yeah, I know. That's not all of it, either. I'd also write and occasionally publish my own scholarly papers and present them at the yearly symposium. And contribute to the Synod's publications. And keep up-to-speed with all of the goings on at Synod, which I already do, anyway."

"Hmmm." I chew on my thumbnail, suddenly worried about the number of hours in the day and wondering how this job would give him any more free time than he already has.

"Dr. G. thinks I'd be perfect for it."

"Professor Northam, huh?"

Wiping sweat from his brow with his right shoulder, he replies, "I don't know. Am I finished doing what I was called here to do?"

"I don't have the answer to that."

"And what if I take this opportunity, then discover I'm not cut out for it, either?"

He pulls his head back to verify Addi's fallen asleep. Then he stares once more into the distance.

I regard his profile for a few seconds. "Are we really talking about this?"

He swallows and returns my eye contact over the curve of our daughter's back. "Yeah. I think so."

While thoughts of relocating and worrying about money and leaving friends and family war with the thrill that comes with starting over, in a community much more similar to my hometown, I shut my eyes.

Brice grasps my fingers. "I know. It's a lot to think about."

Retrieving my mostly empty glass, I sip the ice dregs, then ask as casually as possible, "What does this pay? Generally speaking."

"More than I make here. Of course, it costs more to live in St. Louis, and I won't be receiving a housing allowance, so I'm not sure how that'll shake out. We'll have to crunch some numbers."

"Does it matter?"

"Of course. I want to be able to support us. Hospital bills, among other expenses, have made things tight."

"What else is new?"

"I'm just saying, things might be even tighter there. And we might not be able to live in a house or a neighborhood as nice as this one."

"I didn't marry you expecting to live in the lap of luxury. If teaching is what you want to do, if that's what you feel called to do right now…"

"Being home like this in the evenings, on the weekends, with my family, is what I feel called to do. It's more important now than it ever was."

I squeeze his fingers. "You pray about it some more. I'm with you, whatever you decide."

"Really?"

Loosening my grip on his hand, I trace my fingertip around his wedding ring. "Absolutely. I want you to be happy."

He averts his face, gazing down at the cement between his bare feet. "Dr. G. said the job was mine if I wanted it. His recommendation carries a lot of weight. And apparently, before he even mentioned me, the higher-ups at the Sem had been—I don't know—keeping tabs on me, reading my blog, attending my presentations at conferences and whatnot. And they were impressed, I guess." He blushes at this last tidbit while chancing a glance up at me.

"And you thought you weren't blazing any trails?"

Leg bouncing, he deftly dodges that challenge to his earlier statements. "This is all so unexpected, you know? A few days ago, I was listening to Wes and Ben's plans for the kick-off to the new Sunday school year and researching a vicarage and thinking about calling all the committees together for Advent and Christmas activities, now that people are returning from vacations and preparing for back-to-school stuff, and— If we do this, we won't even be here for most of that."

"When would you start?"

"Early November. Winter quarter classes start at the beginning of December."

I chew the inside of my cheek and calculate the logistics but don't comment. Oh, my gosh. We're really talking about this. November/December? That means... Dare I dream about it? A nice, relaxed holiday season. Well, as relaxed as the lead-up to Christmas is for laypeople. A lot more relaxed than it ever is for us, that's for sure. I assume we'll be active members of another church with its own activities, but Brice won't be leading those activities. We could even—gasp— skip some of them, if we wanted. Maybe by December 26 of this year, I wouldn't feel like I've been trampled by a thousand manic Lutherans. What would that be like? Oh, yeah. I remember how Christmas used to be, before this was my life. Christmas Eve candlelight service and Christmas morning church. That's it. The rest? Food and family and time off from work. You know, leisurely.

Fortunately, before I can get too caught up in the rapture of all the possibilities, Brice speaks again. "We'd only have a couple of months to sell this house, find and buy and move into a new one, and get settled. It's a lot. And I'm not sure you—we—can handle—"

"We can handle anything just fine. Focus on the decision first."

He takes a deep breath and blows it toward the darkening backyard. Since Max, Brooks, Harris, and Aidan have abandoned the sprinkler to chase fireflies, I hop from my chair and turn off the water at the spigot on the back of the house. Returning to the patio, I pluck Addi from her dad's shoulder and transfer her to mine. It's time for potty, pajamas, and prayers (or what Brice and I ruefully and simply refer to as the dreaded "Triple-P").

"I'll be right back with towels after I put her down," I tell Brice, who stands and stretches.

"Okay." He steps into the grass and snatches a firefly from the air, carrying it in his closed hand as he approaches his sons.

When I open the back door, I hear him say, "Check it out, guys! I caught one!"

Their gasps of delight trail me inside.

4

WEIGHING THE OPTIONS

*H*ow do I feel about the Concordia call? How do I feel about it?

So many feelings. Mostly, I'm ecstatic.

Of course, I won't tell Brice that until the decision… er, call… is final. Heck, I won't tell myself that, consistently. Every once in a while, though, I catch myself daydreaming about a life where my husband has a job that more closely resembles a normal occupation. With standard working hours, no calls in the middle of the night, and real weekends, not this Friday and Saturday b.s., which really means Friday and half of Saturday, because the second half is devoted to getting ready for Sunday. Or no weekend at all, when it's wedding season. Or Advent. Or Lent. Or there's a baby boom. Or a rash of deaths (hey, it happens).

Since that first tough year of adjusting to life in the ministry, I've rarely questioned those things (out loud, that is), because they just are. They go with the territory. Complaining about any of it would be like resenting that I need oxygen to breathe.

But the thought that life doesn't always have to be like

that, that life could realistically not be like that, is a heady, fantasy-inspiring concept. I scorched the oatmeal to the bottom of the pan this morning while staring off into space, imagining it.

Most of the time for the past twenty-four hours, though, I've kept this bubbling excitement at bay. Because what if he decides not to do it? What if he chooses to continue with his ministry here in Springfield, at Peace? Then all of these dreams would be about as productive as the time I spend on the Internet planning tropical, kid-free vacations. Only the realization that it's never going to happen will be even more bitter because, while I always know in the back of my mind that those vacations are unattainable, this call from Concordia is all too attainable. But it could be snatched away just as easily.

Plus, I feel pretty guilty about wanting to escape this town. I tried. I really did. I've even grown to accept it for what it is, so it's not that I think it's the worst place in the world to live. It's just not for me. And I hate that. It makes me feel like there's something wrong with me, like there's something I'm missing, some qualification for living here I don't possess. I'll never be a member of The Club here. Whatever that entails. Other people, people I love and admire, seem perfectly happy here. Why aren't I?

Peace has been a great church for us, too, for the most part, not counting run-ins with a certain former associate pastor. It's been a heck of a lot smoother tenure than Brice's time at Messiah, that's for sure. Even I recognize that. As a matter of fact, the only thing that would make the prospect of Brice teaching at Concordia even better would be if we could take Peace with us to St. Louis and attend it as regular members. I'd jump all over that chance. But that's about as possible as those vacations I price once a month.

And while I may be burning breakfast during my occasional lapses into undisciplined daydreams, there are parts of the Concordia plan that range from giving me pause to downright terrifying me.

For one thing, the thought of leaving Brice's mom makes feel awful. She packed up everything, sold the house in St. Louis, where she lived with Augustus for their entire marriage, the house where Brice was raised, and moved here to be near us. That was just over a year ago. Not only that, but she tirelessly took care of the boys while I was in the hospital, and Brice was spread so thin he was practically translucent. Are we going to repay her for her trouble by turning around and abandoning her? The situation makes me uneasy, at best.

And what about our friends? I'd miss all of them, too. Mitzi, Jared, Marianne, Clark, Lucy, Ben… even Wes. They're precious to me, although I'm horrible at expressing that effectively or often. We have a support system here that doesn't exist elsewhere, not even in Chicago. I try not to take it too much for granted, but it's inevitable to do so in a busy life.

Chances are, we'll make new friends, but they won't be like these friends. And what if we don't? Making friends, for me, is not a given. Brice will definitely fit right in; he always does. But what if I don't? What if I'm just as much of a misfit there as I am here, only without the handful of people who know and love me in spite of my quirks? What if I have nothing in common with the other professors' wives or the members at our new church? What if I never interact with anyone older than the age of four? I'll go insane.

Because here's the next thing: the workload Brice described last night sounds relatively intense. It's not that I don't think he can handle it, but if part of the draw of this job is that he spends more time at home, that means cramming all of that responsibility into a standard forty-hour work week. Which could be stressful. Which could result in a crabby husband spending more time at home. Which would defeat the purpose, no?

Then there's the money. I finally got a more concrete answer from Brice about his salary, and I Googled "cost of living" for the St. Louis area. The results weren't encouraging. If it were just him and me and a sane number of kids, we'd be able to live fairly comfortably, with responsible budgeting. Factor in how many kids we actually have, and we slide into an income bracket that feels more confining, especially when you take into account real estate prices in that area compared to what we can expect to get for our house in this area. As much as I'd rather not know too much about our finances, it's impossible for me to know nothing about them, and what little I do know, particularly about our medical bills, is worrying. Like I told Brice, I don't expect to live in luxury, but I also don't want to trade one stress for another.

I'm thinking a lot about logistics. Not only money, either. I'm thinking about selling this house, finding the time and opportunity to go to St. Louis to look for another house, packing and moving our family of seven… It's already giving me a stomachache, and it's not even happening yet. It may never happen.

Since when has that stopped me from worrying about something, though?

So, I guess my feelings about this new prospect are much more complicated than I originally thought. Typical.

∼

"We need a list," I say, plopping onto the couch, the force of my weight on the cushions nearly catapulting my husband into a different room.

He tightens his grip on his phone, then shuts down the social media app he was so diligently studying.

"I went to the grocery store yesterday morning. But I forgot coffee," he admits, his forehead crinkling like a paper fan. "And tangerines may not have been the best choice in fruits. The boys are eating them like crazy. It's made for some not-so-pleasant diapers and potty visits," he adds on a mutter.

I swat his shoulder. "Not a grocery list. A pros and cons list. About your decision."

That statement receives a groan, paired with ample eye-rolling.

I set my jaw. "I don't know what you have against lists. A practical, logical guy like you should love them."

"I'm not against lists! I use them, too. But you're obsessed with them."

"They're helpful, and if you'd use them, you wouldn't forget stuff at the grocery store."

He bestows upon me a playful glower that makes me laugh.

"Are you saying you don't need help sorting through all the information involved in making a decision about Concordia?"

He looks remarkably like his oldest son staring down a plate of spinach. "It's a call. I'm not really deciding anything."

"You have to decide whether to answer it. So between prayers and waiting for God to tell you what to do…"

"Careful…"

"It's a lot to consider. That's why we should write it all down."

His head drops to the back of the couch, and he moans at the ceiling.

I rise and stride to the kitchen. "Forget it. You'd obviously rather cut me out of the process, as usual."

"No, wait. I'm kidding." He rushes after me. "I do want to talk to you about it."

As he arrives in the room, I scowl at him around the edge of an open cupboard door, where I'm retrieving a glass. Crossing to the fridge, I say while pouring myself some water, "Are you sure?"

"Yes! I keep going back and forth."

"What? You're getting mixed signals from The Big Guy?"

He doesn't seem amused by my question, so I hurry on. "Isn't this the same as a call to a church? And when you've been called to churches in the past, haven't you felt obligated to answer those calls?"

He rubs his hand on top of his summer-short hair. "I guess… But it doesn't feel the same. And I'm driving myself nuts. One minute, I'll think I've finally hit on the deciding factor; then I'll think of something else for the other side that makes it just as—or more—confusing as ever."

I process all of this while sipping my water. Finally, I pull the glass away from my lips. "It doesn't sound like you're doing much praying about it. Sounds more like you're analyzing it and trying to make the decision yourself." I open the dishwasher, wedge my glass between the tines and the other dirty glasses on the nearly full top rack, toss a detergent cube into the appliance, and shut the door, pressing the button to start the cycle.

When I get no response from Brice, I face him once

more. "Instead of a congregation calling you, the next generation of Lutheran leaders is calling, asking you to share with them all you know, all you've learned in the field, so to speak. They need your wisdom and leadership just as much as churchgoers do, only in a different capacity."

"True."

"Is it something you'd like to do?"

He looks like he's confessing to something heinous when he says, "I think I'd love it."

"Is it because you want to go that you're hesitant?" Before he can answer, I point out, "Because, you wanted to come here, and that didn't give you pause. At all."

"I— Maybe it feels like I'm giving up. I just always thought I'd be a pastor."

I pull my lips sideways and wrinkle my nose. "Unless I have something wrong and don't understand how all this works, you'll still be a pastor."

"You know what I mean, though." He drops into one of the chairs at the kitchen table and slouches with his back to me and his forearms flat against the surface.

Walking up behind him, I place my hands on his shoulders and knead the tight muscles under his t-shirt.

"It feels like I'm giving up," he repeats more surely, bending one of his arms and stroking his eyebrows with his thumb and pinkie.

Instead of jumping right in to reassure him otherwise, I take a deep breath and ask instead, "Have you given Peace your all while you've been here?"

"Yes," he immediately answers. "Of course."

"Would accepting this new challenge be a revocation of your vows?"

His head shakes from side to side.

"Do you feel like, by leaving, you'd be leaving Peace in

the lurch?'"

He pauses, his shoulders tightening under my hands. Eventually, he grumbles, "No."

I lean down and kiss his cheek, murmuring against his skin, "Then do what you think God is telling you to do. Go with your gut, your heart, whichever body part generally gets involved when He's trying to tell you something."

I expect him to at least smile, but he stares straight ahead for a while, not reacting at all. When he abruptly swivels in the chair to face me, I back off a bit, but he pulls me toward him by both of my hands.

"Do you want to go?" he asks, his eyes beseeching.

Even with permission-bordering-on-begging for me to say, "Yes," I'm hesitant to let him know how much I want this. Because what if he ultimately decides not to do it? Then, on top of wondering if he made a huge mistake, career-wise, or if he's incorrectly interpreted God's will, he'll worry about having disappointed me.

I trace my index finger along the deepest furrow in his brow. "Oh, you know me. I go where you go; I stay where you stay."

"I'm serious. I'm asking you." He pulls me into his lap, his eyes locked on mine. "Yesterday, when I told you about this, you didn't give much away. Today, you seem more like you want me to say yes. But if you have any doubts about going—or if you just don't want to—that's my answer."

I gulp. "No pressure," I mutter.

All this time, I've wanted him to include me more in making big decisions. But if he had, we wouldn't be living here. And as much as I hate to admit it...

"We have it good here."

What?! I nearly look over my shoulder to see who the

hell said that in my voice. But now that it's out there, I realize it's right. I'm right.

Tears glisten on his lower lids. "We do. We're so blessed. But…" He stops, breathes through flared nostrils for a few beats, then lowers his eyes to my lap. "We're so busy. Too busy."

"In all fairness, we'll probably be busy in other ways with this new thing. Pastors don't do 'idle.'"

His jaw sets as he shakes his head. "No. That has to change."

"But—"

Lifting his head, he chokes, "I almost lost you."

"Oh, hon. Please…"

"I know, we don't talk about it. Most of the time, I can't talk about it. But while you were—" He shakes his head, unable to say the word. "I knew that if you never woke up, I'd have regrets. Major regrets. I'd have had to live with knowing I didn't spend as much time with you as I could have. And that… that terrified me. Still does."

My throat aching with pent-up tears, I have no choice but to hear him out, no matter how painful it is to remember how close we came to the end of our time together—here on Earth, anyway. And since I still haven't told him I heard him begging me not to go, begging God not to take me, and I don't feel able to tell him that now, I owe it to him to let him say what he feels he needs to say.

Anger creeps into his eyes and his voice. "Just a couple of months later, I'm back to spending fifteen hours a day away from here. Sometimes, I come home after everyone's in bed. And I say, 'Well, that's just how it goes,' in an effort to justify it, but it's not justifiable. And even more inexcusable, when I am home, half the time I'm not mentally here. I'm thinking about what needs to be done tomorrow, next week, next month. I'm thinking about the people on the prayer lists or the members I haven't seen in a while who I should touch base with but I know I won't, because I don't have time. After all, if I don't make time for my own family, how can I make time for people I rarely see and barely know?"

"You do the best you can."

"It's not good enough!"

Rather than continue to argue, I bite my lip and resume listening.

"So this is our chance. My chance. My chance to do what I was called to do, but maybe not so much at my family's expense. Because I made a commitment to you guys, too. I supposedly make it every day. And consequently break it."

I swallow. "Just promise me one thing."

Resting his forehead against my shoulder, he muffles into my shirt, "Anything."

Wow. I should ask for something a lot bigger than what I was originally going to say. This is quite the opportunity. But as a testament to… what? Growing up? Taking advantage of a new lease on life? Lack of imagination? Whatever. I say, "Promise me you'll be more forgiving of yourself when it comes to the many, many things you can't control."

He lifts his head, thinks about it for a second, then rubs the heel of his hand against his eye. "Um, okay. But I have control over a lot more than I think sometimes. And less control over other things. I just need to do a better job of sorting them out."

"Fine. I'll accept that as a yes."

Taking a deep, shuddering breath, he focuses his red eyes on me. "So. That still leaves a decision to be made. Do we stay, or do we go?"

My heart stutters as I realize I can no longer put off giving voice to what I've been thinking, nearly non-stop, for more than twenty-four hours. "Part of me thinks we're crazy, now that we've finally settled in, now that our family is complete, now that we're surrounded by people we love, to consider starting over again somewhere else."

"Good point."

"But 'sane' isn't one of the character traits we most identify with, is it?"

He chortles, then blinks and sniffs. "Hmm… let's see. We have five very visible pieces of evidence proving our insanity."

I hug his shoulders. "This isn't walking away from your service to God or giving up; this is serving in a different way, a way that was presented to you by an institution just as in need of filling a vacancy as a church would be."

Finally, that clicks. The left corner of his mouth lifts, followed by the right corner, resulting in a full-on grin. "It's going to be different."

That word is becoming one of my least favorite words in the English language, but I say, "Okay."

"I don't know what to expect any more than you do."

"You know more than I do, considering I've never set foot on a seminary campus before. And St. Louis is your hometown, so it's not a totally foreign place."

We touch foreheads. "True. But this isn't like when I was called here, and I'd already been through the process a couple of times. This is new. For both of us."

"Are you trying to scare me?"

"Nope. Just managing your expectations."

"Consider them managed. We'll stumble through this together. It'll be fun."

And the crazy thing is, I actually believe that.

5

MARY'S BEAU

*S*unday mornings are the worst.

Dressed-for-church children have a short shelf life. They sour faster than a glass of milk on a sunny window sill. And there's no point getting dressed and ready before the kids, because you'll get pooped on, peed on, drooled on, or barfed on. Or all of the above. Not to mention it's a sweaty business.

That means it's a forty-minute sprint to dress the child most likely to stay clean (varies, depending on which developmental stage he/she is in) to the least trustworthy one; then the grownups have to take turns keeping watch while the other parent makes him or herself halfway presentable. It requires patience, a good sense of humor, and teamwork, none of which ever seem to be in great supply on Sunday mornings.

I prefer fun Saturday nights like the one Brice and I finally enjoyed last night, the sort of fun we've seldom indulged since Addi's birth and my recovery. The sort of fun that you can only experience when a huge weight's been lifted from your shoulders, when you feel young and carefree and full of hope again. When a fresh start stretches ahead of you.

But even the brightest of post-coital glows can't survive wrangling a caboodle of kids through breakfast and into church clothes before 8 a.m. It's not conducive to bonhomie but more likely to end in divorce. Or the bodily harm of one or more involved parties.

Today, I give up on all hope of peace (because I'm insane like that and still begin every Sunday morning with the hope it can happen) after Brice appears in our bathroom doorway holding Aidan in a pair of khaki pants that are so small they look more like shorts.

I blurt, "Good grief! Do I have to do everything?" while I pull my hair through the flat iron and set the small appliance on the bathroom counter with a clank.

Brice shoves the two-year-old at me and snaps, "I guess so, because your idiot husband can't find anything that fits in all the outgrown clothes you insist on keeping."

"I just haven't had a chance to sort through everything and give stuff away!" I shout toward his retreating back while shifting Aidan to my hip.

"Fine. Then you get the kids dressed. I don't have time to sift through stacks of clothing, peering at numbers on tags." In our room, he pulls open his sock drawer. "I don't have my own clothes on yet, and we have to be out the door in ten minutes."

"All you had to do was ask nicely!" Barefoot, I stomp past him, carrying a bewildered toddler. "My bad, thinking you had it under control, for once, so I could get ready uninterrupted."

The slammed dresser drawer is the only response I receive.

So, he's on edge, and I'm on edge, and I hate that I get

all bitchy and turn into wifezilla when we're pressed for time in the morning before church. It reminds me of chaotic Sundays with Dad yelling at all of us to "Get in the damn car!" But I'm not a morning person to begin with, so this new routine of going to the early church service, presumably so the two of us can work together to get the kids ready, would be harrowing under the best of circumstances, simply because of the hour of day in which we're doing it.

And can I say how much I loathe being in the middle of an argument with Brice on Sundays? Everyone can tell. They read into the cool kiss on the cheek or platonic hug he gives me in the receiving line after the service; they notice I don't laugh at his little jokes in the sermon, or if I do, it seems perfunctory. Not that we ever make out in the line or that I roll in the pew at everything he says. But there's a definite difference in our demeanors, no matter how hard we try to conceal it. The tension is obvious. If it wouldn't be more trouble than it's worth, I'd skip church today. But it's necessary for me to be here.

Any time I don't attend, people freak out. They bombard Brice with questions about my wellbeing. They inundate us with offers of assistance and well-meaning drop-ins that only serve to throw off the kids' routines and exhaust me more. They bury us in casseroles. It's easier for me to suck it up and make my appearances. With every foray into public life, I'm saying, "See? I'm fine! You can all stand down now and go back to thinking about people more worthy of your concern. Like the homeless and the hungry. And reality TV stars."

Today after the service, in the fellowship hall, Marianne's compliment about Brice's sermon practically meets with crickets from me. Honestly, I barely listened. I was too busy wondering when I'm supposed to find the time and energy to sort through baby clothes to determine what can be handed down to the next child in line, what's beyond salvageable and needs to go straight in the trash, and what's already been through the entire succession and has somehow survived in good enough condition to go to charity.

"It was a great sermon," I finally supply dutifully with a frigid smile toward my husband's unreadable face.

Well, unreadable to anyone but me… I hope. Because I can read it. And it says, You're full of shinbones. (He probably doesn't curse in his head, either, the goody two-shoes.)

Marianne may not be getting the full transcript I'm getting, but it doesn't take an expert in social interaction to know this is awkward-with-a-capital-"A." She mutters something about Clark and her having us over for dinner soon and excuses herself.

My mother-in-law isn't as tactful. "What's going on with you two? Did you both get up on the wrong side of the bed? And step all over each other in the process?"

At her open arms and wagging fingers, Brice hands over Addi. His arms don't stay empty long, as Aidan tries to clamber up his dad's trouser leg to fill his sister's vacancy.

"It was a hectic morning," is all Brice says, hefting his youngest son onto his hip.

Mary lifts her eyebrows at me. I avert my eyes, preferring not to get into it in the middle of the fellowship hall before my third cup of coffee. Or anywhere. Ever.

"I hope you snap out of it before I come over for dinner tonight. I was going to bring a friend, but if you're going to be sourpusses, forget it."

That sufficiently steals Brice's attention from the petty gripes he has with me. It even garners more consideration than his youngest son's obsession with his ear hair.

"A friend? As in, a female friend or a guy… friend?" he queries carefully, pulling his head away from Aidan's probing fingers.

Mary touches her index finger to Addi's nose and laughs when the infant crosses her eyes and coos. Avoiding her son's scrutiny, she replies, "A gentleman, if you must know."

Brice blinks. "I guess I would have found out when you showed up."

"That's just it; I'm not bringing him if you're in a mood, kid. I don't want you to embarrass me."

He tries to laugh off the idea, but the noise that escapes him sounds like something from an elephant with a sinus infection. "Embarrass you? We're not going to embarrass you. Your friend is welcome, and we'll be on our best behavior. Right, hon?"

I gulp, working furiously to filter out the mental image of two white-haired people making out like teenagers on the sofa in my mother-in-law's apartment.

Finally, I mutter, "Right. Of course. We'll all get naps before then. Or something."

Thankful for a distraction, I turn to scold the twins for running through people's legs in the crowded room.

Max tugs at the hem of my skirt. "Can we go to Sunday school now?"

A glance at the clock tells me it's, indeed, time to head that way. I call the twins to my side and take one of their hands in each of mine. "Let's go, guys."

Max runs ahead of us, yelling, "Green light!"

Mary and Brice trail behind us with the two who will go into the nursery, rather than a class. From my line-leader position, I hear Brice say to Mary, "What's this guy's name, anyway?" and her quick, matter-of-fact answer, "Bob."

Bob. Of course.

That's the last I hear before we go our separate ways for the next hour, Mary to her seniors' Bible study, Brice to the summer teen class he co-teaches with Ben Eiffler, the youth director, and me to set up Communion and prepare the altar and the sanctuary for the late service with some of the other members of the altar guild.

And now I have to think of a special dessert to make for tonight. Something tells me we're going to need it.

~

Well, this is interesting.

And Brice. Bless his heart. He's trying. So it's not like the evening has been an unmitigated disaster. But it's been typically "meet-your-mom's-boyfriend" awkward. If Mary and Bob weren't so natural and cute together, like they've known each other for years, it would be a lot worse.

Dinner went well. Brice grilled tri-tip steaks, and I tossed a salad and opened a container of store-bought potato salad. But I pulled out all the stops with dessert: a home-made apple pie. Okay, fine, the crust and the apple filling came from cans. But I had to put it all together, including the latticework crust on the top, which I sprinkled with cinnamon and sugar. I also had to bake it at the right temperature for the right amount of time. So, I'm not a complete slacker or fraud. It was an effort for me.

Bob seems suitably impressed, anyway. As we sit eating our pie and drinking coffee, after dismissing most of the children to the living room to play, Bob compliments the dessert, then says, "Now, 'Northam.' That's... English?" With a gleam in his eye, he adds, as if admitting to a guilty pleasure, "Ancestry fascinates me."

Mary pats Bob's hand. Brice observes the intimate

gesture, then stares into his coffee cup, almost successfully hiding a grimace in a polite smile as his mom answers, "Yes, Northam is most definitely English, although my relatives hailed from Germany and Switzerland."

"Swiss! Now that's something you don't hear every day!" Bob cries, as if she's told him she descended from royalty. Or Martians.

"Bob here is a Scot," Mary explains.

In a decent Scottish accent reminiscent of Sean Connery, he supplies, "Abernathy means 'mouth of the river Nethy.'"

"He even has a kilt!"

"I'm Irish!" I blurt to detract from Mary's uncharacteristic giggles—and all they imply in conjunction with the kilt tidbit.

Bob turns his attention to me, switching from his Scottish accent to an Irish one. "I woulda known that from a mile away, lassie. That skin, that hair…"

I don't bother informing him "that hair" is called "Spiced Tea," comes from a box displaying a picture of a carefree model, and has little to do with my ancestry or genes.

Brice covers my hand with his and squeezes my knuckles. "And if you get to know her better, her temper will confirm it."

Glad he's engaging in the conversation and attempting jokes, even if they are at my expense, I laugh. The others follow suit.

He rises to clear the dishes from the table. On his way past a restless Addi in her swing, he pauses to restart the music and tap the mobile to life above her.

"You have a beautiful family," Bob remarks, his eyes on the baby. "Your Addison reminds me a lot of my Elizabeth. She was a gorgeous baby. Blonde curls, big blue eyes…"

"Does your daughter live here in Springfield?" I ask the logical question.

"Oh. No. She's no longer with us."

Splat. And that was the sound of me stepping in it.

Brice backtracks into the doorway, wiping his hands on a towel. "Sorry to hear that, Bob. Was this recent?"

The older man shakes his head while Mary rubs his back, obviously having heard all this before, judging by the resigned look on her face. "No, no. She's been gone more than thirty years now. She was only ten when she was diagnosed with leukemia. Made it long enough to get a bone marrow transplant, but her body rejected it. Died the day after her twelfth birthday." He smiles sadly. "We had a party for her, around her hospital bed. We knew by then it wouldn't be long. But we didn't want her to feel bad about making us sad. So we pretended like it was any other birthday. Not that she was aware by then, anyway. But you know, you do what you have to do to get through it, although in hindsight it seems silly."

I gulp. As if sensing the shift in mood, Addi ramps up her crabbing to full-scale fussing. Brice takes a step toward her, but I intercept him, needing something to keep me busy.

Bob chuckles and blinks his misty eyes. "Sorry, folks. Didn't mean to hit the heavy stuff on the first date."

Brice closes the gap between himself and Bob and squeezes the older man's shoulder. "You're with friends. I'm glad you told us."

Mary leans over and stage whispers, "I told you they were good kids."

"I had no doubt," Bob replies.

"I did, the way they were acting this morning at church," she mutters, winking at me.

I smile wanly.

"And before you worry there's another sad story involving a dead wife," Bob says, his easy tone returning, "don't. Nancy and I divorced amicably a few years after Bethie passed away. Losing a child either makes a couple stronger or... doesn't. In our case, it didn't. But it didn't make us hate each other, either. We just drifted apart, each dealing with the loss in our own ways, instead of together." He shrugs at Brice. "I know, being a pastor, you probably frown on divorce."

"It happens," Brice says, with a final pat to Bob's shoulder. "I don't judge."

Shortly afterward, the guys leave to poke around the woodshed, while Mary and I clean up the kitchen and wrestle the kids into pajamas. You know, women's work. (Who, me? Bitter?)

When the youngest two are tucked in their cribs, and the oldest three are finally settled in front of the TV, I retrieve the Bailey's from the high cabinet over the fridge and add liberal splashes to two coffee mugs. I set one in front of my mother-in-law and keep the other one. Plopping onto a chair at the kitchen table, where I have a clear view of Brice's woodshed through the back window, I say, "Now, let's talk about you and Bob."

Mary sucks one cheek between her teeth, then lets it go with a click. "What's there to tell, kid?"

"How long have you two been—" *Don't go there; don't go there; don't go there!*—"an item?"

Instead of answering my question, she cranes her neck toward the backyard, as if trying to see into the woodshed, and asks, "Do you think Brice is giving Bob a hard time out there?"

"What? No. I mean, how do you mean?"

"You know." She twirls her wrist. "Asking uncomfortable personal questions?"

"I highly doubt it. They seemed to get along at dinner. They're probably out there looking at tools. And wood stuff."

"Brice was very close to his father. That's why I haven't told you guys about Bob or brought him to church. But we've been seeing each other for more than a year."

"A year?!" I mop alcohol-laced coffee from my lips.

She defiantly lifts her chin. "Yeah. He was one of the first people I met when I moved here. It just never seemed like the right time to say anything."

"But... but how did we not know?"

Regarding me as if she thinks I must be slow (or deaf or insane,) she repeats deliberately, "Because. I didn't tell you."

I wave off that too-logical explanation. "Yeah, yeah. But we should have known. We should have been able to tell. Women in relationships are busy, and they glow, and they daydream."

She laughs. "I'm a bit old for all of that. And I do spend a lot of time with Bob. I just do it around everything else. When you're retired, there are a lot of hours in the day, kid." Glancing furtively from the tabletop to my face, she murmurs, "Are you going to tell Brice?"

"Hell, no! That's... that's your job."

"Would I be the worst mother in the world if I never told him?"

"Never is a long time."

"Longer for you than for me."

"That's not a given."

"True." She raps a knuckle on the handle of her mug. "Oh, dear. Well, he's going to be hurt when he finds out. But there's been so much going on for the past few months. And before that, I wasn't sure there was anything to tell. It wasn't worth saying something until I was sure it was serious."

"It's serious, then?"

She nods. "Bob wants to get married. Now, don't look so horrified!"

Apparently, my poker face is officially a thing of the past.

"I'm not horrified," I lie, because I don't know why I'm horrified. But I am. Maybe it's the idea of dealing with Brice's reaction to this news. Maybe it's because I'm an ageist jerk. Maybe I don't want to share Mary with anyone else. None of these reasons are acceptable, though.

"You look like someone just showed you a picture of mutilated kittens."

More like geriatric porn. But mutilated kittens would produce a similar reaction, so we'll go with that. My mother-in-law doesn't need to know I'm obsessed with sex.

She nudges my foot with hers under the table. "Not everything's about that, you know."

Oh, so she already knows. Excellent.

I hide my blush in my coffee cup, then ask, "Do you want to marry Bob?" before taking my next sip.

She holds my eye contact over the rim of the mug. "Yes. I do. Very much so."

I swallow. "That's, uh, settled, then. When's the big day?"

Fortunately, I wait to take another drink. Otherwise, I would definitely choke when she answers, "In a couple of weeks."

~

Is it selfish of me to hope I never have to go through my own mom's re-coupling? I know it's too soon to think about something like that, but seeing Mary tonight, six years after Augustus's death, happy with another man, reminds me that time goes on for those of us left behind.

I still have flashes when I forget Dad's no longer alive, and in those moments, he's the guy who could infuriate me like no other. But the awful moment always arrives when I remember he's not alive. It's been known to make me lose my bearings, drop things, sit abruptly wherever I am, or break down crying at the most inopportune moments.

Seems like yesterday, he was telling me how lost Brice would be without me, and how beautiful Addi was. Of course, it wasn't yesterday. It was never, as a matter of fact. But sadly enough, that dream is the most comforting "memory" I have of him.

Surely Brice has fonder real memories of his dad, which must make it difficult to see his mom with Bob.

Tonight, by the light of the alarm clock, I scoot over in the bed until I'm practically on top of my husband, who's finally settled onto his stomach after much tossing and turning. He grunts. I sneak my hand down the back of his underpants and give his bottom a playful pat.

"What are you doing?" he muffles into his pillow.

"Objectifying you," I murmur next to his ear.

"I thought you were mad at me."

Oh, yeah. I'd forgotten about that. The events of a typical day tend to do that, much less an evening like the one we just experienced. It's true, though, that we barely uttered ten words to each other after Mary and Bob left, only enough to get us through Triple-P with the boys, so it makes sense he would still have that impression.

"I wasn't mad at you." I kiss his earlobe.

"Coulda fooled me."

"Well, I was miffed before church, but that's nothing new. I hate Sunday mornings." I move my hand from his butt to his waist and rest my cheek against his shoulder blade.

Without moving, he says, "I told Jared and Wes what we talked about last night."

My tummy hops, but I tell it to settle down. I refuse to hope; I refuse to get excited. Not until we're to the point of no return, possibly not until we're driving away in the moving van. The thought of driving away in a moving van, though, fills me with giddy glee that won't be stifled.

"Did you hear me?" Brice checks, turning his head toward my side of the bed.

"Yep. So, what does this mean?"

"We should fear and love God—"

I tickle his side. He flinches and yelps, then laughs.

"You're such a goober."

"Sorry. It's a reflex answer to that question."

After I slide off of him and back to my side of the bed, although still facing him (and still technically on his side of the bed), he turns over so we're face-to-face. His eyes still sparkling but his expression more serious, he says, "But really, it means, I guess, that this is happening. If you still want it to happen. I'm going to call Dr. G. tomorrow."

I gulp. "Okay, then. I'm still in if you are."

"My only other reservation was leaving Mom here. But now, with Bob…"

Must not react.

Brice smiles wryly. "The guy asked me for permission to marry Mom. In the woodshed."

"He wants to marry your mom in the woodshed?" I say, to cover my non-surprise.

He rolls his eyes.

I finger the lines radiating from the corner of his right eye, then rest my hand on his shoulder. "What did you say?"

"It's not my permission to give."

"It was nice of him to check you'd be okay with it, though."

"I think my mom would dump him for even asking."

Don't be so sure.

Struggling to remember everything I'm not supposed to know, I ask, "Don't you think this is kind of sudden? After all, we just met the dude."

"That doesn't mean they just met." He smirks. "I know, okay? You can stop pretending you don't."

I release my pent-up breath. "You seem okay with that."

"Bob told me they were waiting for 'things to settle down.'"

"And then they gave up on that notion, because that's never gonna happen?"

"Right? I guess they figured this was as 'settled down' as it's gonna get."

We're both quiet for a few seconds. Then I summon the nerve to ask, "So, how do you feel about the two of them?"

His pursed lips indicate he's trying to decide whether to be diplomatic or frank. "It squicks me out," he finally blurts.

Frank, it is.

I clamp my teeth together to keep from laughing.

Chagrined, he says, "I'm sorry. But it does. I want her to be happy. I just wish she could be happy without him."

"He seems like a decent guy, though."

"I know. It's not about him, personally."

"What would your dad think?"

He moans. "Really? Let's not go there. I just… I can't… I mean, that's all I've been able to think about."

"He wouldn't want her to be alone the rest of her life." In contrast, I know for sure my dad would be okay with my mom never finding anyone else. He wanted to be the one to make her happy. Or miserable. Nobody else. Not even in Heaven would Dad accept her finding a replacement for him.

We all know there is no replacement for him, anyway. And that's not necessarily a compliment.

Brice argues, "She's not alone. She has us. A lot of us."

"We're leaving, though."

After the tiniest of pauses, he reveals, "I thought maybe she'd go with us. Not to live in the same house with us, but, you know, nearby, just like here."

"She loves it here, though. And she wouldn't want to move again so soon."

He adjusts his head on his pillow. "Yeah, I know. But I was worried about leaving her. Not because she can't take care of herself, but because it feels like we're abandoning her. Taking her grandchildren away from her."

"I felt the same way, but now… This takes some of the pressure off, doesn't it?"

Sighing, he reluctantly admits, "Yeah. Now, she has Bob Abernathy, the Scotsman, to…"

"Keep her busy?"

"Please," he begs, placing his hand over my mouth. "Stop it."

Now I do laugh, then push his hand away. "What are you, twelve? Anyway, not everything's about that, you know."

"I don't think it is. But you're—" He shivers. "Let's drop it."

Abandoning the teasing tone, I say, "Fine. But let's say you die."

"I already hate where this is going."

"And I meet someone else."

"I liked it better when you weren't talking to me earlier."

"Are you saying you'd rather I be alone for the rest of my life than remarry?"

"Honestly?"

"Der. I'm not asking so you can lie to me."

"Yes."

"Brice!"

He looks as disappointed in himself as I'm pretending to be. "I'm sorry. I know, it's selfish and awful."

"I'll need help with all your kids!"

"Let's hope they're grown up and taking care of you by then."

"Even if they are. Especially if they are, that's all the more reason to remarry," I say. "I'll be lonely."

He pulls me against him and rests his chin on top of my head. "Please, stop talking about this. I did the right thing; I told Bob I was happy for him and Mom. And I will be. I just have to get used to the fact that there's a 'him and Mom.' And I will."

"'Atta boy."

"Now stop trying to kill me off."

I nuzzle against his chest, closing my eyes. "I'm only kidding, you goof."

"Well, it's just not very funny to me right now."

I pat his pec. "Okay, okay. Sorry."

Kissing the top of my head, he says, "It's okay. My sense of humor isn't what it used to be about certain things."

"Understandable. I still love you, anyway. Good night."

He shifts under me to get comfortable against his pillow. A smile in his voice, he replies, "I love you, too. Good night."

I'm glad I caught myself before making that remark about everyone knowing I'll be the one going first. Something tells me that wouldn't have ended well.

6

PACKING UP

"*H*ey, Sis. I have a question for you," Jason says two months later, poking his head through the opening between the living room and kitchen.

Without glancing up from the stack of plates I'm wrapping in newspaper, I reply, "No, I don't want to build a snowman."

"Aw, man! Why do you always have to ruin my jokes?" The rest of his body, complete with slumped shoulders, joins his head in the doorway.

Still wrapping, I grin and stick out my tongue at him. "It's bad enough I can hear that damn movie in here."

"Dustin seems to like it. And I've never seen your kids so quiet." He advances farther into the room and stacks the boxes I've packed and sealed so far. "Brice and I are finished with the computer stuff. You need help in here?"

"I could use a hand. And some conversation to drown out that movie," I accept, then direct him to the next cupboard I was going to tackle.

He grabs a stack of newspaper for wrapping and

packing the drinking glasses and says, "Oh, come on. It's not that bad."

"Say that after you've watched it or listened to it every single day for months on end. People wonder why I'm off."

"We don't wonder."

Following a few minutes of amiable silence, Jason says, "Anyway, I hope Dustin's seeing that having kids can be fun."

"Still wrestling over that decision, huh?" I ask sympathetically.

He merely nods.

"Being around our kids isn't the best thing for your side of the argument."

He laughs. "Actually, he loves those guys—and gal. We both do. Other people's kids aren't the problem. He just doesn't want to be tied down with our own."

Not really sure about it, I say nonetheless, "He'll come around. He knows how much it means to you. And it's not like you have to worry about your biological clocks."

That earns me a glare. "Dustin's already pointed that out several times, thanks."

"Sorry. Only trying to make you feel better."

He softens. "I appreciate it. Anyway. Let's talk about something else. The pictures of your new house look... nice."

I laugh at his diplomacy. "It will be nice. Eventually."

"I couldn't get Brice to say much about the place other than, 'It's all set up for Wi-Fi,' and, 'We got a great deal on it.' What's the neighborhood like?"

I bite my lip. Glancing at the room's entrances to make sure my husband is nowhere within earshot, I reveal, "The house is in the 'hood." When he snorts, I add, "Brice doesn't appreciate when I say that, but it's true. And as of now, our house fits right in with its surroundings."

"Love at first sight" is definitely not how I would describe my initial reaction to the place when Brice pulled the van up to the curb in front of it that hot Saturday back in early September.

"Well, this is it," he said, leaning over from the driver's side of the minivan to get a better view through my window.

I pushed his face away from my shoulder. "Ha. You're hilarious, Reverend Funny Guy. Now, let's get out of this neighborhood and get to the real house, before we're late for our meeting with Ed." Or mugged.

Brice opened his door, setting off the persistent alert chime. "Seriously," he said. "We're here."

Movement in the side mirror on my door grabbed my attention as a black Lexus pulled up to the curb behind us. If I hadn't recognized it as belonging to our realtor, Ed, I would have wondered if we were about to be shot for being on a dealer's turf. I shook my head, annoyed with myself for being so small-minded, but I couldn't shake the fear.

Alighting from the van, Brice greeted Ed with his customary smile and good humor. "You weren't kidding about it needing some work."

I opened my door so I could hear them, but I didn't move from my seat onto the hot sidewalk.

"Don't dismiss it right away," Ed urged while shaking Brice's hand.

He would say that. He probably had a bet with his realtor buddies to see who could unload the monstrosity.

I debated staying in the van and refusing to go any closer to the spooky house, but, on second thought, I didn't want to be alone on the street, either, so when the guys advanced up the overgrown walkway leading to the small front porch, I scrambled to catch up to them. At the sound of my door slamming, Brice paused and half-turned, holding his hand out behind him.

I grabbed it while taking in the outside features of the place: two stories; red brick; solid front door; burnt-up 'landscaping'; patchy front lawn; gray, streaked, asphalt-shingled roof (that is, on the sections not covered by blue tarps); and flaking concrete porch and steps. I shivered at the idea of what the house had seen over the decades. Pee-soaked mattresses and heroin-shooting vagrants sprang to mind. And those were the more pleasant, non-violent visions.

As he unlocked the front door, Ed launched into his realtor spiel: "Six bedrooms, three bathrooms, eat-in kitchen, unfinished basement, baseboard heating."

"Is it safe to go inside?" I muttered.

He laughed. "It's not condemned. Just unloved. It's been on the market a long time. And it's listed for a song."

"You don't say."

Brice nudged me with his elbow. "It has great bones."

"It does! And the neighborhood is up-and-coming," Ed continued singing the structure's praises while standing aside to let us walk into the house ahead of him. "Several young families have bought properties in this neighborhood in the past few years." He gestured to some nearby houses, festooned with scaffolding. "They're not just renovating and reselling, either. They're settling here. It's a trendy area, one of the last neighborhoods near Forest Park that hasn't already seen a revitalization. Prices around here won't be this low for long."

Before I could roll my eyes at all the real-estate speak and tell Ed to save it, that I grew up hearing it and know The Code, the interior of the house took hold of my attention and gave it a sustained shaking.

"Oh, my gosh."

Brice seemed to mistake my utterance for one of wonder, not the horror it was, and gushed, "Wow. What a place!"

I wanted to turn and run away, but I couldn't move. I was standing in something from the set of a scary movie (or a nightmare), with its peeling wallpaper and gouged floors and mildewed carpets. As Ed led us on a tour of the home, each room creeped me out more than the last. The only thing missing was an abandoned nursery containing a shelf of dirty china dolls with broken faces.

At the end of the viewing we reconvened in what I assumed was the living room, a tiny nook off the entryway. Ed looked expectantly at us, already mentally spending the money from the commission, I could tell.

"Well? What do you think?"

Rubbing his chin and turning in a circle, Brice surveyed our surroundings.

"It will require a ton of sweat equity," Ed conceded, using another one of my least-favorite realtor buzz phrases. "But if you're willing and able to do it yourself, it's a steal."

Brice stopped spinning. Jamming one hand in his shorts pocket, he rested his other hand against the side of his face and addressed me. "I think it's doable."

We'd gotten to know Ed pretty well over a couple of long weekends of house-hunting, but I still didn't want to tell my husband he was out of his frickin' gourd in front the guy. So I turned to the realtor and asked, "Do you mind giving us a minute?" with a sweet, serene smile.

As soon as Ed exited through the front door, and I could see him messing with his phone by his car, I said to Brice, "You're crazy if you think we're going to live in this house, in this neighborhood."

"Aw, come on! It's not that bad. Don't be a snob."

"I'm not being a snob; I'm being practical, something you usually pride yourself on being."

"This is practical," he insisted. "We can get this house for next to nothing and use the profit from our house in Springfield to fix this place up. The only things wrong with it are cosmetic."

"Did you see the tarps on the roof?"

"We'll take care of that before we move in."

Trust me; I heard the "will," rather than the "would," in that declaration. And that's when I knew: this was our new house.

That didn't stop me from continuing to plead my case. "And this neighborhood…"

"It's a little rough around the edges," he conceded in his typically diplomatic way that would have made me laugh if my future weren't at stake.

"People have bars on their doors and windows."

"I think those are historical artifacts. You heard Ed. The neighborhood's seeing a rebirth. It's probably safer than most of the neighborhoods in Chicago. Or Springfield."

He kind of had me there. Sort of. Springfield once won the dubious honor of being named the most dangerous Midwestern city. The only security we have there is of the false variety. But since when have I let facts cloud my judgment?

"It feels more dangerous here."

"We'll get an alarm system. And build a privacy fence." Before I could say another word, he grasped my hands in his. "The location is perfect." I scoffed but let him continue. "Really. I could walk to campus. You could walk to Forest Park with the kids."

"Not that we'd want to," I grumbled.

"And you can't beat the space. All of the kids would have their own rooms—except the twins, who wouldn't want to be separated, anyway—and I'd have a dedicated office. The backyard is huge for a city lot. There's room for me to put a shed for my woodworking stuff and build a play set for the kids. We've been talking about doing that for such a long time. Here, I'll actually have time to build it. And that kitchen. I can make that kitchen into something you love."

Chin lowered, I let my eyes do the talking.

He laughed. "I know. Sorry. That was an unevolved offering, wasn't it?"

I couldn't help joining in his amusement. "Uh, yeah. But I appreciate your trying. And you spend as much time in the kitchen as I do, so stop acting like it would be my special sanctuary. Are you sure you want to take on all this work? I'm willing to squeeze into a four-bedroom house in the 'burbs."

"I don't want to commute forty-five minutes every day. And I'm sure we can do this. A couple of weeks of hard work before we move, and we'll have it in shape."

"You're so naïve."

Not sure why, but that semi-joking statement wiped all evidence of amusement from his face. Determination set up residence in the set of his jaw. "Maybe." Before I could get too worried about having hurt his feelings, he moved on, his excitement taking hold. "But we can realistically have the carpet torn up, the roof replaced, the wallpaper stripped, and the floors sanded and refinished before move-in. The rest we take our time doing on the weekends."

I flapped my shirt front against my sweaty chest. "Let's hope the air conditioning works."

He took that as a yes and pulled me in for a sweaty hug. "Aw, hon! It's gonna be great!"

Instead of telling Jason all of that now, I simply relay, "The realtor called the area 'up-and-coming,' if that tells you anything."

"Oh, that tells me everything. That used to be one of Mom's go-to phrases."

"There's not much we can do about the neighborhood, but the house is coming along. Brice has done a lot of work on it, and when he sends me pictures, I have to admit, it's exciting to see the transformation. His enthusiasm is contagious."

"Are you just putting on a brave face for him, though?"

I tape the box of plates and bowls and slide it as far as I can toward the neat stack Jason made near the garage door. "Of course. Somewhat. But mostly, I mean it. I knew we'd have to make some sacrifices to get the size house we needed close to The Sem."

"Oh, it's 'The Sem,' now, is it?"

"That's what everyone calls it."

"You're hip to the jive?"

I pretend I'm going to throw a stack of plastic containers at him.

He doesn't even flinch, merely continues wrapping. "You guys are going to be so cute, in your fixer-upper, in your gentrified neighborhood, near 'The Sem.' Real hipsters."

I emit a derisive hiccup. "Hipsters. You don't know hipsters until you see the people who bought this place."

"Do tell!"

"Their running commentary as we gave them the tour of the house was comical. 'Love the big backyard! Babe, we can put the compost pile over there and the garden over there. What's the neighborhood association's view on raising chickens?'" I stop myself before I get too carried away with my unkind impersonation. "Not that there's anything wrong with being self-sufficient and growing your own food. But Brice was like, 'I'm pretty sure the association is anti-livestock.'"

I laugh at the memory of their disappointed, then disdainful, faces. I could tell that, to them, we were a couple of philistines, depleting the Earth's natural resources at an alarming rate while contributing to overpopulation. They might have a point.

It's not that I don't admire what they're trying to do. I just don't appreciate the condescension they bestow on those who aren't as committed to their idea of what it would take to make this planet a better place. I can tell their "Tolerance" bumper sticker is aimed at everyone but themselves. That hypocrisy bugs me.

Jason holds a spotty glass to the light before wrapping and nestling it with its brothers and sisters. "I would have loved to have been a fly on the wall. Between your eye-rolls and Brice's muttered asides, it must have been a trip."

"They have, like, twenty 'cycles.' Road bikes, racing bikes, mountain bikes. They're turning Brice's wood shop into a bike shed. You should have seen his face when he opened the doors to his precious inner sanctum, and they dropped that nugget. I thought he was going to turn down their offer on principle. But they loved the house and were willing to pay asking price, so he sucked it up and took one for the team."

"I still can't believe you guys sold the house by yourselves."

"It wasn't hard. Houses go fast in this neighborhood. And we've done a decent job on the upkeep."

"But all that paperwork!"

"Mom helped us, Dillweed.

"Still. Yuck." He wrinkles his nose and shudders.

"You're such a baby. If it doesn't have to do with computers, you don't want to learn anything new."

He smirks. "So what? Knowing about computers is more than enough these days. I don't need to know anything else."

"Cocky jerk."

Unfazed by my insult, he asks, "What's the plan tomorrow when we get to your 'hood?"

"Plan? Ha!" I disappear into the deep cabinet in the island that contains our small appliances and come out with a food processor I've used maybe once. "You want this thing?"

"Nooo! We're not here to relieve you of any of your unwanted junk. We're here to help you move your junk."

I sigh and plunk it in a box, regretting I didn't take Mitzi up on her offer to co-host a garage sale before the move. There was so much already going on: Mary and Bob's wedding (small, but still a wedding), staging and selling the house, goodbye parties (yes, plural), and packing, among other things. Plus, Brice drove back and forth to St. Louis every chance he had to work on the new house, starting with the aesthetic issues that were easier to fix while the place was still empty. The last thing I wanted to do was squeeze a garage sale into the tight itinerary. Therefore, the food processor and the bread machine—and the electric teakettle I didn't realize I had—are going with us.

I should make bread more often. It's so easy with the machine, and it's delicious and smells amazing.

"Are you even listening to me?"

Guilty, I look up from my careful packing of the appliances I haven't given a thought to in years. "Uh, maybe?"

"I said, you should give us the address to your new place, so we can drive ahead with our car and the moving van while you guys deal with the closing. You'll probably catch up to us eventually."

"You're sure you don't mind driving the moving van?"

"Mind? I can't wait!"

"You don't have to oversell it."

"I'm just practicing my fake enthusiasm for when we arrive at Gentrification Estates."

"Stop calling it that! You make it sound like we've appropriated tribal lands."

"Not quite that bad, but you have to admit a bunch of hipsters and yuppies buying houses for a steal from poor people in an effort to 'improve' the neighborhood is slightly presumptuous, if not downright offensive."

"Everything is offensive anymore. You can't take a crap nowadays without being accused of being politically incorrect."

He peeks over his shoulder. "Whoa. Did Dad just walk in here?"

I ignore the dig. "We're poor. We bought a cheap house in need of repair in a neighborhood populated by other poor people. That's hardly gentrifying."

"Sheesh. I was only kidding."

I put my hands on my hips, take a deep breath, and close my eyes. "I'm sorry. I'm tired and on-edge."

He comes around his now-full box of glassware and gives me a side-hug. "It's okay. Just let it go. Let it go!"

Resigned, I let him squeeze me and yell-sing into my ear like a Broadway queen.

"I hate you so much right now," I grouch through my giggles.

7

MOVING OUT

I have no illusions about how our new home appears from the outside, so I'm prepared for the sideways glances between Jason and Dustin as we stand in the driveway that runs alongside the house.

As soon as we free all the kids from their seat straps, Brice leads the way across the bald front lawn and up the concrete front steps with their bubbling paint that may have been white at one time but has faded and dirtied to a nondescript, uninspiring yellowish-gray. He pauses dramatically as he turns the key in the two shiny new locks on the oak front door.

"Everyone ready to see their rooms?"

Max, Brooks, and Harris chorus, "Yeah!"

Aidan mimics his older brothers on a two-second delay, which makes Dustin cackle and declare, "I love that kid!"

Brice swings the door wide and holds the storm door open so we can walk—or run, depending on our age, maturity, and abilities—past him. "Up the stairs! Careful now!"

Carrying Addi, and not interested in being in the middle of a trip-hazard melee, I'm the last one in line. While the others disappear up the stairs, Brice snags my arm on my way past him. "Hey."

I adjust the baby in my arms for a more comfortable grip, wrapping my hand around her thigh, above her knee. "What's up?"

"Happy Anniversary."

I want to puke when I realize he's not kidding.

He laughs at my sick expression. "I see. You forgot, did you? Well, well, well."

Placing a hand on his chest, I say, "Oh, crap. I'm so sorry. With the move, and— It didn't even register when we signed and dated all those papers earlier. Wait a minute." A mental picture of the date in my handwriting on the closing paperwork floods me with relief. "Our anniversary isn't until tomorrow!"

He shrugs. "Close enough. And as soon as you walk through this door, you're going to see your present, so…"

Assuming he's referring to the house, in general, I relax. "Thanks in advance, then." I lean against him and kiss his waiting lips. "And I didn't get you anything."

"You're here, aren't you?" He winks.

I pat his face. "Yes. I am. Gladly. Now, show me what you've been spending all your time doing up here. I plan to be impressed. Otherwise, I'll think you found a girlfriend."

He pats my butt as I cross the threshold.

I'm fully prepared to follow the rest of the group up the stairs, but the sight of the kitchen beyond the stairs stops me as if super glue covers the floor.

"Oh, my," I breathe, my mouth hanging open.

Brice quickly steps up to my side and takes Addi from my loosening grip. "Here. I'll take Ladybug, so you can… not kill her."

As soon as they're free, my hands fly up to my face and

cup my nose and mouth. I swallow thickly. "Holy shi—cow," I manage, taking in the sage green walls, clean, white cabinets, and bright, blonde counters before the tears fill my eyes. I tap the bridge of my nose and laugh at myself for allowing a kitchen to render me so emotional. But this makes everything real. I can see all seven of us in here, sitting around our big table, eating, talking, laughing. At home. This can be home. It is home.

"How'd we do?" Brice asks, and I realize I've been keeping him in suspense.

I nod and throw my arms around his neck, burying my face against it. He transfers Addi to his right arm and tucks her more closely against him like a football.

Chuckling, he says, "I guess that's a 'good job.'"

"How did you know?" I turn my head and peek at the room again, as if it may have reverted to its former ugly self while I was blubbering on my husband. Nope. It's still gorgeous. "I mean... I... This is how I pictured it. Exactly. B...But I never told you that. I thought it would be months before we'd be able to tackle a renovation like this."

And, secretly, I was worried we'd run out of money before we ever got around to it.

He extracts his left arm from around me and taps his temple. "I know you." Grinning, he adds, "And I saw the dog-eared page in a magazine on the coffee table."

"Sneaky!"

"I figured it wasn't a secret. And I was actually worried it was one of several ideas you had and not your favorite. But then I remembered, I've seen this room before."

I turn my head and tilt it in a silent question.

His fidgeting, combined with his, "You know..." and head-bob in Addi's direction aren't much help, so he clarifies, "When I first saw her, she and the boys were sitting at our table, but they weren't in our kitchen in Springfield."

The penny finally drops for me. "Oh."

He steps away from me and clears his throat. "Yeah. The wall color in that magazine picture. I knew that was it."

Since he's clearly uncomfortable talking about it, I choose not to tease him, for once, and instead slink farther into the room and run my hand along the island with the gas range. "This is the best anniversary present ever!"

He gratefully takes my out. "Really? Because I know we have a rule about no appliances as anniversary gifts."

"I'll make an exception this once." As if basking in my allowance, the shiny refrigerator, dishwasher, and stove— now residing where there were only holes a couple of months ago—reflect the glow from the overhead pendant lights.

Sidling up to me, he plants a kiss on the side of my head. "I just want you to be happy. And I know pretty things don't guarantee that. But it's an easy start. It's also my way of telling you I'm willing to work hard to keep making you happy."

"You've proven that plenty over the years." I turn my head and touch noses with him.

A throat clears behind us. "Um, not to interrupt," Dustin says, when we whirl like guilty teens caught necking, "but there are some excited kiddos upstairs wondering where their mommy and daddy are. I told them to wait up there. Wanted to give you two a moment."

"You knew about this?" I question my brother-in-law on my way toward the stairs.

"Yes! Brice showed me pictures on his phone, but they didn't do it justice. And it's been all I could do not to say something all weekend! I'm horrible at keeping secrets." He pats my back. "I'm sorry to drag you away, but the boys can't wait to show you their rooms."

I'm curious to see the changes upstairs in person; I just don't want to leave this room. But I guess I'll have plenty of time later (perhaps the rest of my life) to admire it, so I lead the way up to the second floor.

Brice emailed me pictures of his progress up here, and he and I picked colors and motifs for each room, so I have an idea of what to expect, but the reality is always better. Plus, I know he worked his butt off to get it move-in ready. He even recruited Vince to help him, each of them taking off a whole week right after closing to focus on the bedrooms and bathrooms, with some—but not much—help from general contractors, plumbers, and electricians. Their efforts have paid off, too, I can tell right away. It all looks great.

The older kids love how easy it is to tell which room is theirs, based on stenciling and wallpaper borders— dinosaurs for Max; rockets and aliens for the twins. Aidan squeals over the clouds painted on his ceiling. Addi can't appreciate the sweet femininity of her nursery adjacent to the master bedroom, but I can. Especially because I remember that it was a glorified paneled closet with a filmy window the first time I saw it.

The master suite (a bit of an exaggeration for the small room with attached bathroom) is clean and minimalist, which suits us fine. And the tiny room Brice plans to use as his office, well, they ran out of time on that one, but Brice insists he can "knock that out on a Saturday." The floors at least are finished.

The common bathroom upstairs definitely wins the "most-improved" award, though. Brice tells Jason and Dustin, "We gave this one to the professionals. The tile, the plumbing, the wiring, it all had to be stripped down to the studs. A little out of our league."

I survey the unrecognizable room. "They did an amazing job."

Brice agrees, then wanders off with Addi to check on her brothers. I hear him from the direction of Aidan's room saying, "Hey, Angel Boy, did you see the castles and dragons Uncle Vince painted for you? Right here."

To Jason, I direct while leaning on the door jamb of the bathroom, "So, while I was dogging our fixer-upper yesterday, you knew about the kitchen remodel?"

He sticks out his tongue, barely containing his glee. "Yep. It was a trip, listening to you talk about how nice the house would be 'eventually.' You suck at being an optimist, by the way. I could tell you were super-bummed at the idea of living in a half-finished house."

I narrow my eyes at him. "It was such a mistake to ask you to help us move. Nicole would have told me."

"Yeah, and it would have ruined the fun. Face it: it was an awesome surprise, and you love it." He pulls me closer and rubs his knuckles against my head, tangling my hair.

"Ouch!"

"If it makes you feel better, the outside of this place is still hideous. And the neighborhood, whew! You can continue playing the martyr on that front. You're getting an alarm system, right?"

Brice returns to the hallway and hands Addi to me on his way to the stairs. "How 'bout we fill this place with some furniture and boxes? Ready?"

The two guys follow him, Jason inquiring, "Then can we eat? I'm freaking starving."

Addi seconds his motion with a tiny squawk. I guess I'm about to spend some quality time in that new kitchen.

~

I hoped the adults would have time to hang out after the kids went to bed, but Triple-P was later and took a lot longer than usual, given the disruption to our routine, so by the time we settle the young ones in their new rooms, my fellow grownups and I can hardly muster the energy to say, nearly simultaneously:

"I'm tired."

"I'm exhausted."

"I'm freakin' beat."

"I'm tuckered out."

We laugh, then Brice claps his hands together once. "All right, then. It's unanimous. I'll make up the sofa bed while everyone else hits the showers. Sound like a plan?"

Jason consults me. "Is that on your list?"

I roll my eyes at him. "Sleeping is on my list; I don't care how we get there."

"Dibs on the new shower!" Jason calls, taking the stairs two at a time and leaving Dustin and me in his dust.

"He's not going to get very far without the travel bag," Dustin mumbles with a shake of his head as he moves toward the kitchen door to get to their car, parked in front of the garage out back. "It's exhausting being the only adult in this relationship."

Less than an hour later, the house lies dark and quiet. Well, as quiet as a house can be in the middle of an urban area. The narrow strips of lawn separating the properties don't always allow for enough room to muffle the sounds of neighbors playing music, watching TV, arguing, or quieting crying babies. Then there's the road noise. Cars (some louder than others), eighteen wheelers, motorcycles, emergency vehicles, and buses rumble past at all hours on the highway just a few blocks away. And I'm pretty sure I just heard a gunshot, but I'm going to pretend it was a firecracker. In October.

"I'm so tired, I can't sleep," I whisper into the dark, unfamiliar room that doesn't feel or smell like home yet.

Brice lies on his back next to me, staring at the ceiling. "Same here."

"This is weird."

"A new house always feels weird."

"Yeah, but… I keep having to remind myself where we are. And why. And how what used to be 'normal' isn't anymore. And that this isn't a visit; it's our home. And everyone we know, except for Jason and Dustin, is hundreds of miles away. And that I don't even know what our neighbors look like, much less what their names are or what they do for a living." With each thing I say, my heart beats faster, and my eyes open wider.

Brice is quiet for so long that I think his body has succumbed to sleep, despite his mind's determination to stay awake. As I'm about to glance over at him to check, he says earnestly, "I keep thinking about all those bikes in my woodshed."

I laugh at how pitiful he sounds.

He joins in. "I'm kind of kidding."

"But you're kind of serious, which is adorable."

"This is good, though, right?" he asks, turning on his left side to face me.

I roll onto my right side, ball up, and scoot so I'm nested inside the curve of his body. I bury my nose against his shirt and inhale. It still smells like our old house, which both comforts and saddens me. When I close my eyes, I can almost trick myself into thinking we're back there. I can't believe it, but I'm homesick. For Springfield, of all places!

Into his chest, I muffle, "I don't know," then turn my head to speak more clearly. "I guess we'll find out. I hope we didn't make the wrong choice."

"Not that there's such a thing as a 'wrong choice,' in this case," he quickly points out, suddenly sounding a lot more confident.

"Um…"

"No, really. I mean, there's a reason we're here. I hope we're happy while fulfilling that purpose."

"I'd settle for not being scared. 'Happy' would be a bonus."

He hugs me more tightly. "It's only scary because it's unfamiliar."

"And punctuated by gunshots."

He sighs. "I heard that earlier, too. It sounded pretty far away, though."

"Oh, in that case…"

We chuckle at the surreal nature of our conversation.

At that precise moment, our bedroom door, left ajar so we can hear the kids, if need be, creaks slowly open. Reverend Kung Fu Panda rolls away from me, jumps to his feet on the mattress, and crouches defensively, his feet on either side of my legs as he tries to position himself between the door and me. "Who's there?" he demands in a booming voice that makes him sound about a hundred pounds bigger than he is.

I curl more tightly, burrowing under the covers.

Max's voice rings out in the dark, "Mommy?" His dark head pokes around the corner of the wall that leads to the inset door.

Brice straightens his knees and stands at his full height, his hands falling limply to his sides. "Stinky," he says on an exhale, slightly out of breath. "Come here." He hops from the bed and plucks Max from the floor, holding him tightly to his chest. Twisting at the waist to produce a comforting swinging motion, he asks, "What's the matter?"

"I'm scared."

"That makes three of us," Brice mutters.

"Your heartbeef is fast, Daddy."

I sit up and press my fist against my own "heartbeef" in an effort to slow it down.

"You scared me a little, that's all, Stink." He sinks to the foot of the bed and presses his lips against his clone's hair.

"Daddies don't get a-scared."

"Yeah, we do. Sometimes."

"Because of monsters?"

"No. Monsters are pretend, remember?"

"Yes, I do. So what are you a-scared of?"

"Oh, a lot of things. Nothing you need to worry about, though." He stands and places Max on his feet. "Let's go potty and get back to bed."

"I wanna sleep with you and Mommy."

It's normally strictly against the rules (we have to draw the line somewhere or we'd never be alone), but when Brice sends me a quick, consulting glance, I nod, so he replies, "Okay. Just this once, though," as he shepherds Max into our bathroom. "There's nothing to be afraid of."

I wonder who he's trying to convince.

8

NEW DIGS

*O*ver breakfast the next morning, I'm reenacting for Dustin and Jason the story of Brice, fearless toddler-slayer, when the man himself staggers into the kitchen, looking like he was definitely on the losing end of his latest match-up.

I rise from my imitation of his mattress-top Judo crouch. "I'd ask how you slept, but it's obvious the answer is, 'not well,'" I say, hurrying to pour a cup of coffee and pass it to him.

He wraps his hands around the mug, closes his eyes, and inhales the steam before taking what must be a scalding gulp, based on his resultant wince. "Rules are rules for a reason," he rasps.

I smile sympathetically. "You could have told him 'no.'"

"I didn't want to be the bad guy."

"You wanted me to be the bad guy?"

"You're so good at it."

"You give kids an inch…"

He grunts and takes another huge swallow of coffee. Then he blinks his eyes and opens them widely, attempting a groggy smile while he settles into one of the retro swivel stools at the counter. "Feeling better already. Although…" He fingers the skin near the corner of his left eye. "I feel a shiner coming on. Seriously, he clocked me no less than a dozen times."

"Fewer," I correct with a smirk that earns me a lethal glare. "Hey, if you're going to be a professor, you'd better speak precisely."

Jason slaps the counter in front of him. "Bacon, woman. You promised me bacon."

"Rude," Dustin intones.

I return to the island, where I open the package of bacon I picked up at the store when I snuck out early this morning. "All right, all right. I'm getting to it."

"Not fast enough," Jason says. "The least you can do is make us a huge, artery-clogging American breakfast after all of our hard work this weekend."

"That's what I'm doing!" I root around in three boxes before emerging with the skillets I'll need to make the eggs, bacon, and hash browns. "I'm having a hard time finding what I need, and you three"—I gesture toward the counter, where they're lined up like hungry, expectant dogs—"aren't helping at all."

"That's kind of the point," Jason says. "We did all the work yesterday."

Brice's eyes widen, and he clamps a friendly hand on the back of Jason's neck. "Whoa, brother. Danger, danger."

"Uh, yeah," I say with a good-natured grin. "I entertained five kids with no TV or toys or artificially flavored snacks all day yesterday and kept them out of your way, when the only thing they wanted to do was run between your legs."

"I'd haul fifty real-wood dressers up those stairs rather

than have that job," Brice says, hopping from his stool and crossing to the coffee maker, where he pours the last of the carafe into his cup and starts making the next pot.

"Butt-kisser," Jason says.

"Yessireebob," Brice agrees unapologetically.

Inspecting the permanent marker scrawled on the side of one of the boxes to try to glean its contents before going to the trouble of unsealing it, I say, "He knows what's good for him. And if you did, you'd shut up and help me find the box with the large cooking utensils, specifically the whisk and the spatula."

Grudgingly, Jason comes around the island and does exactly that, unstacking boxes and cutting through packing tape with the tip of his car key.

Amused, Dustin observes us. "You guys crack me up. I wish my family was like this."

"Rude and irreverent?" I whirl and snatch the whisk Jason has found and is now poking between my shoulder blades.

Posture straightening, Dustin answers, "Yeah! It shows you like each other, no matter what. Love's unconditional, not based on whether you behave well."

I shoot Jason a questioning glance, but he merely shakes his head as if to say, "Don't get me involved."

He hardly ever talks about Dustin's family, but from the few things he has said—and the many things left unsaid—I've gathered they're not the warmest people. I met them at the reception Jason and Dustin threw for themselves after their civil ceremony, but everything was hazy then, as I was still recovering from Addi's birth and the resulting complications, and we were all still reeling from Dad's death. Dustin's parents and sister didn't seem overly friendly, but then again, it was the first time we'd ever met, so their standoffishness wasn't offensive, either. Not everyone can walk into a room of strangers and have an instant rapport with them.

The only person I've ever known who can is rubbing his stubbled face and peering intently out the kitchen window.

He lifts his hand and gives a casual wave to whomever's out there. Then he says, "Our next door neighbor's trying to tell me something. I'll be right back," and leaves through the back door. "Hi there," I hear him say as he pulls the door closed.

And it starts.

Dustin takes over at the stove as I abandon the sizzling bacon and eggs to finish my husband's half-assed coffee-making, keeping my eye on the exchange over the rusty chain-link fence between our driveway and the neighbor's.

It all looks amiable enough: the customary shaking of hands; some gesturing toward our house by the neighbor, a guy who appears to be in his early fifties; laughter from Brice, then some familiar body language that generally accompanies his humble downplaying of something or other. Who knows what? The guy doesn't take credit for anything, not even the five kids he sired. Although that's understandable some days. After another handshake and a final loud, "Thanks for the heads up, Harvey! It was good to meet you," that I can hear through the double-paned window, he turns and jogs back toward the house.

He brings in with him a gust of chilly, autumn-scented air, but since it appears there's already a conversation going on in this room—one I haven't paid a bit of attention to since he left, I might add—he merely retrieves his cooling coffee and retakes his seat at the counter.

"…And that's just how they've always been." Dustin is winding down now while I tune back in. "I didn't realize it was odd until I was old enough to spend some time around friends' families. Most of them were like you guys: relaxed around each other, not always weighing your words." With a fork, he transfers greasy slices of bacon from the skillet to a paper towel-lined plate. "Even your dad, who wasn't the most accepting guy and could get blustery when he disagreed with someone, seemed a lot less judgmental than my dad, with his disapproving silences."

"Kent Stratford, not accepting?" Brice quips, launching Jason and me into our repertoire of Dad stories. When we get through the ones from our childhood and early adulthood, it's Dustin and Brice's cue to add their own experiences with Dad's irascibility.

"Remember the first time he met me?" Dustin asks, giggling at the memory. "Oh, man."

"I'll never forget the time he thought Peyton and I were —" Brice says. His smile quickly fades, though, and he clears his throat.

Not sure why he's pulled up, I look from him to Dustin to Jason, and back. "What? It's okay. Everyone here knows."

Brice shakes his head tersely. "No, it's not that. Never mind. I— We shouldn't make light of that, actually."

"It's funny now, in hindsight. I thought he was going to kill one or both of us that day. It's a miracle he didn't stroke out a lot sooner than he did."

"It's really not funny," Brice insists, rising once more. "I'm, uh… gonna go check on the kids. I think I heard something up there, and I don't want any of them falling down the stairs." With that, he strides from the room and rushes up the steps, trilling, "Yoo-hoo! I hear a bunch of monkeys who need morning kisses!"

Out of the indistinct giggling and shrieking above, we hear Max's strident declaration, "Daddy, your breff smells like coffee!" and Brice's "Mwahahahaha!" in reply.

Jason points to the ceiling and says to Dustin. "See? That. That's what I want."

Dustin smiles. "Yeah, that's pretty darn awesome," he says. "It's the lifelong responsibility—and bodily waste—that always seems to outweigh that other stuff."

Figuring we've transitioned away from my husband's odd behavior of a few seconds ago (and somewhat relieved of it, since I don't understand it, myself), I plate the scrambled eggs and lobby for the two of them to take a couple of our kids.

By the time Brice and his merry men—and not-so-merry little lady—enter the kitchen, Jason has set the table, and I've poured orange juice into sippy cups and regular glasses.

And this is our new life. Sort of.

"Do you think we're targets for a drive-by in this window?" I ask, my listless tone belying the seriousness of my question.

Jason and Dustin left for Chicago after helping Brice return the moving van to the rental place, so we've been on our own, officially consigned to our new life, for a couple of hours now. The kids are in their own beds, hopefully for the whole night. And I couldn't unpack another box if my life depended on it. I'm done.

Brice, sitting with his back braced against the other side of the bay window, his left leg hanging off the edge of the sill, finds the energy to lift his head and level his eyes with mine. "You need to stop making jokes about stuff like that. The people in this neighborhood are hard-working folks, like you and me."

"Is that what—what's his name, again?—Harvey told you this morning during your fencepost tête-à-tête?"

He rolls his eyes. "You're so snide. And no, that's not what Harvey told me. But it wasn't long ago that your main objection to moving somewhere was that it wasn't diverse enough. Well, here we are. Diversity abounds."

"Diversity doesn't have to equal danger."

"You're right. And vice versa. Springfield proved that point quite well."

I narrow my eyes and say through gritted teeth, "What did you and Harvey talk about, then?"

After a slight hesitation, he answers, "He said he was glad a nice family, like ours—"

"He's in for an unpleasant surprise."

"—bought this place, and he's excited we're fixing it up. Apparently, the last tenants were not very neighborly."

"No!"

Brice gently kicks my right butt cheek.

"What else?"

"That's it."

"No, it's not."

His jaw twitches.

"C'mon. Out with it, Northam. You can't lie worth a shit, so don't try. What else did he say? Why did you thank him for the 'heads up'?"

"Were you spying on us?"

"You were talking out in the open, and you said that last thing loud enough for them to hear you at the Arch."

"Oh, by the way, I promised the kids we'd go there sometime this week. I think it's supposed to be sunny and not too cold on Wednesday."

"Mmm hmm."

"I was thinking we could pick up some pumpkins and

carve those sometime this week, too. They'll look cute on the front porch."

"Stop trying to change the subject, Reverend Deflection. What did Harvey give you a heads up about?"

He runs his hand through his hair, which will definitely need a cut before he starts his new job. "It's not a big deal."

"I'll be the judge of that."

"He said there's been a rash of car break-ins and thefts lately, so police have upped patrolling in this area at night."

"Oh. That's actually a good thing. At least, the increased police presence is comforting."

"He advised against parking our cars on the street, even for a few minutes, and said the garage is the only safe place. For the cars, that is."

"Great."

"Like I said, it's not a big deal. There's no reason for us not to use the garage, anyway. And I'll move building that privacy fence and driveway gate to the top of my to-do list."

"Wait. You have a list?" The smirk takes up residence on my face before I can suppress it.

He shifts, bearing his weight on his left leg to retrieve his wallet from his back right pocket. From the wallet, he produces a hardware store receipt, the back of which bears a sizable list in his neat, minuscule block printing.

Before I can take in any of the details, he tucks it into his wallet once more. "There. See? You don't have the monopoly on lists."

"I never thought I did."

"There were too many things to remember, and it was hard to prioritize them when they were all up here." He taps his forehead. "So I wrote them down. Don't get too excited."

"Don't tell me what to do—or not do."

He returns his wallet to his back pocket, but instead of staying on his side of the window, he pushes my bent knees apart and wedges himself between them, leaning forward for a kiss.

"Brice. The whole neighborhood can see us."

One of the first things on my to-do list is to get a covering for this massive window, but it hasn't happened yet.

He presses his lips on mine, and although I'm not relaxed, I kiss him back. Tentatively. He pulls away after a few seconds. "I don't care. We're not doing anything wrong."

"It's private."

"It's just a kiss."

"Still. Kissing leads to other things."

"I hope so."

"Not here. In the window."

He gives me some breathing room but doesn't retreat to his original position. Instead, he perches on the edge of the sill and sets my feet in his lap. "First you forget our anniversary; now you're uncomfortable with PDA. This has been a weekend of role reversals."

"Oh, my gosh! Happy anniversary! For real, this time."

"I didn't want to say anything, but yeah. Happy anniversary."

I close my eyes and pause a second to say a silent "Happy Birthday" to Secret, too. Brice's supporting foot-squeeze brings me back to the room. I open my eyes and smile at him, knowing he feels that same bittersweet tug I experience every year on this day.

Before we can get bogged down in sadness, though, I clear my throat and explain lightly, "I'm all screwed up. I keep forgetting it's Sunday, because we didn't go to church."

"Yeah, about that... We need to see what's close. None

of the churches we visited while house hunting felt like home."

"Where'd you go growing up?"

He screws his mouth to the side. "That one would be a bit of a trek every Sunday. And I'd like to go somewhere new to both of us. Start a new tradition."

I sit up and grab his hand. "I'd like that."

"The church on campus is nice, but I've been there before, too. I attended it all through Sem, and I'll be going to chapel there daily as part of the job. I'd like to be a member—a regular member—of a church family. That's going to be a nice change."

Tucking a piece of hair behind his ear, I say, "I think it will be, too." I haul myself to my feet, groaning more than saying, "I need to clean up the kitchen before bed."

"I'll transfer that load of laundry you started earlier to the dryer," he offers.

"Much obliged, kind sir."

By the time he's finished in the laundry room, I've started the dishwasher, and I'm almost finished wiping down the counters. As I drape the dishrag over the divider between the two halves of the sink, he walks up behind me, grasps my upper arms, and kisses the crown of my head. "Wanna christen the kitchen?"

"Interesting word choice, Reverend," I tease, turning to face him. I pluck at his t-shirt and gaze at him through my eyelashes. "And we don't have to do that. I know it's not your thing."

"It's very much my thing right now," he says huskily. He walks over to the switch on the wall and kills the lights, plunging us into private darkness.

"I don't know," I hedge, hating how reticent and middle-aged I've become.

"Fine then," he states matter-of-factly. I think he's going to turn on the lights and abandon the whole venture, but he pulls me through the room to the door that leads to the pantry. "You give me no choice, I guess."

He opens the door, flicks on the switch inside, and tugs me inside, yanking the door shut behind us. Once inside the tiny, windowless room, he pushes me against a wall of mostly empty shelves and kisses me in a way he hasn't in... a while. I moan into his mouth while pulling at his clothes.

He chuckles against my lips. "Oh, boy. This is gonna be good."

Best anniversary ever.

9

LITTLE PONIES AND SWEETHEART DONKEYS

*L*ife is crazy. And Brice hasn't even started his new job yet. But maybe that's why it's crazy. Maybe our lack of routine is preventing us from settling down. That's what I tell myself, anyway. It's not that life is crazy-bad, but it's not necessarily crazy-good, either. It's crazy-unsustainable. As much as I'm enjoying all of this time with Brice, none of it feels like real life yet. I'm both excited and afraid to see how it will be when this extended vacation ends in less than a week, on the first Monday in November.

In the midst of all of this, I haven't had a chance to ask him why he got so weird sharing the memory of Dad confronting us about what he suspected was an illicit affair between pastor and parishioner. When we're alone, which is rare, we tend to be doing things that may be deep and probing but don't lend themselves to deep, probing conversations. If I didn't know better, I'd think that was the point.

We're still in full-on moving mode, too. It's a seemingly never-ending process. If we're not putting away our stuff, we're fixing the stuff that came with—or on or in—this house. And when we're not doing something related to moving and settling and fixing, we're making it up to the kids that we're home-improvement-obsessed.

So far, they haven't had too many questions about what's going on, and we don't volunteer any information. We wait until they ask ("Where's Gammy?") and hope our answers ("Gammy's in Springfield with Grandpa Bob, but she'll come visit us soon") don't upset them. Keeping them busy and engaged in their new world is the main component of our St. Louis immersion strategy.

To that end, we chose a fair-weather autumn day to drive about a half hour west to a farm, where we went on a hayride, and each ambulatory kid picked out a pumpkin and ran through a corn maze. All five of them had their faces painted, which made bath time that night a messy, melodramatic nightmare ("I don't yanna wash my face off!"), but we all slept well that night, in spite of the neighborhood's ambient noise.

We also visited the Arch, as promised. I'd never been, but when I saw the size of the pods that would take us to the top, my claustrophobia quickly vetoed the venture for two of us. I stayed on the ground with Addi while Brice took the four boys up.

This week, leading into Halloween, we went to Grant's Farm (where I got to touch a cow again) and the zoo, both of which have a ton of kid-friendly, cheap activities for this time of year.

In the van on the way to the zoo, Max asked, "Does Daddy have to go to church to work now?"

Instead of going into a long explanation, Brice said, "I'm on vacation, Stinky."

"What's baycation?"

We laughed at his mispronunciation, but Brice

explained, "It's when grownups don't have to go to work, because they're taking a break."

"And you get a new house?"

"No, that's not part of a normal vacation. We just got a new house before I went on vacation. This time. One time only."

"Oh." Mini-Brice thought about that for a few minutes. As we were circling the parking lot, searching for a space, he asked, "Can I go to school on baycation?"

"You'll go after my baycation," Brice replied.

"Yay! I'll see my friends! And Mr. Pastor and Uncle Pastor…"

Brice and I exchanged panicked glances at Max's mention of Wes and Jared. Then Max started listing the entire Peace staff, and paralysis set in. The last thing I wanted to do was say something that would trigger a melt-down before we started our family outing.

When I seemed incapable of finding a way to explain the changes in a way a four-year-old could understand, Brice dropped lightly as he pulled the van into an empty space, "You're going to go to preschool at our new church," and I braced myself for the fallout.

Bethany, the church we've decided to attend regularly, is fifteen minutes from our house. Attached to it is a preschool, much like the one at Peace, but children Max's age attend five days per week, in preparation for kindergarten. We've enrolled him to start the same week Brice starts at The Sem, which could be a stroke of genius or an epic fail. We'll see.

"What about Hailey and Sara and Luke?"

"You'll make new friends," I offered lamely, quickly interjecting, "Hey! We're here. Who's ready to see some animals and spooky Halloween stuff?"

"Meeeeee!"

"Nice save," Brice muttered while we unloaded the strollers and ten tons of other gear from the back of the van before freeing the kids from their seats.

Fortunately, none of them are going to remember this. That's what I keep telling myself, anyway, since I don't have memories from before kindergarten. I hope Max doesn't prove me wrong and tell me when he's an adult that the way we handled this transition scarred him for life. "What about Hailey and Sara and Luke? What happened to them? I have no closure!"

Now it's Halloween, and we've decorated the house for the holiday, something we didn't have the time, energy, or inclination to do in past years. The process involved some time-intensive crafts, but there was nothing else to do on that rainy day, and I figure if you have a house that appears haunted, it's criminal not to capitalize on that at this time of year. It's the one time it actually looks cool.

As for our Halloween plans, Bethany is hosting the traditional Trunk-or-Treat, but we've decided to take a break, after years of obligatory ToT attendance. Plus, being new to the neighborhood, we feel it's important to participate as members of this community. And I'm a little worried someone will egg our house if we abandon it for the night. We've already lost two pumpkins to midnight mischief-makers. I can only imagine what happens to houses not brightly lit on a night when unfamiliar people roam the streets in large, costumed groups.

"Looks great, Stinky!" Brice calls now to Max, our little pony, who gallops away from us with a parting, "See ya, suckas!"

"Next," I say to the line of rowdy children from my seat on the side of our bed. After some jostling, Brooks emerges victorious. He hands me his bumblebee costume.

As I pull the body suit over Brooks's head, Brice checks to make sure Max is gone, then says quietly to me, "I'm not sure about Max's costume."

"Don't be a sexist jerk."

The rule about Halloween costumes in our house is that as long as it's age-appropriate and we can find it cheap or free, we let the kids choose for themselves. Most of tonight's attire came from the trunk of dress-up clothes we've stocked over the years with garage sale and second-hand shop finds. Max's costume was a slightly different story, since he wanted something ultra-specific. But it still met the basic guidelines, thanks to my mad Internet shopping skills.

"No, it's not that," Brice defends himself against my accusation. "I don't care that he likes My Little Pony. You know, there's a whole group of male fans of the show. They're called 'bronies,' a hybrid of the words 'bro' and 'ponies.'"

I laugh. "No, I didn't know that. How do you?"

He shrugs. "I researched it."

"Why?" I straighten the pipe cleaner antennae on top of Brooks's bee hoodie.

Brice sits next to me and traces his finger along a line in the pattern on the bedspread. "Okay, at first, it did bother me that he liked the show. You know, I was a kid when those things first came out, and they were for girls. Only. No exceptions."

"If I didn't know you better, I'd accuse you of talking like my dad." What was supposed to be a light-hearted jab falls flat when my voice falters on the last word. I clear my throat and rush ahead, "Anyway, aren't you the one who always says, 'Things change'?"

He bobs his head in a way that's neither a nod nor a

shake. "Yes, but— Anyway, I Googled 'My Little Pony' and ran across the term 'bronies.'"

"So, the term legitimizes his fandom?"

He flicks my thigh. "No. But it helped to know he wasn't the only one. And he'll hopefully outgrow it before he reaches adulthood, unlike some of those other guys."

"There are adult bronies?"

He lowers his chin and lifts his brows. "Oh, hon. You have no idea. Just Google it. Knowledge is power. Or something. Anyway, that's beside the point."

I pat Brooks on his stinger. "You're good to go, Screamy."

He buzzes out the door, yelling, "Max! I'm a bee!"

To Brice, I say, "What is the point then, other than moot? The costume has been purchased after I scoured the Internet for a used one, the kid is wearing said costume, and trick-or-treating commences in less than twenty minutes." I beckon Harris forward. "Yo, Squeaky. What do we have here?"

He holds out his chosen ensemble. "'Inja!"

"Like father, like son. C'mere, and we'll fix you right up."

Leaning closer to me, Brice ignores my dig and says conspiratorially, "The problem is, Max insists on calling himself the character's name."

"Yeah? So? 'Rainbow Dash' isn't manly enough for ya?"

"That would be fine. But he thinks the name is Rainbow…" He pauses, then stage-whispers, "Gash."

My hand slips from the sleeve of the nylon one-piece jumpsuit I was tugging over Harris's under-layer of clothing. He loses his balance and sprawls onto the floor.

Without missing a beat, Brice grabs the elastic waistband of Harris's sweatpants and hoists the stunned three-year-old to his feet, finishing the job I've abandoned to fall backward on our bed and howl at the ceiling. I can't concentrate on anything but our oldest son inadvertently calling himself an offensive—yet, literally and figuratively, colorful—slang term for a part of a woman's anatomy.

"Yeah, it's funny here in the house," Brice admits, positioning the spandex balaclava so Harris can see through its oval-shaped eye-hole, "but not so funny in public."

I sit up to survey the results of Brice's work on Harris's costume. The "ninja" strikes a pose reminiscent of the one his dad struck atop the bed a couple of weeks ago. He looks more bowling ball than Bruce Lee but runs off to show his brothers.

"Actually, I'm surprised you know to be embarrassed by that word," I say to Brice, blinking away tears.

Haughty, he states, "Just because I'm too classy to use certain terminology in my everyday vocabulary doesn't mean I'm unaware of it."

"Too bad. It would be less humiliating if you were clueless in this case. Because you know how stubborn Max is; if he decides he's Rainbow Gash, he's Rainbow Gash. And you can't very well explain to him why he can't be, now, can you?"

"Exactly. So every time someone asks him tonight, 'And who are you?' he's going to introduce himself with a stripper's name."

"Stop it!" I shriek, collapsing again and slapping the mattress.

Aidan drops his Thomas the Tank Engine foam poncho at Brice's feet and clambers onto the bed next to me. "Mommy!" he cries, obviously worried.

I wipe my eyes and sit, hugging him to my chest. "It's okay, Angel Boy. Mommy thinks Daddy's funny."

Brice retrieves the train costume from the floor and holds it up. "Hey, Aidan. Let's do the locomotion."

Satisfied I'm okay, Aidan slides down the side of the bed and allows his dad to slip the costume over his head. His railroad cap in place (and pinned to fit well enough that it won't fall off or slip over his eyes every time he moves), he receives a parting pat on his caboose from Brice to move him along. "Go hang out with your brothers in Max's room. I'll be there in a minute."

"Choo-choo!" Aidan says, as he runs from the room.

Bracing my weight on my arm behind me, I meet my husband's concern with amusement. "I'm not sure what you want me to say or do."

He rubs the back of his neck. "I don't know, either. I guess maybe I just wanted you to be aware. That way, if you notice any of the neighbors staring…"

"He's a kid. Everyone will know he's mispronouncing it. For all they know, he has a speech impediment."

"His obliviousness doesn't make it any less shocking."

"Since when do you care what people think? That's usually my specialty." I stand and cross to the door to Addi's nursery. "Now, if you don't mind, I have a little mermaid to get ready before the doorbell starts ringing."

He waves me away, then pulls a Concordia hoodie from the dresser and over his head. "I'll just stand behind him and yell 'Dash!' louder than he says G-A-S-H."

I backtrack on the threshold of Addi's room and raise my eyebrows at him. "Oh, now that the kids are gone, we're spelling it?" When his pithy comeback is to stick out his tongue at me, I address the other part of what he's said. "Anyway, your plan won't make us seem any less weird or make a much better impression with our new neighbors."

He laughs. "Hey. Maybe I have Tourette's Syndrome."

"But you don't."

"They don't know that."

"Don't be such an apologist. You need to own that you have a four-year-old profanity-spouting son who likes to pretend to be a blue-winged pony with rainbow-colored hair."

"Wanna trade places? I'll stay here with Addi and hand out candy."

Since he's only kidding, I don't bother answering. Instead, I simply say, "Have fun. And don't let them eat anything until we check their bags and sort out the stuff I want for myself."

"Yes, my bride," he mumbles, punctuating it with a grin and an irreverent blown kiss. "We'll be back in a half-hour, tops."

"I'll listen for the laughter to keep track of where you guys are!" I call after him as he disappears into the hallway.

Hours later, I'm no longer laughing when, drenched in sweat and out of breath, I wake from a nightmare, nearly weeping with relief that I'm home safe in my bed.

I slip into the bathroom to recover without disturbing Brice, but when I return to the bed, he props himself on one elbow and pinches at his eyes.

"What's wrong? You okay?" he mumbles.

"Fine," I answer, then feeling about five years old, add, "I had a bad dream." I tuck my legs under the covers but remain sitting.

He flops against his pillows and yawns. "Is that all? I was worried."

I half-heartedly apologize for worrying him while the

emotions resulting from the nightmare float around the edges of my sleepy brain like gasoline fumes. "It's just— It was so… awful. I was pregnant."

"Dear Lord. 'Nuff said."

In a spacey voice, I continue, "Only it felt like the first time. The first time."

Brice sits up and cups my shoulder in his hand. "Oh, hon. I'm sorry."

"I was working at Smart Art. And Marshall and Stefan were demanding all these changes to the gallery, changes I didn't agree with. They thought my lack of cooperation was incompetence and kept saying, 'If you don't think you can keep up, we'll find someone who can.' I tried to explain that it had nothing to do with my skills but more to do with my disagreeing with their ideas. They went into Marshall's office to discuss things further and told me they'd keep me updated on their decisions. I sat at my desk, feeling hopeless and overwhelmed. Then the donkeys—"

"Whoa, whoa. Wait a minute. Donkeys?"

"Yes. Dozens of tiny donkeys, about the size of small dogs, ran into the shop through the front door. I scooped up as many as I could and tossed them back onto the sidewalk in front of the gallery."

The bed shakes with Brice's silent laughter, but I'm still too wrapped up in the frustration of the dream to see the humor. "When I'd turn to catch more donkeys, the ones I'd already thrown out would head-butt the doors open and rush back in. I finally managed to get all of them outside and lock the door. Then I immediately logged onto Face-book and updated my status with: Never imagined my day would include catching sweetheart donkeys."

"Sweetheart donkeys?" Brice barely manages to catch his breath through his laughter.

I finally smile faintly. "Yeah. That's what those miniature donkeys are called."

"You mean, the imaginary miniature donkeys in your dream?"

"Yes. In my head, they were a true breed, and they had that name. Like teacup poodles."

"Priceless."

"It's not funny. It was horrible."

"Sorry. I'm just— Sorry." He sniffs to compose himself, then clears his throat. "Is that all?"

"No. After I got rid of the donkeys, I went to the bathroom, and while I was in there, Marshall and Stefan kept walking in on me to tell me their latest plans."

"While you were sitting on the toilet, peeing?"

"I wasn't peeing; I was—"

"Nasty. I think I've heard enough."

"You think I'm nuts."

"No, I think you need to stop eating nuts—or Halloween candy—before bed."

"It was all so vivid. The emotions! It was like being sent back in time, when I was young and unsure of myself and... The frustration!"

"Nothing's worse than being kept from taking a poo. Man. Did you have to mention that part?"

Blushing in the dark, I flap the front of my t-shirt to try to cool myself off. "It was an important part! Because it was humiliating. It was a level of shame I haven't felt since... back then. I dunno. I just needed to talk about it."

"Oh. Okay."

"And, you know..." I pick at the comforter. "Maybe see what you think it might mean?"

He sighs. "It means you're experiencing a lot of change

right now, so your sleep patterns are wacky. And maybe you're constipated?"

When I glare at him over my shoulder, he grinds his fists into his eye sockets. "It's two o'clock in the morning, hon. And I'm a pastor, not a dream interpreter. You want me to tell you it means something about your life, your current mental state, and possibly your spiritual wellbeing? I'm not going to be able to do that. Because I don't believe it."

"I admit, it's not as dramatic as a technicolor dreamcoat or a burning freaking bush, but—"

"You do realize *Joseph and The Amazing Technicolor Dream-coat* is a musical, not the actual Bible story, right?"

"It was based on the Bible story."

"Well, yes. But 'technicolor' wasn't really a thing in Biblical times."

"Why do you have to be such a stickler?"

"Biblical accuracy is, uh, kind of my job."

"Which brings me back to my dream, about my job."

"But that's not your job anymore. You have a new one now. And it's a lot more important than protecting artwork from rogue miniature donkeys." He pulls a strand of my hair away from my damp neck. More gently, more seriously, he says, "Some of your everyday challenges are bleeding into your sleep, that's all. Don't read too much into it. Any of it. What do we tell the kids when they have nightmares?"

"'It was only a dream.'"

"Exactly. It was only a dream. Heck, I bet you're just frustrated you're never allowed to use the toilet alone. Simple as that."

Rubbing my face, I groan. "Gosh, you're probably right."

"Now, go back to sleep." He kisses my cheek and lies down, turning over and effectively leaving the conversation, but not without muttering, "Sweetheart donkeys," one more time and snorting.

I stare at his ear for a few seconds before sliding farther under the covers and pressing myself against his back. Within minutes, his light snores vibrate against my cheek through his shirt.

It may have been just a dream, but the emotions that fed it are real. And they're not going anywhere, no matter how much I try to ignore them on my best days.

10

NEW BRICE VS. OLD BRICE

*O*n my best days, this life of mine is so full of laughter and love that I feel like I'm in the middle of a great dream, or I'm starring in a sitcom from an era when shows only featured families whose problems could be solved in twenty-two minutes.

Other days, like today, I wake up, and I feel weighed down with the kind of permanent, hopeless problems that only exist in my worst nightmares. And nearly every time that happens, the thought immediately accompanying that feeling is, I don't have a dad. He's dead.

And that, my friends, is the most insurmountable of obstacles.

Before I can even think to hold them back, the tears arrive. But they're not tears borne out of grief. They're hot and angry and resentful. And guilty. I'm mad at a dead man for dying. How messed up is that? I suppose it's better than being angry at my infant daughter, whose birth prevented me from attending his funeral. Or worse, angry at God for taking my dad. No, I'm angry at Dad, and not just for being dead, either.

That bastard. The last few years of his life, he was nothing but a pain in my ass, at best, and an affection-with-holding asshole at worst. But I never doubted he loved me. And I never stopped loving him. Most of all, I never stopped believing we'd eventually return to the relationship we once had. Before everything.

No, not before "everything." Before Secret. Before Brice. Before the scales fell from my eyes, and I saw him the way many others had already known him for decades, because they'd dared to defy him at some point. Like I did when I told him about Secret. Like I did when I refused to beg for his forgiveness. Like I did when I fell in love with someone who was the total opposite of him. He took all of those things personally, as if I was doing them to make a statement to him.

And then he had to go and die.

Some days the *How fucking dare he?* is so loud in my head that I swear I've said it out loud.

But I rarely speak of it, much less in such angry terms.

And it seems like the days when I can least afford to be distracted by that hopeless, heavy, choking grief are the days it chooses to strike.

Since today is Brice's first day at the Sem and Max's first day at preschool, I say an extra prayer while sitting on the side of the bed, before getting up and telling Dad to do something sexual to himself. (I say that last part after the "Amen.")

There's no room in the house for my bad attitude, anyway. Nerves and testosterone-fueled melodrama are the occupants of the day.

"A little help here?" Brice asks with less than his usual patience when I enter the kitchen to find him putting the three youngest boys into their booster seats with one hand while holding Addi in his other arm. Max, already kneeling in his booster-less chair, is providing the musical accompaniment to breakfast.

"I don't wanna go to a new school! I want Uncle Pastor and Mr. Pastor and Luke and Sara!"

I guess Hailey was easy-come, easy-go.

I relieve Brice of the baby. Leaning down, I aim to kiss Max on the cheek and whisper something comforting to him. Before I can say anything, however, he swats his hand in my direction, missing me but hitting his little sister in the face.

Addi lets us all know how she feels about the unfairness of her brother's wrath. The swift arm of justice—that is, Brice's arm—descends. On the end of that arm is a hand that clamps onto the back of Max's pajama shirt, yanking the preschooler from his chair like one of those claw games popular in arcades.

"Put your feet down," Brice orders his son through gritted teeth.

"No!"

"Fine. You're still going in time out; whether you walk there is your choice."

"No time out! No!"

"It was an accident," I say over the howling, but Brice carry-drags our oldest child from the room and plunks him in the small chair next to the first-floor bathroom door on the other side of the stairs, the official Northam time-out spot.

When he returns to the kitchen, he says in that ultra-controlled voice of his that never fails to suck all the air from a room, "I know he did not mean to hit her; he meant to hit you. And that is not acceptable."

I kiss Addi's nose and bounce her to soothe her, then say

to my husband, "You forgot your contractions in the other room. You're scaring the children."

"Good. Then they'll never pull a stunt like that." He rolls his head on his neck, closes his eyes, and works his jaw back and forth.

I hold up his daughter so he can see her. "She's fine. See?"

She blinks at him and pops her thumb into her mouth. His expression immediately softens. He palms her velvety head with his giant-by-comparison hand. "Hey, Ladybug. You okay? He didn't mean it. He's just grumpy, because he's nervous."

"Sound familiar?"

Dropping his hand, he smiles sheepishly. "Maybe."

Nobody says anything—a true first—while I prepare Addi's bottle and Max continues his bellowing on the other side of the stairs.

Finally, into the white noise of Max's raging about everything from his "stupid" new preschool to his "mean" daddy, Brooks bellows, "Be quiet, Max! You're being 'noying."

"I'm not talking to you, Brooks!" Max screams back, but he stops crying.

Still standing across the room, near the sink, Brice and I exchange wide-eyed looks, pull our lips into our mouths, and clamp down on them with our teeth, then slowly turn our backs to the table to hide our silent mirth from the boys.

Finally, Brice composes himself enough to turn and call, "If you're ready to be nice, you can come back to the table, Max."

"I don't want to!"

Brice takes his coffee to the counter. "Suit yourself."

Conversation resumes at the table, with Harris and

Brooks debating which Teenage Mutant Ninja Turtle is the best one. ("Purple!" "No, blue!")

Remaining by the sink, I lean my lower back against it and feed Addi her bottle while standing. I study my husband, then carefully say, "You look... the same as always."

His forehead furrows as he pauses, pre-sip. "Is that a good thing or a bad thing?"

"Good. Just unexpected."

"Am I supposed to look different? I got my hair cut." Setting down his coffee, he pretends to fluff the back of his neatly trimmed 'do.

I laugh. "It's very nice. No, I was talking about your clothes. The same black pants, shirt, and clerical collar as usual. I thought—"

"You thought I was going to wear a tweed jacket with suede elbow patches and smoke a pipe?"

"No!"

"This is what I wear. It's one of the perks of the calling: no complicated wardrobe choices in the morning."

"Do you have to wear it?"

"No. I choose to wear it."

"Oh. I just thought— I don't know what I thought." I stop talking, because his expression is hovering somewhere between "confused" and "crestfallen." "Never mind. You look nice. Although..." I bite my lip.

"What?"

"Why do you wear the collar? You've never given me a serious answer."

"Never?"

"No. You've told me you wear it to get free coffee, to pick up nuns, to get preferential parking, to scare people, to make yourself feel pretty..."

He laughs at his own cleverness.

"All hilarious answers," I agree. "But not real answers. It seems like 'to wear or not to wear' would be a matter of conservative—or traditional—versus lib— less conservative," I quickly amend at the glower regarding one of his least favorite words. "But you and Vince are not what I'd describe as traditionalists, so that theory doesn't hold with you two, who both wear your collars when you're 'on duty.'" I shrug. "I've often wondered, but since I never get a serious answer from you, I've given up asking."

"I guess I never thought you were seriously asking. Being a lifelong Lutheran, I assumed you knew, and you were looking for silly answers."

"I'm looking for a serious answer now. If you're free to choose, and some people do, and others don't, what's your reasoning?"

"I honestly like being instantly recognizable as a man of God. I think it serves as a non-verbal witness, which is often a lot more effective, let's face it."

"But on a seminary campus, isn't that like preaching to the choir?"

"It also serves as a reminder to me."

"Sometimes you forget you're a pastor?"

He pinches his lips sideways, obviously amused but not wanting to encourage my snideness. "You ask for a serious answer, then you make jokes?"

"Sorry. Continue."

Running his finger between his neck and the stiff white insert, he says, "The dark-colored shirt reminds me I'm a sinner; the white collar reminds me I speak from God. Or should."

"And that's it?"

"There's historical significance, and some guys who take

themselves super-seriously have more complicated justifications, but 'That's how we've always done it' has never been a valid reason, in my opinion, so it doesn't hold water for me as much as the other things I've said."

"Oh. Hm. I guess that all makes sense."

"So, it's okay for me to wear my uniform?" he pretends to check.

"Yes. I'll allow it. I suppose. I thought, though, that you'd want to wear something more comfortable. New job, new clothes, and all that."

"This is plenty comfortable. I feel safe and at peace when I'm dressed like this. Although I may be a bit of an oddball at The Sem. I don't remember any of my professors wearing collars when I attended. But since when have I followed the crowd?" He nods to my bathrobe. "Now, let's deconstruct your uniform."

I set Addi's bottle on the counter and move her to my shoulder. "Well, I'm glad you mentioned it. I have very valid reasons for wearing this. The white hides the baby spit-up, and the belted waist disguises all manner of sins in my physical shape."

He peeks at me through his lashes with his lips against his coffee cup. "Your physical shape is just fine."

"I think you need to remember what you're wearing and temper your thoughts with your Godly words, Reverend Flirt-Face."

On cue, Addi belches and spews a modest stream of curdled formula onto my shoulder, then glares at me like I've done something to offend her.

Brice glances at the microwave clock, then at his watch, double-checking the time. "And now that we've determined we're both dressed appropriately for the day—although you may want to change into some real, clean clothes, at least for Max's first day at preschool—I'd better be off."

"Oh, gosh. Is it really that time?" Seeing that it is, indeed, I lay Addi in her swing, strap her in, and set her in motion. When I straighten to my full height, Brice stands behind me, perfectly positioned for a goodbye kiss.

With his face next to my shoulder, he wrinkles his nose. "You've smelled better."

I turn my head and pooch out my lips to give him a quick peck on his cheek before rushing toward the laundry room. "It's Eau de Baby Barf."

I toss my bathrobe into the washing machine, then root around in the dryer for something clean to wear.

"I'll be home a little after five," Brice calls from the back door. "Hey, knuckleheads," he directs toward the trio at the table. "Be good for your mom." Then louder, "Max!"

"What?"

"Run upstairs, use the bathroom, and get dressed for school."

"No."

"NOW!"

"Fine!"

As I emerge from the laundry room, dressed in four fewer articles I'll have to fold, thanks to my tardiness, Max rounds the bottom of the stairs and stomps up them, using his hands almost as much as his feet to climb to the second floor.

"Be good for your mom and have an awesome day at school, Stink!" Brice calls as a parting peace offering to his firstborn.

Max, as if the past half-hour never happened, pauses near the top of the stairs and calls through the spindles in the railing, "Okay, Daddy! Have fun at work!" before disappearing to dress.

I smile gratefully at Brice. "Thanks. Love you! Have a great first day. Email me or text me later to tell me how it's going."

He blows me a final kiss on his way to the newest chapter in his life.

I wish I had more time to ponder the significance of the moment, but...

"Shoes, everyone!" I implore my offspring, who scatter to heed my call to action.

Classes don't start for another month, so when I picture what Brice is doing on his first day, he's not standing in front of a class of young, impressionable seminarians. I imagine he's sitting in his new (tiny, windowless) office or wandering around the Gothic campus, reacquainting himself with his surroundings.

Brice. A teacher. That's going to take some getting used to. I can picture him addressing a large group of people, obviously. He's done that countless times. I can even picture him teaching, to a certain extent, considering I've attended one or two [hundred] of his Bible classes. But envisioning him at the front of a large lecture hall, delivering not a sermon but an academic lesson? That's difficult for me to wrap my head around, for some reason.

Maybe it's because I've never known him as anything but a senior pastor. The first time I saw him was when he was installed at Messiah. And back then, he was just some dude taking over for Pastor Niedermeyer, the only other pastor I'd ever known. I was probably thinking more about how tired or hungry I was, daydreaming about what Mom was making for lunch after church, and wondering if the service was going to be longer than usual, due to the installation. I guarantee it never crossed my mind—never—that I might get to know him as a person, much less marry the guy and have his kids and, you know, see him naked on a regular basis.

That makes me laugh out loud in the laundry room, where I'm folding one of the plain white t-shirts he wears under those oh-so-meaningful pastor shirts of his. Not in my wildest dreams did I think I'd be doing that guy's laundry someday.

Oh, my gosh. What if...? What if I'd somehow seen a flash of my future that day, staring at Brice's back while he knelt before whomever that guy was who said all the fancy words to make Brice Messiah's newest pastor? I would have freaked the heck out, that's what. Like, you know when you have an inappropriate dream about someone you don't even think about in that way, and you can't look that person in the eye for a while? It would have been like that, to the tenth power. My brain could not have handled that information. I probably would have never gone back to that church.

As it is, I sometimes still have a hard time believing "that guy" and Brice are the same person. It's like there's a pre-Secret-era Brice and a Secret/post-Secret-era Brice, and they should never be allowed to meet each other, because it could screw up the space-time continuum. Or something. Now an even newer Brice is emerging. Professor Brice. And I can't quite reconcile him with the other Brices I've known.

Dad always used to say, "Those who can't, teach." And he would totally attribute that to his son-in-law right now. He might as well be in this room with me saying it, that's how vividly I can still hear his misguided, malcontented maxim.

The memory of his smug face while uttering that ignorant sentence makes me clench a pair of my husband's underwear in my fist, then brace my hands against the washing machine in front of me, and stare down my straight arms, breathing audibly through my mouth.

What did you have against Brice, anyway, Dad? Was he too good for you? Too good for me? Was the contrast too obvious when he stood next to you? Was that it?

Because he doesn't need to wear a special uniform to remember who guides his every thought, word, and deed. And now that you're gone, he can't even bring himself to say anything negative against you. Why? What does he owe you or your memory? Nothing. You were nothing but a thorn in his side.

A thorn in our sides.

Are you up there, having a party with Wayne Long, patting yourselves on the back about how "right" you were about him? Well, you weren't right. You were wrong. And Brice may not always be right, but even when he's wrong, he's still a hundred times more right than you were on your best day. He's a devoted pastor, son, husband, and—most of all—father.

Brice would never, will never, ever, ever, ever put any of his children through what you put me through. He'll never look at them the way you looked at me that night or on countless occasions after that. He'll never shun them or withhold his affection from them. No matter what. There's nothing they could do to deserve that treatment.

What did I do to deserve it?

Mere minutes after I'd thanked you in front of God, Brice, and everyone for never expressing disappointment in me, you proved me so painfully wrong. Some days I still feel like I did that night, more than seven years ago. At times like this, it may as well have been just days or hours ago. It still hurts like it did right after I told you about Secret, and you looked through me in that parking lot like you didn't know who I was. Like I wasn't the same little girl you bounced on your knee; I wasn't the honor student or the artist or the career girl who made you so proud. When you looked at me that night, I was a stranger to you. And you were a stranger to me.

Your love was conditional. I just had no idea it was until I presented you with a condition that didn't follow your rules.

"Mommy? Da bideo runned out," Brooks says, with a tug on my yoga pants. He points toward the living room, where he and two of his brothers have been watching TV while Addi naps and Max is at preschool.

I sniffle, blink, and pat his head. "Okay. I'll be right there."

"Don't cry, Mommy. You can fix da bideo."

I chuckle at the simplicity of a toddler's life. "You're right, Screamy. I can fix it. Give me a minute to finish folding these—"

CRASH!

Or not.

"Aidan!" Harris shouts, his tone telling me he's more exasperated than scared.

Still, the absence of any sound from my youngest son hastens me to the living room, where I groan at the scene. Aidan waddles over and points to the mess behind him, in case I missed the toppled floor lamp at first glance.

"Oh, no! What happened?"

"Aidan bwoke it," Harris tattles helpfully.

"No kidding. Why can't you guys sit quietly and be still for five minutes…" while Mommy has an emotional break-down and verbally bitch-slaps your dead grandfather? "Huh? Is that too much to ask? You have toys—so many toys! And videos and shows and— and everything. I just don't get it."

"I hafta poop," Harris announces, holding the back of his pants in a way that tells me the deed is done.

I press my hand to my forehead. "Everybody, upstairs. Harris, wait!" I tiptoe through the broken glass from the shade and lift him, stink and all, over the shards. He follows his brothers up the stairs, muttering, "What the hack?"

Aidan sing-songs, "Sawee! Sawee, guys!"

What to do first, follow the kids or clean up the lamp? I check the time on my phone, then shove it back into my hoodie pocket. "Sonofa…" It's already nearly 11:00, but Addi's not awake yet (amazingly, considering the sound that lamp made when it fell), which means I'll have to wake her to go pick up Max from preschool.

"Shit, shit, shit," I hiss, scooting the glass with the side of my sneaker, careful not to scratch the wood floor in the process. When I have the busted green shade in as small a pile as I can manage quickly, I turn and run up the stairs.

I smell it before I see anything. But the nose knows when something awful has happened or is happening. And I'm afraid both may be the case.

At the top of the stairs, I turn immediately to my right and see all three boys through the bathroom door, "helping" Harris with his messy diaper. And when I say, "messy," I'm sparing you the gory details.

"Guys! What are you doing?" I shriek. "No, no, no, no, no! Freeze! Hands up! Step away from the poop, and nobody gets hurt."

My Poop Police act wakes up Addi on the other side of the wall, but I remain focused on the boys and block out her cries. My crazed expression must tell the guys I'm not screwing around, because they uncharacteristically do exactly as I say, complete with hands in the air. "Oh, my gosh! What am I— Okay, deep breaths." Through my mouth.

With no time to spare, I hoist all three of them into the tub and strip them like their clothes are on fire. Once they're naked, their clothes lying in a heap on the floor behind me, I stand and unclip the detachable shower head, pulling as much slack into the nozzle as possible. After regulating the temperature, I hose them down, hoping they don't think this is a game but knowing by their giggles that they definitely do.

"This is very, very bad," I keep repeating, then add, "Mommy is very disappointed and sad and... and... grossed out."

When I've done the best I can do in the time available, I turn off the water, drop the sprayer into the bottom of the bathtub and bellow, "Don't move!" as I reach behind myself into the cabinet below the sink for towels. I lift the dry kids one by one from the tub and shepherd them around the pile of soiled clothing in the middle of the streaked floor. "Keep moving. Nothing to see here," I mutter to their naked backs while following them to Aidan's room.

In there, I wrap the twins in towels and tell them to sit while I dress their little brother before he pees—or worse— without his diaper on. Then we caravan down the hall to the twins' room, where I dress them, followed by backtracking down the hall, through the master bedroom, to get to Addi's crib-side. "Everyone keep their hands where I can see them," I order while changing the nearly hysterical baby's diaper and wrapping her in a bunting for the chilly trip from the back of the house to the garage.

Once in the minivan, with all the kids strapped in and Addi sucking lustily on a pacifier that will only pacify her for maybe half of this expedition, I heave a huge sigh, trying not to worry that I can still smell poop, which means it's probably on me somewhere.

"You guys are going to be the death of Mommy, you know that?" I grumble, backing from the stall and onto the driveway. "First the lamp, then the bathroom. We're picking up Max, eating lunch, and going down for long, quiet naps. All of us. That is, after I clean up the glass and the poop and run an extra load of laundry. And shower. And decide what we're having for dinner. Yeah… I'm not getting a nap, am I?"

"Noooo," Aidan responds solemnly.

I'd laugh at his sweet comedic timing, but that would require energy I don't have.

11

DRAMA, DRAMA, DRAMA

*H*aving finished sweeping up the broken glass, I feel my phone buzz in my pocket as I carry my rubber gloves, bucket, mop, and cleaning supplies upstairs to the crime scene... er, bathroom. Assuming it's Brice checking in, I transfer everything to one hand and answer without checking the display.

"Hello?" You know, in case it's not him (learned that the hard way).

"Is everything okay? I normally hear from you by now, but ever since you moved, your calls have been so erratic. And it makes me worry. Jason told me your neighborhood isn't the best. Honestly, I wish Brice had just settled for a longer commute so you could live in a safer area."

On the threshold of the feces-smeared bathroom, I close my eyes and take a deep, instantly regrettable, not-so-cleansing breath through my nose. Coughing, I reply, "Mom. Not really a good time."

"Why? What's happening? Is something wrong with one of the kids or Brice?"

I set down my bucket and lean the mop against the wall. "No. Everyone's fine. It's just— It's been a bad day."

"Bad, how? Are you unwell?"

That would be one way to describe how I'm feeling, yes, but I answer, "No, Mom. I'm not unwell. I have five small children. Isn't that recipe enough for a bad day every once in a while?" To allay her fears about our health and wellbeing, I recap the morning (leaving out the part about hating on Dad), finishing with, "And I'm just getting around to cleaning the bathroom, so now it's not only a mess, it's a dried mess."

"You don't have to be so graphic."

And I thought I was glossing over the details.

"My life is graphic," I say in my defense.

Since it's obvious she's geared up for a long conversation, and the disaster in front of me is only getting nastier the longer it sits, I put the phone on speaker and place it on a clean spot on the counter. "Anyway, how's it going?"

After snapping on the rubber gloves, I line my cleaning supplies on the counter next to my phone. In the bathtub, I fill the bucket with hot water, adding plenty of soap, so the bubbles foam over the rim, some floating through the air around me.

Breezily, she answers, "Oh, fine. I had some people come by and take away your dad's good suits and some of his newer clothes. They resell them at a boutique downtown for people getting back on their feet after losing a job or recovering from stuff like house fires, you know."

"That's nice," I answer automatically, dunking a scrub brush into the hot water and slinging it into the epicenter of the mess. With both hands, I scour without thinking too much about what I'm doing. It's better to go on autopilot in situations like this.

Too busy visiting my happy place to hold up my end of the conversation, I continue to let Mom lead. "So, today is Brice's first day at his new job?"

"Yep."

"Exciting! Although I think it's odd he'd leave Peace after such a short amount of time there. Well, maybe not so odd. He did the same thing at Messiah. Were things unpleasant at Peace? I always got the impression he was well-liked and well-received there and was happy. Is there something you haven't told me?"

"Everything was fine," I say shortly, annoyed we're having this conversation—again. We already covered this ground plenty when she was helping Brice and me with the sale of our house. "Concordia called; he answered."

"He'd better be careful. I've been on enough call committees to know it's a major red flag if a pastor is never in one place for long."

"That's fine, since we're not hoping to impress any call committees right now."

"I guess it's good, too, for you guys to get this wanderlust out of your system before the kids start school. You can't be uprooting them all the time, you know. They need consistency."

"Got it."

"Why are you being so short with me today? I'm only making conversation."

"I'm cleaning up shit right now, Mom. 'Short' is the most pleasant attitude I can muster. Would you like me to call you back later?"

"No! I need to talk to you about Thanksgiving."

I can't think about Thanksgiving right now. Food? No. Having a bunch of people in my house? Double no. In as few words as possible, I convey it's not a good time to talk about it.

"You're still hosting, though, right? Because if not, it would have been nice to know before now. I could have been planning, but you said you had it cov—"

"Mother. I didn't say I didn't want to host." Although I don't. "I merely said I can't think about it right this second."

"But I need to know what you want me to contribute, so I can give you my shopping list, and you can pick up the stuff I'll need. I'll pay you back, of course. I just don't want to drag that stuff with me all the way from Chicago."

At the rising hysteria in her voice, I point out, "It's still a month away."

"Three and a half weeks."

"Still. I'm not going to shop for your ingredients for another three weeks."

"Don't leave it too late. I want to make this special quinoa salad, and some of the ingredients may be hard to find."

I wipe away the suds on the floor with a rag to ensure the caked-on doo-doo is no longer there, then rinse the scrub brush and go to work on the hand tracks on the vanity cabinets. "Are these hard-to-find ingredients perishable?"

"No."

"Then bring them with you in your suitcase. I'll get everything else."

"Okay, but we need to coordinate, then, who's getting what."

"Some other time, Mom, all right?!"

"Excuse me!" she retorts, the tears audible in her voice.

I sit back on my feet and blow my bangs from my eyes. "I'm sorry. I'm up to my elbows in crap. Almost literally. And kids. And crappy kids."

"Nobody put a gun to your head and told you to have those kids. Don't take it out on me that you're having a bad day because of your poor choices."

I stare at the phone on the edge of the counter.

"Hello? Are you still there."

"Barely."

"What does that mean?"

"It means I'm about to hang up on you before I say something I'll regret or you say anything else you should regret."

"What did I say?"

Incredulous, I answer, "You called my children, your grandchildren, 'poor choices'!" I rip the gloves from my hands and grab my phone as if to throttle it.

"No, I did not! You're twisting my words. Your father and I simply wondered why you and Brice—"

"You know what? I don't want to hear it."

"We worried about you. Especially your father. He—"

"No. I don't want to know what you two sat up in bed talking about every night. I don't want to hear about your idle wonders or armchair quarterbacking. Because, frankly, I don't give a shit."

"Peyton! I don't understand what you want."

"I want to have a normal conversation with you that doesn't make me want to scream. Is that too much to ask?"

"When I warn you about overdoing things, you complain I'm smothering you; when I tell it the way it is, because that's what you seem to want, you get all defensive and hurt."

"I don't want to host Thanksgiving this year," I blurt, rather than address her accusation. "I thought it would be fun, in the new house, in a new city, to show you guys around the Sem, but it's not a good time. It's too much, too soon."

"But it's just as much trouble for the seven of you to travel here, so—"

"We won't be going anywhere. I think it's best if we spend this Thanksgiving here, alone, as a family."

"We're your family too. And stop interrupting me!"

Hang up now. Hang up now. Hang up now.

"I really have to go now. Goodbye, Mom."

I press the button to end the call, silence the phone, and set it back on the counter. Donning my gloves once more, I robotically return to my life's work.

By five o'clock, my 'poor choices' and I are the picture of tranquility, playing a matching game around the dining table, when Brice enters through the back door.

The boys scramble from their chairs and rush him like the winning goal-scorer at a soccer match.

"Hello, hello! What a nice welcome home."

"Daddy, I went to school today!" Max announces.

"Yes, I know, Stinky. And did you meet lots of new friends and have fun?"

"I was pwayer leader."

"Oh, wow. Now, that's a big responsibility." He lifts Max and supports him with crossed arms under his butt so they're eye-to-eye. "What did you pray about?"

"Jesus."

"Always a good choice." Setting Max on the floor, Brice then kisses each of his other sons and wades forth into the kitchen. "Let's go sit around the table and talk to Mommy, too."

"I need help matching these cards," I say, lifting my face for a kiss. After Brice and the boys settle in their chairs, and the kids go back to their game, I ask, "How'd it go?"

"Fine. Great. It's... different." When I cock my head to coax more information from him, he waves a dismissive hand. "Oh, nothing bad. Just different than it was when I went there."

"Well, yeah. That was a while ago."

"Not that long ago!"

I smirk so he'll know I was kidding. "Anyway what's so different?"

He pooches out his lower lip while he considers his answer, then shrugs when he can't seem to put his finger on it. "Just different. It's hard to explain. A vibe, I guess. More scholarly, less relaxed. Or something."

"Hm."

"It's probably because I'm there in another capacity and seeing things from the other side of things."

"Yeah. Maybe."

He removes his collar and slaps it against his hand. "Everyone seems sort of defensive. And protective. Like, territorial. Of tradition and history and the doctrine in general. When I attended, it didn't feel that way. We were all there because we wanted to be there."

"You mean, because you were called to be there."

He peers sideways at me, as if trying to gauge my sincerity. I must pass inspection, because he relaxes and continues, "The background stuff was a given. There was no need to be defensive. Nobody questioned the tradition or doctrine, because, well, we were all Lutherans. Based on stuff I heard from other faculty members today, students now are either there to prove something—God isn't dead; Christianity's not giving up without a fight; the Lutherans will never abandon ship or compromise our beliefs! Rah-rah-rah!—or disprove everything and reform the church from the inside."

"Sounds tense."

"A little." He shakes his head, like he's clearing it. "Anyway. Probably just first-day jitters. I'll have to wait and see for myself when classes start next month."

"Good idea. It's never wise to take someone else's word for it. Good to be forewarned, I guess. But not worth it to worry about it until you experience it for yourself, right?"

He nods. "Exactly. It was a good day, overall. Busy, though. Sorry I didn't call or text. I wasn't alone for a single minute. Well, I used the bathroom a couple of times without a chaperon."

"That may have been for the best."

"How was your day?"

"Best not to ask. We're having pizza for dinner. Should be here any minute."

"Oh, one of those, eh?" Seeming unconcerned, he points to a card on the table and whispers to Harris, "Try that one; I think the fox is under there." When he's right, he pumps his fist. "Yes! Still got it." Abruptly, he rises. "Do you mind if I go for a quick run after dinner? I'll take Ladybug with me in the stroller," he throws in to sweeten the deal.

"That's fine. The boys have already had their baths. Part of the long story you don't want to hear."

He winces. "Yikes. I wondered why everyone, including you, was already in their pajamas."

"That's a different story."

"There's more than one story?"

"Isn't there always? Which reminds me: we're not hosting my family for Thanksgiving."

"That's… interesting."

I smile tightly. "Just another boring story."

He walks to the stairs, pauses at the bottom, leans into the living room, then says back at me, over his shoulder, "Do I want to know why that lamp doesn't have a shade anymore?"

"Nope."

"Okay. I'm going to change my clothes, then. I'll be right back."

I watch him bound up the stairs like a Labrador and envy his energy.

I was so tired, both mentally and physically, after cleaning the bathroom, I had to sit in the shower for a few minutes. On the floor. That scared me a little, but I felt better afterward. I still wanted to go straight to bed when I was finished, but I didn't feel shaky anymore.

Unfortunately, the older kids were waking from their naps. I managed to fake enough enthusiasm for a "special game," in which we raced to see who could put on their pajamas the fastest and "climb into Mommy and Daddy's bed… go!" Max won, of course, and I had to help the other three, but I made them all feel like finishers at a marathon, and we snuggled under the covers with some picture books for the rest of Addi's nap.

When Addi woke, ready to eat, I released the boys from the bed, on the condition they play games or color nicely together at the table until their dad got home from work. Young children love to push the boundaries, but they're sometimes surprisingly astute when it comes to sensing the grownup in charge has reached his or her limit. Maybe that makes their unruly behavior the other ninety-five percent of the time that much more unacceptable. I choose to simply be thankful for that five percent of the time they're good when I need them to be. They came through for me this afternoon.

Especially Max. He channeled his bossiness into a more constructive tone with his younger brothers as he coordinated the games at the table and even retrieved Addi's dropped toys for her without my asking. I hope I made a big enough deal about his helpfulness to encourage him to behave like that more often.

Now I'm in the homestretch of the day. In a couple of hours, they'll be tucked away for the night, recharging their batteries for another day of mischief.

I'm pretty sure I'm going to be okay.

It was nice of Brice to offer to take one of the kids off my hands for Triple-P, but by the time we finish dinner, it's too dark and chilly to take Addi jogging with him.

"Next time, Ladybug," he says on his way past her swing to the door. "Twenty minutes," is his promise to me.

"Just be careful," I can't help but implore, knowing I'll be counting every one of those twenty minutes and in mental agony for every minute he inevitably goes over that time limit.

"I have my phone. And I'll stick to well-lit streets."

I wave him away, not wanting to belabor it. If he stays for one more second, I'll have to resort to begging him not to go. And that would be embarrassing for everyone.

The TV acts as my babysitter while I clean up the kitchen for the night, loading the dishwasher for its final cycle of sippy cups, bottles, glasses, and plates. This time, I keep a better ear open for the "dangerous quiet" that precedes trouble. It's plenty loud in there, all voices accounted for.

And it's about to get louder.

I lift Addi from her swing and kiss the spot where her chubby jowl meets the place where her neck will be someday under all those rolls. "Well, girlie, let's go break the bad news to the guys." At the bottom of the stairs, I lean around and say over the back of the couch, "Bedtime, boyos."

The usual grunts, groans, and whines greet this announcement, but I talk louder. "Yeah, yeah, yeah. I know. Your mom's awful. You should think about getting a newer model. Till then, you're stuck with me."

"We want Daddy!" Harris says with a cheeky pout.

"He'll give you kisses when he gets back from jogging."

"Jogging is stupid," Max declares.

Although I tend to agree, I reply, "Daddy likes it."

"Then Daddy is stupid."

Good deductive reasoning, but… "Max! Don't say things like that."

He mutters something under his breath I can't hear, because Brooks has interjected, "Daddy's not stupid; you're stupid!"

"Okay, enough of the name-calling."

"Stupid, stupid, stupid!" Harris chants, making Aidan giggle.

"Enough!"

Addi flinches and cries.

"Great. You made your sister cry," I grumble, not above deflecting blame. I point up the stairs. "Everyone, up! Line up at the sink so we can brush teeth."

Fifteen minutes and several stall tactics later, I flick the final light switch and say the last goodnight. Downstairs, I flop onto the couch, stretch out along its length, and fling my arm over my eyes. If every day were like this, I would have tendered my resignation a long time ago. I'm not cut out for chaos and drama, from kids or grownups.

The thought is hardly fully formed in my head when the back door crashes open, then closed again. "It's just me," Brice announces before I have too much reason for alarm, but not before I'm annoyed.

I pull my arm down and watch the spot at the bottom of the stairs where I expect him to come into view. "Hey! You mind holding it down? I just got the kids to— Oh, my gosh, what happened to you?!" I bolt upright, ignoring the slight vertigo caused by the quick change in position.

While it's typical for him to be sweaty after a run, even one on a chilly night like this one, he generally doesn't come home bleeding.

"I'm fine," he insists, waving me off.

"You're bleeding!"

"Still?" He licks his swollen lip.

"What do you mean, 'still?' What the fu—"

He disappears into the bathroom under the stairs, where I hear the water running. I follow him as far as the door and persist with my original question. "What happened?"

He dabs at his split lip with a square of toilet paper, then inspects the dots of blood on it. "I was running..."

"I figured that much."

"I hadn't gotten far at all, maybe five minutes away, and there were some other people around, like usual. Then a guy walking kind of fast up ahead of me sped up and grabbed a lady's purse from her shoulder and started running. Or tried to. But she managed to get a grip on the purse strap before he got away, so he sort of slingshot back toward her and tried again to yank the purse away. By this time, I was sprinting toward them and yelling at him, and people were staring. But my yelling distracted the woman who was being mugged, so she lost her hold on her purse, and the guy started running. I already had a pretty good momentum going, though, so I caught up to him right away and grabbed him by the shoulders. He turned around and hauled off and punched me."

"Brice!"

"It barely landed. My own tooth did most of the damage."

"I'm not worried about your lip. He could have had a gun!"

"He would have used it by then to make the woman give up her purse."

"Not necessarily."

"Anyway, he didn't have a gun. I grabbed the purse from the guy and ripped it from his hand. That's when he gave up and ran off. I returned the purse to the lady, made sure she was okay, waited with her at the bus stop, then talked to the bus driver about what had happened so he could keep an eye on her, make sure she really was okay."

"Was she old?"

He purses his lips while considering, then winces when the expression tweaks his cut. "Not really," he answers. "Not, like, elderly and stooped over and frail, but…" He pauses, then reveals, "Big-ish. She was out of breath for a long time. A lot longer than I was. I was worried about her."

I step forward and punch him in the shoulder. Hard.

"Ow! What the helter skelter?"

"That's for being an idiot."

"An idiot? Everyone else stood and watched it happening. I wasn't going to let that lady lose her purse to some punk."

"That's it; no more running."

"Honey!"

"No. If it's not a car, it's a mugger. That's enough. I'm

not going to sit here, scared to death, every time you go out to get your precious exercise."

"It's important to me."

"Use the treadmill I got you. It's down in the basement. We can move it up to our room."

"We've been through this; I don't like running indoors on a piece of equipment."

"Too damn bad!"

He backs me up, gently pushing on my shoulders to force me to perch on the narrow edge of the claw-footed bathtub. Sitting next to me with his legs spread, he places his elbows on his knees and turns his head to study my face before saying, "Listen to me."

"I'm done listening to you about this." The sob builds painfully in my chest, then breaks like a hiccup when I say, "Please. I can't—"

Straightening, he slips his arm around my shoulders and pulls me against his sweaty side. "Shhh…"

It's more of a comforting sound than actual shushing, so I allow it and try to bring my emotions under control.

"Hon…"

The only noise I can make is a pathetic whimper as I press at the tears gathering in the corners of my eyes and threatening to spill over.

He gives me a minute, rubbing my upper arm with his cupped hand. Finally, he says, "How about a compromise? I'll run on campus from now on, before coming home. Okay?"

I nod tearfully, still too choked to speak.

"It means I'll be home later."

"I don't care. That's fine. It's worth it."

"Okay. Come on, don't get so upset. I'm fine. And

everyone else involved is fine. Including the jerk who tried to steal Sharita's purse."

"Sharita?"

"Yeah. That was the woman's name. She lives one street over. We're practically neighbors. She has two boys in college, and she cleans offices at night."

"Did you tell her your life story, too?"

"I told her a few things while we waited for the bus. It seemed to calm her to talk about normal stuff."

I wipe under my eyes and nudge him. "I'm still mad at you."

He laughs. "I guess I'll have to live with that, because I couldn't not help."

"You're lucky to be alive to live with that."

"I feel that way every day, no matter what happens." He pats my upper arm once more, then says, "Are we good now?"

"No." I wrap my arms around his waist and bury my nose in his shoulder, never so happy to be close to a not-so-fresh armpit in my life.

"I'll tell you one thing."

"That you're a numbskull?"

He ignores me. "No more procrastinating; I'm calling the security company first thing in the morning and having someone come out here to install a system."

"Those are expensive."

"We'll get something bare-bones. Just something that will alert us to someone in the house and call 911 when the alarm goes off." He removes his arm from around me and pokes gingerly at his clotting lip. Satisfied it's stopped bleeding, he balls up the toilet paper in his hand and tosses it at the wastebasket under the pedestal sink. He misses. "And this neighborhood needs a watch program."

"Let me guess. You're going to organize that in all your spare time?"

"Someone's gotta do it."

"Like 'someone' had to run after that asshole to get Sharita's purse back?"

"Exactly."

"Why does it have to be you?"

"Because nobody else is doing it. And when I want something to happen, I don't wait for someone else to do the work. Something like a neighborhood watch, once it's up and running, runs itself. But someone has to take the first step and organize it."

Resigned, I heave myself to my feet. "What do you need me to do to help?"

He hops up, eyes sparkling. "Really?"

I roll my eyes while picking up the bloody toilet paper and dropping it into the trash. "Yes. Before I change my mind."

"You could design some fliers for me to put up around the neighborhood. And we'll have to host the meetings here."

"Meetings? Wait a minute…"

"Not too often. Just enough that people get to know each other, and we can talk face-to-face and exchange information."

"Okay," I concede, stifling a sigh.

"This'll be good, hon. Trust me."

I'd say that's been my biggest downfall for the past six years, actually. Before I can joke about that, he turns his head into his shoulder. "Phew. I'm ripe. Adrenaline is kind of stinky. Gonna run upstairs and shower."

"Yeah, yeah. Go."

I'm going to bed before anything else can happen today.

12

NEIGHBORHOOD WATCH

"Design some fliers" turned into a much longer list. Yes, a list. One I showed Brice so he'd understand what an undertaking this neighborhood watch venture is going to be.

His response? "Don't worry about it. Here, give me that list. I'll knock it out myself."

And he did. For the most part. He posted the fliers I made and contacted the closest police precinct to schedule a community safety officer to talk to the group about some basic things we can all be doing to reduce the likelihood of crime in and around our houses. He started a Facebook group. And for tonight's meeting, he's printed an agenda, sign-up sheets, and maps of the neighborhood, labeled with property owners' names from the most recent assessor's records. So no, he hasn't been slacking.

But there are plenty of things he's had to delegate to me. Like taking the calls from people saying they're interested in the group but can't attend the meeting, for whatever reason, and would like more information some other way, usually by email. And guess who gets to send out the emails? Of course, I was also the logical person to get the house ready for the meeting, including refreshments.

In addition, after I expressed discomfort with having so many strangers in our house, I dragged a promise from him that we won't always host the meetings. There wasn't time to find a public venue on such short notice, but future gatherings will be at a community center or church. Push comes to shove, he can call in a favor with a pastor. Surely.

For tonight's meeting, though, our house is the place to be.

"Maybe nobody will show up," Brice says, as he straightens the already-straight sign-up clipboard on the dining table. His nervous chuckle lets me know this scenario actually matches one of his nightmares about tonight. "You never know. It may be just you, me, the police department rep, and Harvey. And you know Harvey."

Sort of. If "know" means nodding to him while herding the children to or from the garage or waving across the fence while supervising the kids' backyard time. He could still be a serial killer or a child molester—or both. I don't know him at all, really. And Stanley Tucci seemed like an okay guy in The Lovely Bones, didn't he?

But I don't say any of that, because it would only make Brice more anxious than he already is. Plus, the kids are in bed, and nobody has any reason to go upstairs, considering there's a bathroom on the main floor. And you'd better believe I'll be sitting on the bottom step, making sure nobody tries to go up there, but it still makes me uneasy.

What if someone attends the meeting, posing as a concerned citizen, all the while casing the house? Nobody will be able to tell at a glance that even our nicest stuff has been sullied in some way by the kids. That Ritz cracker Harris shoved in the DVD drive of the laptop, rendering it useless even after an extended session with the vacuum's crevice tool, is undetectable to someone looking for shiny things to pawn for a quick buck. Therefore, anything portable and of potential interest—including the children—has been stashed upstairs.

The doorbell rings while I'm arranging the broccoli, carrots, cauliflower, and celery on a large, round platter, a bowl of hummus in the center. Brice opens the front door to a police officer in uniform.

She flashes us a bright, eager smile. "Reverend and Mrs. Northam?"

Brice shakes her hand and steps aside to let her in. "Yes. Hi. Come in. I'm Brice; this is my wife, Peyton."

"Officer Felicity Milner. I've been assigned as the community liaison to your neighborhood watch group."

"Of course. Feel free to set up wherever you'd like. The living room's on the small side, so we thought the kitchen and dining area would be best."

Officer Milner sets her briefcase on the kitchen table, then strides over to me to shake my hand. Her utility belt creaks with each step. I try not to stare at her gun.

"Nice to meet you," she says, taking in her surroundings. "Wow. No offense, but I didn't think it would look like this in here."

Brice laughs. "Oh. Yeah. It's a work in progress. Did the inside first. Exterior work commences in the spring."

"Did you two do all this yourselves?"

I pull lemonade, tea, and water from the fridge and place the pitchers next to the red plastic cups on the island counter. With a bob of my head in Brice's direction, I answer, "He did. With help from a friend."

"Impressive."

Brice blushes. "I hired professionals to do the plumbing

and electrical work, and a general contractor did the kitchen and the upstairs bathroom. I basically sanded and refinished floors and trim work. And stripped wallpaper and painted walls."

"Sounds like a lot to me."

"I like working with my hands."

I turn and pretend to be busy with the coffee maker to hide my snicker when his color deepens with that statement.

He clears his throat. "Anyway."

He's saved by the doorbell, which I cross the room to answer while he and Officer Milner go over the meeting agenda and some handouts she's prepared with the neighborhood's official crime stats. When I swing the door open, a surprisingly large group of people waits on the porch.

"Oh. Hey. Uh, hi," I greet the assembly.

"This where the neighborhood watch meeting's going on tonight?"

Harvey pushes to the front of the crowd. "Yes, yes. I told you it was. The Northams are my next-door neighbors."

"Good for you. Brice saved me from a nasty mugger. Does that give me the right to push other people out of the way, too? Rude!"

I step aside. "Come in, everyone. Harvey, good to see you."

He nods on his way past.

Close behind him is someone who can only be... "Sharita?"

Her grin competes with the porch light for wattage. "Yes! And you must be the lucky lady who's married to my knight in sweaty gym shorts."

I laugh at her description. "That would be me. I'm Peyton."

"I hope you weren't too mad at him for coming to my

rescue. Then again, if that was my husband—or son—I would've given him a beat-down. But I sure did appreciate his help."

"It was the right thing to do," I say. "But yes, I gave him an earful for taking the risk."

She pats my arm. "Good girl. You and I are going to get along fine, I can tell. Now let me move my fat carcass outta everyone else's way." She steps across the threshold and looks around, nodding her approval.

"Sharita!" Brice cries, stepping away from Officer Milner and folding his new best friend in a bear hug. "I was afraid you'd have to work and wouldn't be able to make it."

"I traded a weekend shift with a work friend. She and I do favors like that for each other when we have stuff to do." She pulls back from his hug and beams up at him. "I hope you don't mind my saying, but you smell a lot better tonight than you did when we first met."

He tosses his head back and laughs, then says, "I'm glad. And I'm glad you're here. Do you know Harvey?"

"We met on the porch," she drawls, narrowing her eyes at our neighbor, then softening. "No hard feelings, Harv."

"I should think not," Harvey replies, none too graciously.

"Am I going to have to separate you two?" Brice inquires lightly.

I return my attention to welcoming the other people entering the house. Within minutes, nearly twenty people have crowded into our usually spacious kitchen and dining area that now feels about as roomy as a coffin.

Brice stands on his tiptoes next to me near the front door and cranes his neck to see over the heads. "Hey, everyone, thanks for coming! I know we're tight on space, and there's not a chair for everyone, but make yourselves as comfortable as possible. For future meetings, I'll try to find something bigger, but there was kind of a time crunch tonight."

When the assembly quiets, he continues at a more conversational volume, "There should be a sign-up sheet going around on a clipboard. Please put your contact info on the list, so we know how to reach each other. I've also started a Facebook page. I'll send the link to you in the follow-up email after this meeting.

"As soon as we're finished talking business, we'll get to know each other more informally. First, though, let's go around and introduce ourselves."

Starting with Harvey, each person says his or her name and where they live in the neighborhood. Derek and Stacy Fox, a couple in their early thirties, live across the street in one of the houses currently being renovated. They have two daughters, eight and three. Jimmy Nash lives a few doors down from us with his mom, who rarely leaves the house, due to health problems. Dick and Janet Hildebrand, our next-door neighbors to the south, whom I've not met or seen until now, are retired high school teachers. We also meet a handful of others, like Sharita, from surrounding streets and farther down our street.

Finally, it comes back to us.

"I'm Peyton," I say simply, ready to leave it at that.

Of course, my husband can't let that stand. "And I'm Brice. We've lived here almost exactly a month, although I was born and raised in St. Louis, then moved all around after seminary before coming back here to teach at Concordia. Peyton and I have four sons and a daughter who are hopefully upstairs sleeping, not coloring each other with pens from my office, which they've done before." He waits for the polite chuckles. "Um, what else? Oh, yeah. I wanted to start this group for a lot of reasons, but the biggest motivator was an incident a couple of weeks ago. Do you mind if I share that, Sharita?"

"Go ahead! My heart still races when I think about it." She winks and fans herself.

He smiles coyly at her, then tells the story of the would-be mugging, downplaying his heroics, of course, and finishing with, "I love people. And I like to believe that people are generally good. But there *are* bad people out there. Or at least there are people who do bad things. The good people outnumber the bad, I think, but that's hard to tell sometimes, because those of us who are good don't stand up and show ourselves. We have to take action when we see something wrong. That's how we build community. There was no way I could see what was happening to Sharita and turn away, thinking, 'Better her than me.' Because it was me. A member of my community was being victimized. Might as well have been my wife. Or one of my kids. We have to send a message to people who think we're easy targets. We're not going to be victims anymore."

Sheesh. Maybe he should have painted half his face blue for that speech. Too bad we can't fit a pacing horse in here.

He clears his throat and rubs the back of his neck after his impassioned mini-sermon. I clutch his hand at my side and squeeze it. He smiles briefly at me and the others.

"Sorry. You know, I've been away for a while, but it wasn't that long ago that I was a kid in this city. I rode my bike all over the place and never felt afraid. Nothing ever happened to me or anyone I knew, either. And if something had happened, everyone would have been shocked. So what's the difference? Indifference. Wrongdoing has stopped bothering us, for some reason. Or maybe we've decided it's not worth our outrage. But it is. It's worth it to us, and to each other, and to our kids.

"I want crime in this neighborhood to become news again because it's no longer the norm. Now, is that a fantasy? Maybe. But I hope you find it worth your time and energy to work toward that goal. I promise, it won't be a lot of time and energy. And the payoff will be tremendous.

"Who here wants to be able to walk with their family up and down the street?"

Some hands rise.

"And who would like to be able to let their kids play outside?"

More hands.

"And who would like to invite people over without their guests feeling uneasy?"

More hands.

"And what about property values? Who wants to see theirs go up, not down?"

All hands.

"I want to be able to go away for the weekend and not wonder what I'll be coming back to," Janet Hildebrand pipes up.

Brice points to her. "Exactly! And I think that's doable. Heck, Janet, you can do that next weekend, if you want. You come over here—or go across the street to the Foxes, or wherever—and tell us you and Dick will be out of town, and we'll keep an eye on your house for you. Pick up your paper and your mail and hold it until you get back. It's the least we can do for each other, right? And it's not a huge imposition. It's just neighborly. And right."

He turns to Harvey. "You need help planting a tree or painting a door or fixing some loose shutters? You call me." Looking across the room, he calls, "Sharita?"

She flinches away from the veggie tray and covers her chewing mouth. "Hmph?"

Brice pretends not to notice. "You want to put up Christmas lights before your boys come home from school for Christmas break? You call me.

"Derek, you need a babysitter? Don't call me. I have enough kids." He pauses for the group to chuckle. "But we should all know each other well enough that you can call someone else on the list. Or private message some of the group members on Facebook. Or text. Or call. 'Hey, Harvey, your barn door's open—and so is your garage.' The point is, we need to communicate!"

He spins so he's facing Dick and Janet again. "You guys, I had no idea who you were until tonight. And that's not a criticism; I'm as much to blame. We live right next door to each other, but we might as well live on opposite sides of the planet! I want to know you. And you. And you," he adds, going around the room and randomly pointing at people. "The more we know about each other, the more receptive we'll be to helping each other and looking out for each other. Hopefully. Who knows? Maybe after this, you'll be like, 'I never want to see that weirdo again.' But I hope not."

He searches the room, trying to see over heads. "Where's Officer Milner?"

"I'm here." Her voice floats from over by the table. She and her squeaky uniform wade through the bodies to get to us.

By way of introduction, Brice says, "I've invited Officer Milner here to partner with us in this project. We need help in an official capacity for this to work. She's going to tell us what we're doing right, what we can do better, and what the city police force can do to help."

"Thanks, Pastor. Can everyone hear me?"

"We can hear you; seeing you's another story," Sharita cracks.

Brice hurries into the living room and returns with the coffee table, which he places in front of the door, patting it to encourage the diminutive cop to stand on it. "Really. You can't do anything to it the kids haven't already," he says when she hesitates.

Stepping onto the low table, she asks, "Is this better? Good. I want you to know what I look like, because I plan to be around here a lot. And I want you to get familiar with me so you feel comfortable talking to me and any of my colleagues. We're already around more than you realize, but we tend to blend into the background." She looks down at Brice (which is hilarious) and asks, "Do you mind passing out the pamphlets and the statistics packets?"

"Not at all," he answers, springing into motion.

Officer Milner leads the rest of the meeting, presenting the statistics on her handout and taking questions from people before stepping down from the table.

Then Brice takes over once more. "That's about it, everyone. Don't forget to put your info on the sign-up sheet. Otherwise, make yourselves at home and stay a while for refreshments and to visit."

He edges around some people and meets me on the stairs, where I crept during Officer Milner's presentation. "What do you think?" he asks me, surveying the buzzing room.

"I think you're crazy," I say bluntly but with enough affection in my tone that he knows I mean it in the nicest way possible.

He seems to take it as a high compliment, anyway. "Yeah, I know. But this is good. Better than good. Excellent."

Someone's in his element. I'm glad one of us is.

13

THANKSGIVING

*T*he neighborhood has responded positively to Brice's ideas, and I've noticed a big change on our street already. People wave to me when I drive past them (usually running late to drop off or pick up Max at preschool). Last weekend, Harvey helped Brice finish our privacy fence. Brave souls, Derek and Stacy invited our whole family over for dinner, and it was really nice (albeit hectic). I don't think they regretted it, either. In any case, they accepted our return invitation, so we must not have been too overwhelming.

Meanwhile, I've been swamped with the aftermath of the meeting: securing a bi-monthly assembly room reservation at a nearby community center, sending out the promised follow-up email with the phone tree list and meeting schedule, managing the Facebook group, and basically being Brice's secretary, as I try to help him juggle all the requests for help that have come in since he so generously offered his free honey-do services.

On top of all that, we're still hosting Mary and Bob for

Thanksgiving. After all, I couldn't very well un-invite them, just because my mom pissed me off.

And that. For the past three weeks, my every-other-day to-do list has included one less item: call Mom. Although she was definitely in the wrong for saying what she did, I've been wracked with guilt for reacting the way I did. She's still trying to cope with losing Dad, and now she has an over-grown teenager (that would be me) on her hands. But I can't seem to make myself call her and say I'm sorry for what I said and tell her all's forgiven for what she said. I'll get there, though. Hopefully before one of us dies.

Brice thinks Mom, in her infinite wisdom and coddling, decided for herself that my hosting both families this year was too much for me and moved the Stratford half of the venue to her house. Actually, I don't think he believes that for a second, but he's so distracted and nervous about the winter quarter starting on Monday that he can't be bothered to dig for the truth, for once. I'm sure I'm only experiencing a temporary reprieve. As soon as he settles into a teaching routine, he'll press me for more details. But maybe by then, it will have all blown over, and there will be nothing to tell.

In the meantime, I'm going to try not to think too much about it. So far, I've been successful. Too busy to obsess, anyway.

Getting ready for Thanksgiving has been typically exhausting but fun, too, in its own way. The kids did a great job helping me with the decor. Lots of hand-print turkeys and construction paper Pilgrim hats and cornucopias. I didn't realize they had kiwi (at least, that's what I hope that round brown thing is supposed to be) at the first Thanksgiving, but I applaud Max's efforts to broaden the Pilgrims' diets, even if it's a couple of hundred years after the fact. I've seen adult depictions rewrite history in worse ways. The boys wanted to make a centerpiece from real leaves, pine cones and acorns found during one of the Saturdays they "helped" Brice and me rake leaves, but I convinced them the construction-paper versions of those things would be less buggy, so an afternoon's work (for me; they got bored after five minutes and wandered off to destroy their bedrooms) encircles a pumpkin-scented candle in a jar in the middle of the dining table. The whole atmosphere is cozy and quaint.

And quiet.

And empty.

I miss my family.

Bob and Mary are here, though, so it still feels somewhat special.

Actually, "special" is a good word for it. Or, more accurately, for my husband's strange behavior since returning from a round of golf with his new stepfather. I'd love to get a minute alone with him to ask him what the deal is, but he's made that impossible, fluttering around the kitchen with his mother and me.

"You need me to mash those potatoes?" he asks now.

I pause with the electric mixer poised to obliterate the spuds in the pan in front of me. "Um, no? But you can check on the yams in the oven. And set the table. And check on the kids, because they're suddenly really quiet."

"Bob's with the kids," Mary pipes up with her head in the oven, where she's basting the turkey and consulting the temperature on the meat thermometer. "And the yams look fine. We might take them out in a few minutes and cover them to keep them warm."

Brice nods. "That leaves the table, then. I can do that. You want to use the good stuff?"

We both crack up at the concept, but Mary says, "You know, you should have some nice things for special occasions, kids. Or quiet dinners for the two of you."

"That's the newlywed speaking," I tease.

Brice scrunches up his face. "Currently, I'm spending all of my disposable income on diapers."

I groan at his pun and turn on the beaters, folding butter, sour cream, cream cheese, and salt into the potatoes. He's right, though. I can't imagine purchasing fine china, crystal, and silver right now. Where would I store it, safe from monster hands? And when would we be having these romantic dinners? After we put the kids to bed, I guess, but the idea of making a meal for them, then a separate one for us, is ludicrous. I barely have the patience for one dinner and its associated cleanup.

By the time I'm finished with the loud mixer, the topic has died, so I ask while transferring the potatoes from the stock pot to a serving dish, "Are we going to take a drive around The Sem later, show Bob and your Mom your new digs?"

Keeping his eyes on his flatware placement, Brice answers, "Nah. We're supposed to get rain this afternoon. Plus, the kids will be napping. And anyway, Mom's seen it all before."

"Yeah, ages ago."

"It hasn't changed that much."

"What about Bob?" I press, inwardly giggling at the inadvertent movie title mention.

"What about him?"

Mary slides the yams onto a couple of hot pads on the counter and covers the casserole dish with a clean towel. She closes the oven. "Bob's never seen the campus. He was looking forward to it."

"Maybe tomorrow the weather will be better, and he

and I can walk there. That way, we don't have to drag all the kids out."

Stopping everything, I study my husband.

"What?" he asks.

"I thought you were excited to show everyone around."

"Well, everyone's not here, are they?"

"I guess Bob and I are chopped liver," Mary quips, her tone not coming off as lightly as I think she intended.

Since her back's turned to us, I issue Brice a wide-eyed look and mouth, *What's wrong?*

He ignores my attempts at subterfuge and says at a normal volume, "I'd rather watch the game after we eat. We'll all be tired from the cooking and cleaning—and golfing." His cheeky smile at that last thing signifies he wants it to be the last word on the topic.

Mary turns around and gets the same hint, apparently, because she brightens and inquires, "How'd that go? Who won?"

"Oh, Bob shellacked me. But what do you expect from a Scot?"

Mary chortles. "Yes, he takes his golf seriously."

"And I haven't been on a course in a couple of years, so it was no contest. Plus, my hip was stiffer than I thought it would be."

My head snaps up. "Really?"

He waves away my concern. "Yeah. But whatever. You'd think having a titanium body part would be an advantage, but not so much." He sets down the last wine glass and stands back to admire his precise table-setting. "Perfect. Too bad we have to introduce the chain gang to this scene."

"But we do. Feeding them is one corner we can't cut." I head upstairs to get the kids and Bob while Brice slices the turkey and Mary sets the rest of the food on the table.

Within minutes, the boys have bellied up to the table at their usual spots and are chanting, "Hungry, hungry, hungry!"

Bob smiles indulgently at them. "Now, boys, haven't your parents taught you any table manners?"

Brice exchanges our beloved centerpiece for a platter of turkey and replies bluntly for them, "They have an excuse for being socially incorrect once in a while: they're kids."

I exchange a glance with Mary, who quickly transfers her attention to the yams in her hands. Clearing my throat, I say, "Anyway, boys. Grandpa's right; you should—"

"Hey! Let's pray and eat; then there'll be no need for any lectures about patience or manners," Brice interjects. Since he refuses to show me anything but his profile, I can't convey to him my displeasure at being interrupted.

"Okay," I mutter under my breath. Louder, I say, "I think everyone and everything is here at the table."

"Great. Let's pray." We all bow our heads and close our eyes while Brice says a prayer that sounds more perfunctory than usual. He and I remain standing to help the kids load their plates, but even when we finally sit, nobody says anything.

Trying to entice Addi to try some new solid foods, I poke sweet potatoes at her mouth while she sits in my lap.

"This is nice," Mary tries after several minutes of nothing but clanking silverware and the occasional unintelligible utterances from little people.

Bob blinks, not seeming as sold on the niceness.

Brice doesn't react, merely shovels food into his mouth with his eyes on his plate, as if scouting for his next bite.

What the hell is going on?

Something must have happened while Brice and Bob were golfing, but what could that possibly be? Until now,

Brice's biggest beef with Bob has been that he's not Augustus, which isn't Bob's fault and isn't like Brice to make Bob suffer for it. And Brice is a competitive guy when it comes to board games, but I've never known him to get bent out of shape about sports. Especially golf. That was my dad's modus operandi. He'd invite someone to play, then get pissed off if that person played better than he did. Brice couldn't care less about his golf handicap, whatever that even means. I think he learned how to play as another "in" with people, a way to get them to lower their guards and talk to him about the things he thinks are really important, like Jesus and stuff.

And surely Bob didn't say something against Jesus during golf. As a matter of fact, before Bob and Mary were married, he became a Lutheran and goes with her every Sunday to Peace. He's involved, too, from what I hear, having joined the Board of Trustees. And he and Mary both regularly attend the seniors' group events. Brice can't ask for much better than that, can he?

We also can't find fault with the way Bob treats Mary. Unless new information came to light on the links, the two retirees are very much in—gulp—love, and while that may make Brice feel "squicky," he's not the type of person to put his own feelings before his mother's happiness. He sees how Bob opens doors, pulls out chairs, and basically does everything for Mary. So I doubt it has anything to do with that. I thought Brice was getting over that initial weirdness about the whole thing. But I'm dying to know what it is that's caused such an arctic front to pass through in the past few hours.

When the silence becomes too dense for me, I say with more enthusiasm than I feel (mostly for the kids' sakes),

"Hey! I know! Let's go around the table and say what we're thankful for."

Brice puts down his fork and wipes his mouth, but I don't need to see his pinched lips to know he's not in the mood for this exercise. Too bad.

"Max, you go first, so your brothers know what we mean. What makes you happy?"

"*My Little Pony!*" he cries without hesitating—or waiting to swallow his mouthful of food.

The grownups laugh, which makes the boys giggle, despite probably not understanding what we think is so funny.

Brice rubs his eyebrow. "Well. That's great. I guess. How about you, Brooks? What makes you happy?"

Our serious thinker considers the question for a while, then answers, "Addi Grace." Four hearts melt on the spot. Then he adds, his eyebrows pinched together, "'Cepts when she cries and poops."

"Keeping it real. I appreciate that, Brooks," I say with a wink across the table at him. "Harris? What makes you happy?"

"Mashed 'tatoes!" he blurts with a mouth full of them, as if to prove it.

Bob, shaking with laughter, slaps the table, then wipes his eyes. It's impossible to witness his amusement without joining in.

The boys, feeding off the grownups' reactions, toss out simultaneously:

"Punkin pie!"

"Table!"

"Light!"

"Pilgrims!"

"Whoa, whoa, whoa!" Brice manages through his chuckles. "Now, you're being silly. And it's Aidan's turn."

Aidan squeals, "Poop!"

"Hey!" I rap my knuckles on the table like a judge trying to restore order with her gavel. The giggling boys quiet. "That's enough. Aidan, please tell us what really makes you happy."

Chastened, he plunks his cheek against his fist and mumbles, "Gammy."

Mary presses her hand to her heart and tucks her chin to her chest. "Oh, you sweet boy! I'm going to get up right now and kiss those cheeks!" She rises from her chair, trots around the table, and delivers on her promise. Then she kisses the other boys and Addi, too, to make it fair. After she returns to her seat, she asks, "Is it my turn?"

"If that's what you want," Bob replies.

She practically glows. "This. This makes me happy. I'm glad to be here; I'm so proud of each and every one of you; and I can't think of anywhere else I'd rather be." When we think she's done, she rushes before Bob takes his turn, "Oh, and I'm most especially thankful for my husband." She turns to him and grasps his hand.

I stretch the boundaries of my peripheral vision so far to get a glimpse of Brice that my eyes ache. If he were a hologram, I'd think the computer had frozen. He doesn't even blink while Mary continues, "I'm thankful God still has happy surprises in store, even for us old folks!"

Bob beams. My eyes sting with proud tears for the sweet couple. Brice manages a thin half-smile.

"How can I top that?" Bob booms, startling Addi, who spits green bean onto the front of her shirt.

I scrape the green blob onto the spoon, which I shove

into her mouth before she can get too attached to the idea of crying.

Bob continues, "I guess, to avoid repeating what's already been said—'mashed 'tatoes' was going to be my answer—I'd have to say I'm most thankful to be part of a family again. It's— Well, it's special."

Mary pats his hand on the table. "Aw. We're glad to have you in our family. Aren't we?" she consults the rest of us.

"Yes!" I immediately supply.

Brice's previously stony expression softens. "Of course," he says quietly, then more confidently, "Of course we are."

Mary's chest puffs out as if her only son has announced he won the Nobel Peace Prize.

"Your turn, hon," I say to Brice.

He shifts in his chair and avoids our eyes. "I'm thankful for all of you, that we all have our health, and…" Now, he looks up. "I'm thankful for fresh starts." He turns to me. "And last, but definitely not least…"

Although I could choose to go all deep and emotional after the year we've had, I decide to keep it light. "I'm thankful for a quiet, relaxed day with you guys. And pumpkin pie. Whoever said that earlier was a genius."

Several hours later, finally alone, Brice and I tuck the sheets around the sleeper sofa's flimsy mattress and prepare for a night of camping out in the living room (because you don't make two people in their late seventies sleep on the couch).

I toss my pillow at the head of the "bed" and ask, "Are you going to tell me what's wrong?"

He pauses, then says too casually, paying close attention to smoothing the sheet on his side, "What? Nothing. I knew

I shouldn't have mentioned anything about my hip." He straightens, meets my eyes, then mimics a golf swing and winces. "See? It's the back-foot pivot-and-swivel action that's the problem. Not used to moving that way. And my hip wanted to let me know it wasn't happy about it. Anyway, that's only one of many excuses for playing so poorly."

"I'm not interested in your golf score."

"I know. I just don't want you to worry."

Pulling back the covers, he slides under them and almost immediately grumbles while closing his eyes and squirming to get comfortable, "Hide-a-beds should be illegal. That metal bar. Who the heck thought that was a good idea?"

I remain standing, looking down at him. After several seconds, he opens his eyes and lifts his head from the pillow to squint up at me through the lamplight. "Is there a problem?"

"You tell me. What happened on the golf course? And I'm not talking about bogies or your sore hip, either. Out with it."

"I'd rather not talk about it."

After turning off the light, I take my place in the bed next to him and stare at the ceiling. "Too bad. If you don't tell me, I'll ask Bob tomorrow."

"It's better if I keep it between him and me."

"Better for whom?"

"Everyone. We had a disagreement; it's over."

"A disagreement about what?"

"Asiughdubggfhjkl!" he grunts. (At least, that's what it sounds like.)

"Excuse me?"

He flops from his back to his side but immediately regrets the dramatic action when the aforementioned bar fails to yield under his ribs. "Oh, fudgesicle," he hisses, rolling once more to his back and clutching his side.

I watch his display, then ask dully, "Are you okay?"

"I think so."

"Good. Now tell me what you and Bob argued about."

"It wasn't an argument per se."

"You want me to punch you in your other side?"

"What's the deal with your punching me lately?"

"I haven't done it tonight yet. Say 'per se' one more time, though, and that may change." I sit, but my tailbone grates against the bed's support bar, so I scoot closer to my pillow and draw my knees to my chest. "Come on. Stop avoiding the question. You know I'm going to find out eventually. It may as well come from you. Heck, Bob's probably telling your mom all about it right now."

Brice scowls. "He won't, if he knows what's good for him."

"You afraid she's gonna take his side?"

"She most definitely won't."

"If you're so in the right, then, tell me what happened."

He blows a huge breath through puffed-out cheeks. "Fine. Bob's a…"

"Serial killer. Martian. Secessionist. Packers fan. *What?* Spit it out already. The suspense is killing me."

"He's a— Well, he's a bigot."

My backbone curves as my shoulders slump and relax. "Oh."

"Oh? That's all? Just 'oh'?"

I cock my head toward my right shoulder. "Yeah. 'Oh.' He's— Well, he's old."

"So? That doesn't make it okay!"

"I didn't say it did. But it makes it less surprising. What did he say or do to make you think he's a bigot?"

"You don't believe me?"

"Of course, I do. I just want to know details. Did he use an epithet? Tell a questionable joke? What?"

After a sigh, Brice says, "I guess he figured that since I'm a pastor, I hold certain views. You know, about politics and stuff. 'Please God, and God will reward you; anger God, and you'll be punished.' That type of hooey. So he made a few comments about our neighborhood and our neighbors that I let slide, because… Well, you make jokes about it all the time."

"Not racist jokes! And I don't imply that people who struggle in life do so because they've pissed off God somehow."

"No, but he didn't say anything overtly racist at first, either. It was more general than that. Elitist, I guess. It made me uncomfortable, but more in a defensive way. We live here, too, you know?"

He pauses; I wait.

"I just thought, if I don't encourage him, he'll get the hint and talk about something else. But he didn't. Then he said something about 'those people,' and I felt something in me snap. Like I felt when Max hit Addi, only I couldn't lift Bob by the back of his shirt and put him in time out. Instead, I was like, 'Those people? You mean, people-people?' and he kind of ha-ha'ed and said, 'Now, I'm not lumping you in with them. I know you're trying to bring some respectability to that neighborhood, and I respect your efforts.'"

"Yikes."

"Yeah. Then he said something about mixing races, financial assistance programs, and the moral bankruptcy—and subsequent downfall—of our country, and that's when I told him to shut up."

"You actually used the words 'shut up'?"

I hear him swallow in the dark. "I said a lot more than that. My exact words were, 'Shut up, Bob. The biggest problem in society right now is people like you who hold outdated, ignorant views and attribute them to Jesus.'" The cringe is strong in his voice when he says, "I lost my temper, big-time."

"Sounds pretty justified to me."

"I should have risen above, though, and chosen my words more carefully."

"Hey, some expressed views don't deserve a tactful response."

"There's more."

"Oh." I hold my breath.

"Of course, he defended himself and said he didn't believe in paying lip service to political correctness and that there are statistics to back up what he believes about certain segments of the population, which, according to him, 'includes more than just the blacks.'"

I resume breathing, mostly so I can release a chagrined moan. "Who talks like that anymore?"

"Bob Abernathy. My mom's husband. My... stepfather."

"Oh, hon." I lie down next to him and put my head on his shoulder. "What did you say to that?"

"I told him if he breathed any of that garbage around my kids or in my house, that would be the last time he'd be welcome here."

My eyes widen, but I give no other indication he's shocked me, and since he's not looking at me, I may as well have not reacted at all.

"I mean, my word!" he defends himself. "What if your family had been here today? I'm sure Bob would have plenty to say about your brother and Dustin."

"Yeah, so? A lot of people do."

"I just wish everyone would shut up about everyone else and focus on their own crap, for a change. Everyone. On both sides of all the issues."

"Shh…"

"Oh, whatever." He flaps his hands in a double-waved gesture. "I have half a mind to go on the front porch and yell it from there. So the whole street can hear it."

"That would definitely cement your reputation as the neighborhood eccentric," I say, patting his pec. "Listen. I agree with what you said to Bob. I'm glad it all came out on the golf course, too, when you two were alone. And who knows? Maybe what you said resonated with him. He didn't seem to be holding a grudge at dinner."

Brice snorts. "Dinner. When he said that stuff about being glad to be part of a family again, and I felt about three inches tall? That dinner?"

"Do you think that was calculated?"

"No!"

"Shhh! If you wake up the kids with your outbursts, you're on your own with them."

He scratches his head, then repeats more softly, "No. I don't think he was trying to make me feel bad. But it had that effect. And what am I supposed to do? I won't apologize for setting him straight. 'Hey, Bob, sorry I got mad about you being an intolerant dinosaur'? Not happening."

I giggle while imagining that conversation. "If you feel bad enough, though, you could apologize to him for losing your temper. Sounds like that's what you most regret."

"Exactly. How hypocritical is it of me to demand he respect other people, regardless of whether or not he agrees with them, and then I spout off like that?"

"He's lucky to have a stepson who recognizes that."

He groans under me. "Please. Oh, and do we have to encourage the kids to call him 'Grandpa'?"

Carefully, I reply, "It's the easiest, least confusing thing for them. They never knew your dad, and now with my dad gone… They like having a grandpa again."

"I suppose."

"Plus, whether you like it or not, he is part of the family now."

"I know. And I don't dislike it."

"Yes, you do."

"I'm trying not to, though."

"That's all anyone can ask right now. And he needs to know that if he's going to be part of this family, it's best if he keeps his opinions to himself about certain things. Sounds like he respected you for being upfront with him. That's what families do. They care enough to let each other know when they've crossed the line. Then they forgive and move on. At least, that's how it's supposed to work."

Man, I'm so insightful when it comes to other people's family problems.

14

MORE DRAMA

I gotta give Bob credit; he didn't tattle on Brice to Mary and try to spin it like her son was being mean to him. I know this, because when we all meet up in the kitchen this morning for a post-Thanksgiving pie-and-coffee breakfast and Brice says to Bob, "I'm sorry for the unkind way I expressed my point-of-view to you yesterday," Mary regards her husband and son with a knitted brow that conveys one thing: cluelessness.

Bob glances at her but immediately returns his attention to Brice's outstretched hand, which he grasps and pumps. "No hard feelings. I spoke out of turn."

Brice grins. "Great. Moving on. Is there any peanut butter pie left?" He crosses to the counter, where I've lined up the foil-covered pie tins straight from the fridge.

"What's all this about?" Mary questions.

Not eager to witness her finding out she's the only one in the room who doesn't know, I keep my back to everyone and watch the coffee drip into the nearly full carafe.

Bob answers casually, "Just a misunderstanding."

"Actually, we understand each other quite well, I hope,"

Brice says, his tone still friendly—too friendly. "But we don't need to belabor it."

"Belabor what, exactly?" Mary tries again.

I spin and hold the carafe at eye level. "Coffee, anyone? Freshly brewed. Tongue-scorchingly hot."

The room's three other occupants ignore me during their stare-down.

"Well, I'm going to drink some." I pour a mug for myself, replace the pot on the burner, and weave my way through the others. "And eat some pumpkin pie. Everything is better after coffee and pie." I nudge Brice so I can access the desserts, muttering from the side of my mouth, "Do something. Say something."

He pushes away from the counter. "Bob and I discovered while golfing yesterday that we disagree—fundamentally—on some things. Important things. But now we know where we stand, and there's nothing more to discuss. We've agreed to disagree."

"About what?"

"Not saying anything else, Mom. Just drop it. You guys can talk about it on the way home. But I've spent enough of this weekend thinking about it."

"Well, good for you! But you don't get to dictate what I think and talk about." She points to Bob, in case he thinks he's exempt. "Nobody does."

He holds up his hands in mute surrender.

Brice shuffles his feet like a teenager being reprimanded in front of his friends. "I just meant—"

"I know what you meant. You're used to getting your way all the time. What you say goes. You decide when to shut down the conversation. And that may be okay for some people"—she glares at me—"but it doesn't fly with me. I think you forget who you're talking to, kid. I gave you life."

The deep wrinkle between Brice's eyes could grip my coffee mug handle. I'm oddly tempted to try it, if for no other reason than to break the tension and change the subject, but I resist the urge and merely chew and swallow my pie. Something tells me it's better to fly under the radar in this conversation, anyway.

"I didn't mean—" He takes a deep breath and starts again. "I'm sorry. I'm trying to avoid any more unpleasantness about this."

"Then you should have made your apologies privately."

"You're right."

"I know I am."

"You're right that I should have apologized privately." He pours a cup of joe, his movements executed with exaggerated precision, his face hard and closed. "And while you are not right about me getting my way all the time, I will have my way this time. If you and Bob want to talk about this, that's your choice, but I'm not going to." He leaves us with an unapologetic, insincere smile and a sip of his coffee. On his way up the stairs, he says, "I've got the kids."

I look from Bob to Mary while licking the last of the pumpkin pie filling from my fork. Placing the utensil and my plate in the sink to deal with later, I say, "I'll leave you two alone, then," and exit as quickly as possible. A nice, long, world-avoiding shower sounds good about now.

At the top of the stairs, none of the usual voices and noises greet me. The doors to the boys' rooms remain closed, and all is quiet and still. Intrigued, I poke my head into Brice's office. Empty. I turn and walk the other way down the hall, toward our room, where I hear the deep timbre of his voice, if not the actual words. Creeping closer to the source brings me to the threshold of Addi's nursery. I linger on the periphery, out of sight, hoping to hear something insightful. Or, at the very least, heart-warming.

Instead, what I overhear puzzles me.

"Oh, you know me, up with the birds. Plus, between the kids and the old folks, there's no sleeping in…. What's that?. . . Oh, yeah. Livin' the dream…. Never mind. You called me; what can I do for you?"

Ohhhhhhhhhhhh… Whew. Phone call. For a minute there, I thought he'd gone off his rocker, talking to Addi and silently filling in her side of the conversation. I tune back in to figure out from context clues who's on the other end of the line.

Brice is quiet for a second, then says, "Uh, I don't know. I'd have to check the academic calendar, I guess. I can't take time off, but I'll have some time around Christmas, when campus shuts down for the holidays. Why?"

Addi fusses, and he clicks his tongue at her.

"No, no. This is probably the best it's going to get around here today…. Yeah, she's here somewhere. Let me finish changing Addi, and I'll go find her."

Oh, shit. I think "her" is me. Why does this person want me? And why did they call Brice, if they needed to talk to me? And why am I still standing here?

Thinking fast, I run to the bedroom door, then back through it, making plenty of noise as I open and close dresser drawers, choosing underwear, socks, and a sweater.

Brice pokes his head through Addi's door. "Oh, here she is…. Yeah, probably eavesdropping on me." He laughs at the person's response to that—and my scathing, yet guilty, expression—then says, "Oh, I'm used to it, trust me." He pulls the phone away from his mouth. "Vince is on the phone and wants to talk to both of us about something." He hits a button on the phone and sets the device on top of the dresser. "You're on speaker, Brother. What's up? And just a warning, I have a hungry baby here, so I hate to rush you, but time is of the essence." He bounces Addi to delay the inevitable pre-breakfast meltdown.

Vince replies, "Okay, gotcha. Jen's here, too, by the way, and you're on speaker, as well."

"Great. Got it."

"Happy Thanksgiving!" I greet the two of them.

Brice widens his eyes at me and nods at Fusspot, but I stick my tongue out at him. It only takes a second to be sociable.

They return my wish, then Vince says, "Jen's sort of shy about telling you two this, but I finally wore her down, and…"

"We're getting married!" my "shy" friend shouts loudly enough to distort the sound from the phone's speaker.

After we congratulate them, Brice asks, "When?"

"Well, that depends on you," Vince replies. "That's why I was asking about your schedule. Because you owe me, Brother."

"Yes, I do," Brice says with a grin. "Where's the blessed event taking place?"

"We wanted to do it on the boat, just a handful of us, you know? But…"

Brice winces. "I gotta be honest; a trip to Florida's gonna be hard for us to swing anytime soon."

"Yeah, that's what the 'but' was for. Plus, it's a little chilly in December to stand on a boat deck."

"So, where does that leave us? You want me to call you guys back when I don't have the world's hungriest baby on my hands?"

"Yeah, that'll work."

They arrange a time to talk later, and I promise to call

Jen when I get a minute to myself, possibly during afternoon naps.

Brice hits the button to disconnect the call, pockets his phone, and says to me on his way to the bedroom door, "Took long enough for them to figure it out."

I snort. "Right? Sounds like they're in a rush now that the decision's been made, though."

"Someone else is in a rush, too." He nods down at red-faced Addi. "And I hear the boys in their rooms." Pausing in the doorway, he turns and walks back toward me, leaning close to me and murmuring, "Don't leave me alone with Bob and Mom today, okay?"

Addi pitches herself backward, letting us know how fed up she is with not being fed.

"Okay. Take Aidan downstairs with you. He'll be a good distraction for your mom. She won't want to argue in front of Angel Boy. I'll get the other boys and be down as soon as I'm dressed."

His forehead furrows. "Just don't be long, okay? Please?"

So much for that nice, long shower.

Without the kids, the morning and early afternoon would have been interminable, but it's amazing how much of a diversion children—especially our children—provide. To the uninitiated, it's not obvious most of the adults in residence aren't speaking to each other beyond the bare minimum. Unfortunately, I'm initiated. And my shoulders are feeling the strain.

So when the boys finally go down for their naps after a morning running around a cold Concordia campus with the quietest tour guide ever, I take my cell phone into the master bathroom and draw a hot bath. I realize that means I'm leaving Brice alone with his mom, who's not talking to him, and Bob, who's also receiving the silent treatment from Mary, but the guilt associated with that lasts about three seconds and is quickly outweighed by the need to get away from the tension. My husband's a big boy who shouldn't be so afraid of his mommy, even if she is kind of scary when she's ticked off.

Plus, I promised Jen I'd call her. I can't go back on that, can I?

As soon as the water fills the tub, having reached the perfect, just-shy-of-skin-searing temperature, I lower myself into it, almost immediately feeling the sweat bead along my hairline and on my upper lip. Ah, yes. Baths and sex: the only times sweating is enjoyable.

I turn off the taps and retrieve my phone from the folded towel on the floor next to the tub, careful to wipe my hand dry first to prevent dropping the device into the water.

I dial Jen's number and, after the initial niceties, say, "I trust that 'I finally wore her down' isn't a euphemism."

"What are you implying?" she replies, feigning innocence.

"You know what I mean."

"My sex life—or serious lack thereof—is none of your business."

"Since when has that mattered?"

"I'm about to be a married woman. According to you, that means no more kissing and telling."

"Hmm… yes. That wasn't intentional. It just happened." I stretch my legs, resting my ankles on the rim of the tub, pointing my toes, and flexing my weary calf muscles. The water tinkles around me.

"Are you peeing?"

"No! I'm in the bathtub. Escaping for an hour."

"Vince said Brice didn't sound very thankful on this day after Thanksgiving. Did you and Mary do any Black Friday shopping?"

"I'll be lucky to have the energy to do all my Christmas shopping online. And don't even get me started on the money."

"You're still tired all the time?"

"Yes, but I don't want to talk about it. It makes me tired."

"Oh. Okay. Good. Back to me. So, Vince and Brice haven't had a chance to talk yet, but I think it's safe to tell my matron of honor we're going to get married there in St. Louis, sometime the week between Christmas and New Year's."

I roll my head on my neck. "Nice."

"Don't get too excited there, P."

"I'm sorry. I'm just, well, you know. I'm so happy for you. Really, I am. Despite how it sounds. I've been waiting for months for the phone call Brice and I got this morning."

"You have?" Her voice bubbles with girlish excitement.

Closing my eyes, I answer, "Oh, yes. I could tell when you came back from Florida to visit me in the hospital that you and Vince were in *lurve*."

"Nuh-uh! I didn't even know then."

"That's what made it so cute. You two were all, 'We're just friends,' but I said to Brice, 'They're more than friends, whether they know it or not.' But I think Vince knew it before you did. Because Brice acted all shifty whenever I talked about you two, like he'd already talked about it plenty with Vince and didn't want to say too much to me without permission."

"We sound like a bunch of teenagers."

"I know," I say wistfully, remembering vaguely what it felt like to be young and stupid and bursting with hormones.

"And don't worry; I'm not going to need a lot from you in the way of matron of honor duties. This is going to be super-low-key."

Jen and "super-low-key" generally don't go together, so I open my eyes and protest, "No, no, no. You tell me what you want; I'm there for you. Like you were for me."

"It's not the same."

"Why not?"

"Because Mitzi and I were co-maids of honor at your wedding, and neither of us were married or had kids. In this case, it's all you; I'm not sure Mitzi and Jared can make it."

"What?!"

As if I'm a simpleton, she explains, "Jared's up to his eyeballs in stuff at Peace, since—ahem—Brice abandoned him. And you know how it is at a church around Christmas. I offered to wait until January, but Mitzi said it won't be any better then, because the new senior pastor they called starts then, so Jared will have to be around to show him the ropes."

"Oh. Well—"

"I'm not waiting longer than January."

"I see."

She giggles. "Sorry."

"No apologies necessary."

"It's not just about that, obviously."

"Another bride-to-be thought she had to tell me that recently, too. What the heck?"

"Everybody knows you're a nympho."

"Thanks. Tell me what you're thinking about for colors. Do you already have a dress picked out? What do I get to wear? Mitzi made me look like an eggplant. You're not going to do something like that, are you?"

"Gosh, no! I told you, this is going to be ultra-casual. Like, if we could get away with not having a church wedding, I'd totally get married down here by a justice of the peace and just have a party there in St. Louis, so most of our friends didn't have to travel too far."

"That would go over like the proverbial fart in church."

"I know, right?" She sighs. "A church wedding, it is. Vince wants Brice to marry us, anyway, which will be a sweet touch."

"It will. Those two have been friends a long time."

"Not as long as us, though."

I sink farther into the water, submersing my shoulders. "We have to figure out a way to get Mitzi here. It'll be tragic if we're not together on your wedding day. We're the Trippin' Trio!"

When she doesn't chastise me for using the nickname but simply says, "I know. It's gonna kinda suck, actually," I rush to reassure her. "But I know you're in a tough spot. By the way, how's Vince going to swing being away from Zion at such a busy time of year?"

"All the retired pastors here love filling in. And he'll be here for Christmas Eve and Christmas Day. Then, when we get back from our honeymoon—"

"Oooh! Where're you going? Somewhere warm and sunny, I hope."

"Nope. Paris. We've both always wanted to go, so we're doing it."

"Wow. Jet-setters." After a pensive pause, I say, "This is going to be so great," the tears suddenly stinging my sinuses.

She sniffles. "Right? I can hardly believe this! Sometimes I think about where we all were ten years ago, and if someone then had shown me our futures, I would have told them they got some serious psychic wires crossed."

"Tell me about it."

"I mean, I would have bought Mitzi being married to a pastor, but you and me?"

"Never."

"Never in ten million years."

"When I went to see my pastor for advice about how to break the news to everyone about my predicament, the last thing on my mind was whether that pastor would make a decent future husband." I chuckle at the memory. "And he thought I was there to ask him about premarital counseling and officiating at my wedding, because that was typically what women my age came to talk to him about."

"What?" she shrieks. "You never told me that!"

"Yeah, he said he was pretty bummed about it, because he'd been trying to get up the nerve to have a real conversation with me, and he figured he was too late."

"Who was this hypothetical fiancé of yours?"

"Dunno. But Brice said he had an irrational, instant dislike for the guy."

"Awww, he was jealous! If he'd only known how many conversations the two of you would share in the coming months—years." We think about that for a second; then she says, "So, when you told him you were pregnant but wanted nothing to do with the cretin sperm donor, he was relieved, in a weird way?"

The thought makes me laugh. "Maybe for a split second. But he realized pretty quickly that the real issue was a much bigger complication. Boyfriends—even fiancés—can be dumped. But what I was telling him…"

Jen clicks her tongue. "Oh, P."

Must not allow us to go there.

I brighten my voice. "And romantic relationships between pastors and parishioners are highly frowned upon, for obvious reasons. Did you know there's a seminary class about stuff like that? Ethics and dos and don'ts?"

"Something tells me they won't be asking Brice to teach a section on that." Delivering her best Brice imitation, she quips, "'Do as I say, guys, not as I did, m'kay?'" In her regular voice, she gushes, "Wow. That's a really sweet story. And romantic as all get-out. Plus, it explains a lot about why it took him so long to make a move. He was working up the nerve to talk to you, worried about doing something he'd been taught was a big no-no. That guy... God broke the mold with him."

"Strangely enough, God seems to know what He's doing. Fortunately, we don't have to understand it all at the time."

"Premarital counseling. Ha! That's priceless." She trails off dreamily, then sucks in a shallow breath. "Sheesh. That reminds me. Vince and I need to do our counseling with Brice at some point."

"Vince did ours online. Just a couple of sessions. Not a biggie."

"There's not enough time to do everything!" she laments.

"But the moral of the story is, it'll all work out, right?"

"Absolutely."

Still, I think we need to make a list.

15

HECTIC HOUSEHOLD

*F*or the first time in our married life together, I only know it's Advent, the season before Christmas on the church calendar, because we go to services on Wednesday evenings, in addition to Sunday mornings. There are no other deviations from the schedule. My husband is home each night at his usual time, and—

Wait. Can we stop a second to marvel that my husband now has a "usual time" to be home? It's still a novelty, one I keep expecting to wear off. But it hasn't yet and doesn't seem like it will any time soon.

When Concordia's winter quarter began, I thought, Here we go. He'll start getting home later and later, wrapped up in grading papers or talking to colleagues or holding office hours or whatever he does there. But nope. Post-work jog or not, he's home at 5:30—almost on the dot —every single night. Sometimes earlier. No more Don't hold dinner for me text messages when I'm expecting him to walk through the door any minute. No more apologetic phone calls ("I got held up at the hospital, then lost track of time getting caught up at the church" or "So-and-So passed away"), sometimes hours after I'd been expecting him. None of that. It's incredible.

For the first month, I had to resist the urge to give him a standing ovation every evening when he walked through the back door. But I resisted. Because what kind of precedent would that set? We don't want the man getting too full of himself, do we? I mentally applaud, though. And hop up and down and squeal.

And this month, I don't know what I'd do if he was late every night or if he came home exhausted and unable to do much more than eat dinner and lie on the floor, half-asleep, "playing" with the kids. On the contrary, he walks through the door full of energy, ready to pitch in with dinner prep, then participates enthusiastically in the sometimes-rowdy table conversation and takes charge of baths, before sending the kids, naked and pink, to me to be dressed for bed. Without that evening teamwork, I'd be in trouble.

Because between neighborhood watch business and being Jen's "boots on the ground" as she plans her wedding at the end of the month, it's a miracle I haven't dropped more balls around the house than I have. And I've dropped plenty.

One of the biggest balls is the tangled mass of clean, unfolded laundry now on the living room floor.

After tucking in the kids, a whistling Brice trots down the stairs and stops short at the sight, the last note of his tune sliding from his lips and landing sickly at his sock-clad feet. "What the—" he breathes toward the mountain of clothes.

"I've gotten a little behind," I explain. That's an understatement.

Shoulders slumped, he stands, frozen, at the threshold to the room. "Um, yeah. B...But... How— I mean, I had no idea!"

Avoiding his eyes, I confess while folding a tiny pair of jeans, "I've been doing your clothes separately and making sure they're put away every day."

"Why?!"

He tiptoes through the folded, sorted piles I've already started and plucks the first thing he finds, a set of pink footie pajamas, from the top of the unorganized mound in the middle of it all.

I shrug. "I didn't want your clean clothes to get wrinkled. You're the one who has to look presentable every day. I used to be good about washing and folding two loads a day. But with everything going on, I've let it slide. I'm still washing. Folding, not so much. I've kept the laundry room door closed so you didn't have to see the mess, but I ran out of room in there."

He laughs. "Ya think? If I'd had any idea, I would have been helping you in the evening."

"I don't want to spend our quiet evenings together folding clothes."

"If we did it every night, though, it would only take, like, fifteen minutes. This is going to take hours." He pulls more articles from the jumble and folds in double-time.

"Please. I have this. And it won't take as long as you think."

"I'm not going to sit here and watch TV or read a book while you do all this alone."

"I don't mind. It's my job. I meant to do it before you got home, but… Well, obviously that didn't happen."

Instead of arguing further, his answer is to continue plucking and folding. After a few minutes, when we still haven't made a dent, he stands and gathers as much of the unfolded clothing in his arms as he can manage.

"Hey! What are you doing?"

Struggling to hold onto the unwieldy heap while bending over to collect stray socks and onesies, his face nearly purple with the effort, he rasps, "This can wait."

"What?! No, that's the whole point. It's waited too long!"

He ignores my protests and strides from the room, dropping one of my bras in his wake. I pick it up and follow him as far as the dining table, then wring the undergarment in my hands as I watch him throw the clothes on the floor in front of the washer and dryer. He steps back through the doorway and closes the door. Turning to me, he smiles tightly. "Don't do any more of that without me. We'll do it this weekend."

"You're crazy!" I say on a tired groan. "I have to do it. Tonight!"

Gently, he removes the bra from my hands and drapes it over the back of one of the dining chairs. "Stop."

"It's stressing me out to have it hanging over my head."

"Then stop thinking about it."

"That doesn't solve anything."

He grips my shoulders and turns me in a circle so my back presses against his warm front. "Look at this place."

"It's a mess, I know. I try to keep up, but—"

Poor choices. Poor choices. Poor choices.

"That's not the point I'm trying to make." Leaning down and placing his cheek against mine, he murmurs, "This house isn't unsanitary or dangerous. It's lived in. It's loved in. It's home."

I turn to face him. "This is how filth starts, though."

He holds my gaze. "They won't be babies forever."

"Thank God!"

"Yes. I do."

Actually, I have a confession. Half the time when someone reminds me our kids won't be babies forever, it makes my heart hurt. I like them as babies. The one who's technically not a baby anymore is kind of a pain. Independence is overrated. It comes with mouthiness and willfulness. Or maybe that's just our kids.

I pay lip service, though, to the idea that I have a paper chain for each child, that I'm counting down the days when all of my kids are school age. Because that's what people expect. It makes me feel like a freak to acknowledge I'm not excited for them to grow up.

Brice's expression slackens as he seems to notice for the first time, "You look tired, hon!"

My jaw clenches.

"Now, don't make that face."

"I'm not making a face," I say, not releasing a single pound per square inch of pressure on my molars to utter the words.

"You are. And it's adorable. But you know I'm right."

"Putting off that laundry for another day isn't going to make me less tired, though. It's going to make me more tired, when there are two more loads added to it."

He shakes his head. "I'm serious. No more laundry until we get that stuff folded, and no more folding until I can help you. It's just one night. We'll knock it out while the kids are napping tomorrow."

"Tomorrow's Saturday."

"I'm well aware."

"Well, Saturday means projects around the house. And I have other things to do during their nap times tomorrow. Max needs a freakin' shepherd costume for Bethany's Christmas program, and Jen's asked me to meet her wedding photographer at the church so he can scout a few things, and I haven't even started the Christmas cookie baking for this year. Plus, look around! Ten days before

Christmas, and we don't have a single decoration up yet. Except the Advent calendar, which taunts me every day with its countdown. We don't have the tree up, or anything! And we have to put up lights, because otherwise, this house will be the Grinch of the block."

He presses his hand against my mouth. I can still smell the orange-scented kids' shampoo from bath time. No longer appearing the least bit amused, he says, "Enough. Don't make me hunt down your latest, greatest list and burn it."

Ha! Shows how much he knows. It's on my phone, so there'll be no burning of anything. I'm organized and tech-savvy.

He continues calmly, "We'll manage to do what needs to be done tomorrow, including the laundry. In the meantime, you put the ten pounds of clothes we tackled tonight into a laundry basket, set it aside, sit on the sofa, and wait for me to bring you a glass of wine." I blink at him. "Nod your agreement, and I'll move my hand."

Reluctantly, I do as he says. He drops his palm from my mouth, but before I can do much more than take a breath, he leans down and kisses me. Like he means it.

I close my eyes and wrap my arms around his neck, holding tightly to keep from falling backwards. He cups my butt in his hands and pulls me closer.

Separating my lips from his for a second, I say breathlessly, "I don't really want that wine," then go back to drinking him instead.

He's right; the laundry—and everything else—can definitely wait. Right now, I'm hot for preacher-teacher.

∾

In addition to being so busy that the days pass in a blur of diapers, naps, and mealtimes, part of the reason I haven't been as full of the Christmas spirit as usual may have something to do with the lingering tension between my mom and me. And Brice and Mary. The last time I checked, Brice still didn't know his mom's Christmas plans or if she'll be at Vince and Jen's wedding.

At least I'm talking to my mom again. Sort of. My nerves can't handle calling her every other day, but I try to call her once a week. Nothing has been resolved, and we talk about nothing significant and seem to be tiptoeing around each other, but that's relatively normal for us, so I'm calling it good for now. It's the Stratford way.

Even after years of being an honorary member of the Stratford family, Brice still doesn't understand our propensity for grudge-holding or problem-burying. When he finally couldn't stand not knowing the whole story, he seized what I'm sure he thought would be his opportunity to fix it with one golden piece of insight.

Standing at the pedestal sink in our bathroom early one morning a couple of weeks ago, when we were still the only ones awake in the house, he sprayed a blob of shaving cream into his hand and, lathering his face, asked, "Are you ever going to tell me what's going on between you and your mom?" He rinsed his hands, picked up his razor, and regarded me with raised eyebrows through the mirror before leaning forward and making his first stroke down the right side of his face.

I used emptying the hamper as an excuse for not answering promptly, as I debated whether I wanted to get into it right then. I had a feeling he already had his "Love one another; don't let the sun go down on your anger" speech ready (although the sun had gone down nearly thirty times at that point). While I stalled, he made short work of the shadow on his cheeks, chin, and neck, splashed water on his face to rinse the remaining foam, and patted himself dry with a hand towel.

Massaging lotion into his newly smooth skin, he turned to face me, rested his hand on his towel-clad hip, and said, "Well?"

Arms full of dirty clothing, I told him what she said, word-for-word, to upset me.

His Adam's apple clicked, his face hardened, and he left the bathroom without a word. There ended the sink-side sermon before it began.

Maybe I shouldn't have told him the part about Mom and Dad questioning our "poor choices." But I needed him to see my pique has been justified, and none of his platitudinous proverbs would apply this time.

He hasn't said anything more about it since then, but I'm sure Mom's words were part of the inspiration last night for him chucking the laundry out of sight for another day. Maybe he's determined to turn our poor choices into doable, right ones. If that means helping with the laundry, whether or not I want him to, then he'll help with the laundry. Desperate measures, and all that.

This morning, still half-asleep, I peel the covers away from my body to get up at the first sound of Addi stirring, before the sun is even up, only to have him bolt upright in bed, mumble-yell, "I've got her!" and practically yank the covers over my head, patting blindly at my hair while saying, "Go back to sleep."

I don't have to be told twice. I figure it won't be for long, anyway, since my to-do list is crying at me a lot louder than Addi ever could.

But the next time I wake, two hours later, the clock

congratulates me on my ability to sleep through the most persistent calls from my responsibilities. I stretch like a newborn just figuring out she's no longer confined to her mother's cramped—albeit secure and cozy—womb. I take my time showering, dressing, and brushing my teeth, then saunter downstairs.

On my way down, I glance over the banister and into the living room just long enough to do a head count. All accounted for, including the biggest one, holding the smallest one while overseeing his cartoon-watching clones from the couch.

I hang a left at the bottom of the stairs and make a beeline for the coffeemaker. After serving myself, then topping off Brice's quarter-full abandoned mug next to the sink, I carry the two cups into the living room to a chorus of "Mommy!"

"Hey, guys!" Their warm greeting is a pleasant surprise; their rapid exit is a perplexing development. "Hey, where are you going?" I say to their bobbing heads before they disappear up the stairs. "Was it something I said?" I ask Brice.

He sips the coffee I hand to him. "I told them they had to be quiet until you got up; then they could go upstairs and play."

"Oh. So they weren't really happy to see me; they were just happy to see me."

"Something like that," he confirms.

I set my mug on the coffee table next to his propped foot. "Okay. Hand me that sweet little Ladybug. I bet she'd like to give her mom some snuggles."

"You sure? I think she's filling her pants."

I laugh. "Sheesh! This is quite the 'good morning' all around," I say, while lifting Addi from her dad's lap and holding her aloft long enough to get a substantiating whiff of her bottom before cuddling her to my chest and kissing her chubby cheek. "Hmmm. I think I have a few minutes before the load drops." I settle into the couch, closing my eyes and breathing in a huge whiff of her baby, clean-for-now smell.

"How'd you sleep?" he asks.

"Fabulously," I answer, opening my eyes and grinning at him. "Ready to tackle that laundry, for sure."

"Excellent."

I glance at the phone in his hand, then do a double-take when I realize it looks suspiciously like… "Hang on a second. Is that my phone?"

He simpers at me. "Maybe."

"What are you doing with my phone?" I demand, swiping for it and missing, due to the load-dropping load in my lap. Addi giggles at the jostling.

Brice holds the device away from my reach, which is also coincidentally far enough that he can view the screen without the reading glasses he refuses to wear for anything but bedtime reading. "I thought I'd access your precious must-do list to see what's on it, besides the dreaded laundry."

"For you or for me?"

"For both of us. We're in this together, babe."

I roll my eyes and at how much he sounds like Lonnie, whose incessant use of that endearment for Nicole has landed it on my list of verboten words and phrases, right up there with "per se."

Brice titters at my disgust.

"That's an invasion of my privacy!"

"If you're so worried about that, you should screen lock it. You got hot sexts on here from someone?"

"No, the only person who would sext me uses terms like, 'expressing our love,' which is hardly sexting material."

He grits his teeth. "I am never going to live that down, am I?"

"Nope. Now give me back my phone."

Seemingly unconcerned about the consequences of disobeying me, he replies, "Not yet. Let's see. Oh, my— You do have a rendezvous with another man today! Smack-dab in the middle of the day, too."

Leaning forward, I retrieve my coffee from the table and take a bracing gulp while considering the weekend's highest priorities. "That's the wedding photographer, thank you. I'm meeting him during afternoon naps."

"How brazen!"

"Shut up. And give me my phone."

He continues perusing the list, swiping his thumb against the screen to scroll through it. "Oh, I see I'm getting the Christmas decorations from the attic and putting up the outdoor lights. Good to know."

"Yes, but not while I'm gone, please." I picture him, lying at the base of a ladder, and shudder.

"Yeah, yeah. Next item. Yikes. You're on your own with the shepherd costume. The sheep would have no respect for a guy wearing anything I'd design."

"I already know what I'm going to do; I just need time to get it together," I reassure him.

"Tell me it has nothing to do with pastel ponies, and I'll consider it handled."

"It's a traditional costume, dork. I got the pattern from one of the other preschool moms."

"You're going to sew?" He bites his bottom lip, suddenly seeming more worried about that than at the prospect of a pony-bedecked bedsheet costume.

"No sewing necessary."

His teeth release his lip. "Okay, then. 'Nuff said. I'll leave that one to you."

The boys clatter down the stairs, making train noises. "I da caboose!" Aidan pronounces proudly, trailing several feet behind his older brothers, who come to a hissing stop in front of the TV.

"All aboard!" Max, the conductor (complete with my discarded bra from last night wrapped around his head), bellows. "WOOT WOOT!"

Addi twitches, toots, and squawks.

Brice waves my phone at his progeny. "Boys, boys! Hold it down. Your sister's trying to poop."

"Ewww!"

After a comforting squeeze from me and a productive push from her, Addi quiets.

With a flourish, Brice returns the phone's screen into view. "Moving on. I also see something about…" He transmits a furtive glance at the now-quiet convoy, then finishes, "C-O-O-K-I-E-S."

"'Cookie' starts with 'C,'" Max helpfully provides, adding a "Woot woot!"

Brice mutters, "Stinkin' *Sesame Street*."

"Good job with the letters, though," I make sure to praise Max. "You're right," I say to both him and Brice.

Max beams.

"I yaunt a cookie!" Harris interjects.

Brice and I ignore him. Brice is too busy making fun of my ultra-specific list ("'Gas'? You have to remind yourself to have it, or what?"), and I'm too busy defending myself and breathing through my mouth to avoid the eye-watering smell now coming from our daughter ("Pump gas. Into the van. Nerd").

I stand, hoping by the time we make it to the changing table in her room, Addi will be finished with the biggest job on her to-do list.

With his eyes, Brice follows our movement toward the stairs and waves his hand in front of his face to dispel the dirty scent ions we've left in our wake. The boys immediately mimic him, coughing, gagging, and plugging their noses with their free hands.

"Yeah, yeah. I'm taking care of it," I grumble, but Brice stops me two steps from the bottom by saying, "Oh, I also promised Sharita I'd put up her Christmas lights."

"You were kidding!"

"No, I wasn't. And I've been putting it off for a couple of weekends now. I told her I'd be by sometime today." His tongue peeks from the corner of his mouth as he thumbs that entry onto the official list on my phone.

"Are we gonna have lights, too?" Max asks.

Brice drains his coffee, probably grateful for the diversion and an excuse not to meet my withering eye contact. "Yep. They're going to be beeyootiful."

The boys cheer and dance, although I don't think Aidan knows what they're supposed to be so happy about. He's just happy his brothers are happy.

"Red and blue and green and purple and... and..." Brooks's forehead wrinkles in consternation as he tries to think of more colors.

"Orange, black, brown..." Harris lists what sounds like the ugliest string of Christmas lights ever.

Brice explains matter-of-factly, "Our lights are white."

"Awww!"

"They're still pretty, though!" he tries to convince them.

They stare blankly at him.

His tongue clicks once. "Anyway, you guys are going to

help with the Christmas tree, too, right? There are lots of ornaments. Your mommy and I can't do it without you."

The monkey dancing resumes. Max contributes a sassy, musical, "Oh, yeah! Uh-huh!" before he remembers, "And the manger?"

"Yep. The nativity." Brice sets my phone on the coffee table and rises with his now-empty mug, which he nudges in the direction of the bay window ledge. "I think it should go right over there this year, don't you?" he checks, as if he and I haven't already discussed and decided where to put the display of miniature ceramics.

"Yeah!" his design team cheers.

I set my jaw but say nothing as the conversation continues below me, the boys each claiming the pieces of the nativity they'll be in charge of setting up. I guess now's not the time to get into a lengthy discussion about my husband's propensity to overextend himself with community service projects at hectic times of the year.

But this year was supposed to be different than all the other years before it! Sure, I still expected to be busy, but not in the ways we've been in the past, to the point of exhaustion and irritability and bah-humbugness. I hope he's not trying to fill the holes left by his absent church responsibilities with neighborly good works.

As the debate over who gets to place the baby Jesus heats up, I tune back into the action.

Brice soothes, "We'll figure it out later, okay, guys? Maybe we let Addi handle Jesus, since they're both babies."

All four boys loudly voice their displeasure with that disastrous idea.

"Fine, fine! Just a suggestion." He passes the bottom of the stairs on his way to the kitchen and glances up at me.

"We're gonna need to fumigate if you stand there much longer."

I turn and make my muttering way up the rest of the stairs with my stinky parcel.

All I want for Christmas this year is my husband's time and attention, damn it. I think I've earned it.

16

SATURDAY NIGHT FIGHT

*I*ntermittent gusts of cold air blow through the house for the rest of the day as we come and go. We fill the hours with tree trimming, laughing, playing, arguing, baking, feeding, eating, napping, and costume designing/modeling, followed by climbing, light-hanging, and oohing and aahing. Brice was right that we managed to get it all done, even the dreaded laundry.

Now, for the youngest of us, there is sleeping. And silence.

Relative silence, that is. Bing and friends croon from the speaker on my cell phone on the coffee table, keeping Brice and me company as we balance the ornament distribution on the twinkling Christmas tree. Brice's tongue pokes from the corner of his mouth as he finds new homes for the bunch of baubles currently clumped at toddler level.

On the other side of the tree, I marvel at how many ornaments the children were able to cram on one branch and wonder if it's a skill they can parlay into something more practical later in life.

Following another one of my amused mutterings, Brice peers around the tree at me. "You okay over there?"

I shake my head. "Yep. Just getting a kick out of how cute our kids are."

He smiles. "Yeah. It was a good day."

"It was." I chuckle at how surprised I sound, then add, as if he's asked me to defend it, "I mean, exhausting, but good."

Keeping a focused eye on the tin snowflake hanging from his index finger, he offers, "Take a load off. I'll finish this."

I wrinkle my nose at him. "Huh? Why?"

"You know," he replies casually, stepping toward the back of the tree, where I can no longer see his face, "you shouldn't overdo it."

I can't help but sigh and roll my eyes at that statement. "You're the one who climbed up and down a ladder most of the day, at two different houses, hanging lights. And you were up two hours earlier than I was."

"I took a power nap while the kids were napping and you were meeting the photographer. I haven't been as on-the-go as you have." He has no choice but to venture into view to grab another ornament for relocation.

I stop everything I'm doing, study him, and put my hands on my hips. "Have you been talking to my mom?"

"No! And even if I have been—which I haven't—you make that sound like a capital offense."

"I don't want you guys talking about me behind my back, like I'm some wilting flower in a freaking Victorian novel. I'm fine."

"You don't look fine."

"Thanks!"

"That's not what I meant!" He steps around the tree,

sets a ceramic teddy bear in a Santa hat on the coffee table, and moves to touch me.

I flinch away. "Don't."

He pulls back his hand before making contact with my arm. Instead, he runs his fingers through his hair. "I didn't mean it like that. I just meant— I'm worried, that's all."

"Great. Looking bad enough to make someone worry is awesome."

"You don't look bad. Would you let me explain?"

Why, suddenly, does everyone, including my husband, seem to think it's okay to constantly remark about my appearance, for better or worse? Is that all I am? A conglomeration of physical traits that dictate everything else about me, including my wellbeing and my intelligence? Plus, do these people think I never look in a mirror? I see the dark rings under my eyes and the dullness of my skin and the occasional acne breakout.

But spa weekends and makeovers aren't in our family budget. Heck, I haven't had a professional haircut in months. I've been cutting my own bangs (and it shows) with a pair of the kids' safety scissors.

I blink at Brice, then away, staring at the white light on a branch in front of me. Its burning filament blurs while I fail at my attempts not to cry, and Rosemary Clooney implores us to have ourselves a merry little Christmas.

Fortunately, Brice keeps his distance. One touch, and I'm gone.

"You don't look bad," he repeats softly. "Someone who doesn't know you wouldn't have a clue there's anything wrong. But I know you. I know your face better than my own." He pauses, then offers as an example, "For starters, you've lost a ton of weight."

I had noticed my jeans and yoga pants weren't cutting

196 | THE SECRET KEEPER FULFILLED

me off at the waist anymore. But I had a lot of weight to lose. And sure, I'm not exercising to lose the weight, but who needs an exercise regimen when you run after four active boys and an infant all day long? I may not be sweating it out at the gym with a personal trainer on fancy equipment, but I'm burning more calories than I'm taking in, and I'm lifting more weight than I ever did when I was single and childless.

Do I eat as well as I should? Hell, no. I definitely have different standards for our kids' diets than my own. Some days my lunch is a banana, period. I'm not one of those annoying people who "forgets" to eat, but as crazy as this sounds, some days I'm too lazy to eat. I often don't want what the kids are having for lunch, but I also don't want to bother thinking of what I do want to eat, much less prepare it. Ironically, when that happens, I wind up eating the least-mangled leftovers from the kids' plates, thereby consuming what I originally rejected but in a more disgusting form than if I'd prepared enough for myself to begin with. But I consider that cleanup more than dining.

Mulishly, I reply to what sounds more like an accusation than a compliment, "That's what normal people do after they have a baby, or five. They lose that weight. It's supposed to be a good thing."

"It is a good thing! Hon, I don't mean to sound like I'm criticizing. Someone who hasn't seen you in a long time would say you look great."

I bite my lower lip. "But?"

"But I don't care how you look."

"Lucky me."

"I care about how you feel. And you don't feel well. I want you to see a doctor when things settle down after Christmas and the wedding." Before I can protest, he says, "I want you to go before then, but I know you won't, and I don't want to add one more thing to that ridiculous to-do list of yours."

"It's not ridiculous! It's how shit gets done around here. Without my 'ridiculous to-do list,' it all goes to hell. Even with it, things fall through the cracks. I haven't scrubbed the damn shower in our bathroom in weeks."

He lifts his arms straight out from his sides, hands palms up and supplicating. "Tell me that stuff. I know how to scrub showers. And toilets."

"Whatever. It's stuff I'm supposed to do when you're at work."

"You're so flippin' independent. And stubborn. And infuriating. A… And impossible!"

"What am I supposed to do? Lie on the couch with smelling salts and a hankie while you do everything?"

"If that's what it takes for you to fully recover, then yes!"

"I'm as recovered as I'm going to get. This is life. Life is tiring. I'm tired. Mostly tired of having this conversation with every single person in my life."

I step between the tree and him, grab my phone from the coffee table, silence it, and head for the stairs.

He follows me with his eyes, but his feet stay put. When I reach the middle of the staircase, he freezes me by saying, "I feel like I'm killing you. Okay? And instead of resisting, you're allowing it, encouraging it, even! You're an active participant in it. And I see it happening, as if I'm having an out-of-body experience, and I try to stop it, but as I pull the knife away, you grab my forearm and yank it back toward you."

The last time he sounded this tortured, I was unable to see him. I might as well be trapped in that bed right now, forced to listen to him all over again.

Choking on tears, I nevertheless have enough voice now to demand, "Stop it."

He must think I'm protesting his perceived melodrama, because he says, "I'm not saying it to be dramatic. I'm saying it because that's how it feels." He perches on the arm of the couch and scrubs at his face with his flattened hands before resting them, pressed together as if in prayer, against his lips.

I lower myself onto the closest step. Openly crying now, I put my hands over my ears in an illogical attempt to block out the memory of his bedside breakdown.

He half-turns to see why I'm not responding to what he's said. When he realizes how distraught I am, he rises from the couch and sits next to me on the stairs, wrapping his arm around my shoulders and pulling me against his side. "Hon. Please. I'm sorry. I didn't mean to upset you. That was the last thing I wanted."

"I know." I sniffle, dropping my hands. "I'm sorry, too. I... I just— I'm so sick of everyone treating me like an invalid. And reminding me all the time of what almost happened. I don't want to remember, not any of it."

"Shhh... Calm down."

"I don't understand what you want from me."

"Nothing. I don't want anything more from you. That's kind of the point." He rubs his hand up and down my arm. "I want you to give it all to me."

I clutch at his fingers and grip them tightly. "Why? So you can be exhausted? So you can be the hero?"

Voice tight, he replies, "I've never thought of myself that way, and I don't plan to start thinking of myself that way now."

He pries his fingers from mine, removes his arm from around me and half turns so he's peering down at me.

When I don't immediately return his eye contact, he coaxes me with a finger under my chin. "I— If anything, it's the other way around, all right?" He twists his mouth to the side while composing himself before continuing, "You're one of the strongest people I know."

"'Strong-willed' isn't the same."

"You're that, too. But you're also flat-out strong. Stronger than I could ever be."

"That's nice of you to say, but I'm not feeling it. And I'm not saying that so you'll keep trying to convince me. You're actually embarrassing me."

He shakes his head and sighs. "Fine. Whatever."

"Don't be mad at me."

"I'm not! I'm not mad at you about any of it. Anything."

"You seemed pretty mad a few minutes ago."

"Frustrated."

"I'm sorry I don't have patience for your concern. I'm sorry I don't seem willing to delegate stuff to you. I—" Frustrated, I huff. After a few more false starts, I finally get out, "This is my office; my domain. I'm not trying to shut you out; I'm trying to make it easier for you to focus on your stuff."

"Please, stop apologizing." He rests his chin on top of my head. "You're making me feel worse than I already do."

"Why do *you* feel bad?"

He hesitates. "I just do," he finally answers vaguely.

Although I'm still not able to see his face, I look toward my bangs, in the direction of his head. "Why are you shutting me out?"

His chin rubs against my hair when he shakes his head but doesn't say a word.

My heart thunders. "You're scaring me." I pull away

from him and angle my upper body so I can see his face. "Come on. What is it? Something bad? It can't be that bad. Right? I need to know it's not."

"It's nothing bad at all."

"Then tell me."

"It's just something I keep thinking about lately. A memory. That's all."

"A memory that would upset me?"

After a considerable pause, he answers, "Maybe. That's just it; I don't know. But it's personal to me, and it means a lot to me, and when I think of it, especially lately, I—" He takes a huge, shuddering breath. "It's haunting."

"Does it involve Secret?"

"No."

"Me?"

"You weren't there," he non-answers.

"Oh." I think about that for a while. "But it does have something to do with me?"

He lifts and lowers his chin, but begs, "Please stop guessing. I promise you, it's nothing bad; it's nothing that affects you."

"Except that you're thinking about it a lot lately and shutting me out. And freaking me out. I guess I'm strong when it suits you, but I can't handle whatever this is?"

"Point taken."

"And I want to trust you on this, but—"

"Why does there have to be a 'but'? When have I lied to you? When have I kept anything from you that wound up hurting you in some way?"

"Well…"

He chuckles. "Okay. Fine. There may have been a couple of times, but this isn't one of them. If you must know, this was a conversation between your father and me before you and I were ever married."

"Now I'm even more intrigued."

"I knew you would be."

"And this has stayed with you all these years?"

"We've only been married six years."

"It feels like forever," I tease.

"We've packed a lot into a short time," he says. "Anyway, yes. You could say it's stayed with me, considering I can probably tell you word-for-word what was said."

"But you're not going to?"

"I'd prefer not to. You wouldn't have appreciated the general theme of the conversation."

I slap his head, and he flinches, as it finally hits me what kind of talk they must have had. "Were you asking him for permission to marry me? Please, tell me that wasn't it."

"Ow! And no. He invited me over to talk."

"I really want to know the rest of the conversation."

"I know you do." In spite of that acknowledgment, he stands and offers me a hand up.

"You're mean."

"I'm tired. Let's finish the tree and go to bed. I promise I'll tell you some other time."

I know a stall when I hear one. "You're full of shin-bones," I say.

He nearly trips on the bottom step and has to hang onto the newel post to keep from falling. Coughing, he demands, "What?!"

Remembering too late that was a fake-curse I merely attributed to him in my imagination, I nevertheless recover quickly and own it. "You like that one?"

"Yes. I'll have to put it into circulation."

"You're still full of them."

"Probably so," he accepts, retrieving the ornament he abandoned on the coffee table and searching for an open spot for it.

I follow him and resume working on the other side of the tree. "Jackamuffin," I mutter.

"That's another classic."

"You are."

"You are."

We lean around the tree and narrow our eyes at each other at the exact same time, which tickles both of us.

When our laughter subsides, I wipe away the last of my tears and say, "I love you."

His grin slowly fades to a bemused smile. "I love you, too, my bride."

17

SHARITA'S VISIT

*I*s it killing me, wondering what Dad could have possibly said to Brice all those years ago that still pushes him into frequent bouts of introspection? Of course. But I'm not going to harass my husband about it. That would be immature and would signify a major lack of trust, wouldn't it? And if there's one thing we've learned during our years together, it's that we have to trust each other. Totally. Definitely. Most of the time.

So I jump about seven feet and tinkle in my panties when the doorbell rings during nap time today, as I'm rooting around in Brice's office searching for the journal corresponding to the time during which he and Dad may have had that conversation.

"Sonofa—" I hiss, nearly slamming my finger in a desk drawer in my haste to exit the room and run down the stairs to the door before the visitor rings again and wakes the kids.

I hop the last three steps, coming to a sliding, squeaking halt in front of the door and quickly pressing my eye to the peephole. My brain can't figure out exactly what's happening on the porch, but I can tell who is out there, so I open the door.

"Sharita! What, uh, brings you here?"

She holds up a large caddy of cleaning supplies. "I'm here to offer my professional services."

My jaw drops. "Huh?"

Her arm straightens, bouncing the caddy against her ample thigh. "Brice didn't tell you I was coming today?"

"No! Please, come in where it's warm."

She enters the house and booms, "Men! Let me tell you, they're—"

I scrunch my shoulders toward my ears and grimace.

"Oh, sorry," she whispers. "The little ones sleeping?"

"Yeah. You don't have to whisper, though."

"Gotcha. Anyway, when Brice put up my lights, I told him I'd pay you all back somehow. He pooh-poohed that, of course, but it's the least I can do."

"So you're here to clean our house?" My heart picks up a few extra beats per minute. Oh, Lord. No.

Setting her caddy on the floor so she can take off her coat, she smiles. "Now, now. Don't be shy. And don't go worrying I'm doing this because I think you're dirty, or something. This is what I do." She hands her coat to me. "I can't hang Christmas lights or build a fence, and I have a brown thumb—literally and figuratively." She gives me a thumbs-up and laughs.

I smile weakly. "Well. This is… unexpected. And nice. But…" On auto-pilot, I hang her coat in the closet next to the stairs, realizing too late my action effectively signals my acquiescence to this trade agreement.

"Come on. I insist. Make this worth both of our whiles. Give me your most hated jobs."

I bite my lower lip and spin in a semi-circle. "Um. Geez. I don't know, Sharita."

"Showers and tubs? Nobody likes to do those. Except me."

"It has been a while," I say before thinking better of it.

She rapidly claps her hands, but doesn't make a sound. "Yay! All right, girl! Point me in the direction of my first victim." She hoists her caddy, ready to follow me.

I'm tempted to show her the one in the downstairs bathroom, since we never use it. That way, she won't have to encounter our filth, but she'll also feel like she's fulfilled her end of whatever weird bargain this is. Something tells me she'd see right through that ruse, though, so I skip the part where I insult her intelligence and lead her up the stairs to the kids' bathroom.

Lowering my voice to a murmur, I say, "Here it is. I can't believe you're really going to do this."

"Why not? Brice has done me two huge favors; it's only right that I try to say thank you."

"Just saying it is plenty."

"But I want to do something more. My Christmas lights have never been straighter! They're beautiful!"

I chuckle. "Yeah, he prides himself on a job done precisely. It's the German in him."

She cackles and wheezes. "He's just cute as can be. Now, where's the other bathroom, so I don't have to bother you when I'm ready to do that one?" I lead her to the master suite. She murmurs approvingly. "Very good. You all are neat! Lemme guess, more German traits?"

"Not sure about that. You happened to hit us after a weekend when we actually got things organized around here. Normally, it's not this tidy."

She rolls her eyes and waves a hand at me. "Oh, you

modest little thing. Now, you go put your feet up and don't worry about me."

Uh… yeah, right.

There's no way in heck I'm going to lounge around while someone else cleans my bathrooms. Anyway, I don't know her that well, and my kids are up here. Not that I'm worried. But it would be irresponsible to blindly trust a near-stranger, right? Plus, I should probably stick around, in case she has any questions. That's the nice, hostess-y thing to do.

Since I also don't want to be in her way, I have no choice (ahem) but to return to Brice's office. I stand in the middle of the small room, hands on my hips, foot tapping.

If I were a methodical (anal retentive) pastor, where would I keep my old journals?

Starting on my right, I scan the floor-to-ceiling shelves along the north wall. But all of the books on the shelves are large, hardbound volumes, mostly reference books, or non-fiction paperbacks. Of course, he wouldn't have his precious journals out in the open, where the kids (or someone slightly older) could get their hands on them. No, they won't be exposed. They'll be in a drawer or a closet. Or a trunk.

My eye lands on the wooden chest in the far southwest corner of the room.

I remember the day Brice finished making that thing. "You have one for blankets; now I have one for storage," he said proudly, running his hand along its smooth surface. In our other house, he set it by the front door, a few paces away from his built-in desk under the stairs. Here, it serves as both a trunk and a place to sit, complete with a couple of throw pillows.

Am I doing this? Am I really doing this?

I take one, then two steps. I stand in front of the chest and move the pillows to the floor. I open the lid. I smell the cedar. I focus on the organized stacks of notebooks, each stack containing a different size and style of diary.

Yes, I'm doing this. I need to know.

Before touching anything, I take a mental picture of the trunk's contents. Everything has to go back exactly as I found it. Confident I can recreate what I'm seeing, I lift a small, soft leather-bound book from the pile tucked into the corner. It's just like the one I read without his permission in his office at Messiah, when I was pregnant with Max. Just like the one he probably has jammed into his back pocket right now.

Quickly flipping to the first entry in it, I see it only dates back to six months ago. With maximum willpower, I set it aside. It's tempting to read all of it, but I'm not trying to discover things he has no intention of ever telling me, for whatever reason. I vowed I'd never do that again.

And this reconnaissance mission doesn't technically break that old promise. I'm seeking something he would tell me, will tell me someday, but something I'm not patient enough to wait for. It's a tiny loophole, but it's legit. I think. Maybe.

It's soon obvious the pocket-sized journals are stacked in reverse chronological order. Careful to place them face-down in a pile on the floor next to me, so I can quickly put them back, I remove the top six without looking at their contents (less temptation that way) and open one about halfway through the stack. Still not far enough back, but we're getting closer, judging by entry dates.

My heart stutters. But that's anticipation, not an indication of adrenaline fueled by guilt or conscience. Probably.

I dig two more journals deep, close my eyes, and pause before wrapping my fingers around the book.

This is okay.

But is it?

Yes.

Hmmm... I don't think Brice would agree.

Who says he has to know?

What, I'm going to read whatever I find (a synopsis of the conversation or Brice's feelings afterward or... I don't even know what I'm expecting), then give no indication I've read it? That seems to indicate it's wrong to read it.

He'll tell you eventually.

When I'll have to lie and pretend I don't already know.

Maybe he'll tell you stuff he didn't include in the journal entry. Then you won't have to pretend it's news to you.

Oh, gosh... I don't know.

Do you want to know what happened, or not?

Yes.

Then you need to put on your big-girl panties and do this. What's happened to you? Not long ago, you wouldn't have hesitated. You would know by now. The journals would be back in the trunk, and you'd be on with the rest of your day.

Upset. Or worried. Or infuriated. Or hurt.

Or relieved. And informed.

Brice wouldn't hesitate to tell me if it were something I'd find humorous. If it were a feel-good story or conversation, he would have shared it during any one of my family's numerous memory sessions over the past few months. Not only has he kept it to himself, but the memory consistently makes him mopey. That can't be good, no matter what he says.

Therefore, I should respect the journal. Put all this away. Walk away, not knowing. Patiently wait for Brice to deliver on his promise to tell me.

He never really promised to tell you, though. He just

said he didn't want to tell you Saturday night. There was no guarantee of a future telling. Rather, it was more like when you tell the kids "maybe" about something, knowing full well you're never going to deliver. You can't never know. That's why you have to do this. Then Brice won't have to talk about something that makes him uneasy.

Of course, last time I had to know, the consequences of knowing without being allowed to indicate I knew were horrible.

Well, you're not in danger of giving premature birth this time… for once. A little psychological discomfort never killed anyone.

I flap my lips.

"You okay in here?"

For the second time in this room today, I startle toward the ceiling. Journal to my chest, I whirl to face Sharita in the doorway.

She waits for me to answer her question.

My lips tremble into something I hope is close to friendly. And innocent. "Uh, I —" I straighten my arm, dangling the journal at my side. Dropping it into the trunk, like a guilty kid, I say, "I was looking for something, but I don't think I'm going to find it here."

Her raised eyebrows indicate my explanation is not only unnecessary but doesn't answer her question. "Okay…"

"I mean, yes. I'm fine. Sorry. Are you finished already?"

"Just with the first bathroom. I thought I'd come in here and let you know I hear two little voices in that room over there." She points to the wall Brice's office shares with the twins' room.

Now that I'm not arguing with myself, I clearly hear them, too.

She returns to the hallway and retrieves her cleaning

caddy from the floor. "Wasn't sure how much trouble those two get into when they're left to their own devices for too long. I know my boys were always up to something."

"Are your sons twins?" I ask, trying to gain some normal footing in the conversation while I return Brice's journals to their storage place.

She shakes her head. "No. Might as well be, though. Whadda they call 'em, when they're less than a year apart? Irish twins?" Her eyes widen. "No offense. Is that offensive?"

Amused she would guess my ancestry or think I'd be offended by stereotypes about long-dead forbearers I've never met, I wrinkle my nose. "No. Not to me, anyway."

"Phew. I know people are sensitive about stuff. I tend to open my big mouth and say things before thinking."

I close the chest, return the pillows to the approximate position they held before my snooping session, and step into the hall, stopping outside the twins' door.

Sharita walks toward the master suite, tossing over her shoulder, "I'll be in here. Then you tell me what else you need. This has been too easy. You're gonna have to do better than this."

"I'll be thinking about something truly awful for you to do next, if that helps."

She chortles. "That's a good girl."

I haven't decided yet if I'm annoyed or touched by Brice's back door way of relieving me of more of my household duties. I'm leaning toward annoyed, but I need more time to think about it before letting him know the extent of my vexation. Dinner, bath time, and Triple-P have provided the perfect distractions.

Max has unwittingly tried to buy me even more time by demanding we search for his favorite pony figurine before he'll submit to sleep. I found it almost immediately in the couch cushions, but I've been pretending for the last few minutes that I'm still searching. Unfortunately, he's starting to panic that we'll never find it, so I trot up the stairs with the rainbow-maned toy in my grasp, then drop it in the basket of my son's folded legs in his bed.

Jaw set, Brice flicks off the light. "There. Now, go to sleep."

Max falls backward onto his pillow, curls into a ball, and closes his eyes, his fist wrapped tightly around his blue pony friend.

Outside our firstborn's bedroom door, Brice says, "We shouldn't encourage that kind of dictatorial behavior."

I walk away from him—and his ironic statement—without commenting. I'm definitely not in the mood to talk parenting strategy, which usually entails him telling me everything we do wrong and how I'm going to remedy that all by myself during the day, when I'm in charge of the kids. That way, they'll magically be cured of whatever bad habit or behavior by the weekend, when it's his turn to take part more fully in said parenting.

He follows me, his feet heavy on the stairs behind me.

On my way past the island, I swipe the dirty pots from the stove. I squirt liquid soap into both of them and turn on the water, using the sprayer to work up a faster lather.

"You're mad that I forgot to tell you Sharita was coming today," he says to my back.

When he walked through the door at 5:29, dressed in half jogging gear, half winter wear, his bare legs poking ridiculously from the bottom of his wool coat, he did a double-take at the person sitting at the kitchen counter and keeping me company while I cooked dinner.

I saw the fleeting "Oh, shih tzu," in his eyes before he quickly regrouped, his face brightening as he greeted our visitor with a warm hug.

Before anyone could scold him for forgetting to pass along the details regarding today's plans, he asked if Sharita was staying for dinner. She repeated her answer to my earlier offer ("Thanks, but I have something waiting in the crock pot at home"), so he insisted on giving her a ride home, and the two of them fled like accomplices from a robbery.

As he closed the door behind them, I heard her say, "I think you're in trouble, Mister."

He knew better than to let me hear his murmured reply.

Now, he launches into his defense. "I honestly just forgot. She mentioned wanting to repay me for helping her out, but we started talking about other stuff, and it totally slipped my mind by the time I got home."

"You were over there a long time," I suddenly recall. I turn off the water and let the pots soak while I rinse the plates, cups, and cutlery in the other half of the sink, quickly slotting each item into its tidy place in the dishwasher.

"Nothing inappropriate is going on, if that's what you're implying."

My mouth dropping open, I look up from my task and stare at him. "What?! No, that's not what I'm implying!"

"Good."

"But your asinine preemptive denial does make me think you're guilty of something. Like, possibly complaining about me to her? Perhaps something to do with my Irish temper?

Or, more likely, telling her I can't handle my responsibilities around here?"

There. I said it. I wish I hadn't, though. Because now my stomach hurts. I drop the last fork into the utensil caddy and shut the dishwasher with a satisfying clang and click.

It doesn't help that Brice fails to immediately contradict my guesses. Instead, he shifts from foot-to-foot. "I put up her lights."

"You must think I'm a moron." I edge past him with the tub of cleaning wipes, ready to tackle the sauce-spattered table, which I scrub with a vengeance.

At first, he merely gapes at me. Then he follows me and rips a wipe from the tub a little more firmly than necessary. He steps away to swab the island. "Okay, when I was finished hanging her lights, she invited me in to warm up." He blushes. "I mean, she made me some tea."

"Then?"

"Then, what?"

"What did you guys talk about?"

"None of your business!"

I raise my eyebrows at him. "You're proving my case quite nicely."

"She told me some things in confidence, okay?"

"You're not her pastor!"

He stills for a few seconds, then mumbles, "I'm well aware I'm not anyone's pastor anymore."

I intend to merely glance at him over my shoulder, but the set of his shoulders and the pathetic expression on his face make me study him longer. He works the wipe back and forth an inch with his index finger, staring at the wet spot it leaves on the counter. When I say nothing, he glances up and smiles shakily.

"You better not be trying to get out of trouble by making me feel sorry for you."

His eyebrows nearly touch. "What? No!"

"Because that's not allowed. And anyway, since when are you upset that you're not a congregational pastor? You like your new job! Right?"

He rushes to nod. "Yes! I do. I like it a lot. At the same time, there are things I miss about serving a church." He walks to the trash can, steps on the pedal to open the receptacle, and drops the dirty wipe. After releasing the lid, he leans against the wall, crossing his arms over his chest. "But even though I'm not officially anyone's pastor, I still don't feel comfortable repeating what someone tells me in a conversation about personal matters. It would feel like gossiping."

"Mm-hm."

"I'm telling the truth! I didn't say a word against you to her. Does that sound like something I'd do?"

"Well…" I can't help remembering a time I overheard him venting to my dad about me.

"She served me hot tea and talked to me about some stuff on her mind. That's it."

I rinse the stock pot and saucepan, setting both of them in a drainer on the counter next to the sink. "You're infuriating, you know? You always say I am, but you're worse than I am. You have more altruistic motives for it, so that makes it seem better. But it's not. It's still infuriating. Just in a different way."

"I know."

"And another thing…" (His agreeing with me isn't going to stop me from giving him a complete piece of my mind.) "When Sharita got here today, it was awkward as hell. I had no idea I was supposed to be expecting her; then I was put on the spot to choose what part of our nastiness to show her."

"I'm sure she's seen worse."

"So? Gosh, that is such a male thing to say!"

"You want me to apologize for being a guy?"

"I want you to get your head out of your ass. You claim you want to help me? Well, neglecting to inform me I'm going to have an impromptu housekeeper for the day isn't helpful. What if I hadn't been home?"

"That's why I told her to come during naps."

"What if I'd had my heart set on my own nap today? What if I didn't feel like showing a neighbor our mildew and soap scum?"

"All you had to do was say no or tell her to come back another time."

"Have you just met Sharita?"

He laughs. "All right, all right! I get it!" Like a Benedictine monk, he presses his hands together in prayer and chants, "I'm a nuuuumbskull. Ah-ah-ah-amen," punctuating his silly song by crossing himself.

Keeping a straight face in the presence of his antics is impossible, so I crack up but roll my eyes. "Admitting you have a problem is the first step, I suppose."

He stops clowning around. "But am I forgiven?"

"By Someone a whole lot more important than me, lucky you."

"I want to know if you forgive me."

I groan at the ceiling. "I guess." Leveling narrowed eyes at him, I say, "You don't seem to be able to do anything to make me stay mad at you."

It's not for his lack of trying, though.

18

SISTERLY DISAPPROVAL

So much for that relaxing, idyllic holiday season I've been fantasizing about since August.

Christmas is only five days away. Jen and Vince's wedding, which, as I predicted, is not going to be a "super-low-key affair," is in nine days. That means Jen and Vince will be here in six days, followed closely by our friends and most of my family. And the edge of my sanity should be arriving in… ohhhh, any minute now.

This week, through the magic of technology, I've been carrying Jen around St. Louis, bringing her face-to-face with people and places hundreds of miles away from her, through my phone. She talked to the people at the reception hall yesterday and saw with her own eyes the space where she and Vince will have their first dance as husband and wife.

Today, when her dress made it to my house, shipped from the seamstress in Florida after Jen's final fitting, I showed it to her. Then she helped me select a hiding spot for the dress, somewhere climate-controlled but away from ten little hands that would seek to do it irreparable harm. There is no such place in this house, unfortunately, so she had to be satisfied with me squirreling it away in my closet. I may have lied and said there was a lock on the door so she'd be able to sleep for the next nine days. Thankfully, she didn't ask to see the lock.

It's not that Jen's being a bridezilla; in fact, she's gone out of her way to plan this wedding long-distance, all for my family's benefit, which is why I'm trying to make it as easy for her as possible. I remember those last few days before the Big Day. They're both nerve-wracking and exhilarating. One minute, it can feel like time has crawled to a near-stop; the next, you despair you have too much to possibly accomplish before your deadline. It feels like a week-long manic-depressive episode. Jen's holding up well, and she tells me about ten times a day how much she appreciates my hard work.

It's great that someone appreciates it, because my sister? Not so much. And she's not shy about letting me know in the first conversation I've had with her in weeks. The long-suffering sigh on the other end of the line tells me more than she could say in an entire soliloquy. And that's good, because I don't want to listen to a verbose rant right now.

I'm sure she's going to provide one, anyway, in three... two...

"So, let me get this straight. You flaked on hosting Thanksgiving. Now you're telling me you're too busy with Jen's wedding preps to spend any time with us at Christmas?"

When she puts it that way...

I flop back on the sofa, resting my head on the arm and closing my eyes. "I can't be in two places at once."

"That's a yes?"

"It's one year."

"But this is the first year since Dad— I mean, it's going to be hard. I thought we'd get through it together."

I swallow with difficulty. "Maybe it's best that it's as different as it can be. If we're not all there, maybe it'll seem like he's simply one of the absent ones. Just this once."

"But that's not how it is."

"I'm just trying to make the best of the reality."

The pout heavy in her voice, Nicole continues, "Plus, Brice has time off—at Christmas! That's unheard of."

"Yeah, I know. But this is just the first of many years. Hopefully. Maybe."

That's what I've been telling myself, anyway, to soothe my own disappointment. I'm not at all sure of that, though, after our conversation earlier this week. If he misses being that trustworthy shepherd of the flock already, what's going to happen in a few months' time? Will he be putting himself on the call list again?

I can't worry about that right now.

"Real convincing. And that's not the point. The point is, it's your first year not shackled to the church calendar."

"Nice."

"And we can't even take advantage of it."

"You're coming to Jen's wedding, right?"

"No! Sadie has a science competition that day, and the boys are both participating in a district basketball tournament that week and weekend."

"Well, shoot! How is this the first time I'm hearing this?"

"Maybe if you and Mom talked more often," she mutters under her breath.

"Because you couldn't tell me?"

"Mom's the one who loves to brag about all that stuff. I'm too busy making it happen and managing my kids' schedules to be the town crier."

I understand that. I also rely on Mom to pass along the rare noteworthy information from our family, and I don't even have school-aged children yet. Still, I don't want to take responsibility for being in the dark, so I mumble a lame, "Whatever."

"What's going on with you and Mom, anyway? She won't tell me. She keeps saying, 'I guess I really ticked her off for good this time.'"

Must. Not. Explode.

When not exploding means not speaking at all, Nicole prods, "Hello? You still there?"

"Mom knows exactly what she said and why I'm upset. Don't let her innocent act fool you."

"I don't think she's claiming ignorance about the cause of your anger. She's clueless about how long it's going to take for you to forgive her."

"I've forgiven her."

"Maybe you should send her the memo."

"Maybe you should stay out of it."

"Okay, then."

I take a deep breath and open my eyes, focusing on a section of the ceiling above me. Oh, crap. Is that water damage? I shake my head to refocus on the conversation with Nicole. "Sorry. But you know how she is."

"Yeah? I don't have a problem with her."

"Because you two are exactly the same."

"That usually makes people not like each other."

"Only if there are things about yourself you don't like. And you and Mom love everything about yourselves. And each other."

"I think there's an insult in there somewhere, but I prefer to see that as a good thing."

"It's not a bad thing; I'm just explaining the phenomenon."

"Tell me, what did she say that was so terrible?"

I snort. "Uh, no. Not happening. I'm not dragging you into the middle of this. Like I said, I've forgiven her."

"Yeah, it sounds like it."

"I have! But things were still raw at Thanksgiving, and now I'm too busy with Jen and Vince's once-in-a-lifetime day to host a huge Christmas get-together here or drag my entire family to Chicago. There will be other Christmases."

"Your loss, I guess. You're going to miss out on Mom's pecan pie."

"Tragic, for sure."

"It's the highlight of my year, but maybe that says more about my life than Mom's pie."

"Maybe. Hey, tell me more about Sadie's science project."

Yeah, that's a safe, interesting topic.

19

THE DATE

*C*oncordia's two-week Christmas recess has finally delivered the difference I've been craving in this year's holiday experience. It's been a huge blessing to have Brice home to keep the kids occupied while I wrap presents and perform all those last-minute pre-Christmas and matron of honor jobs.

It's also been helpful to have another adult around to enforce the rules about the kids keeping their toys in their rooms and to share the number of trips up and down the stairs, returning said junk—er, stuff—to its rightful place.

Then yesterday, the day after Christmas, Jen and Vince arrived. It's been harder to enforce the tidiness rules with our grown guests. After all, we don't want to be inhospitable jerks. So we're tolerating the clutter the best we can.

Vince is sleeping on the sofa, because he's still young enough that I don't feel obligated to give him our bed. (Something tells me he's not flattered by that.) Jen's taken up residence in Brice's office. In addition to her unbelievable amount of luggage—"I had to pack for our honeymoon, too, you know!"—she's storing what seems like a wedding supply warehouse's entire contents of centerpieces, party favors, and other miscellaneous decor.

She and Vince were going to keep everything in the van they rented to haul it up here, but Brice tactfully advised against that. "It's not that anyone would want to steal your wedding stuff, but they will want to break into your van to see what's in those bins and decide, 'Nope. I don't want that.'"

Jen widened her eyes and wrinkled her nose at me. When I reluctantly agreed with my husband, the four of us lugged it all inside. Our plan, at first, was to keep the storage containers downstairs, in the kitchen, so we could quickly load them again on Saturday morning, to take to the church and reception hall. But there wasn't enough room there, so we hauled everything upstairs to Brice's office.

That left no room for Vince's luggage, so he has his slightly fewer bags stowed under the stairs. Things keep creeping out into the living room, though. Not sure if that's the kids' doing or Vince's. Or Jen's. She keeps thinking they've forgotten things, so she ransacks their bags until she finds whatever it is and eases her mind.

Then there are the bathrooms. Vince is using the one downstairs. He has a razor, a toothbrush and toothpaste, a comb, and some shower supplies. Perfectly neat and tidy. In contrast, Jen's occupying the kids' bathroom at the top of the stairs. It's like a beauty supply store blew up in there. Now that she has about five-hundred percent less hair than she used to have, I think she uses five-hundred percent more product in it, if that's possible. And she's always been a big supporter of the cosmetic industry, but I'd forgotten how deeply committed her patronage is. She must have brought two dozen shades of lipstick with her. This morning, I caught Aidan eating a tube of "Killer Red."

And there's the rub: we tell the kids to play upstairs to keep the main floor as neat and clean as possible; but what's normally a mostly childproof zone has now been taken over by someone not accustomed to securing her lotions and potions and products made possible by chemistry. I fear someone may not survive the week.

However, that fear isn't going to stop me from accepting our friends' offer to babysit the kids tonight so Brice and I can go on a rare date. When Jen first proposed the idea, I gave her a "We'll see," hoping she'd drop it and would be satisfied with merely extending the offer. But after only two days of this insanity, I need to get out of here. And the kids will be in bed most of the time. Hopefully. If they don't run roughshod all over Aunt Jen and Uncle Vince. But I'm not going to worry about that. Because Jen wants to thank us for everything we've done to help with the wedding. And this is how she wants to thank us, by buying us dinner and watching our kids. Who am I to rob her of that?

I'll even do a convincing job of enjoying myself. For starters, I'm wearing a dress I've never worn before. A brand new dress. Like someone who feels pretty. I also dug out those shoes I've only worn once or twice (because they hurt like a mo-fo), so they still look brand new. And they make me feel about ten feet tall. I'm also wearing makeup. Maybe not as much as some people would wear. But more than I normally do. Enough to cover the darkish circles under my eyes. And I not only washed and brushed my hair, but I styled it, too. I also shaved my legs. (Goes without saying, right? Ha!)

So I'm all gussied up. Because I've been told we're going somewhere nice, somewhere that required a reservation, somewhere we can be reasonably assured will be kid-free. And for some reason, I'm nervous. Like this is our first date, ever, instead of just the first one in longer than I care to try to pinpoint.

Brice seems unsettled, too, now that we're alone on the way to the restaurant. He taps his fingers on the steering wheel at red lights and sneaks peeks at me.

After his fourth or fifth furtive glance at me, he smiles sheepishly. "Sorry. It's just, you— Well, you look great. I mean, you're always beautiful, but tonight, you look really, really great."

My face warms, but I don't give in to the knee-jerk reaction to say something snarky or self-deprecating. Instead, I simply reply, "Thanks! You look pretty hot, yourself."

He wiggles his eyebrows at me. "Why, thank you. I clean up okay."

"Yes, you do."

Cue: conversation officially drying up.

I take advantage of the mostly companionable silence to consider just how well he cleans up in his navy blue suit, blue-and-white striped dress shirt, and maroon tie. He has a fresh haircut, and I can tell by the absolute absence of shadow along his jaw that he shaved in the shower this evening. I barely resist the urge to reach over and feel how smooth his cheek is. Instead, I content myself with breathing in his clean, familiar scent, enhanced by a conservative spritz from the brand new bottle of his (okay, my) favorite cologne, which Santa dropped in his Christmas stocking a couple of nights ago.

He interrupts my silent appreciation to ask for better directions to our destination, so I pull my phone from my purse and use the mapping app to deliver us the rest of the way.

Once inside the dim, cozy restaurant and seated in an intimate booth, we peruse our menus. "It smells so good in here!" I say after I've decided I'll be asking the server for a recommendation, considering I know nothing about French cuisine.

"Yeah, it does." He studies the leather folder in his hands, looking overwhelmed. "Uh, am I having beef or fish?"

"That's your call. I'm going to make the server tell me what she likes."

He wrinkles his nose. "What if she says"—he consults the menu, and I bite my lip when he has to push it farther from his face to read it—"'J'adore the bacon, horseradish, tomato, and bleu cheese mussels'?"

"Then I'll get the trout."

"Oh, so you're going with fish? Now, I feel like I should eat beef, so we're not one of those sickening couples who orders the same thing."

I nudge the laces of his cordovan shoes with the pointed toe of my sling backs under the table. "I'm going with whatever the server recommends. Unless it's the mussels."

"So you don't want an escargot appetizer?"

"No."

"Do you think they'd scoff at me if I got a burger?"

"I doubt the burger here is your typical quarter-pounder."

He points it out to me on the menu. "It's not. And it sounds amazing. But I'd feel like a hick if I ordered that. Kind of like ordering a salad of wild greens and asking for ranch dressing."

"Yeah, but if that's what you want…"

"I'm just not used to eating like a grownup. This is the first place we've been in months that doesn't have a ball pit."

"But wouldn't that be awesome?"

He pinches his mouth to the side. "Sort of. I'd jump in."

"Me, too."

The server arrives, foiling our plot to bring down the mental age of the establishment's clientele. She recommends the chicken pasta for me. Since that's acceptably safe-sounding, I accept her advice.

Brice hems and haws some more. "Geez, I really want that burger, but no!" He closes his menu and hands it to her. "Trout. No, sea bass!"

She smiles at him and promises to be back soon with our salads and wine.

He surveys our surroundings. "Despite not having a ball pit, this place is pretty nice."

"Yes. Definitely not our usual venue."

His eyes light up. "Can you imagine the kids here?"

"No. Max would go table-to-table, making sure everyone prayed before they ate; Brooks and Harris—" I unroll my silverware and drape the linen napkin in my lap. "Never mind."

Brice tilts his head. "What? What's wrong?"

"Nothing." Placing the utensils precisely next to where my plate will eventually go, I explain, "I don't want to talk about the kids tonight."

"Oh." He grasps my hand across the table before I can return it to my lap. "Okay. I can live with that."

I meet his eyes. "I don't want to talk about a lot of things." Curling my fingers into his for firmer support, I lean sideways and, with my free hand, dig my phone from my purse on the floor next to my feet. Straightening in my chair, I smirk across the table at him. "I made a list."

He purses his lips. "Of course you did."

"I wanted to make sure we treated this like a real date. I didn't want to waste this opportunity discussing the price of diapers or Addi's transition to solid foods."

"How's that going, anyway?"

"She has a texture issue, I think. If it's not perfectly smooth— No! Oh, my gosh! It's like I can't stop myself."

He pats my hand. "It's okay, you know? There's no 'off' switch for moms and dads."

"Maybe not, but tonight we're pushing 'pause.' No talking about the kids."

"Fine." He flicks his chin toward the device in my hand. "What else is off limits?"

I pull up the list on the notes app. "Um, let's see. No talking about either of our moms, for obvious reasons."

"A-okay."

"We already covered the kids."

"Quite extensively."

"No talking about your work, unless it's positive and interesting."

"Okay…"

"I just don't want to spend the evening worrying you're not happy."

"Ah. I see. I don't have anything negative to say, anyway, so continue."

I clear my throat. "I'd also prefer if we didn't talk about Jen and Vince's wedding. I want to pretend for a couple of hours that it's over."

He chuckles. "Amen to that."

My shoulders slump. "Okay, good. I mean, they're our two best friends, and I feel guilty even thinking anything bad about them, because we're here tonight thanks to them, and they've gone to a lot of trouble to get married here in St. Louis, so we could all be a part of it, but at the risk of talking about it, they're stressing me out." I suck in a huge breath after that guilt-laden speech. "And they're not doing anything wrong; they're just… there. In my space, moving my cheese, destroying my routines."

"They'll be off to Paris in two days."

Leaving a ton of their junk behind for us to store while they're gone, I think. But I won't say it, because we've already talked more about it than the list allows.

I refer back to my phone. "Okay, so moving on."

"There's more?"

"Just a couple more taboo topics. Like, my health. And the neighborhood watch. And house repairs or renovations."

He scratches the side of his nose. "Hmm… I hope you have a list of things we *can* talk about, too, because I'm going to be at a loss after this."

I glance up from my notes long enough to narrow my eyes at him. "Yes. We can talk about good memories and our future."

He waits, but when that's it from me, he bites his bottom lip, then says, "Uh, okay. Even those are going to be difficult if we're not allowed to talk about the kids."

Our salads arrive, so I stash the phone. Spearing some greens that look fresh from a spring meadow, I say, "Not really. I can think of a few things."

After chewing and swallowing his first bite, he points to me with his fork. "You lead, then."

To avoid talking with my mouth full, I merely lift my chin in a gesture of agreement. That's exactly what I was hoping, anyway. I knew he'd have a hard time talking about anything not having to do with the kids, his job, the house, the neighborhood watch, the wedding, or our mothers' recent tiffs with us. Everything's going according to plan. He's a pretty fast thinker, though, so I can't give him a lot of time to ponder his own possibilities.

Following a few bites of salad, I push the plate aside and fold my hands in my lap. "Like, how did you know—*know*— I was 'the one'?"

"Who's saying I know?" he counters with a smarmy grin.

"Don't make me kick you. These shoes are really pointy."

I swear he takes another bite to prolong the suspense of his answer. Then he wipes his lips and sips his wine. "Hm. I believe I've already told you this more than once."

"Tell me again."

"I feel like you keep asking me to try to catch me in a lie."

"What?" I laugh. "That's not true at all! Anyway, I can always tell when you're lying."

"True. It's just, the answer changes in my head. I'll think I know, but the more I remember, the more hindsight allows me to see more clearly that it was earlier than I originally thought."

"Cryptic."

He smooths his napkin in his lap. "Okay, you want specifics?"

"Yep."

"Like, at first, I would have told you I knew I loved you when I picked you up from that hotel and was sure I could have killed the person who'd upset you that much."

I smile at the memory of me, tear-streaked and rumpled, waiting for him in the lobby of the hotel where Drex and Stefan were staying. He had seemed homicidal when he came through that revolving door, with his sleep-mussed hair and untied running shoes.

"But then I go further back in my memory, and I knew

before then. I knew when we went to breakfast together, and you nearly threw up on the table between us."

I sputter, drawing the attention of some of the reserved diners around us. Covering my mouth, I muffle, "No way."

"Yes way. Because I knew if it came down to it, I would have carried you from that restaurant and let you puke on me."

"Gross."

"But that's true love."

"No, it's not. That's chivalry. Or insanity."

He considers it for a second. "Okay, but anyway, that's not when I knew, either."

"Please, don't give me a love-at-first sight line. I can't handle that."

Raising his hands in front of himself, palms out, he says, "Fine. I won't," then silently returns to his salad.

"Seriously."

His right shoulder rises toward his ear. "Maybe not first sight, but close. Before we ever had enough interaction for it to be logical to feel so deeply for someone." He glances up from his plate.

I blush.

He blushes.

"Wow. So, like, I was just sitting out there, minding my business in church, and you were up there, pining after me?"

His eyes roll. "No. Not exactly."

"Oh, darn."

"I'm being serious here. Like, embarrassingly honest. At the risk of sounding creepy." He rests his fork on the edge of his plate but fingers the end of its handle.

Sobering, I say, "Aw, hon. I know. I'm just giving you a hard time, because that's what I do. It's not creepy. I think it's sweet, really."

"'Sweet': how every man yearns to be described," he drawls, dragging his thumb along his lower lip.

"You have told me before that you talked to your parents about me before I ever came to talk to you in your office about… stuff."

"I did."

"And neither of them told you you were crazy, and your mom's a sane, reasonable person—I'm assuming your dad was, too—so that lends some credibility to your feelings."

"Thanks."

"You're too cute."

"'Cute' ranks up there with 'sweet.'" He takes a fortifying swallow of his water. "All right, Ms. Worldly, 'fess up. When did *you* know? Or should I say, when did you resign yourself to it? Because I know you didn't submit willingly." At my outraged expression, he winks.

"I'll have you know, I have a cornier answer than yours, even." Taking a page from his book, I slowly sip my wine while he anticipates a fuller answer.

Suddenly, he sits forward, throwing his hands up between us. "Wait! Let me guess."

I bat my lashes at him, playing along while knowing he'll never get it.

"Our first kiss."

My snort serves as an answer.

"Okay, no. Um… Before or after that?"

I merely shrug, so he sits back and looks around the dining area, as if the answer's hidden somewhere in this room. "At the lock-in, when you witnessed my awesome Bible Charades skillz."

"If you're going to be silly, forget it. We'll be here all night."

"That was a serious guess, but whatever."

I wave away his dorkiness. "Remember Valentine's Day, when I was stuck at that art convention in Las Vegas?"

"Yep."

"And we talked on Skype, and you told me how you knew what you felt for me was love?"

He scratches his eyebrow. "Vaguely. I was distracted by an emotion masquerading as love at the time."

My jaw slackens.

Tugging on his earlobe, he shifts in his seat. "You were wearing— Well, anyway. You know, you can experience lust and love at the same time, obviously. The balance was just a little skewed that night."

"And what you said that night sounded so heartfelt and pure."

"It was heartfelt."

"Wow. The things we learn."

"But we're talking about you here, remember?"

Our food arrives, and the server takes her time making sure everything has been prepared to our liking before refilling our wine glasses and removing our salad plates.

As soon as she leaves, Brice returns his laser-like focuses to me. "Continue."

"Wait. We should eat before our food gets cold. This is an opportunity we don't often get."

He shakes his head. "Finish your story quickly then."

"Fine." I run my finger along the rim of my wineglass. "Anyway. You told me what love meant to you, and I realized I could say everything back to you—if I'd been able to talk at the time—so that's when it finally clicked."

He looks unimpressed. "A) You've already told me this before; B) How's that corny?"

Maintaining eye contact, I say, "That's not the corny part. The corny part is, once it clicked, I had this weird, like, soul-filling feeling that I'd always loved you. Like…" I avert my eyes, mumbling at the tablecloth, "beforeIevermetyou."

He taps my ankle with the toe of his shoe, but I don't trust myself to move my intense stare from the runaway crouton I've located on the expanse of white.

Finally, he says, "That's not corny. That's kind of… beautiful."

I grab my fork and stab at the butterfly pasta in the shallow bowl in front of me. "Anyway. It was probably more like I'd been waiting my whole life for someone to come along who treated me with love and respect. That's all."

"You don't have to apologize for it."

"I'm not. I'm just explaining it."

Fortunately, he redirects his scrutiny to his food, so I feel less conspicuous, even brave enough to peek up at him with a quiet smile. "You're not the only one in this relationship who knows how to have deep feelings, you know."

"Never claimed I was."

"I just don't feel as comfortable expressing myself."

"I know."

"But you do. That's why it's odd—and a bit alarming—that you're so hesitant to talk to me about the conversation you had with my dad before we were married."

There. I did it. It was rough, and I had to do some squirm-worthy soul-baring to get here, but the way Brice pauses in his chewing, his tongue peeking out to collect the tiny dab of wine sauce in the corner of his mouth, tells me I've played it perfectly.

Not that I really played anything. I meant everything I said, and it was hard to say it, because it's something I've often thought with the realization it sounds fruity and senti-mental. But I am counting on the payout for such a confes-sion to be huge.

Not taking his eyes from mine for a second, he finishes chewing, then swallows. "I'm not sure now is a good time."

"No time like the present."

He rolls his head on his neck. "This isn't relaxing date-night conversation, though. How come this wasn't on the list of taboo topics?"

"Because I make the lists."

He sighs, then resumes eating.

Instead of scaring him off by being too insistent, I follow his lead and return my attention to my food while I wait to hear the story. The pasta dish may as well consist of sawdust and real butterfly wings, as unappetizing as it is to me right now, but I feign nonchalance.

After a few more bites, he sets his fork, tines-down, on his plate and dabs his lips. Then he carefully places his napkin on top of his nearly empty plate. "I knew your dad didn't trust me, didn't like me, didn't... whatever." He pauses, takes a deep breath, and continues, "Especially when it came to you."

"That was my fault, though. If I'd just come clean with him about Stefan... Because I think he always wondered if you and I, you know, were sneaking around, or something."

He shakes his head. "No. He believed us. He just didn't want us to know that."

"Twisted jerk."

"Peyton."

"Sorry."

"Anyway, a couple of days after I told your parents how I felt about you, your dad called me and said he wanted us to talk, man-to-man."

I wince. "Yikes."

"Meh. I wasn't too worried about that. I figured it couldn't be any worse than when he brought you and me before the elders in the church library that one time." He bounces in his seat as he jiggles his leg under the table. "I knew my biggest challenge would be keeping my cool, or I could kiss goodbye any chance of having a decent relationship with him. And that was important to me. I didn't want to be at odds with your dad, a person I expected—or hoped —to be in my life for a long time."

"How gracious of him to take care of that," I quip, earning myself an incredulous stare. "What? Too soon? He was my dad."

He pinches the stem of his water goblet. "Yeah, well, I didn't know what the future would hold. I knew I wanted to marry you, and if you said yes—not something I was taking for granted, by the way—I wanted him to be a positive fixture, not someone whose goal in life was to make my life miserable. So. I accepted his invitation. But I didn't tell you about it, because… Well, you were still mad at me about telling your parents about us and saying what I said to them."

I think back, struggling to put everything in context. I was livid that he'd talked about me behind my back to them, lecturing them about how unfairly they were treating me, interfering in something I felt was none of his business. Then he (reluctantly) told me how my parents—namely, my mom—reacted when he revealed our relationship to them, saying he and I weren't equally yoked, that he was a phase I was going through, and I blew up. Because I wasn't sure she was wrong. I wanted her to be wrong, but based on my history up to that point, she was more likely to be right.

And when I made the mistake of being too honest about that, when I despaired that now that our relationship was out in the open, people would be echoing my mother's concerns, when I admitted I didn't know how to judge the depth of my feelings for him without factoring sex into the equation, he stormed out.

We were both hurt and on edge. And silent for the rest of the week. With each other. Seems Brice was talking to *someone* in my family.

The next time he talked to me was when he came over to apologize. And the day after that, we went off-roading. In more ways than one, almost.

At that flash of memory, I check, "Let me get this straight, then. Before we, uh, almost had sex in the back of your Jeep—"

"Shhh…eeesh!" he hisses, looking around us, his ears reddening.

"Nobody's listening or cares."

He gulps his wine.

"Anyway, a couple of days before that, you talked to my dad about me?"

He sucks his lips against his teeth, then replies, "Yes."

"Wow. Now I really need to know what you guys talked about."

"The two things had nothing to do with each other. I got, uh, carried away in the woods. I definitely wasn't thinking about your dad. Or anything else. Trust me."

I giggle at his sheepish expression. "I see. Well, for days afterward, all I could think about was your underwear."

He laughs uncertainly. "Wha—"

"It was just so cute."

"There's that word again."

"No, really. Like, I'd never seen a pastor's underwear before, obviously, but I had a pretty narrow-minded idea of what kind of underwear a pastor should wear."

"I'm a little disturbed by how much thought you put into clerical undergarments."

"Just yours."

"And mine exceeded your expectations?"

"Very much so. Now, where were we? Ah, yes. Dad invited you over to talk, and you accepted, which means you hadn't learned your lesson as well as I'd thought after the first experience."

"Glutton for punishment." He rubs his knuckles against his jaw. "Yeah, so I showed up right on time, and we sat down in the living room—"

"Where was Mom?"

"Don't know. Not home? I didn't ask. She may have been avoiding me, considering my reaction to what she'd said to me a few days earlier. Anyway, your dad was like…" He lowers his chin, scowls, and deepens his voice. "'I'll get right to the point, Pastor. Save you some sweat.'"

While I crack up at how accurate his impersonation of my Dad is, Brice's phone rings. A few months ago, that sound would hardly be unusual. Nowadays, it's rare for his phone to ring for anything other than personal business when we're together. And lately, personal business is usually unpleasant or stressful business, so my heart sinks. Then it rises into my throat when I remember our children are in someone else's hands for the evening.

Before I can speculate too much, Brice glances at the screen and says, "Hmm… Officer Milner."

That doesn't put my mind at ease. At all. Nor does the sadness on Brice's face as soon as the initial niceties have been observed. But I figure he'd be more horrified or panicked if the call was about our household, so I wait patiently through, "What happened?. . . Oh, man. That's awful…. Of course…. No, no, that's fine…. Okay, we'll be right there."

He hangs up and signals for the check in one motion,

almost flinging his phone across the room. Barely keeping it in his grasp, he juggles it for a few seconds, then shoves it in his pocket.

"What the heck is going on?" I ask.

Our server arrives before he can reply, so he tells her we have to leave quickly. As soon as she bustles away to print our check, he says to me, "Sharita needs us."

20

SHARITA'S TRAGEDY

*T*he twinkling Christmas lights along the roofline of the modest house seem to mock us as we park at the curb behind the police car. Officer Milner meets us at the front door and pulls us aside in the entryway. From a room I can't yet see comes keening.

Oh, gosh. I don't think I can do this. What the hell am I doing here?

Before I can get too far into panic-mode, Milner murmurs, "I volunteered my partner and me to take the call about notifying next-of-kin when I recognized the name and address."

"What happened?" Brice asks, pinching the bridge of his nose and studying his shoes.

"Nelson was home for winter break, but fortunately for Sharita, he went back to his dorm room on campus to do the deed. But he got the pills here. The bottles had Sharita's name on them."

"Oh, no."

"Some heavy-duty painkillers she never used up after a surgery a couple years ago. Tramadol and Vicodin."

He winces. "Did he leave a note?"

"Yeah. Standard stuff. Depression, hopelessness. A few lines about losing a scholarship and worrying about being a financial burden to his mom."

None of this seems like news to Brice, who merely shakes his head and clicks his tongue.

Milner glances over her shoulder, toward the crying, which increases in volume. "She's understandably distraught. But she asked for you personally. Her oldest son, Warwick, is here with her, too."

"Good." Brice pats the officer's shoulder. "Thanks for doing this."

Milner stares at the place where the wall meets the floor. "It's the worst part of the job, but it wouldn't have been right for her to get the news from a stranger." She looks up. "After the coroner gives us an official cause of death, his body will be released to the funeral home."

"I'll help her take care of all those details," Brice reassures her.

She nods. "In that case, there's nothing more for me to do. But keep me posted?"

Brice promises to do just that. Milner smiles sadly on her way past me, then leads us farther into the house.

When we cross the threshold of the living room, Sharita looks up from the shredded tissue in her hands and springs from the velour-and-wood couch. "Oh, you guys!" she says on a sob, pulling us to her in a suffocating three-way hug.

I try to return the embrace, but she's pinned my arms to my sides. Brice met her with arms open, so his mobility is unhindered. He squeezes her to him, rubbing her back. She quickly lets go of me to focus her attention on the expert hugger. Free, I stand by, impotent and no less awkward than when I was trapped. I observe as Sharita shakes and quakes against my husband. He says nothing, simply lets her cry into his chest.

After a few seconds of this, I start to feel weird watching the two of them, so I avert my eyes, which land on a young guy sitting helplessly on the sofa. Bent at the waist, elbows on his knees, he stares at the shag carpeting between his immaculate running shoes.

"I told him it didn't matter, we'd figure somethin' out!" Sharita slurs and gasps. "He was always too worried about me. Oh, this is all my fault!"

Her despair threatens to topple her. Brice sends me a glance over her head as he staggers backward against her weight.

I flinch forward to grasp the grieving mother's arm and restore her balance. "Sharita. Honey, let's sit down, huh?"

The man I assume to be Warwick rises to his feet and helps us walk Sharita to the couch. He and Brice remain standing, so I sit next to her and take up the job of back-rubber. Warwick wanders wordlessly from the room.

After Sharita and I are settled, Brice sits in a chair perpendicular to the sofa and leans forward so his knees nearly touch Sharita's. "Can I pray with you?" he asks.

She nods limply, but as soon as he says "Amen," she opens her eyes and studies us more closely. "Look at you two," she says, swiping her sodden tissue under her eyes. "You're all dressed up. Did Officer Milner call you away from something important?"

"No," we answer together.

"You don't hang out around the house like that." She flaps her hands at our attire. "I hope I'm not bothering you."

Brice cuffs her wrist in his hand. "You're not. Don't ever think that." Warwick's return grabs his attention. He stands and extends his hand. "I'm so sorry. Warwick, isn't it?"

The guy answers affirmatively, shaking Brice's hand. "And you're Brice. Mom's talked about you. Thanks for— Well, you know. Everything."

Brice ducks his head. "Glad to be a blessing." Sweeping his arm in my direction, he says, "That's my wife, Peyton."

Warwick and I acknowledge each other. He takes a deep breath and rubs his close-shaven head. "I, uh... I'm not sure what to do. Or think. Or say. Or even feel."

Brice claps him on the shoulder. "Nothing right now. Just be here for your mom."

"I could kill —" He stops himself and barks bitterly. "See? I can't believe this is happening. I'm just mad."

Sharita shakes with another round of tears. "He couldn't help it!" she defends her youngest. "He was such a sensitive boy. Always trying to be perfect."

"Well, this is perfectly fucked up," Warwick spouts.

"Watch your mouth!" his mom snaps, the flash of anger temporarily interrupting her crying. "You save that kind of talk for your friends. I don't wanna hear it in my house, around my friends."

"It's okay," Brice says, hastening to smooth feathers.

"It's not okay! My baby's dead, and he"—she flicks her chin in Warwick's direction—"says such nasty things."

Spying a box of tissues on a nearby table, I reach and grab several fresh ones and press them into Sharita's hands. "C'mon, now. Everyone's upset. He's upset for you. The last thing he wants is to make it worse for you."

She nods. "I know." She looks up at her son and reaches a hand to him. "C'mere, baby. I'm sorry. I'm just... so... sad."

He accepts her invitation and kneels in front of her,

pressing his forehead against her knees. She pats his head. After a few seconds, his shoulders shake with the tears he's suppressed until now.

I search for an exit.

Brice retakes his seat, appearing relatively at ease, considering. I clear my throat, bob my head, and perform all manner of calisthenics to try to capture his attention and communicate with my eyes that I think we should leave, but he appears to be in a pastor trance, his unfocused gaze fixated on his hand atop the armrest.

Finally, I have no choice but to say out loud, "Brice."

He startles and transfers his eyes to my face.

I tilt my head toward a doorway that leads to a kitchen. "Can we—"

He offers to make some tea, to which Sharita mechanically agrees. Once in the kitchen, I fill the kettle from the stove while Brice opens a cupboard.

"I think we should go," I hiss barely loud enough to be heard over the running water.

"Not yet," he answers succinctly.

"But, hon, they need some privacy."

"They don't want privacy. Trust me. When you have privacy, you have to get on with the business of… everything. And they're not ready for that."

I grit my teeth. "I feel weird out there."

"You are weird." He turns around with a tin box of Earl Grey in his hands.

"Har, har. This isn't funny."

"You're doing fine."

"I want to run away."

He pops open the tin. "That's normal. It's not easy to be in the presence of such grief. But you don't abandon people in their time of need, just because it's not easy to witness their pain."

I set the kettle on the stove and twist the knob on the front of the appliance. The swirly element glows orange. Brice retrieves mugs and places a tea bag in each one. From another cupboard comes a serving tray. And from still another, he grabs a dainty crystal sugar bowl.

"You know your way around here pretty well," I remark.

He smiles sheepishly at me over his shoulder. "Yeah."

"How many cups of tea has Sharita made for you, anyway?"

Loading the tray with the mugs, sugar bowl, and teaspoons, he answers, "A few. I've actually watched her make more tea than I've had to drink."

"Interesting."

He chuckles. "Now, don't get like that. I've stopped by on a few occasions when she needed someone to talk to."

"Oh. So, this, today, isn't that big of a surprise?"

He runs his hand through his hair. "I don't think she expected this in her worst nightmares. Nelson was having a rough time, sure, but this... No, I don't think he gave her any indication he was that desperate."

The water pops in the kettle behind me, indicating it'll be ready any second. "I don't know what to say to her. This is pastor territory."

"It's mother territory."

"No. I can't think like a mother here. I'll lose it."

"She needs you to sympathize and empathize. She needs you to hold her and tell her she didn't do anything wrong."

"How do I know that?"

"Does it matter, at this point? She needs to be comforted. And you're perfect for the job."

I take a deep breath and concentrate on not releasing it

in a huge, self-pitying sigh. What I'd like is to go home and hug my own kids. But how selfish is that? There's a woman in the next room who will never hug one of her sons again. The child she brought into this world, presumably on one of the happiest days of her life, the child whose fingers and toes she counted in awe and delight, the child in whose face she recognized herself and his father and countless other relatives, the child she chased and chastised and hugged and kissed goodnight, is gone. Like that.

I swipe away tears as the kettle whistles. Spinning toward the stove, I stop the intrusive sound by lifting the shiny container from the hob.

Brice walks up behind me and grasps my upper arms. His lips against the back of my head, he says, "Just a little longer, okay?" He pulls away slightly. "We'll take this tea in there. I'll get some information from Sharita, call some relatives of hers to come be with her and Warwick, and then we'll go home."

All I can do for now is nod.

He reaches around me and relieves me of the kettle. While he pours the hot, steaming water over the tea bags in the mugs on the tray and sets the kettle on one of the cold elements on the stove top, I compose myself. He returns to the counter, where he lifts the tray, and turns to face me. "Ready?"

Honestly, no. But I get to go home to my normal life eventually. This is Sharita's new normal. I think I can suck it up for another hour or so.

21

JEN'S WEDDING

*T*he next few days feel like a 90s Hugh Grant chick flick. Except nobody has a charming English accent. And there are way too many kids underfoot. Okay, the only thing that makes it like a 90s Hugh Grant chick flick is that there's a wedding and a funeral on back-to-back days. And Brice and I are heavily involved in both events.

As much as I've been dreading Bob, Mary, and my mom under the same roof (ours, to boot) and comparing notes about how awful we are, they've been instrumental in keeping the kids alive while Brice and I tend to last-minute wedding preps for our besties, including the rehearsal dinner. I'm just trying not to think too much about what our mothers are saying about us when we're out of the house. I'm counting on my kids to keep them too busy for idle chit-chat. Don't let me down, munchkins!

The wedding would be stressful enough, but with Brice also officiating at Nelson's funeral, the insanity level has ramped up about a thousand percent. I told Brice it was crazy to think he could do both of these things, but he aptly pointed out that we can't ask Vince and Jen to reschedule their wedding, and we're not about to suggest to Sharita that she plan her youngest son's funeral arrangements to suit our needs. So, we have to do the best we can. The biggest conflict is Nelson's visitation falling on the same day as the wedding. Since we only have to pop in to the visitation, which is in the afternoon, and the wedding isn't until 7 p.m., Brice thinks we'll be okay.

He's apparently never been a matron of honor.

Fortunately, Mitzi and Jared found a way to make it for the wedding, so they've been serving as our stand-ins when Brice and I have to duck out to support Sharita. However, that means one-year-old Sasha has been added to our brood at the house.

Last night, with everyone—and I mean everyone— already waiting for us at the church for the rehearsal and dinner, I had to physically pull Mitzi through the back door in the middle of explaining her detailed childcare flow chart to my mother. The only specific instructions I had for the parenting pros in charge were for Addi, who needed to drink the bottle in the fridge right before her bedtime, at or around 7:30. Or whenever. At this point, I've resigned myself to the fact that my kids' schedules are so screwed up beyond belief that only intensive reprogramming will fix the situation, and that's not happening until everyone goes home and our life reverts to our version of normal.

From the passenger seat of the minivan, Mitzi grumbled to my profile while I stretched every traffic law to its max, "I only have one kid, you know. I don't want to screw it up."

A lack of sleep and severe emotional overload prompted me to snap, "Yeah, because I'm hoping to just get one of mine right. The rest? Collateral damage."

She sighed. "You know what I mean."

"No, I don't really, Mitz. But I do know we're late. And

for the past two days, I've been switching between 'I'm sorry your son's dead' to 'Yay! You're getting married!' I'm exhausted."

"That's not my fault! And I'm only trying to make things easier for your mom. Sasha doesn't go down easily, especially in a strange place."

"It's one night; she'll be okay. And it's not that I take the safety of my children lightly; but at some point, you have to trust that someone else can do just as good a job keeping them alive as you do, even if it's not exactly the way you'd do it."

"I guess I can call your mom later from the dinner and walk her through the bedtime routine."

I rolled my eyes but kept my focus on the road, navigating the maze of one-way streets.

Once we arrived at the church, the rehearsal ran as smoothly as it possibly could have, considering the officiating minister and the matron of honor were half out of it. The bride and groom didn't seem to care that we were listless and merely going through the motions. They knew we'd bring our A-game to the actual day.

And that's today.

Straight from Nelson's visitation, I drop off my kids in the church nursery without a backward glance. My biggest concern is changing from my visitation clothes to my wedding attire and finding the stylist who's supposed to touch up my makeup and give me an elaborate updo to match Mitzi's. And that all needs to happen in less than thirty minutes, when the wedding is supposed to start.

When I rush through the bathroom door, I find Jen in front of the sinks, still being attended by her mother, Karen, and an aunt I've never met until yesterday.

"Hey!" I say as cheerfully as possible, dropping my tote

bag by the sinks on my way into the handicapped stall with my garment bag slung over my shoulder.

"How'd the visitation go?" Jen asks into the mirror.

I appreciate how understanding she's been about my divided attention the past couple of days, but I honestly don't know how to answer her question. I finally settle on the easiest, most honest option. "It sucked."

She winces sympathetically.

I duck into the stall and hang up the garment bag on the hook on the inside of the door. "But anyway! How are you?" I call while pulling down on the bag's zipper and simultaneously stepping from my sensible pumps. "What's your status? What needs to be done? How are you feeling? What did I miss?"

Karen and Aunt Whoever laugh at my rapid-fire questioning. Jen replies calmly, "I feel great. And everything else is great. Just get yourself ready. That's all that's left to do."

"Great. I'm the egg in the snake?"

I can hear her wrinkled nose through the plywood door. "If you must use such a gross metaphor, yes. But it's not a big deal."

I shuck my simple black dress from my shoulders and let it fall to the floor around my feet. Then I dive headfirst into the ice blue tube of satin I'll be wearing for the next several hours. I detach the straps from my convertible bra (this girl ain't no dummy) and tug upward on the strapless dress to fully cover the undergarment.

As quickly as possible, I join my friend at the mirror, hopping the last few feet as I slide on my shoes. Mitzi click-clacks into the bathroom, stopping on the other side of Jen and turning her head from side to side to make sure her shellacked hair hasn't moved during her prolonged nursery drop-off.

Jen tells her mom and aunt they can go, "now that my real bridal party is here."

With a final kiss to her daughter's cheek, Karen fans her face and leaves, leaning on her sister and murmuring something about "My little girl."

Jen rolls her eyes but smiles affectionately after them.

"Where's your dad?" Mitzi asks.

"Probably raiding the communion wine," Jen answers drolly, tapping out a text. "And avoiding Mom, of course. I think we'll call it a win if those two exchange less than ten words with each other during all this, and none of those words are profane."

I've never known Karen and Jerry as a couple; they've been divorced—bitterly so—for as long as I've known my friend. Karen had full custody, so she was always the parent; Jerry had the luxury of being the buddy. And he was good at it. It created no end of animosity between him and his ex-wife. Karen never remarried ("No, thanks! Been there; done that; got the gray hairs!"), but Jerry has used the intervening thirty years to try to break the record for number of marriages. He's presently between wives.

"Just keep him away from my mom," I demand, darkening my makeup with quick strokes. "Who are you texting?"

"Killian, the stylist. He needs to get in here now and get to work on… that." She merely points to my head.

"Gee, thanks."

"Seriously. Stop with the makeup. He's going to want to start over. Trust me."

"All righty, then." I toss the tube of mascara into my tote bag and twist my dress, trying to get the seams straight. While we wait for this magic stylist, I give Jen a more thorough once-over. "You look amazing. I thought the tiara was going to be over-the-top, but it's perfect."

Her eyes sparkle at me in the mirror. "I know!"

"Vince is going to have a heart attack when you come up that aisle," Mitzi predicts.

"He better not! He has obligations later on."

The three of us snicker at Jen's wiggling eyebrows.

Mitzi walks around Jen's back and fiddles with the already perfectly straight buttons trailing all the way from her shoulders to her butt. "Remember when Brice started crying when Peyton walked in?"

"No, he didn't!" I say.

"Yes, he did!" they say together.

Jen laughs. "How could you have forgotten that?"

"Because it never happened."

"It did," Mitzi insists.

"I think I would have noticed that," I say, doubt creeping in. Because, honestly, I might not have. I was as self-conscious that day as a gawky pre-teen at her first school dance. My powers of observation weren't at their peak.

Mitzi clicks her tongue. "Obviously not. Because it happened. It's not like he was blubbering, or anything, but there were definitely tears, and he was swallowing all spastically." She demonstrates, looking like someone in need of a toilet.

"He was probably trying not to throw up," I mutter. "I know I was."

Jen swats at me. "No, he was happy! I've already warned Vince he better not pull anything like that, because I'm not as strong as you, Peyton. I'll lose it."

"It had nothing to do with strength. I had tunnel vision. I was like, 'Don't stumble, don't fall, don't pass out, don't puke,' pretty much the whole way up the aisle."

"How romantic," Jen teases.

Mitzi nods. "Yep. That sounds about right. I, on the other hand, would have run up the aisle if I could have. I was so excited! And I didn't care about anyone else there." At our mock-offended gawks, she corrects, "I mean, I cared about all of you, but I didn't particularly care what anyone thought about me at that moment. Except Jared. And my mom. I knew she'd kill me if I did something silly. But I had the biggest urge to skip."

Jen flutters her lashes. "Well, I look like a regal princess, and I'm not going to ruin that by crying or rushing up that aisle. And I'm going to make a conscious effort to take it all in, so I'll remember every detail. Vince better not cry, or do anything else that interrupts my concentration."

The stylist sweeps into the women's restroom like he owns the place, not even checking first to ensure nobody's using the facilities. After one glance at me in the mirror, he says, "Oh. Let's get busy," in an Irish accent that would be dead sexy if he weren't bluntly insulting me.

Mitzi and Jen smirk. Then Mitzi pulls on Jen's arm and inches them toward the door, "We're going to go to the staging area to get our flowers and attach Jen's veil. Meet you there in twenty minutes?"

Killian snorts. "I'm good, but you better make that thirty."

I smile tightly at him. "Nice to meet you, too, Killian. Lovin' the guyliner." Actually, he's intimidatingly hot, including the eye makeup. Black leather doesn't usually do it for me—I grew out of my bad boy phase a long time ago, obviously—but he's rocking it.

"You're going to appreciate all of me by the time I'm finished with you, love."

I try not to take that the wrong way or blush to the roots

of my hair, but that's a losing battle, considering...
everything.

He opens a collapsible stool and pats its seat. "Now, sit
down and prepare to be amazed."

Not sure "appreciative" was the accurate emotion I felt for
Killian by the time he stepped back and declared, "That will
have to do. We can't keep people waiting all night," but
"amazed" definitely fit. And Brice was impressed, though he
tried to pull his eyeballs back into his head by directing them
at the open liturgy book in his hands as I walked toward him
and Vince.

Fortunately, my moment in the spotlight didn't last long,
and Jen got the show-stealing entrance she was going for.
Vince didn't cry. But I think the only way he prevented an
emotional outburst was by making silly faces and acting like
a goof while his bride walked to the front of the church.
Probably not what Jen had in mind, either, but she made it
halfway down the aisle before she couldn't stifle her laughter
at his antics anymore.

After Jerry placed his daughter's hand on her groom's
waiting arm, Jen gave Vince's shoulder a playful push,
prompting Brice to say when the music stopped, "Well,
we're off to a good start. Let's pray."

Now we're at one of the rowdiest receptions I've
attended since the days when it felt like college friends were
getting married every other weekend, and it seemed they
were all competing with each other for the most memorable
party. Brice and I originally planned to stay through the
traditional stuff at the beginning, then bug out with the kids,

but after my short and sweet toast to the bride and groom, I find my husband alone at our table.

"Was my toast that bad?" I ask, peeking under the table.

He drains the champagne in the flute in his hand and sets it on the table. "Our moms took the kids home and told me not to bring you home until we'd had a good time." Before I can sit, he stands and pulls me toward the dance floor. "And I always do what my mom says."

"Liar."

We stand on the periphery, watching Jen and Vince's first dance as husband and wife, openly laughing at how hopeless Vince's dancing is and how valiantly Jen's trying, and failing, to save it. Finally, the deejay invites the rest of us to join them, so Brice and I walk onto the floor and sway to one of our favorite tunes.

I'm tired, and we might regret this tomorrow, when we have to be up bright and early and functioning for church, then Nelson's funeral, but something tells me that's what makes tonight even more necessary. Too much about the past week has been sad. Or draining. Or just plain hard work. We need this release.

"You look incredible, my bride," Brice says as soon as the song ends and transitions into the next one.

I gaze into his face. "Better than on our wedding day?"

"Now, what kind of a scary trick question is that?" he asks on a whine that amuses me.

"Just kidding. You should have seen the guy who did this to me."

On second thought, maybe it's best not to go there.

I clear my throat. "He, uh, meant business."

"He somehow managed to improve on perfection."

"Nice save."

He laughs at himself. "I love you." In the cover of the

dim, strobe-lit dance floor, he leans down and kisses my lips more intimately than he normally would in a public place.

After the kiss, I return his sentiment, then rest my head on his chest for the rest of the song.

The next number is a peppy one, and more than half of the dancers return to their tables, but Jen bellows across to Brice and me, "Don't even think about sitting down!" She searches the area for Mitzi and Jared. "You two, either! This is a party, damn it!"

Brice widens his eyes at her, then says to me, "Her majesty has spoken."

So in spite of my aching feet and the fact that I seem to have forgotten how to dance to anything with a fast tempo, I stay exactly where I am, face my husband, and bop to the beat. He can barely dance better than I can, so it doesn't take long before I'm giggling too hard to remember to be self-conscious about my lack of moves.

"You're laughing at me? You should see yourself!" He reaches out his hand.

I grasp it, despite being a little apprehensive about what he has in mind. He pulls me toward him, twirling me along the length of his arm. I whoop in surprise but stay on my feet, coming to rest with my back against his chest. He twirls me back out, then does a snapping move that makes him look like a bad backup dancer in West Side Story or a Michael Jackson video.

"You're such a dork!"

"Yep!"

"Maybe they'll ask us to sit down."

"We can always hope."

Despite the lack of variety in our moves, we have decent rhythm, so after observing and emulating other, more prac- ticed participants around us, we loosen up and start to enjoy ourselves. And break a sweat. And laugh until our sides hurt at our failed attempts at some of the more complicated modern moves. Then Jen, Vince, Mitzi, and Jared boogie up to us. In the loose circle, Brice and I are two of the better dancers. Which is sad. But also hilarious. And gratifying.

Jen hip-checks me and shouts over the music, "Hey! What happened to you? You used to be so much better than this."

"Childbirth killed my mojo?" I hypothesize lightly, not at all offended by her criticism.

She puts her hands over her head, bends her knees, and wiggles her hips, snapping her fingers and turning her head into her toned upper arm. "Remember this move? The guys used to flock when we'd do this."

I raise an eyebrow while watching her, remembering when we'd grind against each other at nightclubs on a weekly basis. "I wonder why."

"Because it looked like we wanted to make out!" she replies earnestly before looking at me and pairing my rolled eyes with my sarcastic utterance. "C'mon! For old time's sake!"

I shake my head at her. "No way."

Despite my protests, she turns and faces me.

"Jen…"

"Don't be such a party pooper!"

I glance over her shoulder at Brice, the deepening redness of his face conflicting with the expression of pure fascination on it. His jaw slackens. Vince sidles up next to him and nudges him back to awareness, then says something close to his ear to make both of them grin like dopes. They assume their best pastor poses to observe the spectacle.

Meanwhile, Jen refuses to give up. "It's my wedding day; you have to do what I say! Now, dance!"

I roll my eyes but figure it'll be easier to simply do what she wants for a few seconds, then retreat to the open bar, where there's a gin and tonic with my name on it. It might have helped if I'd had a few of those G&Ts before this display.

Channeling my inner drunk, I mirror Jen's pose, trying not to visibly wince when my knees crack and creak as I keep them bent at uncomfortably extreme angles while asking them to bear the weight of my wiggling, gyrating torso and butt. As I lift my arms and snap my fingers, I turn my face into my arm and close my eyes. At least this way, I won't have to see anyone's reaction to us. But that means I don't see when Mitzi slides in behind me. I squeal when I feel her crotch bump against my butt, though. Then she wraps her hand around the top hem of my dress, between my shoulder blades, to steady herself.

"This is ridiculous!" I yell when the deejay draws more attention to us by imploring the crowd to "Check out the bride and her besties! Girls know how to get down!" The clapping and whooping draws nearer.

I keep my eyes closed, wishing the song would end, although unable to stop myself from laughing and enjoying myself, in spite of the borderline humiliation.

The air moves in front of me as Jen edges closer still. "And they say pastors' wives don't know how to have a good time?" she shouts.

I merely shake my head. That's when Jen decides to wedge her left leg between mine. Or try to. Our long skirts aren't having any of that. And the skirt on my dress is not only long, it's tight, so her knee bounces off the material and knocks her back on her three-inch platform heels.

At her shrieking laughter, I open my eyes just in time to see her arms pinwheel and her left hand grab at my chest, her shiny new wedding ring glinting as her fingers snag the straight line of fabric straining just above my cleavage line. That pulls the dress so tightly against my back that Mitzi couldn't let go if she wanted to. And I know right then: we're going down.

On our way to the floor, as people around us scatter to avoid being taken out, I say to Jen and Mitzi, as if it's all happening in slow motion, "This was a bad idea!" before we fall into a heap of quivering and quaking satin.

Black-clad legs come into view, but we're too busy laughing (and in my case, trying not to pee my pants) to grip any of the proffered hands, two of which I recognize instantly as my husband's. While a knee belonging to Jen stabs me in the ribs, I muffle into an arm belonging to Mitzi, "The Trippin' Trio strikes again!"

"Stop calling us that!" they yell in stereo.

*A*fter our spill on the dance floor, I figured alcohol was superfluous, so my skipping church this morning had nothing to do with being hung over. However, I made Brice promise to let our moms believe I have a simple hangover, because... Well, I'm not sure. It's less embarrassing, maybe? Plus, they were the ones who insisted we stay and have a good time. I'd rather they think I had too much of a good time, in liquid form, not that I crippled myself dirty dancing like someone half my age.

As soon as everyone else left for church, I began the arduous task of getting ready for our next big event: Nelson's funeral. That involved limping around our bedroom and eating ibuprofen to steel myself for the pain of showering and dressing, followed by sticking adhesive pain-relieving heat patches to various parts of my body—some unmentionable. Now I'm dressed, sprawled on our bed, sweaty and exhausted from the effort. The herd recently returned from church, but as much as I want to help with lunch, I can't.

Brice appears at the foot of the bed and nudges my

pantyhose-clad big toe with his knuckle. "Well? How are you feeling?"

"It took me an hour to get this dress on. And pantyhose. They're Satan's undergarment."

"Maybe you should go to the ER. You might have seriously hurt something."

"Just my pride. Everything else is superficial. And so deserved."

"I'm sure Sharita will understand if—"

"No! Ow!" I moan as I shoot into a sitting position. "Uh-uh. I'm not flaking on this."

"It wouldn't be 'flaking.' You're in agony!"

"Like she's not?"

He tilts his head and blinks at me.

"No. I promised her I'd be there. I told her I'd read Nelson's favorite Shel Silverstein poem. I have it downloaded onto my phone, ready to go. I think I can even get through it without crying. Maybe."

Crossing his arms over his chest, he opens his mouth to rebut, but I cut him off. "I would have gone to church if it had been possible to get dressed in time."

"Can you even walk?"

"Yes. Of course, I can." I stand and perform what's meant to be a catwalk strut but comes across more like a herky-jerky toddler stumble, each step punctuated with a grunt.

"No, really. Can you walk without looking and sounding like a cast member of *The Walking Dead?*"

I hold my breath, take more normal strides, and choke out, "Yes."

"At least tell me you'll wear flat shoes."

"Flat shoes don't go with this dress."

He rolls his eyes, then turns to leave the room. "Whatever. It's your choice. Nobody would blame you for sitting this one out, though."

I'd blame myself.

~

Getting through Nelson's funeral was a cake walk compared to what awaits me: being alone with my mom. It's been too chaotic this long weekend for us to have a single conversation. Not one. If only we could keep it that way.

Do I want to have this discussion tonight? No. But someone's gotta be the grownup here. Someone has to put on her big-girl panties and bite the bullet or address the elephant in the room or any of those other clichés that mean, "Take care of business."

I guess I'm that person.

The trouble is, there's nobody here to act as a buffer. True to her word, Nicole stayed in Chicago to shuttle her kids to their various activities this weekend; Jason and Dustin are on their annual post-Christmas cruise; and Brice doesn't seem eager to get in the middle of my skirmish with my mom, considering the mess he's in with his own mom and stepfather. That leaves me. Just me. And we Stratfords may be pretty good at sweeping things under the rug and pretending problems don't exist, but this particular problem is a major tripping hazard. There's no ignoring it any longer.

Brice, Mary, and Bob have taken the kids for a cold pre-dinner walk that will hopefully tire them out enough that they'll be ready for Triple-P soon after dinner (the kids, too). Mary, Bob, and my mom will leave shortly afterward to spend one more night in their hotel rooms before going in separate directions first thing in the morning. In other words, this is my last—only—chance to do this, while Mom and I heat up leftovers for dinner.

Mom and Mary must have had a cook-off this weekend. I take container after container of food from the fridge and set them on the counter. Mom opens each plastic tub, empties it into a larger dish, and places it in the microwave for reheating. After about three cycles of this, I say, "I'm sorry we haven't had a chance to talk much this weekend."

Okay, so kicking off the conversation with a lie might not be the best strategy. But I gotta start somewhere.

Unfortunately, she waves off my apology with a breezy, "You've been busy. That boy's suicide was just awful timing."

I grit my teeth and try to block out the image of Sharita when I made the mistake of looking at her during my reading of Nelson's favorite poem. She wore the most heartbreaking expression of sadness and nostalgia, like she was recalling the first time she ever read that poem to her baby. Also, I detected a hint of pride on her face that may have been directed at me, and that was even more upsetting. I had to pause a few seconds to breathe, swallow, and compose myself before continuing. Other than that, the reading went without a hitch.

Now, instead of taking offense to my mother's insensitive statement, I keep in mind she doesn't know the people involved (not that it excuses her insensitivity). Plus, like many people who have never experienced mental illness firsthand, she's not particularly understanding.

I wonder what it's like for life to be so definite, so uncomplicated, so lacking in shades of gray?

Before she can further offend with her views on the selfishness of suicide, I peel the lid off a dish of potatoes and hand it to her. "I think the timing of Nelson's death is the least of everyone's concern," I simply say now. "But anyway, I… I want to talk to you before you go home."

She stirs the potatoes while the plate of brisket rotates for the last few seconds of its ride in the microwave. "About what, sweetie? The kids were angels for Mary, Bob, and me. Max says the funniest things! And Aidan's a parrot. But as good as they were, I don't know how you do it every day. It was exhausting! And there were three of us! It's no wonder you look so worn out."

When I say nothing, searching for the right words to get us from here to where I want us to be in the conversation, she rushes forward. "Now, don't take that the wrong way. I know I'm not telling you anything you don't already know."

"Yeah, I know I look like shit."

"You're taking it the wrong way."

"Just because you say 'Don't take this the wrong way' doesn't mean it's okay to say whatever." I push my hair from my eyes and laugh mirthlessly to hide the grunt resulting from the pain of moving my arms too quickly.

"You were gorgeous at the wedding yesterday. It was so cute when the boys kept saying how pretty you were when they saw you at the reception. They're not used to seeing you like that, I guess."

I drop my hands to my sides. "Hey. So. Let's start over, okay?"

She pops the potatoes in the microwave. "Fine. Tell me my lines, and I'll say whatever you want me to say." She turns to face me, tucking her arms under her breasts.

I'm about to tell her I want her to respond like a normal, loving, caring mom, someone who has an ounce of empathy for her child's feelings, someone who isn't always so focused on the superficial, but that may escalate things. On the other hand…

"You know what? That's a great idea. Here we go." I bump the fridge closed with my foot, instantly regretting it as stabs radiate from my hip through my ribs. Still, I persevere. "I say, 'Mom, I've been wanting to talk to you.' Then you say, 'Yes, we need to talk.' And I say, 'I agree. Things have been tense between us, and I want that to stop. I recognize you caught me at a bad time, and I may have overreacted to what you said. I'm ready to forgive and forget.' Then you say, 'Great. I'm sorry I—'"

"That doesn't sound like us at all."

I throw my hands up. "Gaaaaa!"

She appears unfazed by my outburst, a result of equal parts frustration and physical anguish.

"First of all, I'm not sorry for anything. Except that you take offense to everything I say, no matter how well-meaning."

I limp to the island and drape myself across it, bracing my weight on my forearms before my building back spasm renders me incapable of standing.

"What's wrong with you now?" she inquires in a tone falling far short of "nurturing."

"There was a dancing… mishap… at the reception after you left last night."

Lips pursed, she plunks her hands on her hips. "While you were drunk?"

"No. Completely sober. Just… out of practice."

"Maybe I don't want to know." She returns to her inspection of the food.

"It's not important. I hurt myself. That's all. And now this conversation isn't helping."

"Oh, I see. So your physical pain is my fault, too?"

I'm too busy breathing and having flashbacks to Aidan's drug-free birth to reply to her silly question.

"It's not my fault you act like a teenager when you're around Jen. You'd think you'd be past the age of making such—"

"Poor choices," I finish for her. "Yeah. I get it."

The microwave beeps. She stirs the potatoes, tests the temperature, and puts them back in for another two minutes. "That's not what I was going to say. I was going to say 'making such fools of yourselves.'"

"Whatever you call it, it's beside the point. What I really want is to clear the air about that stupid conversation way back before Thanksgiving." I hiss as I inhale a shaky, pain-inducing breath.

"This is hardly a good time," Mom says, but probably more because she doesn't want to deal with it than due to any concern for me.

"I'm fine." I stand at my full height, then bend over again when it's too painful to put my full weight on my legs. "I'll be much better once we get this out of the way."

"Get what out of the way? A fake apology from me, to appease you?"

I grit my teeth. "I'd prefer if the apology wasn't fake, but… I'll take anything at this point."

"Honestly, I don't remember what I said that was so bad."

"That's okay; I remember. You implied my family planning was based on poor choices."

"Well…" She laughs her tinkly, fake, business-party laugh, the one she passed down to Nicole, the one that makes me want to rake my fingernails down her face. If I had fingernails. Which I don't. Because I'd always be breaking them or digging gross things out from under them.

"Mom, so help me God—"

She lines up the heated food on the breakfast bar adjacent to the island, creating a leftovers buffet. "Do I think you and Brice had too many babies too soon? Yes. I'm sorry, but I do. And I'm sorry it came out in that phone call. There. Is that enough 'sorrys' for you?"

"Not really what I had in mind."

She avoids my eyes by covering the dishes with clean dish towels to hold in the warmth while we wait for the others to return. "It was a stressful call, with you backing out of hosting Thanksgiving and snapping at me about everything and giving me a play-by-play of cleaning up Harris's bathroom accident. I slipped and said something I never meant to say to you. Because it's pointless to even talk about it. It's a moot point."

"Exactly! But that's your specialty: second-guessing my decisions, pointing out in hindsight what you would have done or preferred I do. You've been doing it for as long as I can remember!"

"Oh, don't be so dramatic."

"Mom, you questioned 'the wisdom' of my choosing to do my very first book report on *Old Yeller*, because you worried I'd be perceived by my other classmates as a downer."

"It was an extremely depressing, morbid book for a second grader to read and talk about! I still don't agree with the teacher allowing you to do it, even if you were reading at that advanced level. You'll understand someday. I was only trying to protect you."

"You're missing the point."

"You're the one who brought it up!"

Feeling a slight loosening of the muscles along my left flank, I hobble to the dining table and collapse into one of the chairs, keeping my posture ramrod straight. "How about this: how about you just—crazy suggestion alert—be supportive? No matter what?"

"I have been. How have I not been? It's not like I lectured you about your perpetual pregnancies at the time, when it seemed like you and Brice didn't understand what was causing them."

I bark bitterly, then grab my back. "Yeah, Mom. We had no clue."

"Sometimes I wondered! But I kept my mouth shut anyway, even when it was taking a toll on your health. And then—" She frowns, fingering the cross necklace resting against her sweater-covered collarbone. "Then you had to be hospitalized while you were expecting Addi, and every day I thought, 'Is this going to end with me burying another grandchild—or worse—my daughter?'"

I close my eyes and rub my back harder. She comes up behind me and takes over the job, digging her fist into the largest, most problematic muscle.

"I really, really wondered that. Every day. And when you didn't wake up after surgery, I started to take it further. And I'd think, 'Will I love this grandchild like the others? Will I ever be able to forgive Brice if Peyton never wakes up?' Because I don't think I would have been able to. It would have torn our family apart."

"Well, I made it. And Addi made it. So, yay. Can we move on now?"

Her hand stills. "Stop being so flippant!"

"Brice and I wanted a daughter—"

"At any price, apparently."

"We trusted it was in God's hands. All of it."

"No, you figured you were in control, as usual."

"I sure didn't take into account my supposedly Christian

mother's inability to forgive someone for something he couldn't control."

"I'm just being honest."

I shrug off her hands and stand. "I'm so sick of your brand of honesty I could barf, Mom."

"You're the one who wanted to talk about this."

"I wanted to forgive you. But you make it so damn impossible!"

"Who's being un-Christianlike now?"

"I am! At least I own it, though."

She pauses, and I dare to dream that something I've said has finally sunk in.

"I'm owning that I'm worried about you, about your health, about your mental wellbeing. Okay? That's my right, as your mother. You'll never be too old or too in control of your own life for me to stop, either. So get over it."

Hopes: dashed.

"Oh, the infamous 'Get over it.' Almost as great as, 'Because I said so.'" I try to make a dramatic exit up the stairs, but each step is its own special torture, so my ascent is painstaking.

Mom watches in silence until I have to rest four stairs from the bottom. "Look at you!" Her hands fall limply to her sides.

"Nobody's forcing you to watch," I say between grunts, trying to ignore the tears leaking down my face.

Her shoulders droop even further. "Sometimes I'm so jealous of your father. And angry at him. Because he left me here to worry about all of this by myself. It's a thankless, horrible job." She whirls and opens the back door, practically bumping into Brice, who's ducking down to enter with Aidan on his shoulders.

"Oh, hey!" he greets her. "Smells great in here!"

"Excuse me." She pushes past the crowd of family members on the deck and disappears into the backyard.

Brice watches her go, then turns to me, his rosy cheeks falling as his smile fades. I drop to all fours and climb the rest of the way up the stairs, not caring how it appears and hardly registering how it feels. At least it makes the kids giggle.

The ibuprofen's finally kicking in. Good thing, because I've taken enough to put someone twice as big as I am into renal failure. But don't tell anyone that. If I die, I don't want Mom to blame Brice for making the money to buy that super-sized bottle of 200-milligram tablets.

I made it to the top of the stairs before Brice caught up to me, but I batted away his helping hand. "I'm fine. I just need to lie down. Feed the kids. Get them ready for bed. And make sure my mom doesn't get frostbite."

"What the heck is going on?" he asked my ass as I crawled toward our room.

"Back spasms. Big fight. The usual."

"Ah. Okay, then."

That was a few hours ago. I fell asleep about an hour after dragging myself into bed. Later, I woke up and briefly registered Brice creeping through the room with Addi and putting her to bed in her adjacent room, but I was already out of it again before he finished with her version of Triple-P.

Now, Brice is back, only he's removing his clothes in the dark, kicking them in the direction of the hamper by the bathroom door but not making the effort to put them in it.

The house is eerily quiet around us.

"Hey," I croak. "Is everyone gone?"

"Yes. How's your back?"

"It only hurts when I breathe."

"Oh. Great. We're going to the doctor tomorrow."

"No! They'll write me a bunch of prescriptions for drugs that will make me want to sleep all day and will nauseate and constipate me and—"

"Relax those jacked-up muscles."

"Ibuprofen works just fine. Here." I flip onto my stomach with minimal grunting. "Give me one of your awesome massages, and I'll be good to go."

"You think you're going to flatter your way out of this?"

"No. I'm fully prepared to suffer the consequences of my latest poor choice."

"What happened last night wasn't a poor choice. You were humoring a friend. Actually, it was pretty hot... until you guys fell down." He walks across the bed on his knees and straddles my lower back, pushing my shirt up so he can rub his splayed hands against my skin, fanning out from my spine to my sides.

My eyes cross from the pleasure-pain. "The bruises I have aren't hot. We're too damn old for that shit, as I tried to tell Jen before it all went horribly wrong and as my body is making sure I understand today. I think I got the worst of it, because I was in the middle of that... that inappropriate sandwich."

"We'll go to a doctor tomorrow, and he or she will make it all better."

"I don't want any narcotics in the house."

That shuts him up for a while. While he kneads, I can practically hear him formulating his response. Finally, he says, "I know you're thinking about Sharita and Nelson..."

"And every other horror story I've seen or heard."

"…but our kids aren't suicidal."

"No, they're worse; they're clueless. And into everything."

He sighs. "We'll put the bottles up high somewhere."

"Have you seen those kids climb? And if I'm hopped up on drugs, it'll be even harder than usual to keep up with them, and—"

"Shhh… You're tensing up. If it means that much to you, then forget it."

"Thank you."

"I'll be home this week, so you won't have to lift or carry the kids. And you won't."

"Fine. Deal. I probably shouldn't change any diapers, either."

"Whatever."

"That feels so good," I slur into my pillow as he continues to grind his fingers and the heels of his palms into my sore muscles. Sleep reaches for me, beckoning me to return to its warm, comforting oblivion.

"Your mom's fine, by the way," Brice says, startling me awake.

I swallow. "Oh. Good."

"She was pretty upset when I went out to check on her, after fixing the kids' plates, but I finally convinced her to come back inside. She didn't eat, though."

"Is this supposed to make me feel bad?"

"No!"

"Because all she had to do was say she was sorry for calling our kids 'poor choices,' but she couldn't even manage that."

"Do you really think she ever meant it that way?"

"Don't take her side."

"I'm not! She hurt you, and when you finally told me

what she said to upset you so much before Thanksgiving, I'll admit it hit a nerve for me, too. But she loves those kids. There's no denying that."

"Yeah, yeah."

"And she loves us."

"Are you sure?"

"Yes. I am."

"Well, I'm sick of conditional love."

"What did she say to make you think she doesn't love you unconditionally?"

"Everything."

He rises to his knees.

"No! Don't go. Keep rubbing, and I'll tell you what she said."

"I'm not stopping to punish you for making me drag it out of you; I'm stopping because you obviously don't want to discuss this seriously right now, and that's fine. But if that's the case, I'd like to go to sleep."

"Fine."

I roll onto my side and jam one of the decorative throw pillows that usually grace our bed—when I can be bothered to make it—between my knees. In a monotone, I recap the argument, at first leaving out the part about her never forgiving Brice. But then I hear myself saying, "There's one more thing," almost not believing I'm going to tell him but figuring if anyone can take something like that in stride, it's a pastor. "She said if I hadn't made it—you know, after Addi was born—she didn't know if she could have ever forgiven you. Or loved Addi as much as the boys. I mean—" My throat tightens at the mere thought of it. "How fucked up is that?"

He says nothing, and I wonder how long he's been asleep. Without thinking, I turn my head to glance over my shoulder at him. And see stars. "Agggggh! Oh, mother-fuhh..." I clutch at the muscle connecting my neck to the rest of the right side of my body.

He takes over the massaging. "Easy, girl," he murmurs.

"I thought you were asleep. Did you hear what I said?"

"Yes, I heard your potty mouth."

"No! The other thing, what Mom said about not forgiving you or loving Addi the same as her other grandkids."

"Yep."

"And?"

"I already knew that last part."

"She told you that tonight?"

"No, she told me that when you were still unconscious. And I... I understood it at the time. And as much as it hurts, I still understand it."

"How? How can you accept that?"

"For one thing, it never came to pass, so... whatever."

"But the intent..."

"Means nothing. It's the follow-through that matters. And nobody knows if they have what it takes to follow through on something like that until they're faced with that reality."

"How could she say that to you when you were going through that, when you weren't sure if I was ever going to wake up? How could she?" The pent-up tears from the past few hours—heck, for the past six months, going all the way back to when I heard him crying next to my hospital bed—break loose. "And now I'm supposed to forgive her for saying that to you at such an awful time?"

"Shhh..." He stops rubbing but kisses the achy muscle. His lips against my shoulder, he says, "I forgave her. I under-stood where she was coming from." He backs off a bit, his breath whispering on my skin and raising goosebumps. "Think about it. She'd just lost her husband. She was emotional. Thinking in absolutes. Thinking for both herself and your dad, trying to keep in mind what he would say."

"You know, there's a good reason 'What Would Kent Do?' never caught on."

"And I was so full of self-loathing at the time…" His voice chokes to a halt. "I… I didn't have room for anyone else's anger or disappointment. I already hated myself enough for everyone."

My chest aches at the thought of what he was going through. "She had to have known that, though. And she, of all people, having just lost a spouse, should have been sensitive to what you might be facing."

"In her mind, she and I were not kindred spirits. She was a mother, and I was the person who put her daughter in danger. With my 'poor choices.'"

I groan in frustration. "She's a lunatic."

"She's not a lunatic."

"I beg to differ. And she's my mom, so my opinion counts more than yours."

"Now there's some creative logic."

"I can't believe you're defending her."

"I'm not! But I feel like I need to justify my forgiveness. We're told to forgive seventy times seven—"

"She's gone so past that limit!"

"You know it's not literal. And we've all gone past that limit. Which is kind of the point."

"What's next? She's going to imply that Addi would have been a murderer if I hadn't lived?"

"Cut it out." Finally, his demeanor hardens, but his anger seems to be directed at me, not my mom. And that's not fair.

"Well? That's the brand of logic she was employing. Talk about blaming the victim!"

"She would have realized that eventually. And, again, it doesn't matter. Because you're still here. And I thank God for that every day. More than once a day. I—" After a heavy pause, he continues, "I'm too busy thanking Him to hold a grudge against your mother for something she said while she was going through one of the most difficult times of her life. We all were. So just—I don't know—let it go."

"Says the guy in the middle of a month-long feud with his mom."

"What? No. That lasted a week. Tops. I called her the next week and apologized. And she accepted my apology and said she was sorry for losing her temper with me."

"Why didn't you tell me that? All this time, I've thought the two of you have been distant, and it's been stressing me out."

"Sorry. I had no clue. I didn't tell you, because it may as well have never happened. That's sort of what forgiveness is about. And that's what adults do."

"You're not taking into account the lunatic factor."

"Be careful. It might be hereditary."

"What?!"

"I'm just saying, you and your mom may be more alike than you'd like to admit."

"I'm going to pretend you never said that."

"Whatever helps you sleep at night." With that, he gives me a peck on the cheek, turns over so we're back-to-back, and says, "Goodnight."

Well, I never! What. A. Dick.

23

NEW YEAR'S COMMANDMENTS

*W*hy couldn't my mom leave it the other night when she said, "You looked beautiful at the wedding"? Period. Sure, I would have added the silent, "for a change," in my head. But that's just it; she doesn't need to say it. So why does she?

Someone less defensive than I am (basically anyone) would say she's letting me know she cares, that she notices when I don't seem well. They might go a step further and say she points out when I don't look good to underscore it's out-of-the-ordinary. But it feels like nit-picking to me. And it makes me feel more self-conscious than I already am, which is plenty.

But being pretty isn't a priority for me right now. I'm not the mom who drops her one kid off at preschool in the morning, hops in her luxury SUV, and scoots off to hot yoga or Jazzercise, followed by tanning or a mani-pedi or massage or a cut and color. Or whatever. That's not me. It never was me, even before I had multiple kids hanging off me. And I don't think my looking like a zombie should be the crime against humanity it's being made out to be lately. I have an excuse for lurching through life right now. Five adorable excuses.

Five adorable, inordinately quiet excuses, at the moment.

For the past couple of days, I've been sequestered, and Brice and I have told the kids to ask him for most things. The first day was a rough, but they've adapted, so I've been left alone today. Very, very alone. And you know what? It's been lonely! I didn't realize how much I relied on them for socialization and entertainment.

Now, restless and bored, I poke my head around the stairs and nearly melt into the floor at what I see. Brice is lying on his stomach on the floor, propped on his elbows, a throw pillow from the couch jammed against his chest. A soccer match on mute holds his rapt attention. All four of the boys, lined up on either side of him, mimic his pose. At least, I think that was their original intent. Harris and Brooks are holding steady, though their blinks are lengthening; Max has passed out with his head resting in one hand, his cheek smooshed, drool running down his arm; and Aidan has fallen asleep, face down with his forehead against his arms in front of him.

I think Addi was the reason Brice decided to watch the game from the floor, as she likes to sit next to him and play the drums on his butt; however, she's currently slumped over the small of her dad's back, sound asleep, her head turned to the side, her rosebud lips hosting a cluster of tiny seed-pearl bubbles.

My soft laughter at the sweet sight pulls Harris's attention from the TV. "We watchin' soccer, Mommy!"

Brooks rubs his eyes. "I don't wanna take a nap."

I chuckle at his preemptive denial. "Oh. Well, you have

to, because that's how you grow big and strong. Plus, you don't want to be grumpy, do you?"

He shakes his head earnestly.

"Then up the stairs you go, both of you. Use the potty. One at a time!" I call to their rising bottoms before they get any ideas about trying to cross streams into the toilet. They have a hard enough time making it on target when they take turns. As an afterthought, I add, "Sit down to go!"

Max shakes himself awake at the sound of my voice and wipes his drool-soaked arm on the area rug. "I'm not tired!" he whines, flopping onto his back and banging his heels into the floor.

Brice turns his head and regards him, unimpressed. "Puh-lease. You were zonked out over there, Stinky. Use the toilet and get in bed."

"No!"

"If you wake up your sister, I'm going to wear out your butt."

"Don't say 'butt!' That's a potty word! You have to call it a 'bottom.'"

"Whatever I call it, it's going to hurt if you don't march up those stairs right now."

I cast our oldest a wide-eyed wince as I walk over to Brice and gently remove Addi from his back. "I think your dad means business, Stink."

"Naps are stupid!" he says, then runs for the stairs when Brice fakes a move in his direction.

"That's right; you better run, you little stool pickle," Brice mutters under his breath, rising to his feet and lifting Aidan from the floor. "Aw, man! Speaking of turds, we have a dirty one, here."

"Not it," I declare, quickly following the others up the stairs.

He laughs. "Nice."

"Never said I was nice," I toss over my shoulder.

Ten minutes later, when everyone's in their designated nap location, however temporary that may be, I return to the kitchen and my heating pad on the unyielding dining chair that forces me to practice correct posture. My ministrations with heat, cold, over-the-counter pain relievers, and anti-inflammatory medications have paid big dividends.

He trots down the stairs and heads for the fridge, despite the fact that we ate lunch less than an hour ago.

Before I can make any observations out loud about that, he says into the refrigerator, "Christmas break can't end soon enough."

"Sick of changing diapers?"

"That, too. But I do nothing but eat when I'm home!"

"You'd think those two activities wouldn't be very compatible."

"Right? Apparently, my appetite is insatiable."

"Grrrrowl."

He winces. "The only thing 'grrrowl' about it is my noisy stomach." Without retrieving anything from the appliance, he closes it and turns to face me. "You know what? It's New Year's Day."

"Oh, please don't make a resolution to get in better shape, because you're fine the way you are, and buying your nasty health food and cleaning the caked-on protein shake residue from the blender is a pain in the ass."

He slinks toward the table. "That's not what I was going to say, Miss Smarty Pants."

I stick out my tongue at him.

"I was going to say, 'It's New Year's Day, and I never got my kiss at midnight,' because you're mad at me about saying you and your mom are alike."

I clench my jaw. "I'm not mad at you."

"Oh, really? You hardly talked to me at all yesterday, and the proof's in the midnight kiss—or in our case, lack thereof."

"If it makes you feel better, my pillow was the only thing I was kissing at midnight."

Bracing his hands on the table, he leans closer to me, pretends to consider what I've said, then replies, "Nope. Doesn't make me feel better. I think you're mad at me."

"I think you're acting weird."

"Prove you're not mad at me. Kiss me."

Careful not to make any sudden moves to tweak my still-tender back muscles, I crane my neck and place a peck on his chin.

He rolls his eyes. "Lame."

He's right that I didn't talk much to him yesterday, and he's right that it's because I was irritated by what he said, and he knows he's right (about why I wasn't talking to him, not about being like my mom), but I'm also telling the truth when I say I'm over it. I've continued to be quiet today, because that's how I stay off the kids' radar.

"I'm not mad at you. Because there's no point being angry about a completely untrue statement. It would be like being mad at you for saying, 'The sky is yellow.' It's ridiculous."

The corners of his mouth droop downward, then he grins. "M'kay. Good. I didn't say it to upset you. I only wanted you to consider it."

"Consider it considered. And discarded."

He pinches his lips together. "Fair enough. So you're not mad at me?"

"No!"

"Then kiss me. Otherwise, a bunch of sloppy baby kisses

are the only ones I've received today, and that doesn't bode well for the rest of the year."

"As if you believe in superstitions."

"Kiss. Me."

I comply for real this time. He supports the back of my head with his hand, pressing his lips harder against mine. After a few seconds he pulls his face away a few centimeters and wiggles his eyebrows at me. "You feel up for some nap time fun?"

"The back's up for it, but it's my Bye Week."

He straightens and steps away. "Oooh... That's unfortunate."

I grip the edge of the table to keep my seat after his hasty release. "It's not contagious! You don't have to treat me like I have the plague."

Hissing, he makes a cross with his two forefingers and holds them out on extended arms.

"Max is right; you're stupid."

He sobers, dropping his arms and putting one hand on his hip. "About that. I don't know what to do with that kid."

I bite my lip while I decide whether to approach this earnestly or keep up our playful banter. I don't want to start a new argument. However, I've noticed some things after observing him with the kids and staying out of the fray for the past couple of days, and it's going to be hard to point them out without sounding like I've been sitting here, shaking my head in disapproval. I hate when the tables are turned, and he does that to me.

Playful banter, it is, then.

"Well, I think we're supposed to stay the course and keep him alive."

He pulls out the chair at the end of the table and sits, folding his arms in front of him, tapping the insides of his elbows. "No, but really. He's so defiant. And negative. What happened to our sweet little guy?"

"He turned four. He's still sweet most of the time. He's just testing the boundaries, asserting his independence."

"We give him plenty of opportunities to do things for himself, though. So why the attitude?"

I bob my head from side to side.

"You don't think we let him do enough things?"

Tread. Carefully.

"We try. But sometimes we cut in and finish the job for him, and I think that's frustrating for him."

Yes, the royal "we" works well in these situations.

He thinks about that for a while, then replies, "Sometimes we don't have the luxury of giving him ten minutes to put his own clothes on, only to have them be backwards, so he has to undress himself—which takes a while, too—and start over."

I nod. "Yep. I get it. Trust me. I have to get five of them out the door every morning to take Max to preschool."

He smiles sheepishly. "Oh, yeah. I've been doing the dumbed-down version while I've been off, haven't I?" he says, referring to taking Max to preschool alone while the other kids stay with me. When there's been preschool, considering all the days they've been closed for Christmas and New Year.

I merely tilt my head magnanimously. At least he's acknowledging he hasn't been getting the full manic experience, yet he's still having trouble keeping up.

He taps his lips with his forefinger for a few minutes, then shakes his head. "There's nothing we can do about that. Time is finite."

"He'll get faster, if we let him figure it out."

"What are we supposed to do? Get him up at 4:30, so we can be sure he's ready on time?"

I roll my eyes at his hyperbolic suggestion. "No. We supervise better so he doesn't need to start over, for one thing. And on Saturdays, when there's no time crunch, we let him do the whole process himself, as many times as he needs to. That means, we walk away."

"Okay. I can do that. But about the 'tude…"

"We do need to work on that," I concede.

He closes one eye and scratches his neck. "Yesterday, as we were leaving preschool, I asked him about his day, and he said they learned about 'when God 'stroyed the Earth in the flood,' and I was all like, 'Oh, yeah… That's a great story!' and he said, so loud it echoed in the vestibule, where there were a bunch of other kids and parents, 'God is stupid!'"

I press my fist against my mouth.

"It's not funny! I wanted to seep into the floor. And I… I could hardly even react to what he'd said, because the other kids were laughing, and the other parents were like, nervous-laughing but in that way, you know, when you can tell they're thinking, 'That turd's parents must let him get away with murder.'"

"Why, because you think that when kids act out and embarrass their parents in public?"

"No!"

"Then why do you think other people do?"

"It's in the disgusted looks on their faces."

"They're just thinking, 'Thank God my precious little angel isn't the one being a jerk right now.'"

Unsure, he says, "It doesn't seem like it."

"So what did you say to him?"

"I told him that wasn't nice, and we'd talk about it in the car."

"Good. You didn't—I don't know—threaten to spank him?"

He freezes, holds my eye contact, and answers warily, "No…"

"Because that seems to be a go-to threat."

"It gets his attention."

"Not anymore, because he knows you're not going to do it. Ever."

"I don't like doing it."

"Then don't say you will."

He rubs his eyebrow. "Do I really say it that much?"

"In different ways, yes."

"Only with Max?"

"He's the only one who pushes you to that point. For now."

Elbows on the table, he covers his face with his hands. "I'm a horrible parent!"

"No, you're not!"

"Yes, I am. I'm screwing up left and right. And it's show-ing, with Max. The others won't be far behind."

"The others have their own personalities and will react in different ways. Which keeps things challenging—and interesting. Remember how whiny the twins were when they were Aidan's age?"

Brice uncovers his face and blinks. "Yes!"

"Well, he's not whiny, is he?"

"No, he's not."

"See?"

"Yet."

"True. I guess we're not out of the woods, but let's enjoy each un-whiny day as it comes. And as for Max, we just have to be consistent and follow through on the consequences of his defiance. So, is the consequence spanking?"

He sighs. "Oh, gosh. I don't know. I'm not all that comfortable with how often we'd have to swat him. But what other leverage do we have? Time out? Why does that seem so lame most of the time?"

"I don't know. The kids act like it's a huge deal, though." I grab a nearby scrap of paper and a purple crayon from the kids' morning doodle session and write Time out by the number one. "And yes, I'm making a list. And it's going to go on the fridge."

He flaps his lips.

Ignoring him, I ask, crayon poised, "What else?"

He gazes at the ceiling. "How about rewards for good behavior and good attitudes?"

"Yes!"

He lowers his eyes to mine, his forehead smoothing and the corners of his mouth lifting. "Yeah?"

"Totally."

"Because…" He sits taller in his seat. "I feel like maybe he's being a negative jerk all the time because we're negative jerks to him about everything."

"Not everything!"

"No, but it seems like we're always telling him not to do stuff or nagging about how he could do something better, instead of, like, making a big deal out of when he does something right."

"True." I write down Rewards for good behavior.

On a roll now, Brice throws out there, "And maybe we could be funnier. Remember when I used to be funny?"

I pretend to try and fail to recall such a time.

He laughs at my bad acting. "I was! I think. It's been a while."

"I'm teasing you. I still think you're funny. I love listening to you with them."

"I don't feel funny. I feel like I'm all-business. And it's boring. And I'm worried they only know me as that serious guy who tells them what to do all the time."

"You can't always be the jolly good-time man," I defend him. "Sometimes you have to let them know you're in charge. But okay." I write down, Have more fun. "I think this is a good start." I set down my crayon and review the short list. "No need to overwhelm ourselves, right?"

Rising from his chair, Brice comes around the table, takes the paper from me, and sticks it to the front of the refrigerator. "Okay. There it is. Our Three Commandments."

"And the Lord said, 'It was good,'" I intone.

"And Max will say, 'It is stupid,'" Brice adds in a similar, preachy tone. "But we will say, 'How stupid is time out? Because that's where you're going every time you say that word.'"

I giggle.

"And that will be a good strategy, because it is consistent, non-violent, and funny," he declares proudly, stroking the list.

"Yes! See? We're not horrible parents."

"I guess not." He sounds sincerely surprised by that. "Parenting is just so hard!"

I'd like to think it gets easier, but I'm starting to realize that as children grow up, parenting just becomes difficult in different ways.

For some reason, a vision of my mom's face accompanies that epiphany.

≈

Our implementation of The Parenting Commandments effects an immediate change in the house's vibe. And for the rest of the week, I marvel at how well the children behave. And Brice and I get along. And my back muscles uncoil.

Saturday morning, I wake from a dead sleep to the sound of a crash directly below our bed. It's the first time in days I've felt that familiar pit of dread in my stomach at the thought of having to deal with whatever life is going to throw me in the coming hours. Nevertheless, I quickly dress and pad downstairs to see what fresh Hell awaits.

But there's no Hell. Instead, I find most of my family members standing in a line of chairs in front of the pancake-mix-covered counter, with the exception of Brice, who's standing on the floor, and Addi, who's bouncing merrily in her doorway jumper. Each of the younger guys has his own bowl and whisk for maximum mess-making.

My arrival pulls Brice's attention from his cooking lesson, but he only peers over his shoulder for a second to grant me an acknowledging smile and a "Good morning" before continuing his lesson on the art of the perfect pancake.

Wanting to stay out of the way and observe without getting dirty, I forestall my first cup of coffee and take up a position near the pantry doorway after giving Addi a smooch and delighting in her buoyant response.

Brice peers into Max's bowl. "That's enough stirring for you, Stinky. You don't want them to get tough and chewy. Harris, mix up that clump a little better." He cranes his neck to see into the other two bowls. "Brooks, you're good. Whisk down. Aidan... whoa! That's— Hmm... Here, let me just..." He takes hold of the littlest guy's hand and helps him deliver a couple of brisk, effective stirs. "Okay, good! To the griddle!"

He helps each child to the floor, then leads the group to another chair at the island. "It's hot, so one at a time."

One by one, he lifts the boys and helps them pour one pancake-sized serving of batter onto the hot surface. When they've each had a turn, he combines the remaining batter from each of their bowls into one large mixing bowl and whisks it all together. "Great job, guys! Now, watch the master." To their delight, he twirls the spatula, then flips each cake with flair. "Pretty cool, huh?"

"I wanna throw a pancake!" Max says.

"Someday, you'll be able to. But today, we want these to go in our bellies, not on the floor." Before Max can pout about it, he claps his hands at all four of his sons. "Go wash your hands and see if you can get back here before these are ready to eat. Hurry!"

Their bare feet slapping against the floor, they rush from the room.

I take the opportunity to pour myself some coffee, slapping Brice's butt on my way past him.

"Please, don't sexually harass the chef while he's making the magic happen." He punctuates that statement with a cheesy wink and a smirk, then lifts the edge of one of the cakes to check its color.

I survey the disaster area. "What was that huge bang earlier?"

I'm alarmed when he doesn't seem to know what I'm talking about, but his innocent expression falters, and he replies sheepishly, "Harris knocked over the high chair."

"What?!"

I rush over to Addi to inspect her more closely for injuries, but Brice quickly clarifies, "Well, she wasn't in it at the time! Duh." He transfers the first batch of hot cakes from the griddle to a large plate. "No babies were harmed in the making of this breakfast. Which was made with lurve."

"My favorite." As my heart rate returns to normal-ish, I abandon my coffee to dust off the chairs with a damp kitchen towel and return them to their places at the table.

Without an audience, Brice abandons his fancy flapjack flipping and reverts to a more efficient, assembly line style, whistling and singing something that sounds suspiciously like an old Cee Lo Green tune that would require several lyrical modifications to make it suitable for this setting.

As I'm placing the last chair, the kids run into the room and circle their dad. "Are they ready?" Max, the ringleader, demands.

"A few," Brice answers. "Go take your seats, and I'll bring some over after I get the next round going."

He pours six more dollops of batter and circumnavigates the island to reach the table, where the boys eagerly wait. He loads their plates, while I follow behind him with pats of butter and the bottle of syrup, never giving any of them as much as they want, thereby preventing a sugar-fueled night-mare morning and a crash before lunchtime. Brice returns to the stove, and I pour the orange juice.

As I wait for the last batch of cakes to finish browning, I sit at the breakfast bar, sipping my coffee and watching Addi, who's an endless source of twirling, drooling, bouncing entertainment in that contraption. "So she's already eaten?"

"Yes, my bride." His whipped tone earns him a glare over the rim of my mug.

Removing the last pancakes from the griddle, he sets the platter on the counter in front of me, between our two plates.

I prepare my pancakes with more butter and syrup than

I allowed at the table, then cut and spear a bite, holding it in front of my mouth for a few seconds, pretending I'm worried about how it's going to taste.

Brice nudges me with his shoulder. "You're a brat."

Chuckling, I put the bite in my mouth, then chew and make rapturous, bordering on obscene, noises.

Brice bites the inside of his cheek and keeps his eyes on his fork and knife as they slice through the enormous stack of cakes on his plate. "Mommy wants to be tickled," he says loudly enough for the boys to hear.

They giggle, knowing a threat when they hear one.

"Don't you dare," I say with a full mouth.

"You better stop being sarcastic, then."

I swallow. "I'm not being sarcastic!" Swiveling on the stool, I turn to face the boys behind us. "Hey guys, these pancakes are delicious. You did a fabulous job!"

"Daddy helped," Brooks obligingly discloses.

"Well, he did a good job, too. But I think the stirring is what made them so yummy."

He solemnly bobs his head.

I spin back toward my plate, sticking my tongue out at Brice on the way.

He laughs. "Wow. You're full of it this morning."

"You love it, and you know it."

"Maybe."

"There are two things you're really good at," I say wistfully, admiring the golden, fluffy wedge of pancake on my fork's tines. "Flapjacks and fu—"

He clears his throat. "Careful…"

"—un. Der. What did you think I was going to say?" I nudge him with my shoulder.

"Mm-hm." He directs his blushing face toward his plate.

"Repressed," I mutter, popping the latest bite of heaven into my mouth.

With a private smile, he retorts, "I prefer 'mature.'"

"Then why'd you marry me?"

He doesn't immediately supply a witty reply, which surprises and disappoints me, as I was enjoying our game.

The playful smirk fades from my lips when I look over at him and see how earnest he suddenly appears.

"What's wrong?"

He shrugs and attempts a return to his earlier demeanor. "Nothing."

"Liar."

"There's nothing wrong."

"Why so serious, all of a sudden, then?"

"I'm done!"

"I'm done, too!"

"Me, too!"

"I'm sticky!" choruses from behind us.

I sigh. "Just a minute, guys."

Brice, however, pops to his feet and crosses to the sink to wet a wash cloth. "Let me clean you up; then we'll do something fun. Who wants to go with Daddy to the hardware store?"

"Meeeeeeeeeee!"

Brice raises his hands over his head. "Yay! It's unanimous."

"What's inanimus?" Max asks while his dad scrubs his face. "Is 'at like a hippopopamus?"

"Nope," Brice answers. "It means everyone thinks the same thing."

"I like inanimus, then," Max says, hopping from his chair.

"Me, too, Stinky. All right... who's next?"

"I guess that leaves Ladybug and me to clean up the kitchen," I pretend to huff. "Typical!"

Brice doesn't miss a beat. "Addi's going with us, so you're on your own."

"What?!"

"Who else is going to hold my bag of nails?" he quips.

"Very cute. You are kidding, right?"

"Your faith in me today is astounding."

"Just checking!"

He shoos the boys up the stairs to begin the potty-and-dressing process and crosses the room to retrieve Addi, who's been listlessly chewing one of her jumper's straps for the past several minutes. I gather the plates and stack them in the sink, turning on the water to rinse them.

Swinging by on his way toward the stairs, Brice murmurs next to my ear, "Leave the mess. I'll get it later."

"Right."

He backtracks and holds my eye contact. "I'm serious. I think we all need to get out of the house this morning. Go do something you want to do."

I gesture to the chaos around us. "You're crazy."

"Crazy for you," he replies, nuzzling my neck.

I flap my lips, but the rough brush of his morning stubble against my jawline kills any pithy comeback I may have been considering. My eyes flutter closed. My hands fall limp against the edge of the sink. "Mmm…" I hum.

Addi kicks me in the ribs.

And… back to reality.

I flinch away from the baby's toe jabs. "Anyway, what am I going to do? Where am I going to go?"

Brice reaches around me and turns off the water, then strides to the stairs. "Don't know; don't care. It's up to you.

But this all better be exactly the same when I get back from the hardware store."

"What are you even doing at the hardware store? What about taking down the Christmas stuff and putting it away?"

"Epiphany isn't until tomorrow," he says, as if that explains everything. And it kind of does. Except for the trip to the hardware store.

I watch his legs disappear from sight, then survey the room around me. I don't want to deal with this mess right now, if I'm being honest. I don't care if it sits here all day. After a few more seconds of staring at a drip of pancake batter on the floor a few feet away, I push away from the counter and hurry after the rest of them.

"Why are you going to the hardware store?" I call again on my way up the stairs.

Nobody answers me.

24

CONDOLENCES

*T*urns out, you don't have to have a reason to go to the hardware store with all five of your kids on a Saturday morning. At least, I never got a reason out of my husband other than, "It's like the mall for men," which I thought was a ridiculous (and sexist) answer. I'd rather go anywhere (even the hardware store) but the mall on a Saturday—or any day—much less with five young children in tow.

"You're welcome to go with us," he offered safely, winking at my sarcastic laugh. "I thought you'd be thrilled to have some time alone."

And I would be. But my mind went blank when I tried to think of all the things I always want to do when I'm surrounded by diapers and whining, crying, arguing, mess-making kids during the week.

This is one of those times it would probably help if I had some friends. Or even one friend. I know people at our new church and some of the moms at Max's preschool, but when you're not the pastor's wife, people don't go out of their way to invite you to do things. Which I thought would be fine. Excellent, in fact. But that puts the onus on me to be outgoing and take the initiative in making friends. Not my strong suit.

Plus, let's face it, not many parents want to set up play dates with the lady who invades your house for the afternoon with five kids. It's hardly a fair trade-off when you come over with your one little darling the next week. And public venues aren't much better. We tend to embarrass our companions, however inadvertently, with spills and outbursts and stinky diapers. I get it; we're exhausting.

And there are social opportunities for the seminary wives, but my inferiority complex at such events would be crippling. It was hard enough when I was only one of two pastors' wives in residence at Peace, and for much of that time, one of them was my best friend. Not much pressure there, right? I can't imagine being surrounded by pastors' wives. Like, good ones. Eager, helpful, charitable, good-hearted, selfless ones. I'd feel like such a fraud!

I've used my five little built-in excuses so far when the rare invitations have filtered through. For the most part, though, I think people forget Brice has a wife. Which might not be the best thing, now that I think of it. But it's still better than being expected to perform social wifely duties. After all, I trust him. And if you can't trust other pastors' wives... Oh. Well. Anyway. I guess that's a chance I'm willing to take. I'm not worried enough to accompany him to most of the stuff that goes on at The Sem on evenings and weekends, that's for sure. So I haven't met people through his work, either.

And you know, whatever. I'm generally a loner, anyway. Days like this, though, I feel more like a loser.

So here I am.

Sharita's front door must be made of magnets, because it's like I was drawn here against my will. (Darn underwire bra.) Obviously, I had to steer the car and apply the gas and the brake a few times. And pull up to the curb. And get out. And walk across the winter-dormant front yard. But I sure didn't feel in control of any of that. Not that I'm suggesting Divine intervention, or anything. I don't think. Nothing that extreme. Just surreal.

And this is so out of character for me. I don't appreciate when people stop by my house unannounced, without plenty of warning (like, hours; preferably days), so I tend not to do it to others. I know that sickening feeling when the doorbell rings, and you know it's either a stranger trying to sell you something you don't want—possibly even their religion—or worse, an acquaintance who's about to see you when you couldn't swear under oath that you've bathed in the past several days. Neither possibility makes the proposition of opening the door a pleasant one.

Fortunately, Sharita doesn't seem chagrined to see me. She looks sad, since her son's been dead for less than two weeks, but the smile makes it to her eyes when she greets me quietly with, "Miss Peyton," and draws me into her cushy bosom. She smells like gardenia and honeysuckle. (Shower: check.)

After a hug I wish could go on a little longer (yeah, my body has definitely been taken over by something foreign), she holds me at arms' length and eyeballs me. "Look at you! You look good, girl!"

"I do?"

"Yes! Come on in. I thought you were Brice, coming to take down my Christmas lights."

As I follow her into the warm, dim house, I say, "He'll

be by tomorrow afternoon, most likely. He doesn't take down Christmas decorations until Epiphany, not even for friends." When she tosses a questioning look over her shoulder as we bypass the living room and go straight to the kitchen, I remember I'm not dealing with someone who understands the idiosyncrasies of your (not-so-average) average Lutheran, so I explain, "Christmas doesn't officially end until tomorrow, according to the Church calendar."

"Ah. I see. That's fine, anyway. It's going to be even gloomier around here without them."

"If you want to leave them up, tell him. He'd applaud your perpetual Christmas spirit."

She chuckles while slowly walking back and forth through the small kitchen, her plastic-soled house slippers swish-clicking against the spotless linoleum floor as she gathers her tools and materials to make tea. Her laconic movements remind me of a sleepwalker.

"I think that calls for some Christmas tea, then, don't you? I gotta get rid of it before this Epiphany thing starts tomorrow, right?"

"Absolutely."

She keeps the red tin out but puts away the others, then fills the kettle. As soon as she cuts the water, she says, "What brings you here on this cold, gray day? And don't tell me you're here to check on me, because I'm fine, and people have been checkin' on me non-stop for almost two weeks. Like I'm a container of Chinese food about to go bad."

"Just here for a visit," I hastily amend my original answer.

"Good. I like your visits." She pauses while placing the kettle on the stove and turning on the element, then qualifies, "Well, I guess this is the first one besides that other time. I didn't like the reason for that visit so well. No offense." She winces as she lowers herself into the vinyl-covered chair across the table from me, like one recovering from child-birth. (Unfortunately, it's my most common frame of reference.)

At the risk of sounding like I'm checking on her, I ask, "You okay, Sharita?"

At the neighborhood watch kickoff meeting, and a couple of weeks ago when she came to clean my house, I would have placed her in her early- to mid-fifties. Today, she could pass for a much older person.

"When your heart hurts, the rest of the body seems to jump on the bandwagon, you know?"

"Would you be more comfortable in the living room?"

"Nah. It hurts no matter where I am."

In the span of about two seconds, I dismiss about twenty topics of discussion, for one reason or another, but when the silence threatens to drag between us, I panic and say the first thing that comes to mind. "Brice kicked me out of the house this morning."

The statement widens her eyes.

"Not like that." I giggle nervously. "He told me to leave the breakfast dishes—which was only fair, since I didn't make the mess—and do something by myself, for myself."

"And you came here?"

I should say something like, This is where I want to be, but bullshitting a grieving mother is probably the lowest of the low, so instead, I go with honesty. "What can I say? I couldn't think of a single thing I wanted to do. It's like I don't have a personality anymore. And then I found myself at your door."

"Weird," she says, the left corner of her mouth creeping up, her eyes showing a shadow of their usual twinkling.

I laugh. "Right? But I'm not here to check on you," I quickly remind her.

Sharita rolls her eyes and flaps her hands against the table, "Thank goodness. Everyone wants to know how I am, and I want to ask them, 'How do you think I am?' but I have to be grateful for their concern. And I am. I just wish they'd stop asking me such obvious questions. I wish people would remember how to talk to me without thinking, 'Oh, yeah… That's the lady whose son killed himself.'"

All too familiar with that experience, if not the exact circumstances feeding it, I blurt, "That's the worst. When Secret died—"

"Hang on. Who's Secret?"

Oh. Yeah. Shoot. Not the best topic when tiptoeing around talk of children's deaths. Way to go.

However, I don't want her to think I'm talking about my Pomeranian, or something, either, and comparing the death of a pet to her son, so I gulp and stare down at my hands. "My first daughter. We don't have to talk about that, though."

"You and Brice had a baby girl who died? He never mentioned that. Not that he'd have to, I guess. Or that he talks much when he's here. It's always me, blabbing away. But he seems to prefer it that way."

I raise my eyes when she trails off pensively, but she continues before I can speak.

"Oh, honey! I had no idea you two had gone through something so awful. What happened?"

She's right that Brice and I did go through it together, but I feel obligated to correct her assumption. "She wasn't Brice's daughter." Then, learning from other times I've told this story to the unwitting, I explain before she can come to any conclusions more interesting than the reality, "It was before he and I were together. You know, I haven't always been a pastor's wife."

This gets a genuine guffaw from her that lifts the heaviness in my chest. Playfully slapping the top of my hand, she wheezes, "I knew you were a complex one. Still waters, and all that."

"Something like that."

"I'm sorry; I don't mean to laugh. It's not funny, the other thing. And I hope you don't think I'm trying to pull anything juicy from you. But humor an old woman who hasn't been on a date in— Well, maybe ever, since I can't even remember. Tell me about this guy before Brice. Was he a bad boy?"

"He was a gay artist I had a one-night stand with."

She rolls her eyes and snorts. "Okay, okay. I understand. You don't want to talk about it."

"No. For real. That's the truth."

With a turn of her head, she studies me in her peripheral vision, the mother's equivalent of the lie detector test. I widen my eyes and shrug, trying to appear as sincere as possible.

Her eyes return to their normal shape and size, and she regards me head-on once more. "Really," she breathes more as a statement than a question. "Well, I'll be... How did that—"

"I worked with him at a gallery. Sort of. He was one of our contributors. And I didn't know he was gay at the time we... hooked up."

"Did he know?"

"Are you asking if I helped him discover the truth about himself?" I drop my jaw, as if I'm outraged at her suggestion, then I answer, "He knew. He was trying new things. Or something. I don't know. We were also inebriated. Separate from all that, he wasn't a very nice guy, turns out. So I wasn't overjoyed when I found out I was pregnant."

"And you knew the baby was his?"

"Uh, yes."

"Just asking, not judging. Things are different than they were when I was a single woman. Not as different as some people would like young folks to believe—we weren't angels, you know—but there was more of a stigma attached to being with different people. Now, I can't keep track of all of Warwick's girlfriends, and I know they're not just holdin' hands and kissing each other on the cheek. He might think I'm dumb sometimes—at least about that stuff—but just because I choose not to talk about it doesn't mean I'm clueless. I only hope he's being careful."

"There was no mystery who the father was. But the fact that there was a father meant I wasn't smart or careful, in that instance."

She nods. "It happens to the best of us, girl." Not for the first time, I wonder what her situation is and where her boys' father is, but it never seems like the right time, and she doesn't give me a chance to ask now, either. "Anyway, this artist puts a baby in you and walks away? You're right; not nice."

"I already knew he wasn't nice, so I never told him about the baby."

"Oh."

"I told Brice, though. Because he was my pastor."

She perks up in her chair. "Oooh. Now, this is gettin' good." Her face droops. "Except I know the baby part doesn't end well, so maybe I don't want to hear any more."

The kettle whistles. Before she can hoist herself from her chair, I hop from mine and push down gently on her shoulder on my way to the stove. "I'll get it. And you're right; stillbirth isn't the most cheerful subject. We don't have to talk about it."

She swivels so she can keep an eye on me while I pour the hot water over the teabags in the mugs. "I'm interested, though. And I guess it all turned out all right. Maybe I need to know that, that it will be okay someday. Good comes from heartbreak."

I lift my chin and smile. "It does. All the time." I dunk the bags up and down to release more tea into the water, then I let them steep. I stare at the tag on the end of the string trailing from one of the cups and say, "It hurt to lose Secret. But maybe the biggest heartbreak from the experience was the shift in my relationship with my dad. It was never the same after that."

After a regretful "Tsk," she replies, "That's hard. And now, he's… gone?"

All I can do is jerk my head once. When my throat reopens enough for speaking, I try to return the conversation to a more upbeat track. "But Brice picked up the pieces."

Her chuckle brings my focus back to her face.

"What?" I ask.

She shakes her head. "Nothing. It's just interesting to get a different perspective on something you think you have all figured out, you know?"

When I merely stare at her, she expounds, "Brice doesn't say much when he comes over to see me, but what he does say has led me to believe you're the steady one in the relationship."

I scoff at the idea, but she puts up her hands at shoulder level. "Just calling it like I see it. He can count on you. You're consistent."

"Consistently crazy," I mutter.

"What did he do for you after you lost that baby that was so heroic, anyway?" she challenges lightly. "He was there for you?"

"Yeah!"

"Well, that's great, and all, but don't you think he would have been there, no matter what? Because that's what you do for someone you love. But you still had to pull yourself through it. You had to overcome that grief, a sorrow like no other. Nobody could do it for you, not even him."

While I digest what she's said, something I've never considered quite that way, I place the teabags in the sink, then carry the mugs to the table. I set one in front of Sharita but keep my hands wrapped around mine as I retake my seat.

Quietly, hoping it comes out the way I intend, I state, "I never knew Secret, though, really."

"She was still your baby."

I think about it, then allow, "Yeah, and I was sad, but I didn't have any memories of her. At the time, I thought I understood pain, thought what I was going through was the worst anyone could go through. But it wasn't. A few months later, Brice's dad died, and I saw the difference." I stare down into my tea as I try to verbalize the distinction. "When Secret died, I mourned what could have been. When Augustus died, Brice grieved for what actually had been. And that's very different. I've confirmed it this past year, with my own dad's death. It's not that the emotions are different—it's all grief—but the depth…"

I re-focus my eyes and lift my head to make sure I haven't said anything to upset my friend. She merely bites her lower lip and gives me an encouraging head-bob.

"In other words, I don't think you and I have been through the same thing—at all. It's like— like"—I scramble to make a comparison, nearly shouting when one finally lands and sticks—"the difference between a large lake and the ocean! Before I'd ever seen the ocean, I told Brice I expected it to be like Lake Michigan, only salty, and he laughed at me, and I thought, 'Whatever, Jerkazoid. How different can it truly be? It's water for as far as the eye can see, and the eye can't see far enough to know the difference.'" I laugh at the memory of my clueless self. "Then I actually saw the ocean. And experienced its power. And I was embarrassed by my ignorance."

Sharita holds her cup to her lips, but before sipping, she regards me steadily. "You can drown in a bathtub, though."

We let that statement hang between us while we drink, breathing in the cinnamon- and clove-scented brew.

After a few minutes, she sets down her cup with a clink against the Formica tabletop. "So you lost that baby and all your illusions about your daddy, but you gained a Brice. And a second chance at life. And more babies followed. Lots more babies." She cocks an eyebrow at me. "You having any more babies?"

Her summary of our life to date cracks me up, as does her question, which comes with its own implied answer: You probably shouldn't have any more babies.

Sure enough, when I say, "No more babies," she relaxes in her chair and releases a breath I didn't realize she was holding while she waited for my reply.

"You have your hands full, that's all," she says, hastening to defend her reaction.

"Plus, Addi almost killed me. Literally."

Sharita shakes her head. "Mmm-mmm. For real? That sweet little thing? I don't believe it!" She winks at me.

"I know, right? She's all cute and innocent, but I was in a

hospital bed for months before she was born, then in a coma for six days after."

"Whoo-ee! I think you're right to stop, then."

"My mom thinks I should have stopped sooner. Not that she wishes Addi was never born. But, you know…"

"Heavens, yes! Before she ever knew that sweet baby girl, she was worried for her baby girl, that's all."

I say nothing—can say nothing—when I realize how elegantly true her statement is.

Oblivious to my astonishment, she continues, "If I had a daughter with four little boys and another baby on the way, I'd be fit to be tied. God must have known not to give me girls. It would have been ugly."

"It gets ugly between my mom and me—frequently," I recover enough to confirm.

"Is she as quiet and fierce as you?"

I wave a hand at that description. "Me? Fierce?"

"Oh, yes! You're intense! If your mama's half as intense as you, I can see where it would get nasty in a hurry when you two don't see eye-to-eye."

I shake my head and study the reddish film of tea glazing the bottom of the mug. "She and I are nothing alike."

"Then why do you clash so bad?"

"She's always second-guessing me. No matter what."

"Can I say something, and you won't get mad?"

"I hate that question."

She laughs. "I guess I'm gonna say what I'm gonna say and not worry if it makes you mad, because I think you need to hear it. And it'll take my mind off my own problems for a minute, so you have to humor me."

When I don't object, she covers my hand with hers and squeezes it. "Cut your mama some slack."

I clench my jaw.

"She may be doing everything wrong under the sun, but do you think she's trying to do everything wrong? Do you think she sees the result of what she says and does and thinks, 'Yeah, that's workin' for me'?"

"No."

"Do you think you're doing everything right with your little ones?"

I remember the list on the refrigerator and the conversation between Brice and me that led to it. Then I think of all the other times I've questioned myself or wondered not just if I'm screwing up my kids but how badly I'm damaging them. "No."

"Do you want them to love you anyway and give you credit for trying?"

"Of course."

"Then do the same for your mama. I know it's a little different, more complicated, when you're dealing with grown-up stuff, but try to make it less complicated in your head. As uncomplicated as you can. Because, sugar?"

I look up at her and blink the tears from my eyes.

"I know you already know this, and you've had to learn it the hard way: life's too darn short."

She must be thinking of Nelson, and I am, too, but I'm also thinking of many others. Secret. Augustus. Dad. Even Pastor Long. All of them, here one day, gone the very next, with no warning.

I swallow and nod. "I know. You're so right."

"And your life's gonna be shorter than it should be if you don't start taking better care of yourself and cuttin' out the unnecessary stress." She lets go of my hand and pulls her arm back toward herself, running her finger along the rim of her mug.

I sigh.

"Hey, a doctor would tell you the same thing. I just saved you fifty bucks."

Groaning, I say, "You're right again. I know I look terrible—"

"Doesn't have a thing to do with how you look! You're pretty damn fine, considering what must go on in that house of yours on a daily basis. But it's how you feel. How you cope with the unavoidable stuff life throws at you." She squeezes my knee. "It's how you recover from the less-than-perfect ways you may have reacted to something—or someone—in the past. You know what I'm saying?"

"I think so."

"Call your mama."

"Oh, Sharita…"

"She just wants to hear you say you still love her. Trust me. I'd give anything to get that phone call right now. Or to make it. My mama's been dead twenty years. And don't think we always agreed on everything. But if she was here now, she'd hug me and tell me I was a good mom and a good woman, even though she hardly ever said that to me out of the blue. But she's my mama. And the last thing a mama wants to see is her baby hurting."

Her eyes fill, and mine do, too, almost as predictably as a sympathetic yawn.

She stands and takes our cups to the sink, where she stares out the window into the backyard for a few seconds before abruptly turning to face me.

The tears are still there, but she smiles through them. "You know what we need? Chocolate cake."

My pancakes are still sitting heavily in my stomach, but that doesn't stop me from readily agreeing with her needs assessment.

"My cousin Donetta owns a bakery just the other side of Forest Park. I'm sure I can guilt her into giving us some free cake."

I laugh at her tongue-in-cheek scheming.

"Sounds like a great plan," I say, rising and pulling my keys from my jeans pocket. "I'll warm up the van."

25

FORGIVING DAD

a week passes, but I still don't reach out to my mom. I have a list of reasons for not calling her, chiefly that it's the first week back to our normal schedule, and the kids aren't making it easy to follow The Parenting Commandments on the fridge. And just as they've finally realized they're stuck with me all day again, and I'm serious about reintroducing structure to their lives, I had to wake up feeling like this. Calling Mom today wouldn't end well.

It's maddeningly frustrating to be furious with a dead guy. There's no outlet for it. It's probably the strain of the week finally catching up to me, but the cause of the mood isn't my biggest concern. My chief worry is that runaway emotions manifest themselves into a full-on rage I direct at someone who's no longer here to care I'm livid with him—if he ever cared.

Recognizing the feeling within the first few seconds of wakefulness, I took a rare morning shower before Brice left for work. I tried to wash away the anger, but it lingered like wood smoke clinging to hair and clothing. I muddled through the morning and early afternoon, irritable and thin-skinned, praying none of the other moms would try to talk to me when I dropped off and picked up Max at preschool (prayer answered). I barely spoke ten words to the kids during lunch, and I barked orders like a drill sergeant in the lead-up to nap time.

But now... Now that I have a minute to myself, I sit at the kitchen table and give in to my smoldering temper tantrum.

At first, I just bite my lip and mutter obscenities under my breath. That escalates into talking out loud. Then I slap and pound the surface in front of me, as if the wood is my father's face or chest, not a cold, impersonal slab. Hands stinging, I collapse onto my folded arms and yell into the muffling crook of my elbow, "Damn you!" until I'm hoarse.

Imagine my mortification—and momentary terror—when I hear the back door click shut behind me. I whirl in my chair to see Brice standing just inside the house, looking one part alarmed, one part pitying.

Worried I may have fallen into a rage-induced fugue state, I seek out the time on the microwave, but it isn't even two o'clock.

"What are you doing here?" I snap, dragging my palms across my soaked cheeks.

"What are you doing?" he counters.

"What does it look like?"

Taking a couple of tentative steps closer, as if he's worried I'm a danger to myself and others (mostly him), he ventures, "Having a bad day? Did the kids do something?" He searches for evidence of mischief on a scale capable of triggering a complete mommy meltdown. Finding none, he has no choice but to turn back to me.

Seeing the worry and fear in his eyes, I blubber, "I'm sorry. I didn't mean to scare you. I'm just… sad." Propping my elbow on the table, I plunk my head in my hand.

He pulls out the chair next to mine and sits, giving my back a couple of jerky pats. Then, warming to the task after determining I'm not going to bite, he lengthens his strokes. "Aw, hon. Those aren't sad tears. What's going on?"

"My dad's dead."

"Oh. Yes. He is."

"And… and… I hate him."

"Oooh. 'Hate' is—"

"I know! It's wrong. It's so wrong. I'm wrong."

"No, you're not. You're hurt."

Sitting up straighter, I nod. "Yes," I whisper, then go on in a louder voice, "How could he? How could he die before —" I take a deep, chest-shaking breath. "I wasn't ready. I needed him to say some things first."

"Like what?"

Brice's face swims in the pooling tears elicited by the mere thought of the answer. I shake my head and mumble, "I can't say it."

"Sure, you can."

"No. He needed to say it, not me."

"You're going to have to do it for him. Unless you're willing to wait until you see him again."

"He'll never say it, not even then."

"I bet he thought it a million times."

Spittle flies unattractively when I explode, "A fat fuck lot of good that does me. I needed to hear him say it, damn it! But he was never brave enough. Never big enough. Never man enough."

Unfazed by my outburst, Brice asks calmly, "Can you

find it in yourself to be all of those things for him?" He pauses, his hand stilling between my shoulder blades. "Well, except for that last one."

"I shouldn't have to be. It's his responsibility."

"Not anymore, for obvious reasons."

"Well, that sucks." I push my chair back with a loud squeal on the wood floor and a clatter against the side of Brice's chair. "Screw him."

Brice has no response to that, so while I cross the room and mop my face with paper towels absorbent enough for kids' spills but apparently not up to the task of clearing away the tears and snot produced during a gigantic snit, I grumble, "What are you doing home?"

He pinches the bridge of his nose. "I, uh… Why am I home?" he repeats, as if at a loss. Shaking his head, he rises and fingers the white square at his throat. "Oh. I wrote some lecture notes on my laptop and forgot to email them to myself."

"You should use The Cloud. Your notes could be anywhere you are."

"Yes. True." He opens his mouth then closes it again.

"I'm okay. I'm not going to hurt anyone. The person I want to kill is already dead."

With a weak chuckle, he closes the gap between us and circles his arms around me. I want to push him away, want to tell him I'm not in the mood to be comforted, but I don't want to hurt his feelings, so I submit to his hug, counting to ten to distract myself from the immature urge to shake him off.

When he finally pulls away and studies my face, I supply a tight, watery smile. "Get your notes."

He rewards my perceived bravery with an affectionate

pat to my damp cheek. "I love you. And, uh, you've got a little…" He mimes swiping under his nose, then after a final pat to my arm and a kiss to my forehead, crosses to the stairs and quietly climbs them.

About a minute later, he returns, and I expect him to head for the door to get back to work, but he hesitates at the bottom of the stairs.

Assuming he's still concerned about me, I wave him off. "Don't worry. I just needed a moment."

"I'm more worried about your dad, when you finally do see him again."

"Lucky for him, they make you check your grudges at the gates. Or so I imagine." I take a deep, shaky breath and busy myself at the fridge, deciding now's a good time to try to figure out what to make for dinner.

While I stare into the depths of the freezer, it feels like Brice stares into the depths of my soul. I hate when he does that.

"Would you please stop staring at me?"

He shakes his head as if breaking from a trance. "Huh? Sorry. I was thinking."

"Yeah, thinking about what a nutjob I am."

"No."

"Whatever. You don't have to deny it. I think I'm a nutjob on days like this, too. But I can't help it." I toss a family-sized package of frozen pork chops onto the counter with a clink. They slide to rest against the microwave, where they're going to spend the next several minutes defrosting, after I transfer them to a plate.

"Does this happen often?"

"Enough," I admit.

"Maybe you should tell a professional about that." As

soon as the words leave his lips, he braces for an impact that never comes.

"Maybe," I quietly reply.

His posture slackens, and he pulls out a chair at the kitchen table. "Come here and sit with me a sec."

Rooting in the utility drawer for a pair of kitchen shears, I mumble, "I need to get these pork chops defrosting."

In an instant, he traverses the kitchen, grabs the package of meat, and tosses it into the freezer, which he slides closed with authority. "Forget the pork chops. I'll bring home Chinese. Or something."

Shears in hand, I gape at him. "What the…?"

He removes the scissors from my grip, drops them into the drawer, and pulls me by the hand to the table. "Here. Now."

"Don't you have to get back to—"

"Yes." He peeks at the time on his phone, then pockets it again. "But I have a few minutes. And I need to tell you this. I should have told you a long time ago, but— Well, I guess I almost did. Then we got the call about Nelson. But I should have told you before then, even. A long time ago. I just—" He scratches the top of his head. "I'm starting to feel responsible for this anger you have toward your dad."

I stare at my lap. "It's not your fault he was a jerk."

Over the corner of the table, he grabs both of my hands, rubbing the tops of them with his thumbs. Such nice, gentle, capable thumbs. Thumbs that have wiped tears and stroked away hurts and assisted with diaper changes and composed funny text messages and turned Bible pages and typed thoughtful, pensive, sermons.

"I love your thumbs," I blurt. Okay, not a good way to convince him of my sanity. In response to his questioning expression, I shrink in my seat. "Sorry. Not the right time, I guess."

"Maybe not. Although I'm not sure where an Ode to Thumbs would ever fit into a conversation."

I laugh at myself. "Never mind. You were saying…?"

Now that he's about to tell me what I think he's about to tell me, I'm not sure I'm ready. I was prepared those other times—on the stairs after our argument by the Christmas tree; in his office, seconds away from finding the journal entry that may have mentioned the conversation; on our dinner date. In those moments, I would have been receptive to hearing the memory.

Now, I'm less sure. Am I in the right frame of mind to hear a story about my dad? Not really. Not unless it ends in his pain and suffering, and since encounters between Dad and Brice usually had the opposite result, I'm not sure this tale's going to fit the bill.

"Before you say anything," I interject while Brice contemplates where to start, "does this end well for you? Because, honestly, if the story ends with him saying something typically insensitive and asshole-ish, then forget it. I don't want to hear it today."

Brice tilts his head. "It ends with me marrying you. So yes, it ends very well for me."

"That's debatable," I mumble, then smile so he won't waste time with a lecture about how great I am. I can't stomach that, either.

He winks at me and takes a deep breath. "You already have the background. Your dad invited me over to talk man-to-man, or whatever."

"Yes. I have the context."

He swallows. Staring at our linked hands, he watches a memory he seems to know well enough to recite in his sleep.

"Your dad took control right away. He asked me, 'Why Peyton?' and I was like, 'Excuse me? I love her. And why not her?'" He raises his eyes. "No matter how many times I told myself I wasn't going to get defensive— I mean, I was prepared for him to attack me, but I lost all focus when he began the discussion with that question."

I close my eyes.

Brice squeezes my hands. "Hang on. Keep listening."

I breathe deeply, praying the story improves soon.

"Since it was clear his opening question bothered me, your dad said, 'Oh, c'mon. You know I don't mean it that way. I just mean, why do you love her? Not that I think it's strange or impossible for you to love her. But why? What are the reasons?'

"I was still confused and more than a little offended by his probing, so I said, 'You want me to give you some Hollywood, bull hockey answer, like, "She completes me," or "I can see our unborn children in her eyes"?'"

I can't help but snicker, totally able to hear both of them in my head. I open my eyes, and despite my trepidation, I smile. "This is already classic."

He releases a wobbly smirk. "Oh, it gets better. So, he said to me, 'No! As a matter of fact, I want to make sure that's not your answer. I need to hear something concrete, something practical that tells me you're not just sniffing around—'"

"Nuh-uh."

"Right? I had the same reaction. Although I didn't say that, because I was too busy walking toward the front door. I knew I'd made a mistake agreeing to talk to him, and all that would result from the conversation would be more animosity. He stopped me, though. He said, 'You think I want to ask you this? You think I want to have this talk?' I pointed out we were only having the conversation because he'd called me there and was leading it."

He stops, takes a breath as if to continue, then grunts, looking down at the table. "Hm."

"Oh, geez. This is the bad part, isn't it?"

He clamps his lips together. "Mm-hm."

"Maybe you can skip this part? Or give me the gist? Or just... Never mind. I don't need to know."

Chin tilted down, he shoots me a skeptical look through his lashes.

I sigh. "Okay. You're right. I have to know now."

"Keep in mind that you're about to hear some things that are going to chafe. But just let me get through it, okay?" He raises his chin, his eyes grabbing mine and holding tight. "Remember, this was a while ago. None of your outrage now is going to change what was said."

I sigh. "Great. Okay. I promise not to interrupt you or fly off the handle."

My hand receives a rewarding pat for my guarantee. "Good. So, after your dad claimed not to be enjoying the conversation, he said, 'I need to know I'm handing her off to someone who can take care of her the way she deserves to be taken care of.'"

I grit my teeth but don't say a word.

"I immediately challenged him on his wording, especially the 'handing her off' part, and he got impatient with me and said, 'I'm not good with words, okay? You know what I'm trying to say. Why are you making this difficult?' Mostly to move the discussion along, I let it go and asked, 'How do I prove anything to you? What do I say?' He said, 'Do you have any idea what you're doing?' I replied, 'Having a ridiculous conversation, at the moment.' He didn't appreciate my joke, which wasn't really a joke; I was truly at a loss and didn't know what else to say. But he was like, 'Don't get smart with me, preacher boy!'"

I suppress a groan.

Brice continues, "That's when he really let me have it. He said, 'Let me break it down for you. Peyton is precious. And I don't mean it in that snide, sarcastic way folks say it nowadays. It's just the best word I can think of to describe her, but it doesn't even come close to hitting the mark. I love all my kids, and I know you're not supposed to have a favorite, but when you're a father someday—especially if you're ever blessed with a daughter—you'll see. It happens. It's not something you can use a simple word like 'favorite' to describe. But that's what Peyton is to me.'"

I blink and breathe away the tears. "Oh…"

Brice murmurs down at the table, "Yeah." After a pause, he continues, "Of course, I was still intent on winning the argument, so I said, 'Pardon my saying, sir, but you have an interesting way of showing it. As a matter of fact, I know she thinks exactly the opposite is true.' Instead of making him angrier—which was kind of my goal, if I'm being honest—those words seemed to deflate him. He stared at his feet and said, 'Yeah, well, I can't very well go around broadcasting it, can I?'"

I sob/hiccup and rest my forehead on the table.

Brice cups the back of my head in his palm. "I know, hon. I'm sorry I didn't tell you sooner."

I move my head back and forth, feeling the wood warm from the friction against my skin.

He moves his hand under my hair to the back of my neck. "I thought it needed to come from him. I kept waiting for him to tell you that himself. Or something close to it. It felt like it wasn't my place to say, 'Hey, you know, you're your dad's favorite. He just doesn't know how to say it.' And then his chance to say it was gone. And I could never find the right time to tell you about that conversation. I couldn't tell you the good part only. For one thing, you wouldn't have believed me. I had to tell you the whole thing, and most of it wasn't flattering, for your dad or for me. I was so afraid to show you that side of me, a side that would goad another man into feeling such shame. Of course, it's hardly the worst you've ever seen of me, but—"

"Shhh." I wave my hand blindly in his direction and don't stop until I make contact with his face, his eyelashes brushing my fingertips. "Finish your story." I drop my hand to my lap.

He gulps, then clears his throat. "Okay. When I still challenged him about your needing some indication that he accepted you for who you were, he said, 'Peyton doesn't need me to coddle her. She can take care of herself, and then some. She's strong. Sometimes too strong. Can you handle that?' At the time, I told him I didn't plan to try 'handling' you in any way.

"Then he asked me if I fancied myself your savior. When I told him you already had One of those, and I didn't consider myself close to being Him, he finally seemed satisfied with something I'd said. He was like, 'It's good you recognize that, that you don't have some sort of God complex, some notion of "fixing" her. Because she doesn't need you to change her.' Then, like that, he stood up and offered me his hand and said, 'I'm glad we had this talk.' I was like, 'I'm glad one of us is glad.' He actually laughed at that and said, 'You're a good guy. Not good enough for my Princess P, but I guess you're the closest we're going to get. You're an improvement on the others she's brought around.'"

Brice stops. Voice choked with emotion, he declares, "That's probably the nicest thing he ever said to me."

I raise my puffy face. "That's so sad!"

He shrugs. "I'll take it. At the time, I wasn't very gracious about it, though. I told him I wasn't going to ask for his permission or blessing to marry you. Your permission and God's blessing were the only things that mattered. He bluntly told me I was naïve, to which I replied that I was okay with that."

For the second time this afternoon, I rub tears from my face. Brice hops up and disappears, returning a few seconds later with a full box of tissues from the bathroom. After I honk my nose and wipe and dab my face dry, he says, "Do you see now? That's what I think about every time you and I butt heads about... stuff. I remember him asking me, 'Do you think you can handle that?' and how cocky I was when I told him your strength could only be a positive thing, as far as I was concerned. I hate how right he's turned out to be."

Hackles raised, I pull my head back. "What are you saying? That if you'd known how stubborn I could be, you wouldn't have married me?"

His eyes nearly pop from his head. "No! I hate that I sometimes see your strength as a negative, as something that gets in the way of my getting my way. I hate that he was right about it so often be a sticking point in our marriage."

"Sorry!"

"You're not understanding what I'm trying to say."

"I guess not."

"Which makes this a perfect example of what your dad was talking about."

I take a deep breath and make a concerted effort to calm down and be more receptive. After all, the last thing I want is to prove my dad right—about anything. On a shaky exhale, I say, "Please, explain."

His shoulders relax. "You make it so hard for me to be there for you, because you never want anyone—not even me—to know that you could possibly need support. For anything. You think vulnerability equals weakness, and weakness is something you'll never allow in yourself. But sometimes you have to let someone else—me, in most cases—be the strong one, if for no other reason than to stroke my stupid ego."

"But why should I sacrifice my pride to build up your ego? That's not a good enough reason!"

"I'm sure your dad had the same justification."

"For what?"

"For everything. Mostly, for not telling you exactly how he felt about you. And for not apologizing to you about how he treated you after you told him about Secret."

Before I can challenge him on this annoyingly perfect theory, he stands and squeezes my shoulder. "I have to get back to campus."

Mouth hanging open, I tilt my head back to gape at him. "But—"

He winces. "Sorry! I have a lecture in, like, fifteen minutes. I know right now wasn't the best time to tell you, but it couldn't wait, either. I obviously forgot those notes"—he gestures toward the stairs and the general direction of his office—"for a reason. Take that, Cloud."

I sniff resolutely. "Okay. Yeah. I'm fine."

Being alone might be best right now, anyway.

He kisses the top of my head. "I'll bring home dinner, like I said. Try to enjoy the kids after they wake up. Or something."

I roll my eyes. "Yeah. Or something."

At the door, he turns, a mischievous half-smile on his lips and a twinkle in his eyes. "Just out of curiosity, which one is your favorite right now?"

It takes me a second to realize what he's asking, but when I do, I try to muster an indignant noise. "Brice!"

He squints at me. "C'mon. You don't have to be ashamed of it."

Without explanation, I reply, feeling guilty despite his absolution, "Brooks."

"He's a pretty cool customer." He winks at me, and when I think he's going to leave without sharing his own confession, he pulls open the door, bites his bottom lip, and looks down at the floor. "Your dad was right about something else. I love my boys. Love them. I love how Stinky's so sure of himself; I love how the littlest things make Squeaky happy; I love how Screamy's a deep thinker; I love watching Angel Boy try so hard to keep up with his big brothers. And I thought love was love and there was no way I could love one of my children more than the others. And I don't, technically. But Addi, my Ladybug... " He rests his flat hand over his heart. "She's set apart from the others. And there could be a lot of reasons for that. Maybe most of them aren't even good reasons. But that doesn't mean they don't exist. And it's only going to get more intense. As soon as she says my name and greets me after work and rests her head on my shoulder and holds my face between her chubby hands and gives me wet, open-mouthed kisses on my cheek... I don't know why it'll be different than with the others, but it will be."

I dab at the latest tear to try to make its great escape down the side of my face.

Brice, staring into space, either doesn't notice or pretends not to. After a few seconds, he blinks back to attention. "It's just inevitable." Without another word, he walks through the door and closes it behind him.

A few seconds later, I hear the van's engine turn over, and I watch through the kitchen windows as he slowly drives back to the other half of his life, a new academic life that makes him happy and seems a lot less fraught with worry than his previous occupation—or his current home life.

26

DADDY'S GIRL

I was my dad's favorite.

Huh.

Hmph.

Well.

Interesting.

Of course, maybe that's not saying much. Nicole was and always will be Mom's favorite, so she'd already been picked for a team. Jason... Well, you'd think being the only son would make him Dad's logical favorite, but they were never that close. Sure, they'd go to football and baseball games and play golf together, but there was always this underlying tension between the two of them. And when Jason came out, that pretty much sealed his fate where Dad was concerned. Not saying Dad didn't still love Jason, but being gay wasn't necessarily something that further endeared him to our father.

So I was Dad's favorite by default.

There's nothing "default" about "precious," though, is there? That's a word you use to describe something valuable and rare and cherished.

Oh, gosh. I don't think I can handle that.

So Brice dropped that bomb on me, then skedaddled off to his lecture. I couldn't very well call Nicole and Jason. For one thing, it was the middle of a weekday. For another, can you imagine that conversation?

"So, uh, I was Dad's favorite. Can you believe that shit?"

"Duh."

"Figures."

"But... but He treated me like dirt half the time!"

"That's how you should have known you were his favorite."

"Yeah, he treated me like dirt all the time, especially because I refused to let him win at golf."

It's not something you discuss with your siblings. It would feel like bragging, when really, I'm only trying to make sense of it, to get a second or third opinion on it. Like, maybe Brice misunderstood. Maybe he's misremembering. He seems pretty sure of the memory. A little too sure. After all, who remembers a conversation in that much detail?

I hope he doesn't remember all of our conversations in that much detail. Although, that would explain why every stupid thing I've ever said comes back to haunt me. Oh, sheesh. I married a conversational savant. Great. I hope none of our children inherited that trait, or I'm in trouble.

Anyway, I humored Brice and gave him an answer when he asked which of our kids is currently my favorite, but all kidding aside, I don't buy into the "favorite" thing. Having a favorite implies my love for them is conditional, like they can do—or not do—things to curry favor with me. And that's just not true.

I don't love Harris less because he's been slower to potty train than Brooks. I don't love Brooks more because he seems to listen better and obey more readily than the others.

I may enjoy the company of Aidan more than Max right now, because Aidan still indulges me in a cuddle now and then, whereas Max doesn't like to sit still—or shut up—long enough for that. But then again, the other four kids don't make me laugh as much as Max does. And Addi, my miracle baby... She's special to me for so many reasons, but that doesn't mean my love for her is stronger than my love for her brothers.

It doesn't work that way.

That being said, Dad's love did seem conditional, so the fact that he chose favorites shouldn't be all that surprising, should it? I was probably just his favorite because I pissed him off the least. And you know what? No thanks. I don't need that validation.

Actually, it makes me angrier at him, knowing he felt that way about me but withheld the information. He was right not to overtly declare a favorite, but he was wrong to let me go on believing he didn't love me as much as he did. What would it have cost him to say it? Nothing. Yet, it would have made such a difference to me, personally, and to our relationship!

And now I've been furious with him all these months, so in addition to feeling bereft all over again, I have to feel guilty for that and for assuming the worst of him all those years before his death. But what else was I supposed to think? What did he expect? Why didn't he do something about it? He alone had the power to change that, and he chose not to.

But the worst, most devastating thing is that I feel responsible for his death. Because Mom told me he worried about me. And now Brice tells me Dad considered me "precious." If I really did mean that much to him, could he have worried himself to death about my condition? If so, my decisions, my choices, may have killed him.

How the hell am I supposed to live with that?

It used to be that when I was dealing with something heavy, I'd soak it in wine to make it lighter. I didn't resort to it often, and it's been a while since it's been an option, considering I've been pregnant nearly constantly for the past five years, but it's been a rough couple of months. And I'm tired of feeling so sad, so down, so *ponderous*. After a while, a girl just needs to forget about everything for a night and have some fun. Usually, she does this with her best friends. Well, I only have one handy, so…

"I wanna make a toast!" I declare, topping up both of our wineglasses (although his has hardly been touched).

Brice sits forward on the couch and steadies the bottle in my less-than-accurate hands. "Easy."

I giggle and set the mostly empty bottle down with a hard *thunk* on the coffee table. "Sorry. I'm a little tipsy already, I think."

"Just a little," he says with a smirk, lifting his glass in my direction. "But anyway. A toast. To?"

"To parenthood," I intone earnestly.

"Okay. To parenthood." He nudges his glass closer to mine, but I pull mine back.

"Wait. I'm not finished."

Glass still aloft, he blinks and waits.

"To parenthood. And parents. And children of parents."

His lips twitch. "So… to everyone?"

I think about it. "Oh. Yeah. I guess so."

"Can we clink now?"

"Yes."

We tap our glasses together, then drink. Brice holds up his dark red wine to the light after a sip much smaller than mine. "I foresee an early bedtime for you tonight."

"Are you saying I can't hold my liquor?"

"This is hardly liquor. And it's a good thing. You've become quite the lightweight."

I sneer at myself. "Right? It's just as well, though. We can't afford to buy alcohol in the volumes I used to be able to drink. The Trippin' Trio used to put. It. Away."

"Charming." He sets his mostly full glass on the table. "What's all this about, anyway?"

"Why does there have to be a reason? It's Friday night. The kids are in bed—finally. We survived Christmas and Jen and Vince's wedding and Nelson's funeral and getting the kids back into a normal routine. Isn't that enough? We don't cut loose as much as we should."

"Because we live with five people who don't know the difference between Saturday morning and all the other mornings. Except that I'm around. And if anything, that gets them up earlier. And taking care of loud little people with a hangover isn't a good time."

"They won't have hangovers."

In spite of himself, he laughs at my deliberate misinterpretation. "But you will."

"Nah! I'll drink some water before bed."

"I'm not getting drunk with you."

"You're breaking the third Parenting Commandment: have more fun!"

"I think there's an implied commandment that one parent has to be sober at all times."

I drain the rest of my wine, set my glass next to his, and crawl into his lap.

"What are you doing?"

"Having more fun."

He grunts underneath me and flinches when I bounce too heavily in his lap. "Fun, huh?"

I wiggle my eyebrows, my face about an inch from his. His eyes cross, then refocus. "Yes, fun. It's not like I get silly all the time."

"No. Thank goodness," he tacks on the end in a mutter.

"And when I do, you like to pretend you're too above it all to find it funny. But you love it."

He lowers his chin and blinks at me. "Oh, do I? Honestly, I'm not loving this."

"Why not?"

"Because I know this isn't about simply having fun, and before the night's over, I'll have to help you to bed and tuck you in, and worry about whether you're going to be sick. Plus, I'll be dealing with five kids by myself tomorrow morning—not to mention a hung over wife—and… you're smashing the ol' apostles."

I dismount him with a harumph. "Fine."

Adjusting himself, he asks, "Is this about what I told you this afternoon?"

My sullen shrug lets him know he's close.

"Ah. I see."

The couch's upholstery receives my intense scrutiny. "I know I'm proving you right for not telling me about it sooner, too, so you don't have to be all 'I told you so,' either."

"It hadn't even crossed my mind."

"Whatever." I curl up in the corner of the sofa, plunking my fist into my cheek and staring at the dark TV. In its reflection, I see Brice rub the back of his neck, then both see and feel him scoot down the couch toward me.

"Hon." He rubs my arm.

I half-heartedly push him away with my foot. "Never mind."

He doesn't let my churlishness deter him. "C'mon. Getting drunk isn't the way to handle this. You're only going to pay for it later."

"You can never just humor me, you know?" I turn my head to level my accusation at him. Mistake. The concern in his dark blue eyes kills me. "Stop looking at me like that. I'm not some pathetic drunk who gets hammered every night to numb some melodramatic demons." Rushing on before he can call me on my mixed metaphor about thespian ghouls who have indulged in too much Novocain, I say, "I wanted to have a good time, for once. Is that so much to ask?"

"No. But is this a good time?"

"No. Thanks to you, it's not."

He edges closer still, practically sitting on my feet, leaning his weight against my arm. "It's not a good time, because you're forcing it."

"And you're over-analyzing it, as usual."

A kiss lands on my shoulder. "You know I'm right."

"You always are. Why would this be any different?"

Bemused, he points out, "You're determined to start a fight, and I'm not taking the bait. That's definitely not a good time."

"What am I supposed to do with this information?" I ask, hoping he's not too sober to follow my wine-soaked stream of consciousness. It's not a random question for me; I've been listening to it echo in my head all day and evening.

After studying me for a few seconds, he seems to catch up and answers, "You're supposed to use it to help you understand things better. To give you perspective. To help you forgive."

I snort. "Ah, yes. I see. Forgiveness. Redemption."

"Yes."

"I'm supposed to just say, 'Well, you were a miserable bastard, Dad, but you had your reasons, so I guess it was okay'?"

"He wasn't a miserable—" He pinches the bridge of his nose, drops his hand and rolls his eyes in their sockets. "Anyway. He wasn't."

"He made me miserable. A lot."

"I know. But he wasn't all bad. I think you're forgetting a lot of things, things that would make it harder to stay mad at him, things that would make you miss him."

"Maybe some people don't deserve to have people remember the good things about them. Maybe that's their punishment for being a jerk."

"You're not punishing him at all, though."

I let that stand for a while, because I hate that he's right, but also because rushing ahead and pretending to ignore or discount what he's said makes him sound even more right. And I'm smart enough to know I'm not punishing my father by being mad at him. He cut out early, before he could suffer any of the consequences of his bad behavior.

After I'm sure it's obvious to my husband that he's not telling me something I don't already know, I move my legs, tucking my knees to my chest (well, as close as my knees can get to my chest these days) and resting my chin on them. I resume staring straight ahead while I voice something else I've been thinking for the past several hours. "Is that how you treat someone 'precious'? You withhold your affection because you think she's strong and capable enough to live without it? That's just mean. Only a truly heartless person puts their pride before the emotional and mental wellbeing of someone they claim to love. That's not love at all. Not even close."

When Brice says nothing to that, I look over at him, resting my cheek where my chin was. "I don't understand," I manage to whisper before I give up holding back the tears. I close my eyes and press my forehead into my knees so he can't see my ugly crying, and I can't see his reaction to it.

A few seconds later, his arms wrap around me, and I allow myself to fall sideways, shaking against him.

"I don't understand," I repeat quietly, maybe so quietly he can't hear me. It doesn't matter, since I'm not saying it to him, anyway.

When my vibrations reach unbalanced-washing-machine-on-spin-cycle proportions, Brice squeezes me more tightly and brings his right hand up, pressing my head harder against his lips. I feel the breath from his nose in my hair. But he doesn't shush me or say or do anything to try to stop my crying. He simply holds on, like he did the last time my dad put me in a state like this.

Recognizing the symmetry makes me cry harder. It's like the intervening seven years have been a weird, too-realistic, not-always-so-pleasant daydream or a glimpse at thousands of days still to come, in the flash of a few seconds.

The sensation is so vivid, it steals my breath, and I look up sharply to make sure we're not sitting on the couch in my apartment in Chicago.

At my gasp and sudden stoppage of tears, Brice withdraws a few inches. "What's wrong?" He tilts his head toward the stairs, listening, obviously assuming I heard one of the kids above us.

"Nothing. I—" There's no way to explain it without sounding like a lunatic. It's easier to let him continue to think my behavior has a logical explanation.

He reaches for the wine bottle. "You want more?"

"No." I shake my head. "No. Just hold me."

He resumes his embrace, and I close my eyes, concentrating on breathing normally again. My nasal passages are too swollen for me to detect his clean-man scent, but I know it well enough by memory to trick my brain into smelling it. The warmth of his solid arms soothes and comforts. His breath flows through my mussed hair like a breeze through tall beach grass. His heart thrums against my shoulder.

It takes me a few minutes of listening to Brice's breathing before I can say, "I had this dream…"

He murmurs something encouraging, so I continue, "At least, I think it was a dream. Yeah, it was. I'm almost sure of it. But at the same time, it was so real."

"Was this recently? And did it have anything to do with sweetheart donkeys?" He looks relieved when I manage a faint laugh and shake my head, but he resumes an appropriate air of sobriety when I sit up straighter and hold his eye contact.

"It was while I was— Right after Addi was born."

"Oh."

My heart pounds. "Yeah, I know. I mean, it had to have been a dream. Right?"

He doesn't commit one way or the other but merely says, "Tell me about it," and, elbow braced against the back of the couch, curls his fist against his temple.

I swallow. "Well, it was—I was—sort of floating above everything."

His eyebrow twitches, but his lips remain clamped.

"And I could see you and Addi. And me. But we weren't in the same room. You and Addi were with the nurses in one room, and I was in the OR, still on the table. And it was…

not pleasant in there. But I wasn't alarmed. I was just watching. Detached."

He nods.

"Don't you think that's weird?"

"Not necessarily. Is that all you saw?"

I take a deep breath. "No. I saw my dad. And Secret."

It's his turn to swallow loudly. Goosebumps dot his arm, raising the hairs on it.

"Anyway, we talked. Dad and I. And I held Secret. And Dad told me—" I struggle to remember the sometimes hazy conversation. "I think he told me he loved me. But he said I couldn't stay there with him and Secret, because you and the boys still needed me."

Brice's eyes fill.

I try to laugh through my own building tears, but it falls flat. "I think I told him he was crazy, that you'd be fine. But he was adamant."

Brice shakes his head, then moves his hand from his face to the sliver of couch between us. He grabs my fingers and squeezes them. "I wouldn't be. I wasn't. Those days when you were asleep... That was the longest week of my life. I barely ate or slept, and I didn't think of anything but you. I wasn't a good father or son. I wasn't a good pastor. I wasn't anything but a desperate husband, terrified I'd never talk to you again."

"Shhh..."

"No. I need you to know this. I need you to understand."

"I do. Please—"

"I wanted nothing to do with a life without you."

I place my fingertips against his lips. "I know."

He tilts his head, eyes narrowing, eyelids evicting the pent-up tears balancing on them.

On a deep breath, I say, dropping my hand into my lap, "I heard you. A few times. I couldn't move or speak, obviously. I couldn't even open my eyes. But I could hear what was going on around me on a few occasions. And one time in particular, I heard you talking. And crying. Next to my hospital bed." When I pause and look meaningfully at him, realization flickers in his eyes.

His face pales, then floods with blood. "Oh. That's—" He rubs his face. "I see." His gaze falls to his lap. "You've, uh, known this all this time?" He raises his head.

Wracked with guilt but also relieved it's no longer a secret, I jerk my head affirmatively. "I didn't plan to ever tell you, but it seems wrong not to. Because then you feel like you need to tell me. And I don't want you to put yourself through that again. I know how you felt. Some days, I hate that I know. It hurts to know. But for the most part, I understand that I need to know. I heard you for a reason."

He presses his lips together, nodding so fiercely that more tears shake loose and fall onto his leg.

I take advantage of his speechlessness and continue, "Anyway, I heard and smelled and felt and experienced so many things in that strange week. It's hard to know what was real or wishful thinking. Who were the two people I'd most want to greet me when I got to Heaven? Secret and Dad, of course. And that's how dreams work."

Sniffing and blinking, he manages a crooked, sad half-smile. "So, how was Secret doing?"

"She was beautiful," I tell him, purposely using the same word he's used to describe every one of our children to me upon seeing them for the first time. "Seemed perfectly content to be with her grandfather."

"And your dad, did he tell you he was sorry?"

"Are you kidding? Not even in Heaven does Kent Stratford admit he was wrong."

Brice laughs quietly. "Hm. I guess I was wrong about that in his eulogy, huh?"

"But that's just it. Like, if he'd said everything I wanted him to say, I'd be able to believe more easily that it was a dream. But since he was so him, yet not him, I don't know." I sigh. "What am I saying? It was a dream. It had to be."

Turning his head a few degrees, Brice squints and says, "Hmm. Sounds to me like you had a—dare I say it—otherworldly experience. Like a vis—"

"Don't say it."

"Vision." He sticks out his tongue when I glare at him for ignoring my demand. "Does this mean you're going to stop making fun of me now?"

"No. What a dumb question."

He pokes his index finger into the inside corner of his right eye, and dabs at the moisture that comes away on it. "It seems like you're asking me, the resident vision-seeing cuckoo, if what you experienced was a dream or something else."

"I know you hate when I ask you to interpret my dreams. So that's not what I'm asking. I just— I so want it not to be a dream. I want it to be real so badly that it hurts."

"Then it was real."

"But you can't know—"

"It was real. To you. In that moment. Now, was it reality?"

I shrug.

He shrugs back. "Does it matter?"

I think about it. "Maybe?"

"I don't think it does. How it made you feel was real. Your dad said some things to you that you needed to hear."

My chin wrinkles as the corners of my mouth turn down.

"Aw, hon. Don't cry."

"I have to."

"Okay. I'm here." He's quiet for my latest round of tears and sobs.

After several more minutes, when I make eye contact with him again but don't bother wiping my face, he does it for me. "Better?"

I sniff and snuggle against him.

And I know, like I did all those years ago, that as long as he's here, it is well.

FORGIVING MOM

*D*espite being in the throes of a mini-hangover the next morning, I power through. It's not that Brice will say "I told you so" (not this time); it's more that I can't give in to my sadness for another minute. Not one more second. Even if that means I have to ask others for help to make it so.

Most immediately, I need over-the-counter help. I plop a couple of dissolving tablets into some water, enjoy a fizzy drink for breakfast, and ignore the pounding behind my left eye while I listen to a seemingly endless, pointless story from Max about magical animated ponies and their vampire counterparts. (WTF?)

When Brice says, "Stinky. C'mon, Bud. Give your mom a break and go play," I grab the little guy's arm.

"Wait. I want to know what happens next." I endure another two minutes of the story, never really finding out what happens, since I don't understand most of it, but not caring. The point is that I'm here. I'm present. I study his peachy skin and long lashes while I gasp and laugh and murmur in the right places until he abruptly says, "The end," and runs off.

As soon as Brice and I are alone (with the exception of the ever-present bouncing Addi), Brice asks while loading the dishwasher, "How are you feel—"

"Fine. Great. Amazing." I stand and cross the room, setting my glass in the appliance and smiling wanly at him.

"I'm serious."

"So am I. I'm ready to move on, you know?"

He nods. "Sure. Okay. Yeah." A deep breath precedes him opening his mouth again. "But I was talking more about your head and your stomach."

I chuckle at my misunderstanding. "Oh. I'll be better when that stuff I drank starts working, and anyway, I deserve every minute of discomfort. I'm sorry I got carried away last night. But you saved me from a much worse fate."

He waves off my words and places the last plate in the bottom rack. "Bah. Don't mention it." Shutting the door, he twists the knob on the front of the dishwasher to get it started for its inaugural run of the day. "You are kind of cute when you're happy-drunk."

"Don't encourage me. That needs to not happen again."

"If you say so."

I wince as Addi lets loose with a particularly piercing shriek of delight. "My head says so."

He squeezes my upper arm. "Hey, why don't you take a bath while you wait for that stuff to kick in? I've got it covered down here."

"Are you sure?"

"Absolutely. As a matter of fact, the kids and I need to inspect the backyard to figure out where we're going to put my wood shop and their play set and sandbox in the spring. It'll be here before we know it."

"If you already have plans for them, anyway…"

"Totally. A ton of plans." He winks at me, then lets go of me so he can retrieve Addi from the bouncer. "Maybe you could help me get all their coats and shoes on first, though?"

How can I say no to that?

A surprisingly short time later, I'm soaking in the tub, sweating out the alcohol. Thirty minutes later, when I hear the group returning to the house, I drag myself from the water, wrap my body and head in towels, and sit down at the small table Brice set up for me in our bathroom as part of my Christmas present and serves as a makeup vanity.

I'm not a girlie-girl, but I've always wanted a designated makeup vanity, like my mom's. Hers has the mirror surrounded by large, round light bulbs, with settings for daytime and evening. Mine's not quite that fancy. But it's my own space to sit and pamper myself when I feel like it or have the chance, which are admittedly rare occurrences. This is one of the first times I've used it.

I select the perfect shades of eye shadow, blush, and lip gloss for a casual Saturday at home in a warm, bulky sweater and soft, worn blue jeans. As I'm blotting my lips and admiring the improvement in my appearance, my phone buzzes to life at my elbow. A picture of my mom I took last year at Christmas, when she was surrounded by the boys, watching someone else open a present, and completely unaware she was being photographed, pops up on the screen.

For months, a call from her has elicited dread and the irresistible urge to let the call go to voicemail, followed by frantic thinking to devise a cover story when she asks me later what I was doing when I missed her call, then guilt at all these feelings and behaviors. But this morning, some unfamiliar emotions grip me when I see that picture of her. Tenderness. Acceptance. Forgiveness.

Before the feelings fade, I snatch up the phone and breathe into it, "Mom?"

"Of course. Who else would be calling you from my cell phone?"

I chuckle through my tight throat. "I don't know. I guess you have a point."

"I was digging around in the basement yesterday, and I came across all these old—"

"Mom?"

"—tapes and CDs that Nicole says—"

"Mom."

"—are yours, so I was wondering if you—"

"Mom!"

"What? I'm trying to tell you something here. It's rude to interrupt, you know."

"I love you, Mom."

She pauses, then says, "Oh. Well. Of course you do! I love you, too, silly."

"No, it's not silly. I mean it. I'm being serious."

"Are you drunk? Where are the kids?"

"I'm not drunk! It's not even noon!"

"Okay, okay. I believe you. You don't have to get all defensive. Is Brice home?"

"Yes. The kids are with him downstairs. I'm just glad you called. Because I really needed to tell you I love you. And I loved Dad, too. And—" I swallow painfully but finish quickly, "I'm sorry if he worried himself to death about me."

I can practically hear her roll her eyes. "You are so dramatic. I wish I knew where you got that. Sometimes I could swear you were hatched."

"Oh, I think I'm more like you than you'd like to admit. And we both know there's a lot of Dad in me. A lot more than I'd claim most days."

"Your father was a good man."

I consider that for a minute, and for the first time in a long time, I can actually come up with some examples to support her claim. "Yeah. I suppose he was."

"There's no supposing about it. Sure, he had his faults, but he loved you more than life itself. All three of you. And his grandchildren. And his sons-in-law."

"Don't go too far."

"It's true."

Blinking away the tears that would destroy my hard work at the makeup mirror, I suck in a jerky breath. "I just wish…" I breathe out and close my eyes. "Never mind. It doesn't matter. I loved him, too. That's all."

"You were his Princess P."

"I know."

Her voice softens. "And you didn't kill him, Sweetheart. I don't want you to think that for another second, do you hear me?"

A sob hitches in my chest. "I guess I know that, too."

"That's all you need to know." She clears her throat. "Now about those cassette tapes and CDs. Do you want me to bring them to you next time I come for a visit, or should I give them away? I can put these in my trunk right now, so I don't forget them."

"It's up to you, Mom. I'm fine with whatever you want to do."

She snorts, and it's clear she's joking this time—and accepting my declaration and unspoken apology, in her own way—when she asks, "Are you sure you're not drinking?"

FRIGID BIRTHDAY

*I*t's a frigid late-February day in the park, but if not for the dead grass, hibernating fountains, and bundled-up visitors, you wouldn't know it. People are here in droves, enjoying the sunshine and fresh air. Our only requirement is the absence of precipitation. Even then, if it were snowing, there'd still be plenty of brave souls sledding down the hill.

Coffees in hand, Brice and I perch on the edge of the dormant water feature at the bottom of the hill by the World's Fair Pavilion. I lift my face to the sun and pretend I can feel the warmth that glows through my closed eyelids. When my imagination fails my numb face, I hold my steaming coffee cup closer to my chin. Aaaaahhh. There it is.

I hear Brice laughing at me, but I merely smile while keeping my eyes closed and say lightly, "Shut up. This is heavenly."

"And this is really all you want for your birthday? You should get more than coffee and sunshine for your thirty-fif—"

"Shut it. Don't say the number."

"Oh, come on!"

"I've decided that's part of what I want for my birthday: no mention of my age." I open my eyes and squint into the sun. After my peepers adjust to the light, and I can more clearly see his face, it's obvious he thinks I'm being ridiculous. I widen my eyes and remind him, "You practically had a mid-life crisis when you were thirty-fi— Whatever age I am."

"Ha!" He points at me. "You almost said it!"

"But I didn't. Back to you. You moaned about love handles and nearly got yourself killed in a desperate attempt to hold onto your youth."

"That second thing had nothing to do with trying to be younger. It was dark outside, and I was an idiot and didn't look both ways before crossing the street."

I stick out my tongue at him.

He returns the gesture, going one step further, leaning forward and licking the tip of my nose.

Frantically wiping his spit off my face with my gloved hand, I protest, "You are so gross!"

"See, age is just a number."

"Then you're ten."

"That old?"

"Well, yeah. I don't want our mental age difference to be too creepy." I stand and drink my rapidly cooling beverage. "This was nice. Now, let's go home."

He scrambles to his feet. "No!"

I startle at his vehement response.

"Why not? I told Sharita and Warwick we'd be home before the kids wake up from their naps."

"We still have a lot of time before that."

"So? It's cold out here."

"We'll find somewhere warm to go. Come on. We hardly ever get to spend time alone."

Since he's essentially begging, I relent. "Fine, fine. Geez. Calm down. I haven't had a chance to visit the Art Museum yet," I say, feeling like the worst Art History major and former gallery employee in the world.

"Yeah, yeah! Let's do that!" He drags me in the right direction.

After an hour in the museum, I've thawed, but I'm antsy about getting back to the house. Brice checks the clock on his phone but still doesn't seem in any hurry. He lowers himself to a wide platform leather bench in front of a wall holding three huge, nearly identical black-and-white paintings and leans back on his hands, crossing his feet at his ankles. Almost immediately, he pulls his legs up to keep them out of the way of the other patrons wending through the room.

"Would you relax?" he implores me after I stand over him and ask, "What are you doing?"

"I didn't leave any instructions for dinner."

"You're starting to sound like Mitzi."

That shuts me up.

"I'm kidding," he rushes to amend after one look at my face. "But I made arrangements with Sharita. Everything's covered. And I want to spend this time with you. On your birthday." He punctuates that with a sweet smile and wide eyes up at me. With his stocking cap-flattened hair and still-rosy cheeks, he's particularly irresistible.

I sit next to him and try to fluff his hair back to life. "Fine. But I'm sure the kids want to spend part of my birthday with me, too. And you told them they could help you make a cake for me."

"We will. Tomorrow. This is special." His bright expression fades a couple of watts. "I can't believe I have to beg you to spend time alone with me. I thought you'd like this."

Oh my gosh. I'm horrible.

I wrap my arms around his torso and snuggle up to his shoulder. He sits up straighter, snaking his arm around my back to bring me closer.

"I do like this," I reassure him. "I'm sorry. I'm not being very grateful for everything you've done to make this possible."

"It's okay."

I separate from him, my posture stiffening, my hands cupping my knees. "No, it's not. I was trying to be low-maintenance, that's all." I stare at the smudged artwork in front of us and tilt my head.

Instead of prolonging my apology with his profuse acceptance, Brice merely follows my eye line and posits, "A forest at dusk?"

"Depression," I utter, my eyes unfocusing as I stare at the streaks of gray and black and white.

He mirrors my head tilt. "Oh, yeah. Now I see it," he quips. "Looks like trees and swampy water to me."

"Stick to Bible translating." I glance at him from the corner of my eye to make sure he realizes I'm teasing.

He laughs, then after studying the panel and comparing it to its siblings farther down the wall, he decides, "I think we're both right. On two different levels."

"Impressive, Reverend Renoir." Casually, lightly, I add, "Who knows? Since I started taking those magic pills, I seem to recognize depression in everything."

Rather than make a big deal about my acknowledg-ment of my recent diagnosis, something I haven't done so far out loud, he simply remarks, "That's why art is art, though. It says something different to each person, based on their experiences and current reality. What looks like 'depression' to you may look more like 'peace' to someone else. And maybe the artist intended something completely different."

"Most definitely. Artists don't think like us normal folks."

He edges closer to me so our hips and legs are touching. His elbow nudges mine. "We're normal?"

I take a deep breath, and when I exhale, my spine curves, and my hands rest limply in my lap. I drop my head to the side so it falls against his upper arm. "Yeah. I think so."

"How disappointing."

We chuckle together, then rise at the same time, as if following stage directions on a script. Despite the other patrons milling quietly—and not so quietly—around us, it feels like we're alone as we stand facing each other.

He gazes into my eyes and tucks a piece of hair behind my ear. "Where to next, birthday girl?" When I hesitate, he allows, "You can say 'home,' if you want. I don't want it to seem like I've kidnapped you."

"I promise to spend plenty of quality alone time with you later." I wiggle my eyebrows, then grab his hand and lead him from the exhibition hall to the nearest exit.

He grins. "Mmm… Well, only if you want to."

"It's on my list of birthday wishes. After a long, hot bath."

"This list is a lot longer than you originally claimed."

"I didn't want to seem greedy."

On the moderate walk through the park back to the van, which we left at the Pavilion, Brice halts.

I tug on his hand. "C'mon. There's a break in the traffic; we can get across the street."

He doesn't budge. Instead, he yanks me hard enough

that I fall against him, laughing. Then he pulls us off the footpath, a few feet closer to the water.

"Stand with me here for a minute," he says, squinting into the wind and the falling sun.

My first instinct is to whine that it's too cold, but since he's holding me close, serving as a wind-break, it's not that bad. Now that I think about it, I could stand here for a long time.

"This reminds me of our first kiss," he murmurs. "Remember that?"

I roll my eyes. "Nope. Don't remember it."

"Maybe I need to jog your memory," he says, lowering his face toward mine.

I smile and close my eyes. "Hmm… maybe."

The kiss he plants on my lips makes me wish there wasn't a house full of rowdy kids waiting for us at home.

After he pulls back, I say, "That wasn't anything like our first kiss."

More tenderly and less surely, he tries again.

"Yes. That was more like it. Tentative. Shy."

"I was so nervous," he reveals.

"What's to be nervous about?" I look around us. The other people rushing to get to their destinations aren't paying us any mind.

"Not just now!" he clarifies with a squeeze. "Then. The first time I kissed you. I thought, 'This is it. I may be about to ruin everything.'"

"You were so right. Look where that kiss landed you."

He pretends to truly survey his surroundings before returning his attention to me. "Looks pretty good to me."

"Tell me that again next time you step on a Lego with your bare feet." I kiss his chin. "What did you say this morning when that happened? 'Son of a shipbuilder'?"

He snickers, then says, "It was on the stairs! I almost fell! And I was carrying Addi!"

"See? That kiss by the lake almost killed you, when you think about it. It's almost killed you several times."

"That's me; living dangerously."

"I'm glad you don't regret it."

"Not a second of it. The only thing I regret is that the kiss didn't last longer."

"Naughty."

He pulls me closer. "Do you regret it? It's almost killed you a few times, too."

Before he can get too serious—I can see it coming in his eyes—I reply, "Depends on when you ask me. Right now? Seems like it was a good decision to kiss you back."

"You were pretty into it at the time."

"Yeah, well, I was thinking, 'This guy's a decent kisser, for a dorky pastor.'"

He turns his head, stares across the water, and bites his lip, trying not to laugh. I take that as a challenge.

"Then I was like, 'Pastor's got skillz.'"

His Adam's apple flinches.

"And then I thought, 'I wonder what kind of undies he's wearing.'"

Tossing back his head, he lets loose with the sort of laugh he reserves for the things he loves the most.

Feeling pretty good about myself, I giggle with him, then sober and ask, "Well?"

His eyes sparkle. "You had a lot of thoughts in that short amount of time."

"Fast-thinking was just one of the ways I was fast back then. So…?"

"So, what?"

"What kind of underwear were you wearing? I've waited long enough to get my answer."

Again, he laughs. "I don't remember!"

"Oh, c'mon. Did you have that many different kinds?"

"I guess not. So, probably the same ones you saw a couple of months later. And the same ones I'm wearing now. Well, maybe not the exact same pair."

My eyes flutter closed. "Mmm... I love those."

"I'll give you a peek at them later."

"Promise?"

"Absolutely. You can count on it."

"Let's get home then."

Before I can step away, he instigates one more kiss that probably does have a few passersby gawking at us—and telling us to get a room.

"Down, Pastor," I murmur at the end of it.

He ducks his head and wipes his upper lip with his thumb as we rejoin the throng crossing the street in the deepening twilight. "There's something about nature—and you—that makes me forget myself."

Maybe I should reconsider my hatred of camping.

SURPRISE!

*W*e're quiet on the short drive home. Well, I'm quiet. Brice sings along to the radio, like usual. But I hardly hear him as I stare out the window at the cold world passing outside and reflect on the distinct phases of the first thirty-five (yes, I'm thirty-five, okay?) years of my life. If my life had a curve to it, like the developmental charts the kids' pediatrician is always waving under my nose, I'd have to say I've been a slow bloomer. Maybe not in any of the traditional, physical ways, but definitely in all ways emotional, mental, and spiritual. When I met Brice, I wasn't much more than a teenager with a career and her own apartment. That's what it feels like now, anyway, when I look back at that person.

At the time, I thought I was worldly, like I had it mostly figured out, even when my life was a mess. I knew it was a mess, so the fact that it was a mess was just an inconvenience. But sexual experience and cynicism have nothing to do with wisdom. Therefore, in reality, I knew nothing; I just thought I did. And that was dangerous.

Not saying I know a lot more now, either, but at least I recognize how little I do know. That's a start, right?

The closer we get to the house, the more fidgety Brice becomes.

I glance over at him. "You need to use the bathroom, or something?"

"Huh? Oh. No. Well, actually, now that you mention it, yes."

"But before I mentioned it, you were squirming over there because... hemorrhoids?"

He wrinkles his nose. "No! What am I, eighty?"

"Young-ish guys, like you, have hemorrhoids."

"You've taken a poll?"

"No, but I see the commercials."

He drapes his arms over the top of the steering wheel while we sit at the last light before turning into our neighborhood and laughs, but there's a brittleness to the sound that makes me nervous.

"What's the matter?"

"Not hemorrhoids, that's for ding-danged sure!"

"It was just a guess. Sheesh."

He turns his head and assumes an expression I've seen on his sons' faces a thousand times. The you're-not-gonna-like-what-you-find-when-you-go-into-my-room-but-remember-how-much-you-love-me face.

"What have you done?"

The car behind us honks when Brice doesn't immediately accelerate upon receiving the green arrow to turn left.

He simultaneously returns his attention to the road and advances through the intersection. Using driving as an excuse to avoid my eyes, he says, "Uh, well... You'll see."

"Brice Augustus Northam, there are four things on my birthday wish list: coffee, walk, bath, sex. We've already done two, and the other two wouldn't put that look on your face."

"But I wasn't privy to your birthday wish list."

"It's pretty much the same every year."

"Sure, but this is a special birthday."

"No, it's not."

"Yes, it is."

"Why? Because I can run for Pres—" I stare through the windshield at our street, clogged with cars. "Oh, my gosh. What have you done?"

The closer we get to our house, the smaller the strip of drivable road, with cars parked at the curbs on both sides. Cars I recognize, some with out-of-state plates. More specifically, Illinois plates.

Before he can own up to the answer I already know, I mutter, "I'm going to kill you."

"But here's the thing," he rushes to say, the speed of his speech juxtaposed with the speed at which he has to drive in order to safely maneuver the van down our street and up our driveway, to avoid taking out our side mirrors. "It's been a crazy year, and we didn't celebrate Thanksgiving or Christmas with your family, so I thought—"

"This was your idea?"

In the garage, he puts the vehicle in park and turns, pressing his back against his window, as if there really are flames shooting from my eyes.

After a loud gulp and a nauseated nod, he says, "But everyone was super-excited when I proposed it."

"You forgot to mention it to the person whose opinion matters the most."

"But then it wouldn't have been a surprise!" He bravely reaches across the console and clutches at my hand hanging limply off the end of the armrest. "C'mon, hon. You're always talking about how you don't have any friends, but look!" He gestures to the brightly lit house, where all of the people who belong to all of those cars wait for us. "There are a ton of people in there who love you." At the sick expression that must match the feeling in my gut, he hurries on. "Not literally, though. I mean, a lot of people love you, but it's not like there are two thousand of them in our house right now. The point is…" He sighs. "They wanted to see you, and your birthday was a good excuse to get everyone together. To celebrate you."

My eyes fill, and I know if not for the chemicals in my bloodstream, I'd be on the verge of a full-blown panic attack right now. "I can't go in there," I whisper.

"Yes, you can."

"I hate being the center of attention. You know that."

"It'll only be for a minute or two. Then it'll be like any other party or get-together, but all of your favorite people will be there."

"This is the worst birthday present you've ever given me. Worst. Like, worse than the hand-held vac for my car the first year we were married."

"I knew you'd feel that way, at first. But you'll change your mind."

"About the car vac or about this party?"

Rather than give me an answer, he simply tilts his head. Then he releases my hand and opens his door. "C'mon. We'll get the 'scary' part over with, so you can have fun."

This is happening. Whether I like it, or not. And I have to say, I'm not hating it as much as I normally would. My biggest fear is showing the emotion brought on by so many of the people in my life gathering here, in one place, for me. And I'm not even sure who's here. I recognized my family's cars, but it was hard to place the others in the dark. And through my tunnel vision.

Brice waits for me at the back of the van and extends his hand to me. "I told them no yelling 'surprise,' or anything cheesy like that."

I pretend to consider not taking his hand, but we both know by the clamminess of my own palm when I do thread my fingers through his that I need to grip something when we walk through that back door into the kitchen. And it would look weird if I had my hands wrapped around his neck.

As we walk up the back steps, he tightens his fingers against mine. His wedding ring presses almost painfully against my pinkie, but it's a reassuring, grounding ache. At the door, he pauses with his hand on the knob. "Ready?"

"No."

He patiently waits.

A deep breath steadies my nervous stomach and regulates my erratic "heartbeef."

"They're going to think we're making out back here," Brice eventually quips, wiggling his eyebrows at me.

The idea of anyone thinking that—or of us actually doing it after seeing all those cars out front—makes me giggle and chases the last of my irrational fear. "Open the door, Reverend Horndog."

I've finally talked to nearly every single person. But not before I submitted to having everyone sing at me, blew out a fire hazard's worth of candles, ate an elephant-sized portion of cake and ice cream, and mumbled a lame "To friends and family" for the toast I was forced to make.

It's unbelievable how many people are here, in addition to the ones whose vehicles I spotted and recognized when we first arrived home. I can't think about it without getting anxious, but it's healthy to face our fears, right? And as the night goes on, it's less overwhelming and a lot more touching (and fun and exciting) to see how many people took time out of their lives to be here tonight.

One of the neighbors might have called the cops on us by now, if the cops weren't already here, with all of the neighbors. Okay, not all of the cops and neighbors, but close. Milner and the people who live in the houses in close proximity to ours are present and accounted for. Plus Sharita and Warwick, of course.

It was surprising (and smart) that Brice invited so many of our new acquaintances, but they weren't the biggest surprises of the night. I'm not sure if I was more shocked to see Jen and Vince again so soon or such a large contingent from Peace. Ben, Lucy, and Marianne and Clark (and their daughter, Jessica) made the trip together from Springfield.

But I'd have to say the biggest surprise was seeing some faces from even further in my past. I was delighted, then emotional, to see my old boss, Marshall, and Messiah's church secretary, Marilyn. I was less sure how I felt about seeing Justine Heideker, but it was sweet to watch her son, Isaiah, run through the house with our kids. Plus, I soon found out she's not going to be Justine Heideker for much longer when she flashed her ring at me and beckoned over an unfamiliar person, who was talking to Brice at the time, and introduced him as her fiancé, Tim. It was a relief to know she wouldn't be making puppy dog eyes across the room at my husband all evening. Now that would have been awkward.

Finally caught up with my mingling duties, which

weren't as much of a chore as I thought they'd be, I creep behind Dustin and Jason, who had been talking to Ben Eiffler until a few minutes ago but are now whispering to themselves.

"What are you two troublemakers up to?" I hiss between their heads, laughing at the subsequent guilty flinches from both of them. Dustin lets rip one of his shriek-laughs and shakes his spilled drink from his hand.

Jason turns and pushes his hand against my face. "Don't sneak up on people like that!"

I'm too weak from laughter to fight back with my arms, but I do stick out my tongue and lick his palm, which is just as effective.

"Gross!" he nearly screams.

Sadie, sensing some grown-up fun, sidles up to our threesome. "What's going on over here?"

For about the tenth time tonight, I marvel at how beautiful and mature she's become in just a few short years. The fourteen-year-old's appearance may have changed, but inside she's the same bespectacled sweetheart who was more like my practice daughter than a niece. I wrap my arm around her shoulders, level with mine. "I'm trying to figure out who your uncles are snarking on."

Sadie surveys the room, then turns her back to it to face us again and says in a low voice, "Are you guys cracking up about how much Justine's boyfriend looks like Uncle Brice? Because I think that's hilarious."

I quickly verify this observation and gasp. "Oh, my gosh. You're right!"

"It's totes obvi," she says, with a roll of her eyes, before quickly dropping the snotty teen act. "Actually, it's kind of cute. As long as Tim never figures it out, and she really loves him and everything, what's the harm, right?"

Dustin whispers, "She definitely has a type."

"Yeah. Tall, dark, and dorky," Jason mutters.

"I'm going to hurt you," I say, with a smack to his shoulder that attracts a certain pastor's attention. "Oh, geez. Now, look what you've done. Snark time's over."

"This seems like a fun group," Brice says, pulling Sadie out of my grip and in for a hug. "Hey, Sades. What's new?"

She reddens, unable to hide her guilt at being caught gossiping and, therefore, slow to answer his question. She'll learn.

In the meantime, I rescue her. "We were talking about Sadie's plans to go to France this summer with the French Club at her school."

"Ooh, la la!" Brice replies.

Grateful he bought the lame cover story, I say, "Oui."

"Vous vous appelez Monsieur and Madame Dork," Jason sing-songs, earning him a playful shove from me and an appreciative laugh from his brother-in-law.

"Proud of it," Brice says. "So, France, huh?"

Sadie grins. "Yeah. It's going to be awesome."

"I'm sure! You should go talk to Jen and Vince about their honeymoon. Maybe they can give you some pointers." He blushes. "About navigating France, that is. Not— Anyway." He turns her by the shoulders and gently nudges her in the middle of back.

She sends him a questioning glance as she leaves us but obediently heads in Jen and Vince's direction.

She's barely three feet away when Brice turns back to the three of us and says, "All right. What were you really talking about?"

"What are you implying?" I widen my eyes and drop my chin.

"I know mischief when I see it. And you three are up to

no good. If nothing else, you were corrupting your sweet niece."

Dustin cackles. "He has us pegged."

Brice smirks. "I'm gettin' there. Spill it."

There's no way I'm bringing up his resemblance to Justine's fiancé (or, more accurately, vice versa), so I jump teams. "I was just asking these two the same thing when Sadie interrupted us." I raise an eyebrow at my brother and Dustin. "What's up, guys?"

They exchange a look, then Jason says, "We were looking around here at all the kids and congratulating ourselves on our recent decision."

My heart stutters.

Dustin flutters his eyelashes at me. "Don't get too excited, Sis. The decision is to adopt another cat. And not think about kids for a while."

When a glance at Jason verifies he's okay with this, I say, "Hey, I'm happy if you're happy."

Jason smiles reassuringly. "Yeah. I mean, it's not like we're on a tight deadline. And right now, there are still some things we want to do that would be extremely difficult with children around."

"Like using the bathroom alone?" Brice mutters.

I pull him closer to me and drop a sympathetic hand on his arm but focus on my brothers. "What kind of cat are you getting?"

Dustin drains what's left of his drink and nods at Jason. "Knowing him, the scraggliest, ugliest one at the shelter. He's a sucker for the underdog."

"Or undercat, as the case may be," Brice says, eliciting more groans from the other guys. "What? That's a solid punch line. You're just jealous I thought of it first."

Jason rubs his face. "Dude, you're embarrassing yourself."

Before I can jump to Brice's defense, a large group of couple-friends waves us over. Brice mutters something about hoping they're an easier audience as we cross the room, passing what must be a scintillating—and potentially volatile—conversation between Bob and Sharita, to join them.

"Snarking may resume," I toss over my shoulder at Dustin and Jason. "Just remember to fill me in later."

Jason shoots me a thumbs-up.

When we arrive at the circle populated by Mitzi and Jared, Jen and Vince, and Marianne and Clark, Mitzi immediately hands me a fresh drink, and Jen says, "It's about time you came over to talk to us."

I roll my eyes at her petulance and take a few gulps of what I thought was iced tea but is actually sweet tea vodka. My eyes water, but the alcohol goes down smoothly. Too smoothly. I pull it away from my lips and peer down at the dark brown liquid. "This stuff's about as dangerous as that conversation over there between Sharita and Bob."

That earns me a warning nudge from Brice. Oh, yeah. We're not supposed to tattle on Bob the Bigot, since he's technically in recovery. That's fine. There's something else I'd rather discuss, anyway.

Leveling each one of my "friends" with a glare, I ask, "How long has this shindig been in the works?"

Suddenly, the floor is fascinating to all of them, except brave Jared. He pushes his glasses up his nose and answers, "Oh, for ages."

Mitzi pushes his shoulder. "Jared!"

"What? I'm just telling the truth."

"And I appreciate that, Jared," I say gently, stepping across the circle and patting his face. "Thank you for respecting me enough to 'fess up." I toss a mock-glare back at my husband.

Marianne waves her hand at me. "Oh, come on! If you'd known, you would have put the kibosh on it."

"Definitely!"

"And then you'd be missing this. Isn't it fun to be together again with all these great people? I know I'm having a great time. And Jessica missed the boys so much. We can pretend it's not your birthday, if you want."

Jen rolls her eyes. "Don't let her fool you. She's touched by all this. She's just not allowed to show it."

I break out in a moderate sweat. "If I do, I'll cry."

Mitzi steps around Brice and hugs me. "Aw, P! It's all right."

I playfully push her away. "No, it's not! Stop it."

She holds tight, pressing her glossy lips against my cheek. Jen hurries to my other side to make things more symmetrical. Their mouths against my face, they alternately laugh and kiss on me, while I giggle and beg them to stop, especially when I hear Vince say to the other guys, "Is this doing it for anyone but me?"

That's when Jen completely loses it, her hot breath blasting my cheek. "Vincent!" she admonishes her husband. "You're so bad."

"But I'm forgiven."

"Cheap grace!" Jared and Brice shout together, then laugh.

By now, everyone's staring at us, and I feel a repeat of the wedding reception dance fail coming, so I push away from my best friends and say, "Enough. You're making a scene. Again. And my back can't handle another roll on the floor with you two."

"Too bad," Vince mutters, then lightly smacks his own face. "Did I say that out loud?"

"Extra prayers for you tonight, Brother," Brice prescribes.

"What did you do to him in Paris?" I ask Jen then immediately regret it. "Never mind. Wow. You've created a monster."

She smiles affectionately at him. "Isn't he precious?"

Her use of that word sobers me, but it doesn't sting like it would have a couple of months ago. I simply say, "Yeah, he is. Don't forget it."

"I won't. Any other wise marital advice?" she asks with a roll of her eyes.

I think about it for a second and answer, "Yes, as a matter of fact."

"Waiting with bated breath, O wise one…"

"No secrets."

The group lifts their plastic cups. "No secrets!" they chorus before drinking.

Brice and I meet each other's glances over the tops of our cups. With a private half-smile, he winks, and I smirk.

Well, maybe just a few. To keep things interesting.

ACKNOWLEDGMENTS

As usual, there are a ton of people to thank, from family and friends, in general, to more specific people with specific roles in the writing of this book.

I couldn't have written this book without plenty of feedback and information from people who attended Concordia Seminary—and lived to tell about it (haha). Reverends Jeff Sippy and David Oberdieck survived The Sem and were not only willing to share their memories with me, but they were generous and honest and candid about their experiences. Thanks, also, for the wife's perspective from Cheryl Oberdieck. I received so much valuable and fascinating information from the three of you, and while not all of it made it into the book, it all informed the story. And perhaps it will come in handy in the future. You never know!

Online fiction groups, once again, proved invaluable throughout the writing of this book. It was an angsty, emotional experience, for several reasons, and the online writing community was there for me, lending encouragement and providing advice and laughs and sometimes just a listening ear (or would that be "eye"?). Anyway, I truly appreciated it, as always, and can't imagine going through this process without the support of people who are familiar with the odd, challenging, sometimes lonely experience of penning a novel.

I need to write a very special thank-you to a particular friend—without her help, I'm not sure how I would have finished this book. Laura Chapman (author of *Hard Hats and Doormats* and the *Change the Word* website and blog) took time away from her numerous works in progress and other projects to binge-read the *Secret Keeper* series and cheerlead me through the sixth book. When I got stuck, she brainstormed with me. When I couldn't write the blurb without it sounding like a third grader trying to tell a story about something that happened to her at school, she took over and wrote it for me. When I blubbered like an idiot about imaginary people, she didn't judge. At least, her typing didn't sound judge-y. And some of her comments on her beta copy had me laughing so loud at 4:30 a.m. that I was worried I'd wake up the rest of the family. She also told me enough times that I could do it, that I could say goodbye to these characters, that I eventually started to believe it. And I did do it. And this will be a good thing. Thank you, Laura C! Thank you for being such an incredible friend. I hope I can reciprocate.

Beta readers, you outdid yourselves, as usual. Bethany, Laura, Nicole, Kylie, Erin, and Denise, you each brought different perspectives to the read and gave me a lot to think about, all of which shaped the story and improved the book. Thank you so much!

And loyal readers of the series, you've played your part, too. Very well. Thanks for cracking that whip, for continuing to ask when the sixth book would be done, and for urging me forward. There were times when my work ethic would have failed me if it hadn't been for your dedication. If I had started to think people weren't that interested, I may have continued to find other projects to work on, but you did a wonderful job of reminding me that sometimes we do things we don't want to do or things we fear we're unable to do, because others are counting on us. And that's reason enough. I hope the conclusion of the series was worth the wait.

Thank you!
— Brea Brown, 2019

ALSO BY BREA BROWN

The *Secret Keeper* series:

- *The Secret Keeper* (Book 1)
- *The Secret Keeper Confined* (Book 2)
- *The Secret Keeper Up All Night* (Book 3)
- *The Secret Keeper Holds On* (Book 4)
- *The Secret Keeper Lets Go* (Book 5)
- *The Secret Keeper Fulfilled* (Book 6)

The *Underdog* series:

- *Out of My League* (Book 1)
- *Rookie of the Year* (Book 2)
- *Opportunity Knox* (Book 3)

The *Nurse Nate* series:

- *Let's Be Frank* (Book 1)
- *Let's Be Real* (Book 2)
- *Let's Be Friends* (Book 3)

Stand-alone novels:

- *Daydreamer*
- *The Family Plot*
- *Plain Jayne*
- *Quiet, Please!*